# LEAH HALTED JUST INSIDE THE SOLAR'S DOORWAY AND STARED AT THE MAN WHO HAD SEEMED ON THE VERGE OF DEATH.

'Twasn't possible, yet he sat upright, the blanket puddled in his lap. While bracing himself with one arm, his square jaw set in determination, he struggled to free his sable hair from the bandage around his head.

She'd expected him to be impossibly weak, barely able to speak, yet his actions belied all suggestion of frailty.

Troubled sapphire eyes locked with hers—then his gaze slid downward and slowly, thoroughly, inspected her from head to toe and back again. 'Twas nigh impossible not to move, to withstand the tingling his appraisal invoked, to forswear blushing.

The man was *dying* . . . and yet he possessed the audacity to assess her female attributes!

෪

"Anton handles history with a deft hand, even as she spins a tale that will capture the reader's heart."
—*The Literary Times*

Pleas... for a preview ... A Bride.

# The Ideal Husband

## Shari Anton

**WARNER BOOKS**

An AOL Time Warner Company

WARNER BOOKS EDITION

*Cover design by Diane Luger*
*Cover illustration by John Paul*
*Hand lettering by David Gatti*
*Book design by Giorgetta Bell McRee*

Warner Books, Inc.
1271 Avenue of the Americas
New York, NY 10020

Visit our Web site at www.twbookmark.com

 An AOL Time Warner Company

Printed in the United States of America

First Printing: October 2003

10  9  8  7  6  5  4  3  2  1

*I wish to thank the reference librarians at New Berlin Public Library for their patience, tolerance, and diligence in locating the many obscure history books I asked them to find for me. I encourage everyone to visit and support their local libraries!*

# The Ideal Husband

# Chapter I

*England, 1333*

With Dover's chalk cliffs now clearly in sight, Sir Geoffrey Hamelin clutched the rail of the single-masted galley and prayed for continued divine intervention.

A tall, broad-chested, solidly muscled male, whose mere size had helped keep him safe in the narrow, dangerous alleys of Paris, Geoffrey admitted his lack of prowess when faced with nature's superiority. Here was an enemy he couldn't defeat, merely battle to a draw. Perhaps.

'Twould be both painful and humiliating if he emptied his stomach into the choppy Channel below. Especially now, when the tortuous journey was almost over, and when one of God's most beautiful creations stood nearby to witness.

Geoffrey had noticed the lovely lady while boarding ship at Calais, when he yet possessed the wits to keenly perceive his surroundings. She seemed so sad, and from what he observed, also alone. 'Twas rare for a lady to travel without a companion, and the reason for the oddity pricked his curiosity.

He'd almost approached her. However, judging by the nauseating experience of his first and only Channel crossing, he'd headed below deck for privacy. For the few humbling hours required for passage to England, he'd intended to suffer his mortifying illness alone in the cargo hold—an error of judgment. Whether below or above deck, his stomach roiled.

Desperate for distraction, he allowed himself a glance at the intriguing lady.

The same breeze that slapped waves at the ship tugged at her hooded black cloak, giving him tantalizing glimpses of her trim figure gowned in scarlet silk. The hood fluttered about her classically featured face, caressed by hair the hue of spun gold.

While he admired her beauty, he envied her balance. One delicately fingered hand rested serenely on the railing while his own knuckles turned white in a death grip.

Another wave rocked the ship, flipped Geoffrey's stomach and tested his willpower. He took a long gulp of air and met the Channel's challenge. This time.

Damn, he hated ships, almost as much as he hated leaving Paris to return to his father's estate. Only for his younger sister would he suffer so, to ensure her upcoming marriage was to a man she didn't object to. With their older brother off in Italy, the duty fell to him to protect Eloise, if he could, from the snare of their father's greed.

The law might state a woman couldn't be forced to marry without her consent, but Geoffrey knew well his father's disdain for laws that didn't suit his purposes.

Only look at how Father had tried to force his other off-spring into lives that either advanced his position at King Edward's court or added coin to his coffers.

Geoffrey braced for an oncoming wave, gritted his teeth and rode out the tormenting upsurge and agonizing dip. Droplets of sea water splashed his face and mingled with the sweat beaded on his brow and upper lip. His head spun, the dizziness weakening his knees but not his resolve.

Soon the ship would anchor in the harbor. Soon he'd plant his feet on solid ground. Until that blessed event came to pass, all he could do was hang on.

A dainty hand covered his large fist. The warmth of her touch dealt a blow to his concentration, her heat supplanting the chill he found necessary to keep his legs under him and his stomach from rebelling fully.

"You have gone very pale, sir. Mayhap you should go below."

Geoffrey gazed into concerned eyes of amber gems, a color so pure and of such crystalline clarity they sparkled. 'Twas a bold move for a woman to approach a strange man, especially one of his great size. He must appear a pitiful sight if she suffered no qualms.

"Better the fresh air than the stench below."

The pungency of barrels of salted fish had forced him to seek the deck where he had only to contend with the scent of a few horses that milled about in their rough-planked pen.

A small smile touched her lips, but not her eyes. The sadness he'd noticed before yet lingered. "Ah. I beg pardon. Still, I fear you may lose your . . . footing should you cling to the rail. Might I assist you in some way?"

In Paris, at his charming best, he'd have taken the offer as an excuse to get to know this daring woman. Although ill, he felt the pull of attraction, and again the tug of curiosity over why a woman of both beauty and refinement traveled alone.

However, aboard ship, at his absolute worst, he needed no further excuse to send her away. Better to act the cad than risk soiling her fine cloak and leather shoes.

"Begone, quickly, if you have any sense at all."

She removed her hand from his and cast a glance shoreward, her only moves to oblige his wish for privacy.

"Then I may as well stay and keep you company," she declared. "There are those at home who are eager to assure me I have gone completely witless. Mayhap they are right."

Geoffrey knew the feeling. The moment he passed through Lelleford's gate, his father would likely vehemently question the wits of a son gone rebellious. He knew, deep in his heart, that taking vows would have stripped away his wits in short order. He'd done right to shun the priesthood.

"One must do what one must to keep body and mind in balanced humor, despite the opinion of others."

"My father would not agree."

Nor would his own father agree. So, four years ago, Geoffrey had left Lelleford for Paris without his father's permission or knowledge and not returned since. Making the decision to return home, to face his father's censure, had been difficult, indeed. He'd damn near turned around on the dock at Calais, his resolve weakened by the sight of the ship, knowing what was to come.

"Then why go home?"

She tilted her head. "If you are to be my confessor, might I know your name?"

Intrigued by what sin this beautiful woman was about to confess, he answered simply, "Geoffrey."

"Leah. Do you go home, too, Geoffrey?"

He didn't have a chance to answer before the deck rose to churn his traitorous innards and buffet his aching head.

Leah's hand covered his once more. "The waves calm as we near shore. You need suffer only a little while longer."

Another deep breath, another victory. Leah had the right of it. The galley sailed toward a calm harbor. 'Twas possible he'd gain the shore without spewing his guts. What had she asked? Something about going home.

"My sister is to be wed."

"A joyous occasion, then." She gave him another wan smile. "Me, I go home because I have nowhere else to go. Will you return to Calais after the wedding?"

Without doubt, as soon as he was able, he'd leave home again and return to the continent, despite another agonizing crossing to get there. "To Paris, and my studies."

She nodded, giving him the impression she approved. Would that he could gain the same approval from his father. 'Twould never happen.

"Would you return to France if you could?"

Leah sighed, a mere exhale of breath. "Nay. I should not have gone to begin with. I chased a lovely dream. Unfortunately, dreams sometimes turn into night terrors."

"What happened?"

She shrugged. "I was in love. He was not."

Though Leah tried to sound resigned, he heard the underlying pain. Some witless man had wronged her. The fool.

"Then you are best off without him."

Leah smiled fully, a bit wickedly, revealing a spirit trodden upon but not crushed. "So I told Bastian, rather scathingly. I wished him and his harlot the joy of each other before I threw the harlot's garments out the window and filched Bastian's money purse." She glanced seaward. Her fingers tightened their grip. "Hold on."

Geoffrey took a deep breath. The wave hit the galley and tossed the ship upward—higher than before. This time the bow dove deeper into the water, at a steeper angle. Leah gasped and lost her balance. She fell into his side and grabbed fistfuls of his tunic. 'Twas all Geoffrey could do to keep his footing and hold them both upright.

From below deck came the sharp, ominous crack of bursting wood, followed by a mournful groan. Then silence, as if the whole world held its breath. Bile rose in his throat, partly from his sickness, more from the absurd surety the ship was about to sink.

Steady for the moment, he pulled Leah into the narrow space between him and the side of the ship, then immediately regretted the rash impulse. Her lithe body unyielding, with widened eyes she questioned his action, one he couldn't explain because he wasn't all too sure himself.

To protect her from an as yet unknown threat? When he could hardly keep his own footing? More fool he.

Geoffrey closed his eyes when he caught her scent, of lavender perfumed soap preferred by the ladies of

France. A fresh, pleasant aroma that appealed far too much to his senses.

That he should meet an intriguing woman under such dire circumstances struck him as horribly unfair.

His attention pulled back to their predicament, Geoffrey observed the reactions of the ship's crew and other passengers. In stunned silence, everyone clung to some piece of the ship. Listening. Waiting.

Leah eased her grip on his tunic and drew in a deep breath. "I always planned . . . to learn to swim . . . but not like this."

Her attempt at humor made him wonder if he'd reacted overmuch. The ship tilted slightly, but the mast and sail were intact. The water was rough enough to make him ill, but surely not enough to swamp a seaworthy galley.

Still, something unnatural had happened down in the bowels of the ship to cause damage. How much?

Shore and safety seemed a hell of a long swim away.

"There are boats, if need be." Every ship carried a small boat or two, used to haul crew and cargo from ship to shore in ports with harbors too shallow for large ships to anchor at dockside. "We will be all right, I swear."

A thunderous rumble reverberated through the ship.

Then chaos erupted.

The horses penned on deck screamed in terror. Officers shouted orders at the crew to hustle below to bale water. A few seamen slipped down the hatch before another wave hit, tilting the ship to a precarious list.

Geoffrey gripped the railing with every bit of strength he could muster, keeping both he and Leah from tumbling onto the angled deck. On the edge of his vision he saw rats swarm out of the hold, and seamen wrench coverings off a stack of three boats.

Struggling to keep his panic under firm control, Geoffrey nudged Leah. "To the boats. Now."

No one gave the order to abandon ship, but none was needed. Passengers and seamen alike bolted toward the boats, shouted and shoved at each other in panicked fury. A man lost his balance and slid down the tilted deck. Geoffrey didn't watch to see how fast or how far the man traveled. He took each uphill step carefully, easing along the railing, determined to get Leah into a boat quickly.

The biting tang of smoke heightened his dread. His eyes watered and stomach churned. Leah trembled along the whole length of her.

"Only a few steps more until we reach the ladder," he said, offering encouragement as much for himself as for Leah. "The boats are already in the water. Can you see them?"

"I see."

At the edge of the first group of men eager to clamber over the side and down the rope ladder, Geoffrey shouted, "Make way! Stand aside for the lady!"

When the man in front of him didn't move, he grabbed hold of the lout's shoulder and yanked. "Stand aside!"

The man wheeled, his eyes wide with terror, his fist raised. "She takes her turn same as the rest of us!"

Leah took a half step back, seeking succor against the lout's vehemence. Geoffrey longed to toss the churl overboard for simply scaring her.

In a tone of command he hadn't used in years, hadn't

expected to ever use again, Geoffrey ordered, "Stand aside. The lady goes down the ladder first."

"After me!"

"Bastard."

The fist aimed at Geoffrey's chin didn't land. All the training he'd endured in his father's tiltyard, the endless hours spent in weapon practice and learning fighting tactics took over. A shift in stance, a well-timed dodge and accurately delivered shove sent the lout sprawling face down on the deck.

From the boat below came a shout, "Room for one more! Hand down the lady!"

Grateful for the seaman's timely order, Geoffrey pushed Leah toward the ladder. The group of men scurried off to find seats in other boats. Thick smoke now swirled in the air, though he couldn't hear the crackle of fire.

Tears glistened in Leah's eyes. "What of you?"

"There are other boats," he said, hoping he hid his fear well enough to reassure her.

"Come with me."

Geoffrey glanced down. As the seaman had said, there was room for one more person, and that seat belonged to Leah. One of the many men who stared back up at him, surely, would take charge of her and see to her safety on shore.

"No room." He gave her a brief, hard embrace, which she returned with enthusiasm, warming him clear through. In another place, under other circumstances—but the damn ship was going down. "Besides, I know how to swim. I will see you ashore."

"Promise."

"On my honor. Now, get down that ladder!"

He hated to let her go, but with the seaman's help soon saw Leah settled safely in the boat.

Then he heard the roar of fire, and turned to see the lout he'd shoved to the deck lunging straight at him. Then the huge white sail ripped free of its lines. The thick mast snapped.

From the small boat he hoped was well out of harm's way came the sound that clawed at his soul. Leah, screaming his name.

Leah huddled beneath her cloak, her eyes closed and throat raw, oblivious to all but the horrible memory of a gallant man's last few moments of life.

The man Geoffrey shoved to the deck had attacked him just as the mast fell and rolled the ship onto its side. 'Twas the last she'd seen of Geoffrey. Terrified, she'd shouted his name, but doubted he could hear over the deafening noise as the doomed ship caught fire and splintered apart.

All was quiet now but for the lap of water against the side of the boat and the dip of the seaman's oars. He rowed slowly, circling, searching for survivors and finding none. No one spoke, all too stunned for words, all grateful to be alive.

She hoped Geoffrey had somehow abandoned the ship before it sank beneath the surface. Perchance he'd jumped off and one of the other boats picked him up. Leah lifted her chin from her chest and glanced toward the shore still hazy through the smoke. Geoffrey couldn't possibly swim all that way, could he?

She hoped, but doubted he'd meet her ashore.

More likely he'd saved her life, then lost his, and she

couldn't shake the certainty that if not for her he'd be alive.

A tall man, broad in the shoulder, with a masterful square jaw and intelligent blue eyes, Geoffrey had leaned against the rail, pale as cream, his lack of color a sharp contrast to his long sable hair and emerald tunic. So sick, and utterly determined *not* to be sick.

If she'd minded her own damn business he might not have felt compelled to act as her protector and thus saved himself. So now she was safely tucked into a boat, and Geoffrey wasn't, and 'twasn't fair.

"The other boats head toward shore," one of her boatmates quietly commented. "Perhaps we should, too."

Roused from her misery, Leah glanced at the other two boats, hoping for a glimpse of an emerald green tunic—in vain. Indeed, the boats headed for shore, picking a careful path amongst the scattered ruins of the galley.

Fresh tears welled up and threatened to fall. She cleared her throat and addressed the seaman who manned the oars.

"Once more, I beg you."

His expression reflected everyone's thoughts—no hope, useless to search any longer. They all knew who she sought, the man garbed in emerald green who'd hugged her then helped her over the side and down the ladder. Geoffrey, whose name she'd screamed over and over when he vanished from sight.

If the six men crammed into the boat thought her pitiful, so be it. She couldn't head for shore without ensuring a thorough search. If someday, by some miracle, she ever met Geoffrey's sister, she'd be able to give assurance that every effort had been made to find the gallant brother lost to the sea.

"Please. Geoffrey knows how to swim."

The seaman said nothing, merely turned the boat back toward where the ship had gone down. To Leah's relief, none of the other men objected.

'Twas horrifying, the carnage.

Chunks of mast, the ropes and shredded sail entangled, mingled with bobbing barrels and crates and splintered planks. A horse, the mane burned away, struggled to swim toward shore.

And the men . . . dear God the men . . . dead, many burned terribly, but none wore emerald green.

Leah fought the urge to close her eyes against the devastation. The seaman rowed; she and her fellow passengers searched. The afternoon waned. Too soon 'twas apparent they must head for shore or face the night. Sick at heart, Leah made no further plea when they'd made full circle and found no sign of survivors. No Geoffrey.

The seaman rowed hard, picked up speed. The man seated behind her put a hand on her shoulder and leaned in close.

"Look, my lady, ships come. Perhaps they will find your Geoffrey."

Two ships sailed out from the harbor, lanterns burning bright. They'd lower boats, haul in the dead and whatever cargo they deemed worth salvage. Could they rescue that poor horse she'd lost track of? She hoped so.

The nearer to shore, the less debris. A barrel, a piece of railing, a plank—a large chunk of planking bobbed in the water, onto which clung a man garbed in green, she was sure of it. Her heart leapt to her throat, nearly choking off her words.

"There. Bear right." Unable to sit still, she stood up and shouted, "Geoffrey!"

The man beside her grabbed her hand but didn't pull her down, just aided her balance.

"Geoffrey!"

The man on the plank didn't answer, didn't move.

With the guidance of the men forward, the seaman eased the boat alongside the plank and the man who sprawled face down across it, lying too still, one of his legs bent at a disturbing angle.

Leah bit her bottom lip. Her hands shook. A man in the bow confirmed her fondest hope.

"'Tis Geoffrey, my lady. He breathes but appears bad hurt."

Bad hurt, but alive.

Two men stripped down to their breeches and went over the side.

"Ye gods," one whispered into the evening air. "How the hell do we get him into the boat without injuring him further?"

"Can you straighten his arm?" the other rescuer asked. "Have a care for his leg."

Leah's heart sank as the men worked slowly to straighten Geoffrey's limbs, yet still evoked a long, pain-filled groan. Then silence.

"We need something to wrap him in."

"Will my cloak do?" Leah asked, already undoing the ties.

Using great care, the rescuers spread her cloak over

the slippery plank, rolled Geoffrey onto it and bundled him up.

With much coordination of pushing and shifting to keep the boat from tipping, the men hauled Geoffrey into the boat and laid him on the bottom.

Leah eased back onto her seat, reached down to feel Geoffrey's shallow breaths. Reassured, she brushed a hank of sable hair away from his forehead, revealing a gash that needed stitches. Already a huge lump there turned an ugly, deep purple.

Bad hurt indeed, but alive. Badly in need of a physician's tending, but breathing. But his injuries were many and deep. He was so cold, so unearthly pale.

Leah rubbed her arms against the chill, knowing a long night lay ahead. First she'd ensure Geoffrey received the care he required, then seek shelter for the night. Soon enough tomorrow to worry about how to get home to her undoubtedly disappointed father and usually contrary brother.

She'd left Rouen with no more than the clothes she wore and Bastian's purse, given little thought to much beyond going back to the home she shouldn't have left.

Thanks to the man bundled in her cloak, she was alive and unhurt, able to carry through with whatever plan she devised to deal with her troubles. Yet, her troubles seemed insignificant when compared to Geoffrey's. He'd been on his way home, too, to attend his sister's wedding.

Perhaps his sister or another family member even now stood at dockside, awaiting word of Geoffrey's fate. 'Twould be best if that were the case. She had enough problems of her own without taking on the problems of another, even one who'd saved her life.

Fate often wasn't kind, and attempting to control one's own fate sometimes led to disaster. Only look at how she'd muddled her attempt to trade one fate for another.

She probably couldn't influence Geoffrey's fate any better than she'd controlled her own, but she'd do her utmost to give his a nudge in the right direction.

# *Chapter 2*

$\mathcal{S}$ everal hours later, Leah sat beside Geoffrey's pallet in the huge dockside warehouse used to shelter the shipwreck's victims. Though damp and dark, the wooden, dirt-floored building provided a roof overhead and a common gathering place for not only the survivors and the physicians who treated the injured, but friends and families who sought news of loved ones.

No one had yet come seeking Geoffrey, who'd slept while being tended, who, the physicians warned her, might never wake.

Sweet mercy, he was horribly battered.

Both of his broken legs were braced in splints. A swath of white linen sheet encased his chest to protect his cracked ribs. A thick, odorous unguent coated the burns on his arms and hands. The ugly, deep gashes on his forehead and the back of his head were neatly stitched. A thumbful of oil—placed there by a meddlesome priest over her protest—glistened on his forehead.

Disheartened, wishing she could do *something* for

Geoffrey, Leah again adjusted the light wool blanket covering him from the waist down.

His olive-toned skin stretched tautly over the firm, solidly defined muscle of his upper chest and shoulders, containing the strength she well remembered from their ordeal aboard the ship. Strength he'd likely called upon to pull his sorely abused body up onto a lifesaving plank. Had he any strength left to keep his heart beating much longer?

The physicians declared it miraculous he lived this long. They'd forced poppy-infused water down his throat to ease the pain if he should wake, but doubted he would rouse so far before succumbing to his injuries.

No hope, they said. Nothing to do but wait. Praying they were wrong, she waited.

They'd not questioned her right to hover while tending Geoffrey, simply assumed her related to him in some way. All she truly knew of Geoffrey was that he was strong and brave, and that he carried only a few coins and a key in his money purse, which the physician had handed over to her keeping.

Fearing someone might take the notion to banish her from the warehouse upon learning she barely knew Geoffrey, she let them all think what they would.

If Geoffrey never woke up, didn't tell her how to contact his family, she'd not be able to give his sister an account of her brother's struggle to live. She'd not be able to thank Geoffrey for saving her life.

She slipped her hand under his, careful of his burns, and leaned forward to speak softly near his ear. "You must wake up, Geoffrey. How am I to know what to do with you if you do not give me some direction? I need to know your full name, or better, where your sister might be found."

He didn't stir. Leah resisted the urge to shake him, knowing if she did she'd likely hurt him further.

"I know you must hurt terribly. I vow I will not abandon you here, but you must try to help me."

No response, not even the flutter of an eyelash or twitch of a finger. Leah eased back and rubbed her weary eyes, unsure of what to do next.

"Yer cloak, milady."

Startled by the feminine voice, Leah looked up at Mistress Thatcher, one of the many townswomen who'd taken it upon themselves to give succor to the shipwreck's victims by providing food and drink and taking care of small chores. Leah took the cloak, now dry and sun-warmed. Surprised at the warmth, she glanced at the warehouse's open doors. A new day had dawned and she'd not noticed.

"My thanks. And Geoffrey's tunic?"

"Beyond repair, I fear. Surely we can hunt up something for him to . . . wear when the time comes." Mistress Thatcher scrunched down on the other side of Geoffrey's pallet. "How does he?"

"About the same as when you left. Bad hurt, but still alive."

The woman's eyes narrowed. "And you, milady? Have ye slept at all?"

Leah shook her head. She'd considered trying to sleep, but worried that Geoffrey might slip away if not watched. Foolish to think his life depended upon her keeping vigil, but there it was.

Mistress Thatcher put her hand on Geoffrey's forehead. "No fever. A good sign." She smiled. "The angels must watch over this one."

"Let them watch, just so long as they leave him be."

The smile widened. "Plan to shoo the angels off if they get too close, do ye?"

"For as long as I can."

"Then ye need rest and food." She nodded toward the doorway. "There be food and ale outside. A bit of sun will do ye good, too. Go. I will stand guard."

Leah looked down at Geoffrey. Food and sunshine beckoned hard, but she resisted leaving him, even in another's care.

"Go, milady, or we will be calling for the physicians to tend ye."

Reluctant, but hearing sense in Mistress Thatcher's prodding, Leah covered Geoffrey with her cloak, taking care not to cover his burned arms.

Her legs almost refused to unfold, and her head spun from lack of sleep and food. A short walk and crust of bread would ease both stiffness and dizziness. Sleep would have to wait a while longer.

Mistress Thatcher sat down next to Geoffrey and moved one of the cloak's ties to where *she* thought it should rest.

Leah quickly squelched a flash of unwarranted ire. The woman had merely moved a tie, not usurped Leah's place. A place she only occupied because there was no one else to watch over the man to whom she owed a great debt.

"You will send for me if—" Leah couldn't say aloud what she feared might happen in her absence.

"Aye, milady. I will send one of the boys."

The boys fetched and carried for the physicians. 'Twas the boys the physicians sent to fetch the priests with their holy oil and last prayers. Too often those men the priests prayed over expired shortly thereafter.

Leah wound her way around the pallets of the injured, sped past the neat rows of shrouded dead, and broke out into bright sunshine and the tang of a fresh sea breeze.

Heat on his cold chest. Lavender mixed with salty air. Reassuring, both. Something was missing. The voice of the woman. Her soft, dulcet tone had called him back from the edge of a hellish pit more than once.

'Twas still dark, but not horrifying. Terror lurked at the edge of hell, but no longer threatened to swamp him and pull him under.

He dared not move or cry out. He'd tried once and plunged into raging torment. Best to remain still and quiet, float along on this fluffy cloud to . . . where? He didn't know and at the moment it didn't matter.

Wherever *here* happened to be, he was safe. If he drifted too far, she would surely call him back.

She? Aye, the voice was female, one he knew. Whose?

Thinking hurt. Everything hurt. Where was she? Didn't she know he'd perish without her? How could she know if he didn't tell her?

He tested the wall of torment, pushing gently. The pain hit him hard, but 'twas not so bad as before. He'd survived worse, could endure again because he had no choice.

He must break through the wall to call *her.*

Flames leaped up, the blaze blinding him, taunting his

weakness. Overwhelming fear nearly engulfed his resolve. He pounded against the wall, his fists ablaze, the terror and pain increasing. A guttural plea for deliverance reverberated through his head.

Where was she?

The wall moved, pushing him back through the heart of the flame, back toward the hellish pit.

His strength sapped, his will weak, he gave a last push against the wall. It stopped, but he knew it would move again, and he'd not be able to halt its progress without help.

Without her.

Leah drank deep of the sunshine.

A meat pie and short walk revived her body; the sunshine brightened her spirits. She couldn't remember a time when she'd been so weary, gone so many hours without sleep.

The Channel was calm now, the water smooth and peaceful, reflecting sunlight. So unlike yesterday.

She'd overheard one of the seamen tell a passenger about an inquiry underway to find out what had occurred below deck to sink the galley. For herself, she truly didn't care, was just glad the horror was over and she'd survived.

On the dock, salvaged pieces of the sunken ship lay among the barrels, crates and trunks fished out of the sea. Everything belonged to someone, either to the ship's owner, or the merchants or brokers, or passengers.

She had nothing to claim. Did Geoffrey? Did the key in his pouch fit a lock on one of the trunks? If so, she should have it claimed. Perhaps something inside would provide the means to locate his family.

Leah turned to the sound of someone running. A boy. To her dread, he slid to a halt before her.

"Mistress Thatcher says to come quickly, milady."

Telling herself to remain calm, that Mistress Thatcher may simply have other duties calling her from Geoffrey's side, Leah answered the summons with as much speed as weariness allowed.

Mistress Thatcher's smile greeted her. "He moved, milady. Just a twitch of a finger and his lips, but he moved." She got up; Leah lowered into the spot the woman vacated. "I think he missed ye," she added with a wink.

A fanciful thought, but heartening news. Leah slid her hand beneath Geoffrey's palm. "Would you send over a physician?"

A nod acknowledged the request. "Did ye get something to eat?"

"Aye. My thanks for your kindness."

"'Tweren't much. Wish I could do more, but . . ." The woman shrugged. "I will find a physician for ye. Might be the worst is past and ye can get some sleep."

'Twould be wonderful, indeed, if the worst was over and Geoffrey now stood a better chance of recovery. If only he'd move again, speak to her.

She leaned toward his ear and spoke softly. "Geoffrey?"

He didn't stir, didn't answer.

"Mistress Thatcher tells me you moved your hand and tried to speak. Can you do so again?"

Was it her imagination or did his eyelashes flutter?

"Can you wake? I need to know how to send word to your family. Your sister will surely wonder where you are."

To Leah's amazement, Geoffrey's eyes eased open. Her jolt of elation vanished at the agony marring his darkened blue eyes. He suffered mightily, the torment deep and encompassing.

She struggled against tears. There were questions to ask, answers she needed. Except she couldn't bear his misery.

As if he knew his pain upset her, he went back to sleep.

The physician, an old man with kind eyes, knelt down on one knee on the opposite side of the pallet. "He rouses?"

Leah straightened and found her voice. "He tries. A good sign, think you?"

He sighed. "The poppy must lose strength. I shall send over another vial. You must not take his movement as a sign of recovery, my lady. The pain prods him toward wakefulness, no more."

"But surely—"

"Hold, my lady." The physician fixed her with his steady gaze. "Your Geoffrey is beyond hope. His injuries are too great and too many. The blows to his head alone should have killed him outright. He may live a few more hours or perhaps days, but you must prepare for his death."

Leah winced and pursed her lips at the finality.

"I beg pardon for my bluntness," he said, "but you must not cling to false hope. I dare say he may awaken, even speak a few words, but in all my years as a physician, I have never seen a man recover from injuries so severe. A mercy, I would say. Given the blows to his head, I fear his mind would be badly damaged. Better to die than live without his wits." He glanced around the warehouse. "You must also prepare to move him soon. We must give over to the owners by midday on the morrow. Ships are due and the space is needed for cargo."

Take Geoffrey where? She knew no one in Dover who might take them in. An innkeeper would surely object to letting a room to someone about to die. Numb, Leah watched the physician rise.

"You might consider hiring a carter to take him home," he suggested. "Might be best all around."

Except she had no notion where Geoffrey's home might be, and to take him to Pecham—perish the thought. Impossible. Her father would scream the rafters down. Of course, he was going to scold her anyway for running off with Bastian and then having the gall to return home ruined. Her brother would have his say, too, not loudly but more pointedly.

Her head ached. Her heart hurt.

Leah eased her weary body down and rested her head next to Geoffrey's.

"Oh, Geoffrey, what am I going to do with you?"

She got no answer.


The flames disappeared. The pit closed up.

The voice was silent, but she was near.

He didn't care who she was or why she stayed as long as she remained nearby.

He'd caught a hazy glimpse of the lady. Beautiful, as

he'd known from the sound of her voice that she would be.

He hurt everywhere but could bear it now.

She wanted him to wake. He'd tried to oblige. Not possible yet, but soon. Soon.

Geoffrey survived the night. No one had come looking for him and he must be moved out of the warehouse.

Leah saw no choice but to take Geoffrey home with her to Pecham. Truly, she'd rather not. 'Twould further complicate what was sure to be an unpleasant homecoming.

Too, hauling Geoffrey around in a cart, bouncing him over rutted dirt roads, surely couldn't be good for him. The ride could very well kill him. But then, the physician was so very sure of Geoffrey's imminent demise. What matter if he died on a warehouse floor or the bed of a cart?

Mercy, by what right did she take responsibility for another's fate when she'd so blithely wrought havoc with her own?

Still, Geoffrey had saved her life. She couldn't abandon him to uncertain care.

On the advice of Mistress Thatcher, she hired a carter by the name of Alvin—a large man of middling years, his hairy face and lumbering gate reminding her of a bear. After Leah deemed his charges fair, his two-wheeled cart sturdy and the oxen strong, she slipped Geoffrey's money purse from beneath her sleeve and gave Alvin the small key.

"When I was outside yesterday, I saw several trunks on the dock. Geoffrey's may have survived."

"What might it look like?"

She didn't know if Geoffrey owned a trunk much less what it looked like, but if he owned one she wanted it claimed, if only for his own garments to dress him in.

"I am not sure. You will need to try the key."

Alvin looked at her strangely, then ambled off to do her bidding. To her delight he returned within the hour, carrying a trunk made of oak, the iron bands and lock beginning to rust.

The carter set it down with a thud at Geoffrey's feet and handed Leah the key. "Most everything inside is wet, o' course."

Leah knelt, opened the trunk and found what she most sought right on top—clothing. A long tunic of deep blue velvet. A short tunic of brown wool. An ivory sherte now stained in places with brown dye. A pair of black breeches.

He had no need of breeches, not with his legs in splints. Nor did she see any kind of footwear to replace his boots that were ruined—not that he needed them either.

The long tunic might be the last garment he wore.

Shaking off the morbid thought, she gathered up the soaked garments and handed them over to Alvin.

"Pray give these to Mistress Thatcher and ask her to dry them, if she would."

"Ain't got much time afore ye have to have him ready to go."

"Then do hurry."

After Alvin's departure, Leah began to unload everything to allow both the trunk and Geoffrey's possessions to dry out as best they could. She tried not to dwell on the thought that he'd have no use for his belongings anymore.

A leather pouch contained a knife like those men used to scrape whiskers, a whetstone, a smaller knife and two carvings of horses—one not quite finished. The carvings boasted of his skill, the horses sturdy and yet intricately detailed. Playthings for children, perhaps?

Geoffrey's children?

He'd mentioned his sister, not a wife or children. 'Twasn't inconceivable he might be married and a father. Not likely, though. He'd also mentioned studying in Paris. Students rarely married until after they took a profession and could earn a living.

From the bottom of the trunk, Leah lifted a large, heavy bundle wrapped in oiled canvas and bound up with twine. She knew without doubt the packet contained books, which he'd obviously taken added precautions to protect. Of everything in the trunk, these Geoffrey must value most.

Unable to untie the wet knot, Leah slipped the carving knife under the twine, cut it open and carefully unfolded the canvas.

Atop the books lay yet another leather pouch, the edges damp, smelling of lavender. Within were two bars of finely milled French soap, the ends slightly melted.

The three leather-bound volumes also showed signs of their dunking in the Channel. Leah used the hem of her gown to dry the edges as best she could. Once done, she ran a fingertip over the words printed in gold on one of the book's spines.

The language, she thought, was French. But the subject? Truly, she wasn't sure, knowing only how to form a few words of French. As for the other two books, both were written in languages completely foreign to her, the letters looking strangely like symbols.

Geoffrey must be a very learned man to be able to read and understand several languages. What line of study had he followed? What profession had he hoped to engage in? She may never know, not if the physician was right, and Leah had no cause to doubt him.

Everything in the trunk told her something of the man, but unfortunately, nothing provided information on how to send him home.

Leah spread out the oiled cloth to re-wrap the books, then halted when she noticed a folded sheet of parchment marking a page of one of the books.

She eased open the pages and took out the parchment.

Neatly written in bold hand, the words covered most of the page, their meaning defying her grasp. Likely French, likely Geoffrey's writing, likely notations on the subject matter of the book—whatever it was.

Frustrated, Leah put back the parchment and slammed the book shut, irritated by her lack of an education beyond the simple words and numbers necessary to make entries into Pecham's household ledger. But then, not until now did she have a use for knowledge beyond what a woman needed to run a household.

Her father knew French, a skill necessary for doing business with the kingdom's nobility. Perhaps, depending upon whether or not he allowed her entrance to Pecham, she might ask him to look at the book, satisfy her curiosity.

While she returned Geoffrey's belongings to the trunk, Leah pushed aside uncomfortable thoughts of what might happen when she reached Pecham's gate. Better to concentrate on getting herself and Geoffrey ready for the long trip.

From the warehouse's owner she purchased a pallet and blanket. From the physician she obtained unguent for Geoffrey's burns as well as several vials of poppy water, listening carefully to the instructions on their use.

Near midday, with help from Mistress Thatcher, Leah gingerly eased Geoffrey into his tunic, then watched several men bear him and his trunk out to the cart.

When all was settled to her satisfaction, Leah turned to Mistress Thatcher and clasped her hands. "I thank you for your kindness. You made a difficult time more bearable for me."

Mistress Thatcher squeezed Leah's hands. "Ye will face more difficult times in the days ahead."

Geoffrey's death would be nigh unbearable. She felt tears well up, but refused to let them fall. She'd deal with the sorrow when the time came. "I have no doubt. Might I ask yet one more favor of you?"

"What might that be?"

"I hoped a member of Geoffrey's family would come to Dover to meet the ship. I should let someone know I am taking him to Pecham, but am not sure who that someone should be."

Mistress Thatcher thought a moment before answering. "I could inform the tavern keepers here on the docks. That would ensure most everyone in town would hear, even the authorities and guild masters. Where is Pecham?"

"On the northern coast of Cornwall, not far from the Abbey of St. Cleer."

"Easy enough to remember. God go with you."

After a parting hug, Leah climbed into the cart bed to sit next to Geoffrey. Alvin tugged on the oxen's reins to lead them out of town. The cart jerked mightily along the road skirting the waterfront.

Geoffrey's body swayed with the cart's motion, cushioned by the pallet, unmindful of the rough ride.

Leah marveled at how quickly the ruins of the shipwreck had disappeared. Had it been only the morning before when she'd surveyed the remains scattered on the dock? Gone with the debris, as if the wreck had never happened. As if men hadn't died out beyond the mouth of the harbor.

Near the edge of town, alone and forlorn behind a stone wall, stood a horse Leah recognized immediately—the one with the burned-off mane she'd seen swimming toward shore during her search for Geoffrey.

Elated, she called out, "Alvin, hold a moment!"

The cart stopped. Leah climbed out and hurried over to the wall. The dainty mare bore other marks of her battle to survive. Scrapes and burns marred her chestnut hide. A cut slashed across the white marking on her nose. One eye was swollen shut. Despite her injuries, the mare would thrive with decent care.

From the nearby cottage a roundish peasant woman ambled over. "A sorry sight, ain't it?"

To Leah, who'd seen more suffering and death during these past days than she cared to recall, the mare looked utterly beautiful. "She has suffered much. How did you come by her?"

The woman crossed her arms and frowned. "That husband o' mine went into town for an ale and came back with the horse. Said no one claimed it." She huffed. "Ain't no wonder. She will not eat and cannot work. Stew meat on the hoof."

Stew meat? Leah barely withheld a cry of outrage. So valiant a horse shouldn't come to such an end! She stroked the mare's warm, soft nose. There was strength to the horse yet, and a good heart. All she needed was proper food and care—the kind of care her father would be delighted to give a quality horse.

Leah nearly shook with pleasure at her hastily wrought plan. After silently adding up the remaining coins in the two sorely depleted purses she carried, she smiled. Bastian's funds were about to purchase her way back into her father's good graces.

With as much calm as she could muster, Leah asked, "Would you be willing to sell the horse?"

The woman cocked an eyebrow. "Now milady, what would ye be wantin' with—"

"Will sixpence do?"

"The bag of bones ain't worth—"

"Five pence, then?"

"Sixpence."

"Done," Leah said, sealing the bargain, then called back to the carter who yet stood near his oxen. "Alvin, have you a rope to tie my horse to the cart?"

His eyes went wide with surprise, but he fetched a rope while Leah completed the purchase, almost emptying Bastian's leather pouch. With the rope looped around the mare's neck, Alvin coaxed her through the gate and toward the cart. The peasant woman, smiling with glee at the bargain, apparently felt obliged to accompany them. She glanced into the cart and her smile faded.

"So yer the one," she said.

Confused, Leah asked, "Beg pardon?"

"My husband ain't usually one for repeatin' tales, but he told me of what people are talkin' about in the tavern. Ain't a blessed soul in Dover who ain't heard your story, I imagine."

Leah found herself suddenly enveloped in a hug.

"May the Lord give ye strength and watch over ye and yer husband. 'Tis a crime, it is, for one so handsome and brave to die so young. A right proper hero. I will pray for ye."

*Husband? Hero?*

Alvin crossed himself. "Amen to that."

Stunned, Leah realized that while she'd been nursing Geoffrey in the warehouse, the shipwreck's victims had, naturally, become the subject of town gossip. Apparently, they'd heard of Geoffrey's actions aboard ship and his now woeful condition. Leah had been granted the status of his grieving wife. 'Twas the stuff of which legends were made.

She thought to deny her position in Geoffrey's legend, but for some reason paid heed to a little voice that urgently whispered to leave it be.

"My thanks," she muttered.

Alvin headed for his oxen. Leah climbed into the cart and checked on the man who'd unwittingly become the town's hero—and nearly swore aloud.

'Struth, Geoffrey needed all the prayers he could get. His cheeks flushed red with fever.

# Chapter 3

Pecham perched on the northern edge of Cornwall. The three-story, stone keep was fortified on the seaside by craggy, cavern-riddled cliffs, the rest protected by a high curtain wall. From beyond the fortress, Leah could hear the wind-whipped waves batter the shore.

Home. She'd thought to never see Pecham again and didn't particularly want to enter now. The gate yawned open, like the sharp-toothed maw of a giant dragon eager to swallow her whole.

Walking beside Alvin, as she'd done occasionally over the past four days, Leah mentally shook off the vision. 'Struth, whatever happened to her inside the gate couldn't be as wrenching as witnessing Geoffrey's decline.

The peasant woman from whom Leah purchased the mare had kindly thrown a pouch full of marigold into the bargain, which Leah crushed, mixed with water and managed to coax down Geoffrey's throat. His fever had eased but not left him.

'Twas a bit of comfort the mare weathered the journey well, gaining strength and spirit. Nigel of Pecham would be well pleased with the gift, if not with the daughter who presented it to him.

"I wager yer glad to be home, milady," Alvin commented.

Leah evaded a direct answer. With a wan smile, she changed the course of the conversation. "As I imagine you are anxious to return to Dover. My father might have something for you to haul back."

"Such as?"

"Ore from the stannary, or perhaps . . . something else."

For eons the lords of Pecham had wrenched a living out of this rough, windswept land. The tin miners had made their appearance during her grandfather's time, adding to the estate's income but presenting other problems, which had led to the most lucrative business of all.

Smuggling ran rampant along these shores. Fine wine, elegant silk, exotic fur and glittering gems were only a few of the luxuries her father and brother traded for raw ore and then sold to the wealthy of the kingdom at a high profit. She dare not tell Alvin. 'Twas for her father to decide whether or not to trust the carter.

Alvin halted the oxen and glanced over his shoulder. "Ye should climb in and hold yer husband still. 'Twill be a rough ride over the drawbridge."

Leah did as bid, not correcting Alvin's assumption—again. She supposed she should have told the carter of her lack of relation to Geoffrey, but had so easily slipped into the position assigned her by the townspeople, and now begrudged giving up the measure of respect due her as a married woman.

If only that whoreson Bastian had kept his word, she could return home as a woman wronged, not a woman gone wrong. He hadn't honored the promises whispered in the dark of night, luring her away from home.

Not, she admitted with chagrin, that she'd resisted Bastian overmuch. She'd been ripe for luring.

The cart lurched forward. Leah wrapped a steadying arm around Geoffrey, his over-warm body both a cause for concern and a strange sort of comfort. As long as he was warm, he lived.

She ran the back of her hand along Geoffrey's whiskered cheek, the beard of sable tinged with red now soft to the touch. Alvin had offered to scrape Geoffrey's whiskers, but Leah rather liked the beard. The facial hair filled in some of the hollowness of Geoffrey's cheeks.

"Would you have married me?" she asked softly, knowing Alvin couldn't hear her above the rumble of the wagon and expecting no answer from Geoffrey. "If you promised a woman a life of ease and nights of bliss, would you deliver?"

She should have known better than to believe Bastian's promises. Father's warnings to avoid the men whose ship ran afoul of the rocks at the mouth of the cove, had fallen on ears unwilling to hear. The ship's charming, handsome captain, in particular, proved a flame too bright to resist. During the days the crew enjoyed Pecham's hospitality while the ship underwent repairs, Leah listened with fascination to Bastian's stories of far-off lands and exotic delicacies. Of adventures and excitement. Of the pleasure to be found in his embrace and bed. Too easily she'd succumbed to the smuggler's enticements.

Aye, ripe for the luring.

On a moonless night she'd boarded Bastian's ship and slipped away from the dreary stone keep, forever leaving behind her work-filled days and lonesome nights. Or so she'd thought.

The wagon bumped up onto the drawbridge, the rumble of iron-wrapped wheels over the sturdy planks ominously heralding her journey's end. Leah nearly shouted at Alvin to turn around and take her back to Dover. If not for having seen in Rouen the dire fate of women who had neither family to protect them nor enough wealth to provide their own protection, she would.

She'd *not* end up on the streets like the harlot she'd caught in bed with Bastian, a whore with big breasts and copper hair who he'd paid to assuage his lust, despite her rotting teeth and misshapen nose. A woman Leah had once noticed begging for coins near the steps of a church.

The experience had taught her a lesson, if naught else. 'Twould be a long time before she'd be ripe for luring again. Not that the opportunity would present itself anytime soon. Few honorable men wandered into Pecham, mostly scoundrels of Bastian's ilk, and she'd sworn off scoundrels.

The crossbow-armed guard at the top of the gatehouse waved them forward. Alvin guided the oxen through the bailey and straight on to the stairway leading up to the keep's great hall. Pecham's people, consisting of peasant servants and rough men-at-arms, gave no greeting as she passed them by—too shocked to witness the return of the errant daughter, Leah supposed, or unwilling to show her any deference in case the lord of Pecham chose to turn her away. As was his right.

Both her father and brother stood near the stairway.

Father's arms crossed his barrel chest. He frowned, his black eyes narrowed. Short and stout, with thinning silver hair, Nigel of Pecham ruled his domain with a steel fist he wielded fiercely when he deemed necessary. Yet, he could be moved to humor. He wasn't a man devoid of compassion—like Odo.

Nay, that wasn't fair to her brother. Odo had his good moods, but since their mother's death eight years ago he'd become somber, nearly dour. His temper flared more easily. His few smiles rarely reached his hazel eyes. Of a height with her father, his longish acorn-colored hair tossed by the ever-present wind, Odo stood with his hands on his lean hips, no hint of welcome in his expression.

Leah went cold. Neither man would find a kind word for her, but then, she'd expected none, known all along her homecoming wouldn't be pleasant.

By the time the cart halted, she'd gathered both her courage and composure. She climbed out and squared her shoulders, prepared to beg her father's pardon, as a dutiful daughter should, but not cower.

Father noticed everything, Leah knew, from her disabused scarlet gown and unkempt hair, to the man who lay unmoving in the cart, to the sorry-looking mare. She wished he'd open his arms to her, make her return easier, but knew it would never happen. 'Twas up to her to make the first move toward harmony, and though she'd thought about what to say, words stuck in her throat.

Odo broke the silence, his eyebrow forming a derisive arc.

"My, my. Bastian tired of you already, did he?"

Damn but she hated that tone of voice that suggested she was beyond both help and hope.

"Truth to tell, I tired of Bastian."

Leah deliberately turned a dismissive shoulder to her brother to focus on her father, who kept glancing at the wounded mare, a distraction from his wayward daughter. A good omen.

"You were right about Bastian, Father. I should have listened to you."

"Told you he was a scoundrel."

She couldn't agree more. "That he is."

"Perhaps next time you will heed my warnings. You have much to answer for, Leah."

Leah didn't want to think about what he might concoct as a punishment. However, his voice was less gruff than she'd thought it would be. Truly, unless she indulged in wishful thinking, she would swear he was glad to have her home—or at least relieved.

"I believe I have learned from my error."

He was silent for a moment, then again glanced toward the mare. "From where comes the horse?"

"A victim of the shipwreck."

When her father's eyes widened with curiosity, Leah briefly explained, "We were nearly to Dover when our ship caught fire and sank. All three of us are fortunate to be alive."

Leah swallowed the lump forming in her throat. She

and the horse would live, but not Geoffrey. 'Twas only a matter of time before he succumbed to his injuries. She'd fully expected to have to bury him alongside the road, and said a short prayer of thanks she'd been spared that particularly loathsome ordeal. 'Twould be hard enough to lay him to rest in a proper grave, with a priest's prayers for comfort, surrounded by family. Provided, of course, her family let her stay.

She strode toward the mare. Father followed as she hoped he would. Leah ran a hand along the stubble of mane, remembering the mare's valiant struggle to reach shore.

"Her burns and scrapes are beginning to heal," she said of the still ugly and likely painful injuries marring the mare's hide. "I assume her rightful owner died in the shipwreck because no one claimed her. She is strong and stouthearted, and deserved a better fate than butchering for stew meat. So I brought her home, hoping you might restore both her health and spirit."

Father took his time inspecting the horse, from teeth to tip of tail. "She is sound enough." He nodded toward the cart. "What of him?"

She wished her father, or anyone else at Pecham, possessed the skill to heal Geoffrey's injuries, to restore his health and spirit, too.

"I fear Geoffrey is beyond human help. The physician in Dover told me his injuries are too severe for him to overcome. All I can do is see that he is comfortable until . . . the end."

Odo shook his head in disgust. "So you bring home another lover and expect us to shelter and then bury him. 'Struth, Leah, you should have left him in Dover to die."

She stared at the brother who would never understand why she felt obligated to care for Geoffrey. Too, if her father believed she'd again made a grave mistake, he might indeed send her and Geoffrey out the gate. Leah could think of only one way to begin salvaging her reputation and ensure Geoffrey a decent bed to lie in until he passed on.

Dare she lie, continue the ruse?

No one could refute her false claim, save one man, who would likely die without waking to speak to anyone.

Geoffrey had saved her life at the cost of his own. Would he object to doing her one last service?

Leah hushed her conscience. Her reasons for lying might be selfish, but 'twould serve Geoffrey well, too.

"I brought Geoffrey home because he is my husband."

He ached all over. 'Twas the one clear impression in his fog-filled head. Though mightily tempted to drift back into sleep, he needed to know why he hurt so horribly.

He wasn't alone. A female hummed a cheery tune, the melody accompanied by a faint roar he couldn't identify.

The tang of smoke from lit tallow candles mingled with the musty odor of rushes. Familiar scents, yet unsettling.

Gingerly he opened his eyes and blinked through the moisture blurring his vision. Above him, the stout wood beams anchored in gray stone confirmed that he lay in a castle chamber.

He turned his head, the only movement he dared yet,

toward the humming. A white-haired woman sat on a stool near the window slit, using a faint beam of light to brighten the cloth on which she stitched. No name came to the fore.

The haze in his head was more than annoying. Perhaps he should go back to sleep. Nay, there was something important he must do, somewhere he needed to be. Once he woke fully he'd remember what and where.

Hailing the woman meant speaking, but words wouldn't form in a mouth as dry and rancid as old flour. He'd have to move to get her attention. If he sat up, stretched out the muscles and joints he sensed hadn't moved in too long, the pain might abate. His head might clear.

He shifted his arms to brace himself and was immediately sorry. With his grimace came an unintended groan. The sound startled the old woman. She rose up off the stool, her eyes wide with surprise.

"Yer awake," she whispered, then crossed herself. "Blessed be all the saints." She smiled hugely and shuffled toward the bed. "'Tis a miracle, is what it is. Ye stay right there, milord, and I will fetch yer wife. Oh, Leah will be overjoyed, the poor lass. Been a-moping and a-carrying on—" She patted his bare shoulder. "'Tis a miracle."

She turned to leave.

His head spun with confusion. Nothing she'd said made sense. He managed to choke out one word. "Wait."

She halted. "Milord?"

Too many questions begged answers. If only his head didn't hurt so badly he might be able to sort them out. "Drink."

"Of course, milord. Mercy, ye must be near starved, too. I will bring up bread and ale after I find Leah."

The old woman bustled out the door, leaving him alone with his confusion.

Apparently he'd been so near death the old woman considered it a miracle he'd awakened. Ill or injured? Injured, judging from the pain. Obviously he'd suffered a blow to the head. He raised his aching arms—slightly red, coated with unguent. Moving slowly, he touched his forehead and felt a strip of linen. Another wide swath of linen bound tender-to-the-touch ribs around his otherwise naked chest.

Sitting up hurt horribly, but the need to assess his injuries drove him onward. He peeled away the blanket covering him from the waist down. Ignoring the numerous bruises on his hips and thighs, he stared at the wooden slats bracing his legs. Both broken, he realized, but set straight and true. He wiggled his toes, a small motion that brought great relief.

No body parts missing. Everything seemed to be healing. 'Twould take some time, but one day he'd be whole again, he hoped.

Surely he should know how he'd come to such a pass. He eased back down, fighting panic.

Not only couldn't he remember how he'd been injured, but couldn't put a face to his wife, who the old woman had called Leah. 'Struth, he had no memory of anything before waking up in this chamber he didn't recognize.

He couldn't even recall his own name.

\*　　\*　　\*

From her seat at the trestle table, Leah listened to Anna's gleeful announcement that Geoffrey had awakened.

'Twas not the first time he'd opened his eyes. During the past sennight it seemed every time Leah left the bedchamber for more than a few minutes, he became restless. Sometimes he opened his eyes, or tried to move. She was sure that by the time she climbed the stairs from the great hall to the solar Geoffrey would once more rest in peaceful, quiet slumber.

She picked up her silver goblet and swung her legs over the bench to rise. "My thanks, Anna. I will attend him at once."

"What think you, milady? Shall I take him wine or ale?" Anna sighed. "I should have asked his preference."

Leah bit her bottom lip and put a comforting hand on the old woman's shoulder. Anna's knowledge of herbs and the healing arts made her the closest thing to a physician at Pecham, and she truly believed Geoffrey might recover. Leah held no such illusion. Not after watching him waste away until he'd become a wraith of his former self. 'Twas only a matter of time, as the physician in Dover declared, before Geoffrey breathed his last.

"Likely he will be asleep by the time I cross the solar's threshold. Do not worry yourself over his preference, Anna."

Anna shook her head. "Not this time, I think. He asked for drink, and I will take him something to eat as well. Poor lad's innards are likely grumbling something fierce."

A shiver slithered down Leah's spine. "He spoke?"

Anna beamed. "Aye, milady. He asked for a drink. 'Tis a miracle, is it not?"

Leah didn't believe in miracles and she refused to begin now. She glanced at the stairway, the consequences of a miracle where Geoffrey was concerned threatening to overwhelm her. If he recovered, disavowed her claim of marriage—she mentally shook off the horror of her lie becoming exposed.

Answers to most of Father's questions had easily been put off. She'd explained that she met Geoffrey after leaving Bastian, claimed they'd married and were on their way to Pecham so he could meet her family when the shipwreck occurred. She'd managed to avoid further questions by remaining in the solar, tending Geoffrey, being careful to come down to the great hall only when her father wasn't about. Not hard to do. His time was well occupied by his many duties.

To her great relief, Odo had accompanied the carter and a load of goods back to Dover. Whatever he might hear of Geoffrey and the shipwreck would only confirm her lie. After all, the townspeople had proclaimed her as Geoffrey's wife in the first place.

Still, the less embellished the lie, the better.

Leah gave Anna a sad smile. "Bring thinned ale and bread, then. 'Tis the most his stomach can bear, I think."

Anna nodded and shuffled off on her errand. Leah climbed the narrow, tightly winding stairs, hoping Geoffrey might truly be awake enough for her to thank him for saving her life. 'Twas the one thing she'd wanted to do since they'd plucked him off a plank in the Channel.

That and ask him about his sister.

The physician said Geoffrey might awake, might even

speak before succumbing to his injuries while warning her against false hope. Now might be her one chance to give him her thanks and learn the whereabouts of his family.

Leah halted just inside the solar's doorway and stared at the man who, only a few minutes ago, had seemed on the verge of death. Not only was Geoffrey awake, he sat up in the bed.

'Twasn't possible, yet he sat upright, the blanket puddled in his lap. While bracing himself with one arm, his square jaw set in determination, he struggled to free his sable hair from the bandage around his head.

She'd expected him to be impossibly weak, barely able to speak, yet his actions belied all suggestion of frailty.

Nor did Geoffrey appear quite so gaunt or pale. Color had crept back into his face, especially along his high cheekbones.

His olive-toned skin contrasted sharply with the bandage around his ribs, against which his bare chest strained to expand for deeper breath.

He fought against the outward evidence of his injuries, just as he'd fought against his illness on the ship. When he'd been hale and hearty. When he'd possessed the power to pull himself onto a plank though gravely injured.

He noticed her then. Troubled sapphire eyes locked with hers—then his gaze slid downward and slowly, thoroughly, inspected her from head to toe and back again. 'Twas nigh impossible not to move, to withstand the tingling his appraisal invoked, to forswear blushing.

The man was *dying* and yet possessed the audacity to assess her female attributes.

Except he didn't know his defiance against his injuries was for naught, that his next breath could be his last.

Geoffrey had the bandage nearly unwound. If he weren't careful he'd tug loose the stitches. The distasteful possibility of his bleeding again pushed her across the room.

"Have a care for your stitches." She put her goblet on the small bedside table and reached for the bandage.

He released the strip and let his arm drop to his side.

"Tight," he complained. His voice might be throaty and dry, but yet rumbled in the same deep tone she'd admired when they conversed aboard ship.

"The physician wound the bandage tight apurpose to hold your head together, but I suppose we might loosen it if it causes you discomfort."

Geoffrey felt the beautiful woman's fingers in his hair, removing the bandage more gently than he had done. She stood so close he caught the light scent of lavender.

Was this Leah, his wife? If so, he had every right to lay his aching head against her enticing bosom as he was sorely tempted to do. One would think a man would have no trouble remembering a wife of so fair of face and shapely of form.

"This may hurt," she said. "Dried blood mortars the bandage to your stitches."

He acknowledged her warning with a slight nod, noted the compassion delivered in straightforward yet gentle manner.

She worked carefully but swiftly, and soon removed the offensive binding from his head. Almost immediately the ache in his head eased.

Instinctively he touched the head wound. Several stitches marked a line upward from his eyebrow to well into his hair. The worst pain, however, came from the back of his head. No wonder. The lump there was huge beneath a jagged line of stitches.

She tossed the linen on the table. "We can leave the bandage off, for now. You do not bleed, so may have no need for it anymore. Come, lie back down. You should not be sitting up."

A good suggestion, if only because he'd be able to see her lovely face once more. Still, while sitting up hurt, it also assured him that he wasn't completely feeble.

Questions she could answer begged asking. Was she Leah, his wife? Did the woman who possessed caring amber eyes and soft gentle hands belong to him?

Dare he tell her of his unfathomable loss of all memory?

He needed a drink, anything wet to moisten his tongue and throat so he could speak more than one word at a time. He reached for her goblet; she grabbed his hand.

"Nay, not wine. Anna is fetching ale and bread for you. She should be here any moment now."

The old woman's name was Anna. What was his own?

Again he fought a stab of terror so acute he squeezed the hand of the woman who tended him. Her hand tightened around his, sharing her strength until he managed to push aside the fear.

What need he fear? Surely not the woman whose

mere presence offered comfort. Someone else, then? Were his injuries due to an unfortunate happenstance, or inflicted on him by an enemy? Who? Why? He closed his eyes against his confusion.

"Enough. Lie back before you fall over," she commanded.

He might have resisted if not for the push against his shoulder. Damn, but he was as weak as a newly born babe, and too conscious of his precarious state to let go of the woman who yet held his hand while she fussed with the blanket.

The mattress sagged. He opened his eyes. She perched on the edge of the bed, facing him, a sad smile gracing her full, lush mouth.

"I am glad that you woke. I now have the chance to give you my thanks for your bravery. Without your help I might not have escaped the ship before it sank. I am most sorry you pay so high a price for your gallantry."

He remembered no ship much less one that sank, but apparently that was how he'd been injured, aiding her escape from a ship. A chill washed through him, now recognizing the roaring sound he hadn't been able to identify when first waking. Water. Waves dashing against rocks.

Why did his wife so formally give thanks for what seemed to him a perfectly reasonable action?

Exhaustion nearly overwhelmed him. Struggling to hold sleep at bay, he glanced around the chamber, hoping something might jar loose his memory, allow him to go back to sleep in peace.

"You must be wondering where you are," she commented. "I had no choice but to bring you home with me." She glanced over her shoulder at the doorway and lowered her voice to an urgent whisper. "Geoffrey, you must tell me how to send word to your family. Your sister must be frantic over your whereabouts."

He closed his eyes, mulled over the name she called him, and found it sounded right.

From the doorway he heard the faint fall of footsteps.

"Here is the ale and bread, yer ladyship. Oh, has yer husband gone back to sleep?"

"Oh, no. Geoffrey, can you not stay awake a while longer?"

His name was Geoffrey. The beautiful woman who held his hand was his wife. Leah. Enough to know for now.

He gave into the fatigue. Odd, but her begging him to stay awake struck him as familiar.

# *Chapter* 4

*L*eah gazed out the solar window at the sea, allowing the roar of the waves to calm her restlessness. Even as a little girl she'd loved the sound of the ocean beating the shore. Often the rhythm had been accompanied by the clack of her mother's loom. Then Mother died, and the loom had been removed from the solar to the cottage of the dyer's wife.

How many times over the years had she uselessly wondered what her life might be like if her merry, gentle mother had lived? Futile conjecture, but unavoidable sometimes.

Certes, Mother wouldn't have approved of her daughter running off with the captain of a smuggling ship. But then, Mother had married a man engaged in receiving and selling smuggled goods. Leah couldn't remember Mother ever saying a word in either dismay or approval over how her husband earned the greater portion of his wealth.

Indeed, no one questioned Nigel of Pecham's activities, likely because most everyone in the area was either involved or benefited.

From a wedge in the cliffs several gulls took flight, soaring upward and out over the water, the setting sun casting an orange glow on their wings. Leah watched them glide on the wind, knowing why they fled.

A ship was due within a few hours. Already the men were headed down to the cove, preparing to greet the ship.

Father hadn't had to warn Leah, this time, to stay away from the caves in which the goods were stored and sorted, or avoid the men from the ship. Even if she'd wanted to leave the solar she feared to, not when Geoffrey might wake again. She couldn't risk his speaking to anyone else yet, not when he might divulge truths Leah didn't want revealed.

Only two vials of the poppy water remained. Perhaps she should ease the liquid down his throat, ensure he slept until . . . the end. 'Twould be a mercy to him, would it not, to suffer no more pain, to not know he hovered near death? To simply slip into the afterlife without heed or worry of those he left behind.

Like his sister, who would grieve and possibly wish to claim her brother's body for burial. Or would she? Geoffrey hadn't said he and his sister shared affection. 'Twas an assumption Leah made from the tone of his voice when he spoke of her.

Odo would never speak of *his* sister with warmth in his voice as he once might have. They'd been playmates as children, he the older brother who looked out for the little sister who insisted on tagging at his heels. Ever since Mother's death, he'd turned distant and sullen, and of late overly critical.

'Struth, she was relieved Odo had gone to Dover. Had he been here, he'd have given her trouble over Geoffrey. Better he stay away, sell the wine to the tavern keepers and . . . oh, dear. Mistress Thatcher had promised to spread word of Geoffrey's whereabouts through the tavern keepers. Might Odo come upon a member of Geoffrey's family? 'Twas a complication she didn't want to ponder.

*One problem at a time.*

Leah eased away from the window, startled to realize she'd spent so much time within her thoughts she hadn't noticed how dark the room had become. She lit a taper at the hearth, then lit the ring of candles in their large, black iron stand. The flickering glow spread through the chamber.

"Leah."

Leah jumped at the sound of Geoffrey's deep, raspy voice.

His blue eyes shone like dark sapphires, fully open and clear. How long had he been awake, watching her?

"You woke," she said, cringing at the silliness of her own statement.

"Or I dream."

She tried to smile. "Not a dream, else we share the dream."

"Might be."

"Perhaps a sip of ale would convince you otherwise."

"Mmm."

A sound of assent and hope. Leah lifted the tray of ale and bread left untouched since this morning and headed toward the bed. Another look at him reminded her of his pain, so she plucked a vial of poppy water from the small chest of medicinals and herbs sitting near the hearth.

His eyes narrowed at her approach. As she set the tray on the floor near the head of the bed, she asked, "Something amiss?"

"What . . . in vial?"

"Poppy water. Shall I add it to the ale or would you rather drink it as it is?"

Geoffrey's eyes closed, then opened again, as if making that small decision taxed him. "No wonder . . ." He swallowed, or tried to. "Ale first."

He slowly rolled to his side, keeping his long, splinted legs as straight and flat on the bed as he could, then propped up on an elbow. She eased the goblet to his lips. He took two small sips before he eased back down with a sigh.

"No poppy."

The strength of his command surprised her, both in his voice and conviction.

" 'Twill ease your pain."

"Muddles my mind." He patted the bed. "Sit."

She inwardly sighed at his stubbornness. Why contend with pain when not necessary? Men could be so mulish about such things.

Leah put the goblet down and perched on the edge of the bed, not quite touching him, not wishing to bump any part of Geoffrey's body that might hurt. With light fingertips, she brushed his sable hair back from the stitches on his forehead. Warm, but the fever had abated.

So many times she'd perched on the edge of his bed, wiped a cold damp cloth over his fevered brow. He'd never moved, never responded. 'Twas disconcerting to have him staring at her, able to move and speak.

"What happened?" he asked.

The physicians had warned her about the possible effects of a severe bump on the head, that his mind might never be right. How horrible to wake up battered and bruised and not know how he'd come to such a pass.

"Do you remember anything of the shipwreck?"

"Nay, I do not recall . . . nay."

Leah slipped her hand beneath Geoffrey's, palm to palm, as she had so often during those days in the warehouse. His large hand engulfed hers with a firm grasp, solid and sure—as protectively as his arms had been when he'd held her upright against the ship's railing. How confident he'd been then of their coming to no harm.

"You were my hero, you know."

He raised a questioning eyebrow.

"Our ship had nearly reached Dover's harbor when something horrible happened below deck. A loud blast shook the ship, and then we smelled smoke. When we realized the ship was about to sink, you guided me to one of the small boats and forced the men to give me a seat. I shall forever be thankful for your gallantry. I am alive and in one piece because of your quick thinking and ability to fell a man with one punch."

He took a few moments to absorb the information. Leah realized she mustn't relate the tale too fast, to give him time to understand.

"I did?"

"You were magnificent. Smacked the lout in the jaw when he refused to get out of our way." Leah recalled those terrifying moments when she'd last seen Geoffrey whole and hearty. "I was already in the small boat when the sail ripped. Then the mast fell. I thought surely—" Her voice caught, envisioning Geoffrey leaning against the rail, the flames rising behind him. She cleared her throat. "—I would never see you again."

He squeezed her hand again. "You did, though."

"Aye, but after hours of searching. I knew you could swim, but we were so far from shore. Even if you escaped the ship I feared you might drown." She sighed. "We found you floating on a large chunk of planking and made for shore."

"Dover."

"The townspeople took wonderful care of all of us. And you are now something of a legend. I would not be the least surprised if your heroics aboard the ship become fodder for a troubadour's tale."

"You jest."

"Never."

*And they all think I am the hero's wife.*

Leah squelched down the pang of guilt over her part in his legend. She didn't deserve more mention than being the woman he'd saved, certainly not as his wife, someone he might have aided out of love.

"Geoffrey, your family must be worried about you. Indeed, your sister is likely frantic. I need to know her name and where to send a message."

His brow scrunched. "Sister?"

"You were on your way to her wedding, remember?"

"Wedding." Leah saw Geoffrey's confusion before his eyes closed. He put a hand to his head. "So hard . . . to think."

He must hurt. Terribly.

"Take the poppy. 'Twill ease the pain and—"

"Nay. No more."

Stubborn man.

"Then a cup of willow bark tea."

"Preferable to the poppy."

Leah eased off the bed. She'd rather he took the poppy but would settle for the willow bark.

"I will find Anna and have her brew a cup. Do try to stay awake while I am gone. We need to talk more."

"I shall try."

Leah heard amusement but couldn't think of a thing she'd said to amuse him. Perhaps his confusion went deeper than she'd realized.

His hand came away from his head. "Need a bucket."

A strange request. "Whatever for?"

"Relief."

Naturally, he needed to relieve himself. 'Twasn't a good idea to have him carried to the garderobe, not with both of his legs in splints.

"I will return anon."

Leah ran through the passageway and down the stairs. She snared the first male she came across, a young man-at-arms, and asked him to see to Geoffrey's needs. To Ned's credit, he agreed to the task without comment.

Only after he'd disappeared up the stairs did Leah wonder if she'd made a mistake. The two men might talk. Ned might learn something he shouldn't. But then, Geoffrey's current condition didn't invite long conversations, much less personal revelations. Still, she should hurry back up the stairs.

Leah spotted Anna sitting in a chair near the great

hall's hearth, warming her bones though the day wasn't cold. Leah crossed the rush-covered stone floor, paying little heed to the servants who briskly readied the cavernous hall for the evening meal. Not until Father returned from the cove would the wine be poured or the bread and stew served. Plenty of time remained to spend talking to Geoffrey, if he stayed awake long enough.

"Anna, pray brew a cup of willow bark tea."

"Ye are hurting?"

"Nay, for Geoffrey. He is awake and in pain but refuses to drink the poppy. Says it muddles his mind. Willow bark will have to suffice."

The old woman rose to her feet, chuckling. "That braw husband o' yers is a tough one, strong-willed. If not for those broken legs he would be up and about before long."

How many times had she explained the severity of Geoffrey's injuries? Why didn't Anna accept that Geoffrey was dying, would never use his legs again?

"Anna, the physician in Dover said—"

Anna waved a dismissing hand. "Ye watch, milady. That physician in Dover makes no sense. Yer husband will live. Best be prepared for long years of marriage."

Anna shuffled off to brew the tea.

Was Anna right? Could Geoffrey live? She'd considered the possibility before and dismissed it. Had she too hastily embraced the physician's opinion?

'Twould be wonderful for Geoffrey if he lived. Anna was certainly right about Geoffrey's spirit. Did he possess so strong a will to live that he held death at bay?

He'd done so thus far.

Or did she cling to the false hope the physician had forcefully warned her against?

'Twould present nasty problems for her if he lived. 'Twas sinfully selfish of her to ponder over the consequences of her lie if Geoffrey didn't die.

Leah couldn't decide whom to believe—an herbswoman whom she'd seen treat and cure the people of Pecham for her entire lifetime, or a physician who'd likely practiced his skills for as many years with the benefit of being schooled in his profession.

The physician had sounded so confident of his conjecture.

But so did Anna.

*Damn poppy.*

'Twas clearly the cause of his confusion. Taking enough of the medicinal over a period of time rotted a man's brain. Geoffrey vowed to take no more, no matter how bad the pain.

Twice he'd managed to sit up and not cause further hurt—at least not much. Near complete exhaustion, aye, but not undue pain. The willow bark tea would ease the nagging ache in his head without further dulling his ability to think, to remember.

Ned had come and gone, leaving Geoffrey alone to wait for Leah's return, with nothing to do but inspect the solar.

Leah's family possessed a measure of wealth. Tapestries depicting knights in battle graced two of the walls. The furniture was heavy and dark, the table's legs and chair backs intricately carved, as were the bed's posts. No drapes hung from the rods between the posts, but

Geoffrey suspected they'd been removed for ease in caring for him.

A huge Persian rug covered the greater part of a polished plank floor. A large chest with a sturdy lock sat under the window slit with its oak shutters.

The door next to the hearth likely led to the lord's bedchamber. Geoffrey wondered why he'd been placed in the solar instead of a bedchamber, but decided there must have been good reason which he'd learn later.

His inspection done, he longed for another distraction from the itch of his burned arms and the discomfort of the splints.

Leah had proved a lovely distraction earlier, standing near the window, still and serene. He'd watched her for a few minutes, almost hating to disturb her.

His wife. So beautiful. Slender and graceful. Her long blond hair hung loose and flowing, skimming her nicely rounded hips. Then she'd moved, lit the candles. Bathed in the glow she appeared an angel, and he'd wanted his angel near.

Leah would be back as quickly as she could, he was sure.

He'd found her request to stay awake amusing—a request delivered as a command. He liked her straightforward manner, found her appealing in many ways. A lovely face. Curvaceous form. Melodic voice. If only he could remember Leah, his wife, and this sister of his she spoke of.

'Twas the poppy's fault. Once the mind-numbing effect wore off and his memory returned all would be well. Since dwelling on it did no good, and caused an unwelcome twinge of fear, Geoffrey concentrated on what he did know.

Leah had gone through the ordeal of a shipwreck, too, a harrowing experience even if she wasn't injured. She'd searched for him, found him, then obviously sought out a physician to set his legs and stitch his head. Somehow she'd managed to cart him from Dover to . . . Pecham? Aye, Pecham, wherever it was. Near the sea, he knew, because he could hear the waves through the open shutters.

Perhaps any wife would go to such trouble for a husband, whether she liked him or no. 'Twas Leah's easy touches that said she cared. The light caress of her fingertips to his forehead. The way she slipped her hand beneath his as if the action were natural.

Then why hadn't he been escorting his lovely wife to his sister's wedding? From what Leah related, he gathered she'd been headed for Pecham while he attended the wedding. Why didn't Leah know his sister's name or know where to send a message to her? Peculiar.

Which made him wonder if some rift existed between him and his family. 'Twas the only explanation he could think of for a wife not knowing her husband's sister's name.

'Twas damn frustrating—all these questions, no answers.

Leah entered the solar, a steaming pewter mug in her hand. She closed the door behind her before coming toward the bed.

"This should ease you."

Her voice eased him more than any medicinal could. Her mere presence in the room soothed him.

Geoffrey began to rise on his elbows.

"Nay, do not move." She sat on the bed and bent over to pluck a tidbit of bread from the tray, which she then dunked into the tea. "This way you can eat, too, and we will not make a mess."

Geoffrey knew he wasn't helpless. He could manage to sit up and drink the tea. However, he wasn't about to pass up being fed tea-soaked bread from Leah's fingers. He lowered back down and prepared to enjoy the experience.

Enjoy he did, perhaps too much. The tea was hot, the bread substantial and fragrant. Each time her fingers touched his lips a bolt surged through him, pricking at male urges he was in no shape to have relieved in a normal manner.

How long had they been married? Had they wed out of love or obligation? Did she come to his bed a willing lover?

Gad but he hoped the poppy wore off soon, very soon.

"I can send for more if you are still hungry."

To his amazement, he'd finished off both the chunk of bread and cup of tea.

"Perhaps later."

"How is your head?"

"Better." And it was. Not so much pain.

"Better enough to talk a bit longer?"

About his sister, his family. He couldn't tell her what she wanted to hear. Dare he admit to his loss of memory? He doubted he could hide this temporary lapse for long. Soon or late she'd ask him a simple question he had no answer for, and his mind was in no condition to concoct evasions.

Besides, who better to trust with the truth than his wife? Perhaps, if Leah knew of his ailment, she might help him lift this shroud that encased his mind.

"Leah, I cannot tell you about my sister. I have no . . . memory of her."

She tilted her head, her eyes questioning. "No memory?"

"'Tis the damn poppy's fault. My mind is so muddled I cannot sort my thoughts properly."

Leah was quiet for several long moments before she said, "Perchance 'tis not the poppy. The physician in Dover said the bump on your head might cause some . . . confusion."

"An apt description."

"What *do* you remember?"

"Not much."

"The shipwreck?"

"Nay."

"Me?"

He steeled for her reaction.

"Above all else I wish I remembered you."

She pulled away, putting distance of both body and mind between them. He couldn't be angry with her for it, but wished he'd either kept his mouth shut or lied.

"But you called me by name earlier."

"I heard Anna say your name. I only know my own name because you called me Geoffrey." At least he thought that's what he'd heard. "My name is Geoffrey, is it not?"

"Aye. Sweet mercy, what you tell me is incredible."

Incredible. Frightening. But it would pass. If he didn't believe that, he'd go mad.

"Leah, I know this must be hard to understand. I am sure it doesn't happen often that a man forgets his wife." He took a risk and held out his hand, and damn near sighed his relief when she took it. "Help me remember you, Leah. I need to remember."

Odo followed the whore up the dockside tavern's creaking, sagging stairway, determined to put out of mind the story he'd heard in the common room about his angel of a sister and that husband of hers—Geoffrey, the glorious hero.

He wasn't surprised Leah had charmed everyone in Dover into cheerfully doing her bidding, as if she were a damn princess due homage and obedience. People loved her without any effort on her part, particularly their father who rarely listened to a word against her. He'd once been fond of her, too, until realizing she stood in the way of everything he desired.

Nor was he surprised she'd found a man to marry her, one who'd been so beguiled he'd rescued Leah before first caring for his own neck. Foolish. Look where heroics landed the hero. Dead and buried. Gone and soon forgotten.

Odo hoped his father hadn't spent too much to put the man in the ground. Grave markers cost a lot of coin better put to good use elsewhere.

The whore opened a door he'd passed through many times before and led him to a pallet he remembered as unyielding.

She tossed her arms around his neck. "How do ye want it this time, dearie?"

She wasn't pretty, had put on extra flesh since his last

visit, but she didn't charge much and was available. Odo figured one female's sheath was as good as another, so why not take the bargain? Besides, if he closed his eyes, he could pretend her someone else, like either one of the ladies who'd turned down his marriage proposal.

The humiliation yet rankled. They'd turned him aside because he might be noble but not knighted. An heir but not to a large estate. To hell with them. When he became the wealthiest, most powerful man in Cornwall, they'd regret passing up the chance to be his wife.

"Disrobe," he ordered the whore.

"Cost ye extra."

He nodded his agreement. Having bargained a better than usual price for the smuggled goods, he could afford an extra treat or two without his father knowing the difference. What he couldn't afford was having his now widowed sister home again.

Odo suspected Leah hadn't brought her husband home solely to meet her family. She'd come back to claim her dowry. He'd wager his extra coin on it. 'Twas a stroke of fortune the husband didn't live to collect. Odo had other uses for the contents of the dowry other than seeing it pass to some other man's hands.

The whore peeled away her gown in a rather enticing and graceful display, producing the desired effect. His loins stirred and sex hardened, readying for the romp. With deft hands she untied his breeches and eased them down just far enough to fondle him.

"Ye got a good prick there, Odo. Stretches out nice and hard. Really fills a woman up."

The whore might be cheap but she knew where he

liked to be stroked, but not too much. He didn't pay for the skill of her hands, after all.

The pressure built, the power surged.

"On your back."

"Whatever ye say."

The pallet stank of sour ale and other men, but Odo was beyond caring. He buried his sex within her warmth and stroked hard but not fast, getting his money's worth, pumping out his lusty urges and recent frustrations.

He needed Leah's dowry, especially his mother's gold brooch, studded with diamonds and rubies of exquisite quality. With the brooch as a betrothal gift, no woman would think to refuse him.

He should have asked his father for the brooch—again—within days after Leah left with Bastian, while their father's anger burned at her desertion, at her disgrace.

But he'd thought he had time to make his claim.

Now Leah was home. Again in his way. Forcing him to wait for what should rightfully be his. He wouldn't wait long.

With a punishing upsurge, Odo found his release, but not relief.

# Chapter 5

*L*eah entered the solar and nearly dropped Geoffrey's supper tray. Not only was he awake but sitting up and grinning as if he'd done something incredibly clever and expected praise.

He'd removed the bandaging from around his ribs, and the sight of his fully bared chest caused both a pang of concern for his ribs and a jolt to her female senses.

Glory be. Dark hair caressed Geoffrey from his collarbone on down, over the wide expanse of a chest she thought more suited to a man accustomed to physical labor than sitting in a university lecture hall. Even after all this time of lying abed, his muscles were still taut and well defined.

He rubbed at the hair to loosen it from his olive-toned skin. "I could not breathe deeply, so I removed the bandaging."

Leah managed to find her voice. "So I see." Though she couldn't help but stare, her concern for his ribs came to the fore. "Was that wise? Perhaps you should have asked Anna first."

His fingers skimmed his lower left ribs. "They still hurt a bit, but I feel no break." He shrugged, emphasizing the breadth of his shoulders. "Since I cannot move far, I doubt I will do them harm."

Leah had to admit he'd not likely harm his ribs while abed. Except, for a man who'd come within a gnat's breath of death and fully awakened only two days ago, Geoffrey seemed determined to be rid of the outward signs of his injuries more quickly than she thought wise.

She set the tray on his coverlet-covered lap, too aware of his state of undress for comfort.

Geoffrey didn't seem to notice her unease. He tore away a chunk of the bread and gave out a long sigh. "Manna from heaven."

Leah smiled at the exaggeration. "Merely bread from the ovens. I shall tell the baker you appreciate her efforts."

"I shall tell the baker myself once I am up and about."

Up and about. Dear God in his heaven!

"Geoffrey, you are not to undo those splints without Anna's permission."

He frowned. "My legs no longer hurt—"

She crossed her arms. "I swear, I will set a guard on you, day and night, if I do not have your oath to allow Anna to remove the splints. She is the only one among us with the experience to know if the breaks are healed."

"You guard me well enough."

She noted his petulance, very aware he didn't know all of the reasons she guarded him so closely.

"Apparently I do a bad job of it. You took the bandage from around your ribs while I was out of the chamber."

"You were gone a long time. Did you have your meal?"

"While I fixed your tray. Your oath, Geoffrey."

He speared a chunk of broken meat with the eating knife before he asked, "How long must I leave the splints on?"

"Anna told me leg bones need six weeks to mend, so the splints must remain for another month or so."

"Too long. I shall go mad."

Leah wondered who would go mad first, he or she.

Geoffrey still slept most of the days away, but those times he was awake were becoming longer and more frequent. She no longer doubted his body would heal fully—a cause to rejoice even though it presented complications.

To keep him content to lie abed, she'd need to find something to occupy his time. Perhaps give him his carvings or books?

Would seeing his own belongings prompt his memory to return?

She inwardly cringed at the prospect. Soon she'd have to deal with the consequences of her deception.

Thank the Fates that Father was too busy to bother with her right now. Between readying the smuggled goods for sale and overseeing the stannary, he rarely appeared within the keep's walls.

Odo would likely return from Dover on the morrow, but he'd have little time to bother with her, either, before leaving again to sell the goods now sorted and stored in the caves.

As for Geoffrey, would telling him of her lie harm his recovery? Could the truth add to his irritation over his loss of memory, put him off his food or disrupt his sleep, both of which he needed?

His possible reaction to her deception frightened her. Geoffrey seemed a man of moderate temper, but she'd seen him fell a man with a single punch when crossed. He might be a man of honor, forswear striking her, but what did she truly know of his temperament?

For all she knew Geoffrey was one of those men who settled all arguments with his fists. He could even be a scoundrel of the worst sort, a charming rogue who used other people for his own nefarious ends.

Would a scoundrel have insisted she take the last seat in the boat, put her safety above his own? Perhaps, if he thought there was something to gain in the end. A reward. Money. Or something more personal, more intimate.

She'd once thought herself a good judge of a person's character—until being so wrong about Bastian.

"Anna will be up anon to remove your stitches. You can ask her about your legs then. You have not yet given me your oath."

His blue eyes narrowed in intense displeasure. "My wife the tyrant. Were you always such?" Leah took a step back, and his ire melted into frustration. "My apologies, Leah. I know you mean well." He tossed an arm in the air. "I have not taken the poppy for two days, and yet my memory eludes me. 'Tis . . . unsettling."

And frightening. He'd never said so, but each time he alluded to the bothersome loss of memory, she heard the low undertone in his voice that tugged at her heart.

"Perhaps, in a few more days, your memory will return. 'Tis useless to dwell on it."

"'Tis nigh impossible not to dwell on it."

Anna bustled into the room, scissors in hand, saving Leah from further comment.

"Time those stitches came out, milord," Anna said. "I wager ye'll be glad to have them out of yer head."

Geoffrey gave Anna a charming smile, as he always did when the old herbswoman entered the chamber. "I will indeed. They itch."

"Ye took the bandage from around yer ribs. Uncomfortable, was it?"

"Aye." He cast a sheepish glance Leah's way. "Leah tells me I must allow you to remove the splints, however."

Anna waved the scissors at him. "Four more weeks, no less, or ye risk a limp, or worse."

Leah moved farther away from the bed while Anna snipped at the stitches and tugged them out of Geoffrey's forehead. He winced with each tug, but held still and made no comment.

"Ye'll have a scar, milord. No hope for it."

Geoffrey touched his forehead. "A bad one?"

"Nay. 'Twill give ye the look of a rogue, is all. Now bend forward so I can reach the others."

Geoffrey did as bid, resting his elbows on his knees, his chin to his chest. Again Anna snipped and tugged.

"There ye be. Hardly a lump left. Feelin' better?"

"Much. My thanks, Anna." He combed the sable strands with his fingers. "'Twill feel even better to have my hair clean again, get the last of the blood out."

"That it will." Anna strode toward the door. "I shall

have a wench bring up water and towels and such. Will you be needing help, milady?"

Leah inwardly groaned. Naturally, she'd be the one expected to wash Geoffrey's hair.

Given the disquieting observations she'd made earlier, she would rather not. 'Twould be best to keep her distance until she could once again view him as her patient, not an enticingly attractive male. Decide if he was actually a charming scoundrel or the honorable man he seemed to be.

Except everyone would think it odd if she didn't perform this simple service for him, including Geoffrey.

"I believe I can manage."

Steeling herself for the task, Leah rose and considered the best—and fastest—way to get the ordeal over with.

Geoffrey couldn't move from where he lay, not even to turn sideways in the bed to hang his head over the edge. This mightn't be a simple undertaking.

"Is aught amiss?" he asked.

"Just deciding how to accomplish the chore without drenching either you or the bed."

"I hate to be a bother but my head truly does itch."

The smile on his face belied his words. His head may itch, but he didn't mind being a bother in the least. Such impudence from a man totally at her mercy.

She crossed her arms. "Perhaps we should just cut it all off. 'Twould be simpler to scrub your shaven head."

She'd have laughed at his horrified expression if it suddenly hadn't turned thoughtful, and troubled. He put his hand to the top of his head.

"Did I ever consider becoming a monk?"

She had no idea. "Not that I am aware of. Why?"

"'Twas a feeling I had, that someone else had threatened to shave off my hair."

Leah felt a chill tingle up her spine. "A memory?"

"Not a memory, more an . . . awareness."

With a mix of disappointment and relief, Leah couldn't help thinking of the waste for so handsome a man to be shut away in a cloister.

One of the serving wenches strode into the solar. Leah took the strips of toweling and soap from Mona's hands.

"Put the bucket near the head of the bed," she told the girl, still unsure of how to proceed.

The wench did as bid, staring at Geoffrey the entire time, then backed away, very slowly, nearly bumping into Leah. Leah stepped aside and rolled her eyes, imagining the tale soon to be bandied about amongst the giggling girls below stairs—of the terribly handsome, naked man sitting up in the bed in the solar.

"You may go, Mona," Leah said.

"Ye'll not be needing help, then? Anna said ye might."

Leah noted Mona's disappointment and waved the young, nubile girl out of the solar. "You may return to your duties."

Mona dipped a small curtsey before she left, which Leah suspected more a stalling maneuver than a show of respect.

A knowing, somewhat arrogant smile spread across Geoffrey's face. "I suspect 'tis not often the lass is confronted with a man's nakedness."

Nor was she, especially not a man of such starkly appealing traits. She wasn't about to let him know that, however.

"Last I heard Mona was tupping one of the stable lads. The girl knows more than she ought."

The servant girls all knew more than they ought, and now that Geoffrey was healing, the girls would find excuses to take a peek at the fetching sight in the solar.

Leah placed the towels and soap on the bed, then pushed up the sleeves of her workaday brown gown. "I cannot properly wash your hair, but can get most of the blood out. Can you lean back on your elbows?"

He eased down. Leah placed several towels at his back. She dunked one of the smaller towels in the bucket, wrung out most of the water and sparingly applied soap. He tilted his head back without being asked.

Leah leaned forward and began the task at his forehead, gently wiping back the sable hair from red puckers where the stitches had been, wishing he'd close his eyes. Her breasts hovered much too close to his face.

"Is it so ugly?"

There was nothing ugly on his entire body. "What?"

"My forehead. You frown."

Her frown had naught to do with his wound but her own discomfort. For all his good looks, she hadn't imagined him as vain. 'Twas bad of her, but she couldn't help teasing.

"Aye, 'tis a hideous blemish. Likely you will frighten dogs and children at your passing. Women will swoon in horror and men will turn their faces."

He closed his eyes. "'Tis as I feared, then. Anna meant to be kind."

Anna meant nothing but what she'd claimed. As honest as the day was long, the old woman had stated true. He'd have a thin, roguish scar, no more.

She wetted the top of his head. "We shall have to hide you away, I suppose. How about up in the north tower, in a small dank room, where no one need see or speak with you?"

The corner of his mouth twitched. His wits may be dulled, but he'd finally caught on to her jest.

"I could be the demon of the tower, howling my misery at the moon."

"And keep us awake all night? That will not do. We will simply shape your hair to cover the scar if it grieves you overmuch." Leah dipped the towel and applied more soap. "Be still now. This will be the worst of it."

She saw his arm muscles bunch, bracing for more hurt. As gently and quickly as possible, she swiped at the blood that mortared his hair to his scalp. He'd have a scar here on the back of his head, too, a truly ugly one no one would see.

"You have tender hands, Leah."

"I try not to hurt you any more than need be."

"I know, and am thankful for your care."

She looked down into his upturned face. His wondrous sapphire eyes stared up at her. Gratitude shone through, as did a potent awareness of their closeness. 'Twas all she could do to resist bending down to kiss full lips that seemed to beg a kiss.

He whispered her name so softly, so sweetly 'twas nigh impossible to resist.

"If you do not come down here and kiss me, I am coming up."

'Twas more demand than request, a very husbandly demand.

One kiss, then. One brief, chaste kiss.

Leah bent over him until their breath mingled. Geoffrey rose up to meet her mouth.

Softly, their lips melded, his full, warm mouth too inviting and pleasurable to back away from quickly. He tasted of ale and bread, and so much more.

He moaned low, deep in his throat—a male's seductive mating call to which her female instincts responded. The tips of her breasts tingled. Heat swirled deep in her nether regions, then flamed when his hand rose to caress the side of her face. Unable to withstand the fierce needs so easily aroused, she opened to the urging of his tongue.

His soft facial hair tickled her nose, not an unpleasant sensation. Weakening knees forced her hand to his shoulder, his skin silky and slick with soapy water.

If she sat down, leaned against him, pushed him against the bolsters . . . ye gods.

Leah abruptly rose, chiding herself for allowing the intimacy, for responding so swiftly and fully to a mere kiss.

Chaste kiss, indeed. Not with Geoffrey.

She'd once before allowed a tempting male to lure her into a grave mistake, couldn't allow herself to make another of similar nature.

Especially not with Geoffrey, who didn't know she wasn't his wife, that he had no right to demand husbandly rights. Who she must soon tell of her deception.

Leah wetted another towel and bent to the task of rinsing the soap out of Geoffrey's hair, resolved to ignore her quickened heartbeat and fluttering stomach.

Geoffrey had hoped for a smile from Leah, but got a frown.

'Twas evident something was amiss between him and his wife.

Why had kissing him disturbed her enough to make her frown? They'd certainly done right by the kiss. Passion flared instantly, bright and hot.

His entire body hummed from their too-brief kiss. Any doubts he might have harbored over his male ability to function were now put to rest. Indeed, his member poked at the coverlet. Willing and able.

He would wager that no matter if theirs had been a love match or not, she'd come to his bed willingly, and he'd rejoice in it if she hadn't broken away with a start and then frowned.

Sweet mercy if only he remembered what their marriage had been like before . . . but he didn't.

If not for his broken legs . . . another month. Far too long.

Her hands felt good in his hair, her nails scrubbing his head. She used less caution now, using a wetter towel to rinse out the soap. Water dribbled down his neck and across his shoulders, the drips landing in the stack of towels beneath him.

She stepped back from the bed. "Finished."

So much relief expressed in one word.

A large, dry towel landed on his chest.

"Best you dry it," she said. "I fear I might rub too hard."

He thought to protest, but damn, he wasn't a babe who couldn't dry his own hair. He rubbed harder than Leah might have. The lump on the back of his head had shrunk, the spot tender but not overly sore. Perhaps, with its demise, the headaches would cease.

And perhaps his injuries, her fear that she might hurt him was the cause of her frown, why she'd backed away so suddenly.

Leah dried her hands, pushed down her sleeves, and picked up the bucket. "Now we need a comb. I will be back anon."

Again he wanted to protest, but neither was he a babe who had to be watched and coddled. Perhaps that was part of Leah's discomfort? Perhaps she'd been shut up in this room with him for far too long, and caring for him had been more strain on her than he'd noticed.

Surely she hadn't planned to spend this visit to Pecham shut up in the solar tending an ailing husband. A husband who didn't remember the woman who'd been in the room nearly every time he woke.

A man who only knew his name from having heard it from his wife's lips.

"Have you a silvered glass?"

"Aye." A bit of humor lit her eyes. "Yet concerned about your scar?"

Not as much as before, but he needed to get to know the man who occupied this injured body, and knowing what the man looked like might be a start.

"I wish to assure myself I will not frighten children."

"I spoke in jest, Geoffrey."

"So you say."

Her head tilted, she studied him for a moment before relenting. "I have a glass in my bedchamber."

She gathered up the towels and left the solar, the soft sway of her hips lingering in his memory long after she left. A memory he'd not forget. A new memory to replace old ones.

He'd been so sure the poppy disordered his thoughts, but he'd not taken the foul liquid recently and his memory yet evaded him. Again he raked his fingers through his hair, now wet and slick, to find the lump. Could a bad hit on the head bruise the brain, cause such havoc? Possibly, but he wasn't sure.

Leah returned with a comb and piece of glass in one hand, an ivory linen sherte draped over her arm. She handed him the garment.

"As long as you think to make yourself presentable, I thought this might aid your cause."

'Twas made of a fine, tight-weave linen. "Whose is it?"

"Yours."

He pulled the sherte over his head, pleased with the quality of the soft fabric. If he could afford garments of good weave, then he and Leah weren't destitute. So why didn't Leah wear a finer gown than the coarse-weave brown? One explanation came immediately to mind.

"Did our belongings survive the shipwreck?"

"A few." Before he could delve further, she held out the comb and glass. "Here."

His curiosity shifted abruptly.

The image was slightly distorted, but the man who stared back from the silvered glass wouldn't frighten children. Dark hair and beard. Eyes of blue. A straight nose and square jaw. The red line on his forehead would fade to a thin pale line.

"Satisfied?" she asked.

Mostly. He touched his bewhiskered face. "Perhaps I should scrape this off."

"But I . . . if you wish. 'Tis your face."

He looked up at Leah. "You like the beard."

"Aye."

No hesitation there. If Leah liked the beard, he'd not touch a hair.

"Then it stays."

She looked away, then back, as if contemplating her next words. "If the beard feels strange, then scrape it off. I allowed it to grow because I feared nicking you with a blade and . . ." She shrugged her shoulders. ". . . the hair made your face seem not so gaunt."

Leah had endured much for his sake. She'd not only plucked him out of the sea but then nursed him back to some semblance of health. He owed her his thanks and probably his life. Leaving the beard on his face seemed the least he could do. Perhaps he'd just trim it some to keep it from looking shaggy.

He handed the glass back to Leah and began the task of taming his unruly hair.

His arms became tired and eyelids grew heavy. Though he knew sleep helped him heal, Geoffrey resisted. True, he'd been awake for a long spell, the longest since waking two days ago. A small accomplishment, but an accomplishment all the same.

He'd start doing what he could for himself, like combing his hair, if naught else but to banish this horrible feeling of helplessness. Being stuck abed meant he couldn't do much, needed assistance betimes, and that wouldn't change until the splints came off his legs.

A month. Damn.

Leah turned her head to look at the solar door. The sound of footsteps, heavy and purposeful, preceded the entry of a short, graying, barrel-chested man. He stopped at the end of the bed, his eyes narrowing on Geoffrey.

Leah greeted the man with a single word edged with wariness. "Father."

Geoffrey lowered his arms and withstood the man's scrutiny, doing his best to present himself in the best light possible. 'Twas not how a man should meet his wife's father, but then, surely they'd met and spoken before. The two of them must have negotiated a marriage contract, and Leah's family likely hosted the wedding. A day he didn't remember. A bargain he knew not the terms of.

"Looks like he will live," her father commented.

"Praise be. Geoffrey, this is my father, Nigel of Pecham."

"Sir," Geoffrey acknowledged his father-by-marriage in a simple manner because he knew not what else to say to the man.

Nigel crossed his arms. "I hear your brain is scrambled."

Now Leah crossed her arms. "Tsk. Father, that is not what I said."

Nigel arched an eyebrow. " 'Tis what others say, Leah. He has no memory of his life before the shipwreck. True?"

"Aye, but—"

Her father waved a dismissive hand. "Damn peculiar, I say, but no matter. Leah, there is a crate in the kitchen I wish you to inspect. Spices, I think, but none I recognize. Remove what you deem worth keeping and I shall . . . dispose of the rest."

"If you wish."

"Do so before nightfall."

Leah nodded.

Her father's attention shifted again. "Now, as for you, Geoffrey, I wish to know how bad off you are."

"Father—"

"Hush, daughter, let your husband answer for himself."

Geoffrey found himself liking this gruff, blunt man, though Nigel ordered his daughter about more than Geoffrey liked.

"Not so bad as before. My legs will keep me abed for some time, I fear."

"The headaches?"

"Nearly gone. Now that the stitches are removed the aches should cease."

"We cannot be sure of that yet," Leah cautioned.

"Makes sense to me," Nigel declared. He pulled a roll of parchment from his belt and held it out. "Can you do these sums?"

"Father, what are you about?"

"A small test."

Geoffrey ignored the two and unrolled the parchment. 'Twas a list of coinage—marks, pounds and shillings— as one might find in the accounts in any keep in the kingdom. To Geoffrey's delight, he had no trouble doing the sums in his head. His memory might be gone but not his knowledge of numbers. What about letters? Could he read? He thought so—nay, sure of it. Were there books about the keep so he could test his conjecture? The prospect excited him.

He held out the parchment. "Eight marks, twenty-two pounds and six shillings."

"Good." A wide smile spread across Nigel's face. "Very good." He rolled up the parchment. "Perhaps you can earn your bed and board after all."

Nigel turned to leave the room, then spun back. "Leah, do not forget about the crate, and I am sending up some men to move Geoffrey."

"To where?"

"Your bedchamber. I want my solar back."

*Nay!*

Leah managed not to shout out the refusal that reverberated through her head and froze her feet to the floor. By the time she recovered her wits enough to move, her father had disappeared into the passageway.

"Father! Hold!"

She caught up with him at the top of the stairway. "You cannot mean to move Geoffrey."

"I did not mean to give the solar over to your use for forever. Only days, not weeks."

"Geoffrey should not be moved. His legs are not yet healed."

"The men will have a care. 'Struth, Leah, you bounced your husband over the roads between Dover and Pecham without further injuring his legs. Certes, a short journey down the passageway will do him no harm."

Leah frantically searched for other compelling reasons to leave Geoffrey in the solar—and came up with nothing short of confessing that the man her father meant to ensconce in her bed wasn't her husband.

"A few more days—"

He held up his hand. "I understood when you asked to use the solar. 'Twould be hard for you to sleep in a bed where someone recently died. I know. I felt the same way about my own after your mother died. Fortunately, your husband will not die."

"Geoffrey recovers, but—"

"No more, Leah. If naught else, think on your reputation. It begins to mend. People see your devotion to your husband and forgive you your disgrace with Bastian. 'Twould be a shame to do aught to again court their ill will. 'Tis best this way, Leah. Do remember those spices."

He headed down the stairs before she could tell him that she *was* thinking of her reputation. And damn, how did she explain without destroying the hint of approval of her actions she'd heard in his voice?

# Chapter 6

"What think you, Boadicea?" Leah said softly, stroking the mare's nose. "How do I tell Father?"

Content within her stall, the mare stared back with soft brown eyes that offered no answer, only appreciation for the attention. She'd struggled so valiantly to heal and regain spirit that Nigel named her after an ancient warrior queen.

Leah wished she possessed half the courage and fortitude of a warrior queen herself, especially the ability to remain unaffected and resolute in the face of adversity, especially after tucking Geoffrey snug and warm in her bed.

Sweet mercy, she'd never thought of her bed as small until now when his big body sprawled across the feather mattress with barely a corner to spare, the splints adding to his bulk. Not that she wanted or needed a corner for herself. Even if they were wed, because of his injuries, she'd be sleeping on the straw pallet now made up in her bedchamber.

Not that sleep would come easy in any case, not with a virile male too nearby, one whose kiss had left her breathless. He looked too damn good in his ivory sherte, nearly as tempting as he did nude. She'd sought to cover him up and only made matters worse. The tight-weave caressed sinew and muscle, complimenting but not hiding his fine form. The serving wenches she'd hoped to thwart would only giggle more and stare harder.

'Twas small comfort that even those gossip-prone females must realize the mistress of the keep wasn't sharing bed and body with the comely patient in her bedchamber.

The move from the solar to her bedchamber had worn out an already tired Geoffrey. Anna now watched over him, though Leah doubted he'd stir until morn. In search of her father, she'd come into the stable, and had to admit pausing to pet the mare an excuse to put off certain censure.

What a coil! Certes, all of her own doing. If she hadn't claimed Geoffrey as her husband, she wouldn't now be wondering how best to undo the pretended marriage. Which she must do, and soon, for everyone's sake. Especially her own.

The mare bobbed her head, instructing Leah to rub a bit higher and harder. Leah smiled and obeyed. If only she could make *everyone* happy with a pat on the nose or scratch behind the ears.

Leah heard the scuffle of footsteps. The son of the stable master, Will had grown some in the few months she'd been away. The observation made her feel old.

Will smiled. "She likes ye, milady."

"I imagine she likes anyone who gives her attention."

He shook his head. "Nay, she be choosy about who she lets touch her. You, your da, and my da is all."

The stable master possessed a special way with horses. Leah wasn't surprised Boadicea succumbed to Thomas's charms as well as her father's.

"None of you lads?"

Will slowly reached toward the mare, who shied to avoid his outstretched hand. "Da says she may come around if we go easy. Ain't happened yet, though."

"How strange."

Will shrugged. "Lots of reasons for a horse to go skittish."

Leah couldn't help wonder if the mare had been abused by her former owner, an obvious reason for skittish behavior. No matter. Boadicea would soon learn she'd not be ill-used at Pecham. Expected to work, aye, but not hurt or endangered.

As if to prove her wrong, from outside she heard thundering hooves that suddenly pulled up short. Only one person allowed on the horses ever regularly rode too hard. Her brother.

Damn. He'd come home a day early. She'd wanted to confess her deception to her father before Odo's return. With a mere look he could make her feel worthless. He did it apurpose, she was sure, as if by lowering her worth he raised his own. She didn't want him anywhere near when confessing to her father.

With purposeful, almost arrogant strides, Odo entered the stable, leading his lathered stallion. Will scurried forward to take the reins.

'Twas too much to hope Odo would ignore her presence, but good fortune hadn't sided in her favor of late. He came toward her, tugging off his leather riding gloves.

"One would think you knew better than to make a spectacle of yourself, Leah. I swear there is not a body in all of Dover who does not now know who you are."

As she'd supposed might happen, he must have visited a tavern and overheard gossip.

"I cannot control what people might say."

"Perhaps not, but Father will not be pleased if your renown affects our trade badly."

Naturally, Odo's concern was for the trade. Just as her father loved the stannary, so her brother loved the trade.

The smuggling must be kept discreet to protect all involved, and any problem with the business, large or small, affected Odo's mood. The ruination of a single ell of silk could put him off his food. Bastian's ship running afoul of the rocks had made Odo so terrified of discovery he'd spent most of the following sennight at the cove, ensuring the repairs done quickly. A good thing, or he'd have driven everyone in the keep to madness.

She hadn't considered discretion when asking Mistress Thatcher to inform as many people as possible of Geoffrey's whereabouts. The helpful townswoman must have done a fine job of it, and yet no family member or friend had come to Pecham's gate.

Had she somehow harmed trade by her actions? Leah didn't see how.

"Surely you overstate."

"Would that it were so. 'Twas cursed uncomfortable to hear your name bandied about in the taverns. One would think you *Saint* Leah from the tone of the stories. But we know better, do we not?"

Embarrassment flushed her cheeks. No one had referred to her mistake with Bastian until now. Naturally, Odo would be the last to let her forget.

She shrugged a shoulder with a complacency she didn't feel. "You know how these tales go. One person tells another, each striving to embellish the next telling. I imagine that soon after the tale has made the rounds, Geoffrey and I will be forgotten."

"Aye, such is the way of men whose heroics get them killed. Did you give your husband a costly wake and burial?"

"Nay, we did not. Geoffrey lives."

The news stunned him, but not for long. "Impossible."

"He is in my bedchamber sleeping. Look for yourself if you doubt me."

"But he was nearly dead when I left!"

"I am sure Geoffrey will be aggrieved he disappoints you."

Odo's expression turned thoughtful. He glanced toward the keep. "Have he and Father spoken as yet?"

Leah thought it an odd question. "Aye, this afternoon."

"Did they settle . . . never mind. I will speak with Father. Where is he?"

She only knew where her father wasn't. "I have no notion. Perhaps at the caves."

"The ship arrived on time, then?"

"Aye. The goods are near ready for delivery."

Odo spun on his heel and strode out of the stable,

stopping only to scoop up the leather pouch that Will must have set outside the stallion's stall. Leah knew the pouch contained the money collected from the sales Odo made in Dover, and guessed from the heft of the pouch he'd done well.

The stable master came into the stables and headed straight for the stallion's stall. Leah gave Boadicea a final pat and went to check on the horse Odo hadn't bothered to ask about.

Tall and burly for a Cornishman, Thomas held the stallion's head while Will rubbed down the hard-ridden horse with hay. Gifted with a voice that could soothe the wind, Thomas had no trouble getting the horse to behave in any way he wished. 'Twas a shame he couldn't convince one particular rider to have a care with the horses.

Leah leaned against the post, admiring the powerful black stallion. "How is Cnut?"

Thomas answered. "Even yer brother cannot ride this one to ground. Two days' rest and he will be ready for another go."

Which was probably when Odo would leave to sell the goods sitting in the caves. For those two days she'd be most content to spend her leisure in her bedchamber— except now Geoffrey lay in her bed, disturbing both her thoughts and her body.

Will gave the stallion's withers a hard swipe. "Musta been in a powerful hurry to get home. Gonna take us forever to get Cnut dried off."

Odo was home a day early, unusual for him. Why? Leah mentally shook off the inquiry. 'Twas useless to guess at Odo's motives and actions. She'd likely find out soon enough. Certes, he may have ridden Cnut extra hard to get home just to complain to Father about hearing Leah's name bandied about in Dover.

Leah smiled wryly, thinking that Geoffrey's legend now had a new ending. The hero didn't die, but lived. Whether the gallant hero went on to live happily hadn't yet been determined.

Still, she'd managed to give Geoffrey's fate a nudge in the right direction. Unfortunately, she may also have given both their fates an almighty shove. Best not to push too hard now, send them both over a cliff.

She had to confess her lie to Father, but preferred to do so when she didn't have to contend with her brother's immediate reaction, too.

In two days Odo would be off for London or York or some other town, depending upon which goods were now stored in the caves and where the men thought they could get the most coin for the least goods.

Aye, best wait until Odo left Pecham to confess to Father, and then to Geoffrey. She doubted either man would take the news well, and she feared upsetting Geoffrey might bring on a relapse. Given a few more days he'd be stronger, better able to deal with the news.

Perhaps Odo's coming home was a good thing, preventing her from blurting out the truth too soon. Leah left the stable with a lighter heart than when she'd gone in, confident that keeping her peace for a few more days was the right thing to do for her sake as well as Geoffrey's.

Geoffrey opened his eyes in time to see the hem of Leah's white nightrail slide down her back and over her deliciously rounded backside to hit the floor.

'Twas a poor viewing. Night had fully fallen and only a single thick candle lit the room, but merciful heaven, how nice to wake to such a vision.

Damn. With better timing he might have been treated to the sight of Leah nude. He could order her to remove the flimsy garment and turn around so he could look his fill. As her husband, he had rights—for all the good they did him.

His loins might stir whenever he saw Leah, but 'twas all that would happen for the nonce. There was the hell of it—knowing ecstacy to be found wrapped in a woman's arms, buried within her softness, yet he didn't remember the singular pleasure of making love with his own wife.

Leah moved about the bedchamber, a lithe spirit flitting about tidying the room before slumber. She'd sleep on the thick, straw-filled pallet spread out a few feet from the bed. Her bed. That she should rightfully occupy. With him. Except the thigh-hugging, hand span-wide splints prevented him from bending his legs to give her room on the mattress.

He hadn't complained when placed in her bed. 'Struth, he'd been exhausted after the short journey down the hall, but not too sleepy to notice the bed smelled of lavender. Of Leah.

Her bedchamber proved smaller than the solar but as nicely appointed. Heavy furniture, a decent-sized hearth, a Persian rug. Tapestries hung on these walls, too, one a delightful scene of cherubs cavorting in a woodland setting of flowering bushes.

He'd offer to trade her sleeping places, but doubted she'd accept for practical reasons if naught else. 'Twas less strain to care for someone who lay in a bed than on the floor.

With a flick of her wrist behind her head, Leah grabbed hold of her long, blond hair and swung the braid forward to hang between her breasts. She turned sideways, an absent movement he was sure, and began unraveling the braid. Inch by glorious inch the braid came undone until at long last she shook her head and the candle-sparked tresses settled in a veil around her shoulders to hang well below her trim waist and caress her hips. She picked up her comb to work out the kinks and tangles, a chore he'd be delighted to do for her.

Had he done so before, run a comb through her hair, allowed those long, beautiful strands to glide through his fingers? He couldn't imagine not taking advantage of such an opportunity.

"Leah."

She turned fully toward him. Through the nightrail he saw the rosy tips of her breasts. He tried not to stare, but oh, what exquisite torment.

"Now is a fine time for you to wake," she lightly scolded.

"Is it terribly late?"

"Nay, only a bit past compline. Need you anything?"

Late evening, then, and no needs he intended to tell her about until he could engage in vigorous movement. Then he'd not only tell Leah about his needs, but show her he was able and willing to satisfy hers as well.

"Not for the nonce."

"Comfortable?"

"My only complaint is the size of the bed. If it were larger, you would not have to sleep on a pallet."

She turned away, set her comb on the table. "I do not mind a pallet overmuch."

"I mind."

Leah pursed her lips, then smiled softly. "You must not concern yourself with my comfort. Certes, where I sleep is of little import."

"I would rather you were beside me."

"Oh." A rosy blush crept up her neck and settled on her cheeks.

Why the embarrassment? Surely they shared the marriage bed. Or perhaps not. Some married couples kept to separate beds. Or perhaps he and Leah hadn't been married long enough for Leah to overcome her maidenly shyness.

Leah? Shy? A contradiction. Fascinating—and perhaps not a road to explore without some notion of where it led.

Why was he so reluctant to explore? Somehow his wariness to further question Leah about his past didn't feel right, either. The memory loss fascinated him, though it frightened him, too. At times he wanted to poke and prod until everything flooded back, at other times retreat from the uncertainty of what he'd remember that might be better left in the darkness.

Perhaps he hadn't been a nice man, nor a good husband.

Still, Leah had nursed him tenderly, and their kiss exposed a shared passion. He'd felt her desire, and doubted any wife desired a disreputable lout.

His curiosity overcame his various fears.

"We have not known each other long, have we?"

She tilted her head and frowned. He hated her frown. "You remember?"

"'Tis simply a conjecture. Am I right?"

"Aye," she said warily. "What made you think so?"

"Not one thing in particular, just an . . . impression that we do not know each other well. I assumed we have not been married very long." Which led him back to what bothered him about the shipwreck. "You said the shipwreck happened before we reached Dover's harbor. Were we in France?"

"We boarded the ship in Calais."

"Were we on a wedding trip?"

She breathed in deeply, then blew out. "We truly need to find something for you to do to take your mind off your lost memory."

She sought to change the subject, which he found vexing.

"I did not think my question so taxing."

Her eyes narrowed, her own ire coming to the fore. "Nay, we were not on a wedding trip. Now you have yet another question for me . . . Why were we in France? Am I right?"

"'Twould seem to follow."

"And my answer will bring forth yet another question." She tossed a hand in the air. "You are right, we have not known each other long, not well at all. Geoffrey, I cannot answer all of your questions because I have so *few* answers."

"Better than *no* answers!"

Her fists went to her hips. "You need not shout at me."

He hadn't meant to shout, but he was sick of feeling

so damn helpless, so damn useless, to himself or anyone else.

"Dammit, Leah, my body is here but my mind is not. I feel like a . . . beast who merely eats and sleeps, without purpose. Perhaps you should truly shut me up in the north tower where I can be a proper beast and howl at the moon."

"You will be whole again."

Would he? That depended on what one considered whole, and he very much feared he'd never be whole again.

"My legs will heal, but will my mind? What happens if I never again know the man who I was, or what I can do?" He laid back on the bolster, his wrist over his eyes, his anger ebbing. Aw, hell, he was feeling mightily sorry for himself, but for Leah, too. 'Twasn't fair she should suffer this horror with him. "You should have left me out on that plank, or shoved me off. Better you should be a widow than tied to a man who—"

"How dare you!" Then, from directly above him, "If you were not already hurting terribly I might . . . punch you in the jaw for uttering such nonsense."

He uncovered his eyes. Stark white and trembling, Leah wagged a finger at him, utterly glorious in her fury.

"I went to a hell of a lot of trouble to get you off that plank, to move you to Pecham, all the while believing you *would* die. You proved me wrong, you proved the learned physicians wrong. You live. You will walk again. And yet you speak of—"

Her voice caught. Moisture sparkled in her eyes. She was near to weeping and it was all his fault. She deflated the moment he grasped her hand, damn near sat atop him as her bottom hit the bed. Then he tugged, and she fell face down onto his chest, and he didn't give another thought to anything except the feel of Leah in his arms.

Geoffrey heard her slight gasp, felt her stiffen, but he'd yearned for this for so long he refused to let her go. He held her gently but firmly, and she soon stilled but for the little gulps of air she took in a vain effort to halt her tears.

He absorbed her warmth, wishing his sherte and her nightrail gone, but unwilling to move a muscle to disrupt the embrace.

Leah was slender yet strong, sturdy yet fragile, and far more vulnerable than he'd realized. He'd hurt her deeply with his pitiful whining, made her weep. But now he knew with certainty how much she cared, and that brought him some peace. No matter what else happened, no matter who he'd been or might one day be, he'd have Leah at his side.

He ought to apologize, but feared another bout of tears.

"I gather you do not wish to be a widow just yet."

She hit him this time, lightly on the shoulder. She turned her head to the side and sniffed. "Daft man."

"You might have told me."

"I just did, yer daft."

The false fierceness made him smile. He gave her a squeeze. "I meant about my dying. I did not realize I came so close."

"Too close." She sighed. "I believed the physician in Dover who said you had no chance to live. I should have known better than to discount your will."

The admission gave him pause. A strong will wasn't a

bad thing unless used wrongly, causing others to suffer. She'd mentioned Dover before, and some silly legend, but not the physician's damning opinion.

Naturally Leah, distraught and believing him dying, would have listened to the physician's advice.

"'Twas the physician who gave you the poppy for me."

"To ease your pain so you slept easily. I thought that was what you would do, just slip away peacefully in your sleep." She moved her head slightly, adjusting against his shoulder for comfort.

Gad, but this felt so good, so utterly right, pressed chest to breast with Leah, her head on one shoulder and her hand on the other. He pushed wayward strands of spun gold away from her face, felt the dampness on her cheeks. It pained him to have caused her tears, but he couldn't be completely sorry because the tears were shed for him.

"I am not going to die."

"I no longer doubt." She eased back, leaving a chill behind. "As I said, you will be whole again, someday."

"I want to believe that."

She licked her bottom lip, a nervous gesture. Did she know 'twas also erotic?

"Geoffrey, I think it best if you allow your memory to return on its own. Nothing I have told you about either your sister's wedding or the shipwreck have helped you. My giving you tidbits only upsets you, makes you yearn for more information than I am able to give."

A reasonable conjecture, but he didn't have to like it.

"Perhaps."

"Can you go back to sleep?"

Not for a while yet, but Leah obviously needed her rest and she shouldn't be denied on his account. He'd rather keep her close through the night, but that wasn't possible.

"Likely," he lied.

"Then I shall bid you a good night."

Leah tried to get up. He held fast.

"Then do so properly. A kiss, wife, to help me sleep."

She stared at his mouth, then wetted her lips. "We should not. Your ribs."

"You worry overmuch."

"I have had reason."

"No longer." Geoffrey pulled her closer, felt her rapidly beating heart. "Come see how well I heal."

His name came out on a small sigh. Resignation? Anticipation? He cared not which, only that she closed her eyes and bestowed on him the kiss he craved.

His elation knew no bounds. With a mere touch of soft, sweet lips she filled him with joy—and sorrow that the kiss signaled the end of their night and not the beginning.

Problems faded away. At the moment he didn't care who he was beyond being the man on whom Leah leaned against and shared her generous mouth. Warm and giving, a treasure beyond measure.

Her hand skimmed along his shoulder, up his neck, her fingers curling into his hair as if seeking succor. Already hard and wanting, his body tingled from the light touch, prompting his own hand to roam. Down her back and up again, along the length of her spine only to begin a slow journey up her side, the heel of his hand grazing the fullness of her breast.

She whimpered, feeding his confidence, urging him onward. He shifted to gather up folds of nightrail, the need to touch her bared flesh overwhelming—and nearly came up off the bed from the shot of pain to his side.

His hand instinctively reached for his ribs and Leah was up and off the bed before he could think to catch her.

Her amber eyes were yet glazed with the fever of passion, her lips wantonly swollen, her breathing hard.

"Apparently you are . . . not yet sufficiently healed."

"Come back. 'Twas but a twinge."

She shook her head and backed away. "Nay. Not again. We . . . forget ourselves."

Aye, he had and moved too far too fast. 'Twas a lesson he'd not forget. Next time he'd exert better control.

Leah blew out the candle flame, plunging the room into darkness. He heard her slide onto her pallet, rustle the covers.

"Geoffrey?"

"Hmmm?"

"You are not a beast."

"Except when I shout at you."

"Even then. Sleep well."

Geoffrey lay in the dark, thankful for an answer to one question at least. Not a beast. Hardly a compliment but a welcome observation.

Still, Leah's aversion to discussing the past bothered him.

Better to lie in the dark and ponder the reasons for her hesitation than think about the delightful interlude he'd ruined by allowing his lust to overwhelm his common sense.

She readily spoke about the shipwreck and the events

after. This morn she'd thanked him for saving her life, called him her hero. Tonight she gave him insights into the aftermath—his sorry condition and the incorrect declarations of the physician.

He didn't want to think about how she must have felt when told there was no hope that he'd live.

Of those things she willingly spoke, but whenever the conversation strayed to what came before, his entire life before the shipwreck, she avoided comment.

Perhaps, however, Leah had the right of it. Those few tidbits she'd tossed his way hadn't helped his memory return, had merely added to his frustration. Perhaps his mind needed the same time to heal as his body.

Perhaps in time he'd remember his sister and whether or not he had other family besides. Then he would know why he'd been planning to attend the wedding but not take Leah with him.

Useless to dwell on it, Leah had said.

Damn hard not to, was still his answer.

# Chapter 7

At Geoffrey's adamant insistence, Leah broke her fast in the great hall. She didn't understand why he'd shooed her from the bedchamber, why he thought it important she spend more time with her family. If she didn't know better, she'd think he wanted rid of her when from all indications he wanted more of her.

Much more.

To her everlasting chagrin, so did she. After that excessively powerful kiss last eve, she'd vowed to stay as far away from the bed as possible. A vow she must keep, except ignoring his allure was harder than it ought to be given her one experience with a man who'd also appealed too hard.

So she'd welcomed Geoffrey's suggestion this morn and now sat in her customary chair on her father's left, spooning in pottage washed down by an excellent wine.

On Father's right, Odo gave an account of his business dealings in Dover, to which she paid scant heed.

Truly, her father's presence at table this morn surprised her. After looking hither and yon for him last eve, she'd finally discovered he'd ridden out to the stannary. Father shunned traveling after dark, and if he lost sense of time while with the miners, he usually spent the night in the nearby village, with a widow he'd frequented for many years. Leah had learned long ago not to become concerned for his safety if he didn't return to Pecham for evening meal. Last eve, he'd not returned home before she'd made her way up the stairs to ready for bed and become involved in that dangerous exchange with Geoffrey.

Mercy, she'd been furious with Geoffrey over his suggestion that she should've let him die out in the Channel. Her temper flashed so hot she'd tossed caution aside to ensure he never uttered such nonsense again.

She'd gotten too close, ended up snuggled against Geoffrey's chest, and enjoyed the physical contact and emotional comfort far too much. The man in her bed tempted her beyond that of an attractive male to a healthy female. He engaged her senses, ignited her fury and then doused the flames within the space of minutes.

She'd spent mere moments wrapped in his arms, enfolded in his embrace, secure and aroused all at once. A dangerous combination she couldn't allow to happen again and fog her common sense—which seemed not too steady these days.

"We need to consider changing our buyers in Dover," Odo said more loudly than he'd been speaking.

Leah braced for his complaint, knowing her brother wouldn't pass the chance to tell her father she'd done something wrong. Except she'd done nothing wrong. This time.

"Are you not getting a good price in Dover?" Father asked.

"Decent, but one of our buyers is asking too many questions on the source of the goods, and dared haggle over the price. I fear others may follow his lead. 'Twouldn't do to have our name and trade besmirched."

Leah rolled her eyes.

Father frowned. "Our buyers are our life blood."

She didn't wither under Odo's glare or taunt. "Aye, they are that."

"Are others disgruntled?"

Odo turned back to Father. "Not that I know of, but—"

"'Tis your duty to know." Father leaned forward. "If you cannot judge the mood of our buyers, Odo, then I shall have to do so myself."

The criticism didn't sit well. Leah struggled not to feel glee as her brother squirmed. He'd sought to get her into trouble and ended up in the mud himself.

"Only the one buyer causes me concern, but 'tis nothing I cannot deal with. Besides, you have enough to do in overseeing the stannary. How goes the digging of the new tunnel?"

Leah wasn't sorry Odo changed the subject, though she knew he hoped to distract Father's concern over the trade. Since Nigel of Pecham's true love was the mine, she wasn't surprised he accepted the change. Indeed, she wanted to hear the answer herself.

She, too, loved visiting the stannary, something she hadn't done since returning home. The miners were a hardy lot, given to good humor—likely to balance the danger of their work. The opening of a new tunnel was always exciting.

"The tunnel is nearly complete. 'Struth, we can sell as much tin as we dig out, so I am anxious to begin full operation," he answered, then shifted his attention to Leah. "Is Geoffrey awake?"

"He was awake when I left him, breaking his fast. 'Twould not surprise me if he went back to sleep after finishing his pottage, though."

"He still sleeps most of the day?"

"Aye. For all he is stronger, he requires much rest."

Father nodded his agreement. "The task I have in mind for the lad should not tax him overmuch and will give him something to do with his waking hours."

Odo's eyes narrowed. "What task?"

"I mean to have him do the accounts for the stannary."

Leah instantly mistrusted her hearing. 'Twas a huge responsibility he proposed to give over to a man he'd seen and talked to but once.

"Is that wise?" Odo asked, echoing Leah's reaction.

"I see no reason why not. After all, he is family now and quite capable of keeping the accounts." Father briefly told Odo of the small test he'd given Geoffrey. "I cannot do sums so fast, and never all in my head. Best the man have a task to occupy his mind other than worrying over his loss of memory."

Leah pursed her lips at her father's perceptive observation. She'd not mentioned Geoffrey's state of mind to him. Not that she'd ever doubted her father's intelligence.

Given enough time Father might see through her lie, too.

On the morrow, Odo would leave Pecham to sell the goods in the caves, she was sure. Then she'd tell her father the truth, that Geoffrey wasn't family, before he discovered it on his own. Already she'd delayed overlong. Not that Geoffrey's working on the stannary ledger would pose a problem. Any number of people knew how much tin came out of the mine and the current price for which it would sell, legally or not.

'Twas the smuggling ledger that was closely guarded and kept secret. Only Father and Odo saw those figures, with Odo keeping the ledger current.

Odo took a sip of his wine. "Your husband's loss of wits is most strange."

"Geoffrey is not witless," Leah declared, her fierce protectiveness not surprising, she supposed, given the situation. "'Tis only his memory that fails him, not his ability to reason and speak."

"Or do sums," Father added, then shrugged. "'Twould be disconcerting, I imagine, to not remember one's past, but no matter. If he cannot resume his planned course in life, then we need find him a place here, if he wishes."

"Surely not," Odo objected. "A man does not marry unless he has the means to provide for a wife and family. Leah, you *did* have some assurance of Geoffrey's means to support you before you entered into marriage, did you not?"

Oh, damn. Both her father and brother were staring at her, awaiting some kind of answer. Her stomach churned. How to placate Odo and not make matters worse with her father?

"Geoffrey is not without means," she said, confident

with the conjecture. One need only look at the quality of his garments and the books in his trunk to assume as much.

"Are you aware of the extent of your marriage portion?"

Like a dog with a bone, Odo wasn't about to let go until he'd torn off every tidbit of meat, but at least here she was on safe ground.

"The usual one-third of his worth, I imagine, though we never discussed the extent of it, nor my dowry. You know a woman cannot legally arrange a marriage contract, Odo. 'Twas a matter for Father and Geoffrey to negotiate, part of the reason we came back to England."

Odo huffed. "Except the man does not remember the extent of his holdings or source of his coin. Perhaps he relies heavily on your dowry."

Much good that would do any man. A few coins. A few jewels. Hardly a temptation.

Before she could say as much, her father rose from his chair. "As Leah says, a matter for me to resolve with Geoffrey at a later date. For now, we will discuss the accounts."

Odo rose and followed their father's stride toward the stairs. Leah tossed down the remains of her wine, needing a fortifying moment before making the same trek. Having all three males in the same room . . . well, Geoffrey and Odo had to meet sometime and perhaps Father's presence might make it easier.

Her father's attitude puzzled her. He seemed so willing to accept Geoffrey as his son-by-marriage, hadn't asked much about him or about a marriage settlement. 'Twasn't his nature to trust readily, a good thing considering his business dealings. Yet, for some reason he was disposed to trust Geoffrey, and Leah doubted his willingness was all due to a matter of saving himself time and trouble.

Before Leah could follow her father, Thuro, the captain of Pecham's guards, entered the great hall and strode toward her.

"Milady, there be beggars at the gate."

"Pilgrims?"

"I did not ask, milady, but 'tis most likely."

'Twas rare anyone came uninvited or unexpected to Pecham's gate, and those who did were rarely allowed inside. Father frowned upon admitting anyone within the walls who might stumble upon something they shouldn't. Every so often a pilgrim on his way to one of the holy wells in the area lost his way and happened upon Pecham.

"How many?"

"A family, milady. Man, wife and two children."

"Did they ask for more than alms?"

"Not that I heard."

Torn, Leah glanced at the stairway, tempted to send out a few crusts of bread, a coin or two, and have the guards send the pilgrims on their way. But as her father's chatelaine, the giving of alms was her duty to attend. Everyone would consider her behavior odd if she gave the chore to Thuro. When this business with Geoffrey was over, 'twould be her value to her father as his chatelaine that would ensure a roof over her head.

"Have them wait outside the gate. I will be there anon."

Leah gathered those scraps of food she deemed suitable from the kitchen, all the while worrying over what was happening up in her bedchamber.

"Is there aught else ye be wantin' milord?"

Geoffrey smiled inwardly at the serving wench's blatant offer. Pottage, gossip and fornication. What more could a man ask for to start the morning? Mona had already supplied the first two and was more than willing to provide the third.

He lifted the tray from his lap. "Nay, nothing more, Mona."

She took the tray, bending forward in a saucy display of feminine assets. "Ye sure?"

Tempting. Had he once been receptive to such offers from the servant girls at Pecham? Mona might tempt him, but he had no trouble resisting. Now, if Leah made so exquisite an offer he'd tear his sherte off and flip up her skirts in a flash. Except Leah wasn't about to make any such offer until sure he'd not hurt his ribs again.

"Nothing more," he said sternly.

As he hoped, Mona heard the warning and backed up a step. She nodded slightly in understanding. Leah was right, the girl knew more than she ought.

She glanced over her shoulder toward the open door. Geoffrey heard steady, solid footsteps in the passageway just before Leah's father entered the bedchamber, followed by a younger man. Nigel carried a large book, his companion juggled several rolls of parchment.

Mona dipped Nigel a curtsey and sent the younger man a wary glance before scurrying out of the chamber.

Nigel called over his shoulder. "Odo, place those on

the table. Leah can fetch them for Geoffrey as he needs them."

The younger man was Leah's brother, then, whose unexpectedly early homecoming last evening apparently set the entire household aflutter.

From Anna, who regularly shuffled in to inspect his bandages and check the splints, and from Ned, who appeared at regular intervals to see to his bodily needs, and now from Mona, Geoffrey had learned more in the past few days about his wife's family than he had from Leah.

Nigel, a widower of long standing, had raised up his son and daughter here at Pecham. Pecham's people were delighted Leah had returned to restore order to the everyday running of the keep—except, perhaps, Odo. Apparently the siblings didn't get along well. No one had said outright they disliked the heir to Pecham, but all gave Geoffrey the impression no one minded in the least when he was away from home.

Tall and lean with angular features, Odo dumped the parchment rolls on the table before turning to face the bed. His arrogant stare judged Geoffrey harshly, piercing pride already badly damaged.

Geoffrey keenly felt the disadvantage of his inability to rise from the bed, to stand toe-to-toe with his brother-by-marriage. All he could do was stare unblinkingly back.

Nigel stepped into his line of sight, blocking what seemed to Geoffrey an odd and disturbing contest of wills with Leah's brother.

Leah's father laid the book on Geoffrey's lap. 'Twas a heavy tome of sheets of parchment pressed between slabs of wood, a coat of arms burned into the cover. Thick string served as binding.

Geoffrey opened the book. A ledger.

To his delight, he recognized every neatly written word and number scrawled on the page. He soon understood their meaning. Nigel of Pecham operated a tin mine—in Cornwall called a stannary. On the pages were recorded weekly weights of ore dug up from the depths of the earth, and the cost and profit of selling the ore.

"You understand what you look at?" Nigel asked.

"Aye. This is the ledger for your stannary."

Nigel clasped his hands behind his back, his expression somber. "In Leah's absence, my time for everything became short. You will note the last page, where the accounting comes to a halt. All of the numbers are here but need to be recorded and totaled."

The parchment rolls contained the figures, Geoffrey guessed.

"You wish me to act as your scribe?"

"If you think the chore not too taxing."

He sensed movement—Odo moving to stand at the end of the bed, his scowl challenging Geoffrey to turn Nigel down. No chance of that. The task would give him something to do and be useful at the same time. A sanity-saving prospect.

Now understood Odo's scowl. Resentment. Keeping the accounts should rightfully fall to the son if the father lacked time to do them. Still, he'd not turn aside the task.

"Since I cannot yet give actual assistance at the stannary, I would be honored to keep the ledger."

"You know something about mining?"

Surprisingly enough, or perhaps not given the way his mind worked of late, he did.

"Somewhat. One digs the ore from the ground, washes it, smelts it, then hauls it off to be made into pewter or for coinage."

Odo crossed his arms. "How is it you know about mining and accounts, yet claim your memory lost? I find that right . . . strange."

So did Geoffrey, so he could hardly blame Odo for doubting. Knowledge seemed stored in his mind, springing forth when prodded. Mathematics. Language. Mining. Yet he didn't know how he'd come to know these things, or who'd tutored him in numbers and letters, or if he'd ever seen a stannary.

"I cannot explain," he admitted to Odo, rather pleased the simple statement didn't come out as a frustrated whine.

"Nor need you," Nigel broke in. "So long as you can do the sums I care not about the other." He waved toward the book. "My overseer writes down each day's numbers. At the end of the week they are delivered to Pecham." Nigel smiled. "'Twill take you a while to do the sums for the missing weeks, I own."

Grateful for Nigel's confidence in his ability, eager to get started, he asked, "How long since the last entry?"

"Late spring."

'Twas now high summer. The account was several weeks' worth of entries behind.

That meant Leah had been away from Pecham for a long while, with her absence felt heavily by her father.

Daughters married, left hearth and home to live with their husbands with little disruption to the everyday workings of the home she left. Apparently, not so at Pecham. One would think Nigel would choose a reliable woman to tend to the tasks Leah did as chatelaine, not try to tend them himself.

Or was Nigel one of those men who disliked giving over control of important tasks to others?

Nay, couldn't be. The proof lay on his lap. After only one meeting and an easy test, Nigel relinquished a critical, sensitive chore, though Geoffrey suspected his father-by-marriage would check the figures for accuracy.

Why hadn't Nigel given the chore to Odo? Perhaps a lack of talent for numbers? Possibly, and none of his business. He'd be grateful for the chore and not worry over Odo's displeasure.

Leah breezed into the room, giving the merest glance at the rolls of parchment on the table and the book on his lap.

"Father, if you are finished, pray come down to the hall. There is a family I want you to meet."

Odo turned on his sister. "You allowed outsiders into the hall without permission?"

Geoffrey didn't like Odo's tone, as if he considered Leah's action a mortal sin. Leah showed no reaction, simply continued to speak to her father.

"I deemed them harmless. 'Struth, Father, the man needs work and knows somewhat about mining. If you are in need of miners, he might do."

Odo tossed a hand in the air. "So now you know how to judge good labor for the mine. Truly, Leah, you must learn to keep your nose out of business that does not concern you."

To Geoffrey's amazement, Nigel also ignored Odo. "What brings the family to Pecham?"

"They journey to the holy well at St. Cleer and wandered wrongly. They have two girls, the youngest is blind."

Parents hoping for a miracle for their child. Since his own recovery seemed a miracle, Geoffrey didn't scoff. Still, he owed his life to Leah's care, not water from a holy well.

"Then you should have given them a crust of bread and pointed them in the right direction," Odo instructed his sister. "If the child lost her sight due to some evil, we have no need of her kind in our midst."

Leah finally addressed her brother. "I am told the girl has been blind since birth. What evil could a babe possibly have committed in the womb?"

"Her mother's evil then. Either way, the family should not be left unguarded in our hall!"

"Thuro is with them. Father?"

"'Twill do no harm to talk to the man, I suppose." Nigel waved a hand at the ledger. "Have a good look. I will return anon to answer any questions you may have."

All three turned to leave. His ire high, after Nigel and Leah passed through the door, Geoffrey seized the chance for a word with his brother-by-marriage.

"Odo, a moment if you will."

The man stopped and looked over his shoulder.

Geoffrey ignored his disadvantage. "You will henceforth have a care when you speak to my wife."

Odo raised an eyebrow. "Why for?"

"Because I do not like your tone. If you speak to her at all, you will do so with respect."

"Respect? For Leah? I think not. Obviously you do not remember her lack of sense and her disgraceful behavior. When you do, perhaps you will not be so tolerant. Or are you one of those men easily led by the crook of a woman's finger? But then, you do not remember that either, do you?"

No, he didn't. Disgraceful behavior? Such as what? By whose definition? If Odo's then he'd pay the accusation no heed. Odo thought Leah's compassion for the family in the hall as misguided. Geoffrey considered her actions both compassionate and honorable. 'Twas Odo who needed to temper his behavior, not Leah.

Geoffrey's fist itched to connect with Odo's jaw. "My tolerance of her faults is mine affair, not yours. A wife's discipline falls to her husband, not her brother. I will not tolerate your disrespect for her."

He didn't like Odo's smile. "You will do well to remember who rules Pecham. You are but a guest, Geoffrey. So long as you remain sheltered here, have a care not to overstep."

Odo ended the confrontation by leaving the bedchamber.

Geoffrey's palm slapped the ledger's wood. It stung, doing nothing to relieve his frustration.

He knew in his bones that he and Odo would have words again, except next time he'd be sure the bastard couldn't walk out on him.

She'd done right to admit the peasant family. Father's willingness to talk to the man told her so. Odo's caution about admitting strangers was well taken, but mercy, how could she have turned the family away?

Especially the girls. She'd never laid eyes on two more adorable urchins. The eldest ten summers, the little one six, both girls needed food and clothing and shelter far more than the youngest needed water from the holy well. Superstition persisted about the water's healing effects, but Leah had never witnessed a miraculous cure. Most often people came away disappointed. Leah doubted the water could cure sightless eyes even if the girl bathed in it.

Both girls clasped their nervous mother's hands and stood behind their father, Michael, who withstood the lord of Pecham's questions most satisfactorily. All of the family's possessions lay near the door, bundled up in two blankets.

"Are we agreed?" Father asked.

With his head bowed, his knit cap scrunched in his hands, Michael answered, "Aye, milord. My wife and me are everlastin' grateful."

"Then report to Garth at the mine. He will show you to an empty hut in the village and assign your labor."

Michael's chin rose slightly. "If ye'll be permittin', milord, we have yet to visit St. Cleer. Me daughter—" he waved his cap at the tyke. "We came so far and with such hope."

Leah's heart hurt for both the girl and her parents. The world was a merciless place for a child. Between illness and common dangers so many died. Without sight, the tyke was more open to danger, unable to see it all around her. Leah understood her parents' wish to ease their daughter's burden, give her a chance at a full life. But sometimes life wasn't fair or easy.

"'Tis a full day's walk yet to St. Cleer," her father

said. "Thuro will show you the path. I would not put too much hope in the water, however."

Michael shrugged. "'Tis the only hope she has left."

After a long pause, Father's mouth curved into a sad smile. "Then, certes, you must visit the well. My little girl grew up whole and healthy. Naturally you wish the same for yours."

Leah swallowed the lump forming in her throat.

Father scrunched down. "Come here, child."

Michael called back, "To me, Eileen."

The girl let go of her mother's hand and unerringly walked to her father's side.

"Eileen, is it?" Father asked.

She dipped into a curtsey. "Aye, milord," she said, her voice soft and sweet, then brought her hands up toward Father's face.

Michael stopped her with a hand to her shoulder. "Nay, Eileen."

As Eileen's hands fell, Father looked up at Michael, questioning the command.

"'Tis how she sees, milord, with her fingers. Eileen forgets betimes she must first ask leave."

"Well, then, I give her leave. The lass should know the face of her overlord."

Leah heard the familiar gruffness and hoped it didn't frighten Eileen. He was usually brusque, both in speech and manner. To her relief, the girl clasped her father's cheeks, staring over his shoulder as her fingers roamed his face.

"What do you see?" he asked.

"Yer face is round and much creased. From your voice I thought ye younger."

Leah bit back a smile, doubting Father appreciated being told he felt old.

Eileen giggled. "Yer eyebrows tickle my fingers."

Father's eyes fair sparkled with humor. "Do they now?"

"And ye've a mark on yer cheek, here."

"That sometimes happens when a man is careless when scraping whiskers."

"Does it hurt?"

"Nay, 'twas a long time ago."

Leah wondered how long ago, and why she'd not noticed the small mark on her father's cheekbone. How odd to see her father now as Eileen saw him. Getting on in years. Gruff but able to remain very still while a little girl satisfied her curiosity.

He'd never been one for overt affection. A hug would turn his cheeks red. Still, he'd rarely raised his voice to her and, she now realized, he'd done the best he knew how to raise his children up whole and healthy. Not an easy task, she imagined, after Mother's death.

Leah fought off a sudden chill, realizing why Father so willingly accepted her marriage to Geoffrey, and Geoffrey himself.

*I have given him another son.*

Someone to share the work load, aye, but more. An addition to his family. A strong man of good looks and bright mind who Father deemed worthy of a place at Pecham.

A man worthy to sire grandchildren.

Leah watched Nigel, lord of Pecham, submit to an intimate study of his face by a peasant girl he'd just met.

Would he allow as much from his own grandchildren? Most likely.

Dear God in heaven. 'Twas an expectation of her father's she'd never considered before. Babes to bounce on his knee and regale with stories. Young ones to raise up whole and healthy and continue the family line.

Except she wasn't married to Geoffrey. There wouldn't be issue from the union that didn't exist. Father might hope for grandchildren, but none were forthcoming in the immediate future from either of his own offspring.

Eileen giggled again, and Father's smile widened.

'Twas a thing of beauty and cause for despair.

On the morn she'd have to tell her father the man he'd begun to accept as family wasn't her husband. There would be no grandchildren for years yet, if ever, given both her and Odo's lack of luck in securing mates.

Nigel of Pecham was going to be more disappointed in his daughter than she'd ever dreamed he'd be.

## *Chapter* 8

*L*eah stifled a yawn and hurried down to the great hall, unable to fathom why her father summoned her at this unholy hour of the morn.

Thuro waited near the door, a lighted torch in his hand.

"Is aught amiss?" she asked.

"Not that I know of, milady."

Which was the same answer she'd received from the bleary-eyed maid who'd slipped into the bedchamber and quietly shook Leah awake. Dressing in the dark, she thought she'd managed to slip out without disturbing Geoffrey.

Leah knew why her father was up and about before dawn. As was his habit, Father accompanied Odo to the caves to ensure his son's leave-taking uneventful, that the wagons loaded with smuggled goods rolled smartly down the road. Surely whatever Father had to say could wait until he returned from the caves, until the sun shone and she awakened naturally.

Leah marched into the predawn bailey, pulling up the hood of her cloak against the swirling, chilling mist. Thuro's torch sputtered and spat, the only sound disturbing the deep silence. Even the ocean was eerily quiet, a hush notable for its rarity. From near the gate she heard muffled voices and jingle of horses' tack, their position marked by the haloed light of torches.

She rushed by Odo, who sat atop his stallion, scowling. She didn't pause to find out why, intent on learning why she'd been sent for so she could return to the warmth of the hall. Most likely he wouldn't appreciate her inquiry anyway.

As a child, Odo had possessed an endearing smile, bestowed sparingly, but often enough that she remembered it. He'd not smiled with true pleasure in years. What had happened to the brother who'd once held a little sister's hand when up on the wall walk, to ensure she didn't fall? When had he stopped asking after her welfare and begun belittling her instead?

They'd all been upset by her mother's death and grieved mightily. Time had passed and they'd all learned to smile and laugh again. Except Odo's smile had dimmed, his mood subdued, and in the past few years he'd become morose, as if he found life itself one disappointment after another.

'Twas useless to wonder over her brother's moods. Nothing made him happy anymore, and she'd stopped trying.

Her father was another matter. With him she tried, and occasionally succeeded. He stood near Boadicea, tugging on his riding gloves.

He looked bone-deep weary.

Images from last eve sprang forth, of the little blind girl stroking his age-weathered face. The man should yet be abed, getting his rest, not out here in the dark and damp.

How odd that she felt protective, as if she were the caregiver of her parent, a father who'd barely noticed her over the years. However, since her return she'd felt a subtle change in their relationship. He maintained his gruff, straightforward demeanor, but seemed to have softened somewhat.

She scoffed at the fanciful thought. Soft? Never. He did what he wished and everyone had best fall in line. What better proof than this summons?

"You sent for me?"

Father took Boadicea's reins from the stable lad. "I have decided to make the journey with Odo. I leave you in charge of Pecham until I return."

Shocked to full wakefulness, she blurted out, "You do?"

"Aye, you hear rightly." His indulgent smile didn't ease her confusion. "A sudden decision, but a necessary one, I think."

Father rarely accompanied Odo on selling trips. Her brother's comment at supper the other night about a disgruntled buyer must have prompted Father's decision to see for himself if the business ran smoothly, a decision that must stick in Odo's craw. No wonder he scowled.

"How long will you be gone?"

"A month, maybe more."

*A month!* He'd left her in charge of Pecham before, but never for more than a few days.

The running of the keep she could handle with ease.

If a problem arose at the stannary or with the guards, her father's capable retainers stood ready to advise her of how to resolve nearly any situation.

However, if a ship came in she'd be most uncomfortable.

"There are no ships due, are there?"

Father shook his head. "Nay, we should be back before another ship arrives."

Leah took a long breath, mightily relieved. "All right, then."

"Should you have need of me, send a message with Ned. We go to York, London and Dover. In all but London we should be easy enough to find."

She didn't bother guessing at who of a number of buyers he wished to see in York and London. In Dover he'd visit whichever buyer Odo believed discontent.

"We shall manage," she assured him.

"I do not doubt or I would not leave for so long." He swung up into the saddle. "Should you need advice, look first to your husband. Geoffrey seems a capable man."

A most natural thing to do for any woman, Leah supposed. Except Geoffrey wasn't her husband, which she'd fully intended to tell her father this morn.

Leah bit her bottom lip. She'd prepared a speech citing all of her good reasons why she lied, fashioned an apology and been ready to accept the consequences. However, now was not the time to blurt out the truth, not as Father prepared to ride out on what he considered a necessary journey.

In Dover he'd hear the same tales Odo had heard. Would they anger him, too? Probably not. Given her father's good will toward Geoffrey, he'd likely feel pride that the hero in the legend was his son-by-marriage.

What a muddle she'd gotten herself into.

Leah shook off the morose thought. Self-pity did her no good. She'd make things right with Father, with everyone, eventually.

With Geoffrey? He might never understand why she'd lied, whether his memory returned or not.

The least she could do was ensure that the heroic tale of him ended as it deserved.

"Father, would you do me a great favor while in Dover?"

He raised a gray, shaggy eyebrow. "What might that be?"

"Seek out Mistress Thatcher and tell her Geoffrey overcame his injuries, that he survives."

"This woman has an interest?"

Mistress Thatcher would be delighted to hear Geoffrey survived and be happy to spread the news.

"She helped me care for Geoffrey in Dover, much as Anna does now."

Father nodded his understanding and consent. "Take care."

"Godspeed."

He nudged Boadicea forward and shouted a command for the gate to open. With a mighty clatter the iron inched upward to allow the lord of Pecham to pass through.

A lump formed in her throat. Her eyes misted. Mercy, no reason existed to get all choked and teary-eyed. Father wouldn't be gone all that long. He'd be back, likely better for the invigorating journey, content the smuggling trade thrived.

Still, she couldn't yet go back into the hall.

Leah took the torch from Thuro. "You may return to your quarters."

He shrugged. "I be too awake to sleep now. If yer going up to watch his lordship leave, I may as well come along."

Either the captain of the guard had taken it into his head to watch over her, or her father had given Thuro orders to pay her special heed. Most likely the latter.

"As you please." She led the way to the gate tower and up the stone stairs. After sliding the torch into a sconce bolted to the wall at the top, she eased out onto the wall walk to watch the small party now passing over the drawbridge.

Father and Odo rode behind torch-bearing guards—Odo straight-backed, her father easy in the saddle. Neither glanced back, but she was sure Father listened for the gate to lower. By the time they disappeared down the path to the caves, all was quiet and secure.

'Twas a heady sensation, knowing she was in charge of Pecham. A bit frightening, too, to realize the safety and well-being of the holding and its people were her full responsibility, a rare duty for a woman.

The men of her family had been lords of Pecham for several generations, as her father was now, as Odo would be upon her father's death.

Leah shivered at the morbid, heart-rending thought, then pushed it aside. Pecham wasn't Odo's to rule over yet. Father might be aging, but retained his health and vigor and would do so for years.

Still, he'd looked so weary this morn.

Lack of sleep. Nothing more.

She leaned against the thick stone wall, cold and wet with mist. A breeze tugged at the hood of her cloak and the ocean began to rumble. Familiar. Comforting.

A month. By the time Father returned, Geoffrey's splints would be off, his legs healed. Would his mind heal as well?

If it did, would he even be here in a month? If he remembered his former life, he might well insist on leaving, in the back of a cart if he must, to rejoin his family.

Leah held no illusions. Father wouldn't leave for so long if he didn't think the holding in good hands, and not necessarily in hers alone. She'd have help when needed from retainers who'd been at Pecham for years.

And there was Geoffrey, who Nigel of Pecham considered intelligent and capable. His daughter's husband. A man to whom he might have given charge of Pecham if Geoffrey were physically able to walk the grounds and ride out to the stannary.

Nay, she'd not consult with Geoffrey on any problem. Now was her time to prove her worth to her father. She'd begin as she meant to go on.

"Thuro, you will ensure the entire guard informed of his lordship's extended absence," she ordered, though quite sure her father had taken the guards into his confidence before telling her. "If any are discontent about the matter, I wish to be informed immediately. I will also require two men as escort to the village after nooning. Father hired a new miner and I wish to see if he and his family are settled in as yet."

"The man with the blind child?"

"Aye."

Thuro nodded. "If you will permit, milady, I should like to serve as one of your escort."

Because Father had assigned him to guard her, or out of curiosity over the girl? No matter.

"I shall be glad of your company, Thuro."

Leah pushed away from the wall. The guard once again anticipated her movements. He snatched up the torch and led the way down the stairs and across the bailey. She entered the great hall to find the servants beginning to stir. Soon they'd roll up their pallets and set out the trestle tables and benches for those wishing to break fast.

The daily cycle at Pecham would go on without pause as it had for eons. Meals would be served and chores completed with a minimum of fuss. Everyone at Pecham had a job to do and knew how his lordship wanted it done. Slackness wasn't permitted, even in his absence.

Leah climbed the stairs and quietly entered the bedchamber.

"You are up early," Geoffrey said, his voice soft but too clear to have just awakened. Had he lain awake all this time, waiting for her to come back?

When had he awakened? Before or after she'd slipped out of her nightrail and fumbled with her gown and boots in the dark?

Twice now he'd nearly caught her in a state of undress.

Leah ignored the thrum of arousal at the prospect, vowing to be more discreet in the days to come. The man tempted her body as thoroughly as his conversation and humor engaged her mind—a disastrous combination.

She removed her cloak, draped it over a chair to dry. "I did not mean to wake you. I tried not to."

"I heard the door close when you left. Is aught amiss?"

Then he'd seen nothing he shouldn't, praise the Fates. Still, the thought of standing naked in his presence, having his eyes on her, again sent a thrill through her blood. Leah quickly quelled the sensation.

"My father left with Odo this morn. He wished to bid me farewell, is all."

Not quite true, but close enough.

"He could not have done so last night?" he asked, clearly irritated on her behalf.

Leah eased down onto her pallet and smiled into the darkness. "In that we are of a mind. Nobody should be expected to rise at so early an hour. The next time my eyes open the sun had best be high in the sky."

He said nothing more, allowing her to go back to sleep as she wished. Unfortunately her mind was too busy to allow slumber right away.

With Father gone, she'd not be able to spend so much time with Geoffrey. A good thing in some ways, particularly given how easily she aroused in his mere presence.

She considered moving him back into the solar, then dismissed the temptation. 'Twould cause too much speculation among the servants, too much distracting gossip. Until Father returned, or Geoffrey regained his memory, she must maintain the pretense of their marriage.

He shouldn't be too bored without her company. He now had the stannary accounts to keep him busy, and since she'd be pressed for time, there was no reason he couldn't do the household accounts, too.

She'd check on him from time to time. Anna would surely visit him. Whenever Ned came up to see to Geoffrey's comfort needs, he tended to stay a while, sometimes to play a game of chess.

Geoffrey would be well occupied. He should be content and out of sight and mind while she went about her work.

A fortnight later, Leah returned from a hasty trip to the stannary, a scroll of parchment in hand—the figures supplied by Garth, the overseer, for Geoffrey to record in the ledger.

Two weeks had flown by with nary a hitch.

The new tunnel was nearly completed, would be done and ready for working by the time Father returned home.

Michael and his family had settled into the village as smoothly as could be expected. The water from the holy well hadn't cured his daughter's blindness, and now the villagers began to accept little Eileen's infirmity as one of the body, not caused by any evil.

Thuro still escorted Leah everywhere except up to her bedchamber. 'Twas irksome, but she understood her father's reasoning and accepted the guard's presence as unavoidable. The man simply followed an order she couldn't undo.

'Struth, everything was going so well she could hardly believe her good fortune.

Anxious to give the figures to Geoffrey, she tossed Thuro the reins of her horse.

"Have Thomas give the horses an extra treat. We rode them harder than we ought." At the narrowing of his eyes, she added, "I am but going straight into the keep. No harm can come to me between here and there."

He glanced at the huge oak doors at the top of the stairway that marched up to the great hall, then relented with a nod. Leah crossed the bailey swiftly, knowing Thuro wouldn't enter the stable until she passed through the door. She gave him a quick smile over her shoulder as she tugged on the huge brass ring.

She stepped inside the hall and froze.

Garbed in his long-sleeved ivory sherte and sapphire tunic, Geoffrey sat in a chair placed sideways at the end of a trestle table. His legs, covered by a blanket, were propped on a cushioned stool. Ned sat on a bench, the chess board angled between them on the corner of the table.

Geoffrey fair beamed at her, a smile of joy she'd never seen before and now had trouble resisting.

Leah couldn't decide at whom to direct a reprimand— at Geoffrey for risking his limbs or at whoever carried him down to the hall. Surely he hadn't walked. The splints had best be secure on his legs or she'd toss a fit scathing enough to be heard outside the keep's curtain wall.

Geoffrey's smile never faltered at her approach.

She crossed her arms and tried to look stern, not sure at all that she succeeded. "How?"

He didn't pretend to mistake her meaning. "Ned and Thomas. I swear Thomas is as strong and surefooted as the horses he cares for, and Ned did an excellent job of keeping my legs straight and together down the stairs. Anna stood by the whole time to ensure I came to no harm."

Leah glanced down at Ned, who had the sense to look sheepish, then looked around for Anna, who was nowhere to be seen. Damn, she couldn't truly upbraid the people who'd given in to Geoffrey's whim.

She should have known he'd try something like this. He'd been hinting at his boredom for several days now, and she'd found tasks for him to do—that apparently gave him no relief, or not enough.

"You sweet-talked Anna into this, did you not, because you knew I would deny you?"

"Aye," he said without a hint of apology for his guile. "You tend to be overprotective."

'Twas selfish, she supposed, but keeping Geoffrey hidden away in her bedchamber protected her more than him. True, his legs weren't healed, wouldn't be for another fortnight. Moving him about wasn't a good idea but apparently didn't harm him.

Beyond that, she was wary of allowing too many of Pecham's people to get to know and like him. At any given moment his memory might return and she'd be caught in her lie. She'd lose the respect she'd regained after her stupid error in judgment with Bastian.

Still, she truly wanted Geoffrey to mend completely. When he walked out of here someday—and he would, probably furious with her for her deception—he'd go home on strong, straight legs if she had anything to say about it.

That assumed he wanted to go home. Leah didn't understand why no family member had inquired after him. Did they not care if he healed well enough to return to them?

"Ned, are you not on duty shortly?"

The young guard took the heavy hint and rose from the bench. "Shall we continue on the morrow, milord, especially since I am winning for a change?"

Geoffrey chuckled. "If you wish."

Ned gave her a parting bow and scurried off.

Leah eased into the seat Ned vacated, examining the chess board. Indeed, Ned had Geoffrey's queen in a precarious position.

"The lad's game improves," Geoffrey said.

She pushed the board toward the middle of the table, careful to not juggle the pieces, and placed the parchment scroll beside it. "The two of you play often. With practice comes skill."

He picked up a castle of finely carved pine and twirled it between his deft fingers. "'Twas odd, the first time we played. I knew how each piece must move, knew the strategy to employ. Yet I know not where I learned the game, or who I played against."

She had no answers for him, causing her discomfort as talk of his past always did.

"I suppose you will now expect to be carried down here every day."

Geoffrey placed the castle back on its square. "I should like to, if you do not mind."

She did, but couldn't tell him the true reason why. A glance at the blanket covering his legs revealed the outline of the bracing wooden splints.

"Are you comfortable?"

A wry smile touched his mouth. "Reasonably."

"Then I will add your cartage to Ned and Thomas's duties."

"'Twill only be for another fortnight."

In a fortnight, the splints would come off and Geoffrey could get up and down the stairs on his own, go anywhere he pleased.

He rested his arm on the table, his palm up. Too easily, she slipped her hand into his. He squeezed, gently yet firmly, making her heart beat faster. She looked into intense sapphire eyes and nearly lost the ability to think.

"I know you worry for me, Leah. I promise I will do naught to harm my legs. I want to walk again as much as you want me to." His grip tightened, his mouth thinned. "I fear, however, that my memory may never return, and I must accept it, as must you. If that is the case, then we must make our lives here at Pecham, and I see no sense in delay. Would it not be best for me to know your father's people and them to know me?"

His reasoning was sound, or would be if Geoffrey were truly her husband.

"You have had no more flashes of memory, then?"

"None, and believe me, I have tried." The tightness of his mouth eased. "'Twas cursed wretched to try so hard to remember my past and have nothing spring forth. 'Tis one of the reasons I asked Anna to have me carried down here. I need to look to the future or go mad."

A future. With Geoffrey. Here at Pecham. Impossible.

Fighting his appeal became harder every day, but she couldn't let the attraction or her emotions lead her astray. She'd done so once, with Bastian, and paid a high price.

Leah didn't think anyone had yet told Geoffrey of her scandalous flight from Pecham with the handsome smuggling captain. Eventually, someone would refer to the tale and he'd likely demand an explanation of the woman he thought his wife.

She could tell him . . . nay, no more lies. Too many lay between them already.

Dammit, he'd saved her life. He deserved better from her.

He deserved to remember, to have his life back as it was before the shipwreck. All she'd given him were half-truths and evasions.

If she couldn't keep him, she'd have to let him go free.

Leah glanced at her hand firmly cradled in Geoffrey's, letting the realization settle. Given the choice, she'd never let go of him. For the past month she'd tended him, talked to him, yet tried to shield her heart— and done a poor job of it.

He jiggled their clasped hands. "You would not have me go mad, would you?"

From somewhere she found a light voice. "Nay, I would not have you go mad. You are enough trouble as it is."

"Then you agree that we look to the future?"

"Aye," she said, knowing she lied once more.

"Might that future include a tankard of ale?"

She had to smile. Here she'd been thinking of the future in terms of weeks, and he of only the next few minutes. Perhaps that was best, to take each moment as it came.

"'Tis possible." She squeezed his hand before she let go, felt the warmth fade away. "Shall I bring the ledger down?"

He glanced at the parchment scroll. "Nay. I will record the figures tonight, after evening meal."

After evening meal they'd be alone in her bedchamber, he in her bed and she struggling not to join him. Best both of them have something to do to take their minds off each other.

Leah picked up the scroll, instructed one of the serving wenches to fill a tankard for Geoffrey, then hurried to her bedchamber.

The chamber seemed so empty without Geoffrey's presence.

She hadn't wanted Geoffrey here, and now that he'd escaped she wanted him back where he belonged. Except he didn't, might never truly belong.

Unless his memory never returned. Or if his memory returned and he could find it in his heart to forgive her.

She'd resisted helping him remember, evaded subjects she thought might prod his memory. Perhaps she'd put it off too long already.

Leah knelt down before the trunk stuffed in the corner, brushed the thin layer of dust from the top and opened the lid. Within were the remnants of Geoffrey's former life. Breeches and hose. His books. The wooden carvings and a knife.

She gently ran a finger over the horse he'd been carving before his world vanished. If she gave him the horse and knife, he'd likely know what to do with them. Would he also remember for whom he made it? If she gave him one of the books, he'd likely be able to read it. Would that jar loose a recollection of attending a lecture at the university? Would he remember the sister whose wedding he'd come to England to attend?

She had no way of knowing, and there was only one way to find out.

# Chapter 9

Once more ensconced in the bed, Geoffrey closed the household ledger on his lap, the week's figures recorded, feeling better than he had in, well, recent memory.

Over the past two weeks since Leah overtook the running of the holding, Anna and Ned had been attentive. But today had passed most pleasantly and quickly amongst the merry bustle in the hall.

Leah hadn't been pleased to find him in the hall, still wasn't by the look of her. She'd supervised his cartage back up the stairs after evening meal with a frown on her face, a frown yet evident nearly an hour later.

She worried for his legs, he knew, but sensed some other concern. Leah sat near the candle stand, the glow haloing her lovely form, embroidering blood-red silk on a pristine white altar cloth she'd begun yesterday, intended for the village church in payment for prayers for the soul of her deceased mother.

She'd removed her circlet and veil and slipped off her

boots, the only attire she deigned to remove in his presence, and propped her hose-covered feet on a small stool. Later she would take her nightrail and go into another room to change. Modesty in a wife might be a desirable trait, yet he longed to see Leah in her full feminine glory.

He'd quelled the temptation, more than once, to order Leah to disrobe within his sight. 'Struth, to see her nude and not be able to feel the length of her beneath him might well snap his sanity.

So he watched her hands, fascinated by the deft flow of her graceful fingers, the rhythm of thread piercing cloth, over and over, rarely missing a beat.

'Twas nigh impossible not to imagine Leah's deft fingers grasping those parts of his body she'd so far avoided touching. In a mere fortnight he'd know the pleasure of making love with Leah, making up for the time they'd lost.

For the memories he'd lost.

The thought no longer pained him as sharply as before. He'd given ample consideration to his plight over the past weeks.

'Twas irritating and frustrating, and while he loathed losing so many years of his life, he'd begun to accept the deprivation. The decision not to fight so hard didn't come easily or without doubts, but he'd agonized over the matter long enough. 'Struth, the past didn't matter so much if he could see a future, and he did—with Leah, here at Pecham, at least until he decided on another course.

Though he yearned to know more of the sister he might never see again, Geoffrey could think of no better way to repay Leah for saving his life than to get on with making a future for them both.

As if Leah sensed his stare, she looked up from her stitchery. "Finished?"

"With both the stannary and household accounts."

A wry smile touched her lips. "Father will be pleased. You do sums with greater ease than anyone in all of Cornwall, and with a neat hand, at that. The ledgers have never looked so good."

He shrugged off the compliment. The talent was a part of him he no longer questioned. Still, while the stannary ledger seemed in order, the household ledger gave him pause. The sums recorded totaled correctly, but the ledger wasn't complete.

"I did note an error in the household account. I know Pecham took delivery of a crate of spices weeks past, but I saw no entry for it."

Leah rose and turned to set the altar cloth on the chair. "Very astute of you to notice."

Another compliment, but he got the feeling she truly didn't mean this one. Perhaps she didn't appreciate his commenting on an error in the ledger she normally kept.

"I only noticed because your father mentioned them in my presence and spices do not come cheaply."

She glided toward him—so lovely, so graceful.

Desire flared and heated his loins. If she deliberately tried to distract him from the cost of the spices, she did a wonderful job of it. Into Leah's outstretched hands he placed the ledger, wanting her so badly he was tempted to pull her down atop him.

He could now. His ribs hadn't given him a twinge in

days. Not even after he'd poked and prodded, twisted and turned as best he could to test for pain.

"Nothing of real value comes cheaply, betimes at a hefty price," she said softly, then sighed. "I suppose I must now find some other task to occupy your time."

What he had in mind he didn't consider a task, but pure pleasure. If not for his splints they could wile away the evening in bed, their bodies joined, their passion high. Soaring to bliss with Leah would be no chore.

His fists clenched.

He'd start with light kisses to her forehead and ease his way slowly and more forcefully downward to her lush mouth, then over her beautifully rounded breasts, until ending his journey nuzzled in the hair between her legs. He'd have her hot and writhing, wet and hungry, on the precipice of bliss before he slid into her to take them both over the edge.

Leah couldn't mistake Geoffrey's blatant desire.

She backed up a step, knowing the ledger clutched to her bosom a poor shield against his palpable need. Heat pooled in her nether regions, preparing her woman's places for the intimacy she yearned for but didn't dare seize.

To think she'd once thought keeping away from him during the day would lessen her growing fondness for him—except she thought about him constantly, could hardly wait to return to the bedchamber that had become not only a refuge but a haven. Whether they simply talked of their days, shared jests or shouted at each other, they'd shared intimate moments more powerful than the mere physical.

Nor had her body's cravings diminished. 'Struth, on

some nights the urge to crawl into bed beside Geoffrey had been nigh impossible to overcome.

She'd resisted because of his injuries, and because she didn't know if the man she had come to know so well was the same man she'd met aboard a ship.

People changed. Odo had passed from kind brother to sullen stranger. Father had mellowed. Bastian, for all his charm and promises, had proved faithless.

How odd, now that Geoffrey began to accept his loss of memory, she wanted to test it.

His notice of the spices made the test more urgent. The longer Geoffrey remained at Pecham, the more he'd become involved in the daily events and people's lives. He'd surely come upon other evidence of the source of most of her father's income. The illegal trade was as much a part of Pecham as the stannary.

'Twould be best for all, perhaps, if Geoffrey's memory was destined to return, that it happened before he learned of the smuggling, before her father came back from his journey, before her emotions became further entangled.

Leah inwardly scoffed. She'd found Geoffrey attractive and fascinating from their very first meeting, a man of obvious strength vulnerable to his stomach's upset. By plentitude of his powerful will alone he'd prevailed. He'd even defied death and won, all the while enchanting her with his easy charm and wry humor delivered in a deep, sensual voice.

Perhaps she liked him so much because he treated everyone from her father to the lowest servant with a measure of respect and thus earned their esteem in return. Or because sometimes he looked at her with a mixture of hunger and reverence that made her feel like the most desirable woman ever born.

But more, when snuggled against him she felt cherished and protected, as if she truly belonged within his embrace.

She might lose all that in the blink of a lash, but better now than later.

Leah put the ledger on the table and crossed to the trunk in the corner. Her hand trembled on the latch, but she pushed up the lid and banished her doubts. Surely she did the right thing, if not for herself then for Geoffrey. She moved aside his garments and studied the remaining items.

Which to choose, the carvings or a book? Which might prove the more potent prod—an activity he'd enjoyed at his leisure or a book he'd used for his studies?

Unsure, Leah pulled out the unfinished horse and the knife she assumed he'd used to carve it. She ran a thumb over the rough edges of the horse's head, believing it would soon be as smooth and beautiful as its mate.

"Leah?"

On impulse, she grabbed the completed carving, too.

As she approached his eyes widened and his hands rose. When she handed him the horses, he took them with reverent fingers. He held them up and turned them around in fascinated scrutiny.

She waited for signs of recognition, her heartbeat quickening in anticipation and dread, but saw only puzzlement.

After long moments, he finally asked, "Are these mine?"

Not knowing for sure, in answer she handed him the ebony-handled knife, which fit his palm perfectly.

He put the completed horse aside, cut a notch on the other horse's mane, then shook his head, as if disbelieving his temerity for putting the blade to wood.

Unable to stand the silence any longer, Leah folded her arms across her midriff. "They are beautiful."

He stared at the trunk. "Are there more?"

"Nay, only these."

His mouth thinned. "I know I made these. My hands remember what my mind does not."

Leah wondered at his calm while she struggled with both disappointment and relief. The carvings hadn't brought Geoffrey's memory flooding back, and she didn't know whether to bless or curse the Fates.

He yet stared at his trunk. "You told me that some of our belongings survived the shipwreck. I assumed 'twas only clothing."

"Not only."

Perhaps one of his books would accomplish what the horses hadn't. She'd taken two steps toward the trunk when a knock on the door interrupted.

Mona stood without, tears streaming down her cheeks. Leah's stomach coiled at the sight.

"Milady, ye are needed in the hall. Anna asks for the medicine chest."

The coil tightened. "What happened?"

"'Tis Will. He got himself kicked in the head."

The stable master's son. "How badly?"

Mona swiped at a tear. "Ye can see where the shoe hit his cheek. He be awake, but befuddled."

Leah fetched the medicine chest. If Will hadn't been

kicked hard enough to knock him unconscious, then perhaps the young man would be all right. She hoped. These past two weeks had gone by without mishap, and now this.

She handed the chest to Mona. "Tell Anna I will be down shortly."

The girl sped off. Leah fetched leather-soled shoes of thick felt from her own garment chest.

"Will is the stable master's son, is he not?" Geoffrey asked.

"Aye. One would think the lad knew how to avoid a horse's kick."

"Mona cares for Will?"

The girl's tears said she did. Gossip held that Mona romped with one of the stable lads, but Leah hadn't known which one. A vision of those two young bodies tumbling around in the hay . . . oh my, had they been doing so when Will got caught by a hoof?

"'Twould seem so." Leah slipped into her shoes. "Poor Thomas. He is likely torn between being vexed and worried for his son."

"As any father would be, I imagine."

Geoffrey yet held the horses she'd always thought of as playthings for children. His own children?

For a very long time she hadn't considered the possibility of Geoffrey being married, a father. He wore no gold ring, nor did anything in his trunk give indication of his status one way or the other. She'd merely assumed that because students rarely married until after taking on a profession and earning an income that Geoffrey wasn't married.

Did some women grieve for a husband who hadn't returned to her, or children cry for a beloved father?

'Twould be loathsome to usurp another's place in his bed and heart, and she'd never know Geoffrey's status for sure unless his memory returned. Except if his memory returned, even if he had no wife, he'd likely be too angry over her deceit to look at her either tenderly or hungrily again.

Her heart heavy, she fetched a wide strip of linen and handed it to Geoffrey. "You can use this to keep the shavings out of the blankets. I may be gone for a long while."

"I shall be fine. Your duty is down in the hall, with Will." He touched her arm, an offer of comfort that proved discomfiting. "The lad is young and strong. If he is up and about, likely there is no enduring injury." He smiled wryly. "We males tend to thick heads."

She tried to smile back. That he jested about his own head injury seemed a miracle. Dare she hope for one more turn of good fortune, that Geoffrey's open mind and kind heart didn't close to her the moment he knew the truth?

Geoffrey longed to know what other items lay in the trunk and cursed his inability to find out for himself. 'Struth, he'd never take the use of his legs lightly again.

More than an hour had passed since Leah left to see to Will. Geoffrey had considered asking to be carted down, but didn't have the heart to drag the burly stable master from his injured son's side, where a father belonged.

Besides, he had the carvings to work on and enjoyed the pastime immensely.

The horses weren't twins. The courser stood tall and proud, capable and eager to carry the weight of his knight—clad in heavy armor and loaded down with weaponry—into either tournament or battle. The unfinished palfrey, sturdy yet more delicate, possessed the heart for a long ride if not overly burdened. Both beasts were so necessary to a knight's way of life they were treated with utmost respect, most often fed and groomed better than the squires who cared for them.

Had he carved the horses for his own pleasure or as a gift or favor to someone? For a knight, perchance, whose beasts these resembled.

Geoffrey tried not to dwell on what he didn't know, to simply carve, to feel the warmth of the wood as it came to life under the sharp edge of his knife. A notch here, a deep cut there, a scrape to smooth a rough edge.

Yet as he worked, his mind wandered, and landed on the ledgers and the seeming oddity he'd noticed along with the omission of the crate of spices, or maybe because of it.

How Nigel of Pecham came by his income and spent his money truly was none of Geoffrey's concern. His task was to record figures, not study his father-by-marriage's financial affairs. However, since taking over the household accounts, he'd learned much about Pecham's finances while recording the income from the stannary and expenditures of the household.

As was natural, as the landholder, the lord of Pecham earned a generous percentage of the stannary's profit. Each of the miners received a share, too, though far less hefty. The more tin mined, the better earnings for all—especially for the earl of Cornwall, Nigel of Pecham's overlord, who reaped a royal share.

The costs of running the stannary and upkeep of the household were all normal ones. Still, Geoffrey had a hard time matching the income and expenditures with what he observed of the keep and its people.

The guards' livery seemed made of finer cloth than it should be, and each of the fifteen men-at-arms and five archers received three sets of garments every year instead of the usual two. The servants might be garbed in rough-weave linen or wool, but no garment showed signs of shabbiness.

At tonight's evening meal, fine white linen had covered all of the tables, not just the ornate lord's table on the raised dais. He'd noted serving platters of pewter, and he and Leah drank robust wine from goblets of silver. The rushes on the floor had been changed recently and sprinkled generously with rosemary.

Both Nigel's solar and Leah's bedchamber were nicely appointed, the furnishings all of simple yet sturdy design.

'Twas not the quantity of Nigel's possessions but the quality that made Geoffrey uneasy.

The stannary income didn't support the evident though not ostentatious luxury. Somehow, Nigel of Pecham lived in a style above his means.

Perhaps the earl of Cornwall paid a portion of Pecham's expenses out of his own treasury—highly improbable. Too, moneylenders eagerly loaned goodly sums at high profit. But if there were outstanding loans, the repayment should be recorded in the household accounts.

Or perhaps the answer lay in inaccurate account entries—or deliberately evasive records. He didn't like to think ill of Nigel, but he wouldn't be the first man to alter figures to his own advantage.

Geoffrey allowed he could be suspicious over naught, of course. 'Twas possible Nigel was one of those men who always made the best of a bargain for his coin. If so, he'd made some damn good bargains.

Hearing footsteps in the passageway, Geoffrey looked up from his carving. Leah walked in and closed the door behind her a mite harder than necessary.

"How is Will?"

"Very fortunate," she declared sharply, striding toward the hearth to set the medicine chest in its accustomed place. "The hoof only nicked the lad, thank the saints above. He surely deserves an aching head for his carelessness. Thomas took him back to their quarters in the stable. He and the lads will take turns watching Will tonight for stomach upset or worse."

Leah approached the bed, the tight line of her mouth softening. He knew her well enough to recognize the seeming anger as really worry for the lad.

As always, his body became alert. The closer she came, the higher the tension.

"How goes the carving?"

He held up the palfrey. "Well, I think."

She ran a finger across the completed mane. "You think rightly. On the morrow, if the weather is fine we might put you out of doors and you can carve without worrying about the shavings." Her hand fell to her side.

"Would you prefer to continue now or shall I dispense with the shavings?"

The thought of lounging in the sun, with knife and wood in hand, pleased him more than he could say. For the delightful prospect tomorrow, he could easily give up the carving tonight. Besides, evenings were about the only time he had to spend with Leah, her duties requiring her attention for most of the day.

"'Tis late, and my fingers begin to stiffen."

"From being wrapped around the knife, I imagine."

She raised one end of the towel, then looked across the bed at the other end. To reach it, she'd have to stretch forward, across him. He hoped she would, and perhaps lose her balance, and he'd have to catch her, and—

"If I try to gather this up, all the shavings will end up in your blankets. Hand me the other end, if you would."

He complied, but not without some chagrin. She folded up the toweling, took the horses and knife, and strode to the other side of the room.

She walked with purpose, but also with a feminine grace that quickened a man's blood. Her bottom swayed with each fluid step, each in balance and harmony. Sensuality in motion, completely innocent on her part, but seductive all the same.

She placed the carvings and knife in the trunk, but didn't shut the lid. "Are you ready for sleep yet?"

"Nay."

Leah hesitated for a moment before pulling out a thick, leather-bound book, the lettering on the spine in gold.

"This might help keep you amused," she said, her voice unsteady.

Amused? More like enthralled. He accepted this new gift with as much awe as the carvings.

"Ye gods, Leah, what other treasure does the trunk hold?"

"Two more books. Your coin purse. The rest is clothing —which reminds me. I asked the cobbler to come up on the morn to measure your feet. You survived the shipwreck, but your boots did not."

Yet this precious link to his past also survived, and raised more questions than he'd yet thought to ask. He flipped through the pages, not reading, simply admiring the lettering, more questions forming—no answers springing forth.

"Why do I own a book of Greek philosophy?"

She glanced at the book, an eyebrow briefly raised in surprise, as if she first learned of the book's contents. "You are a man of many talents and interests."

So it seemed. The carvings were pleasant diversions, but this book, heavy in his hands, called to his soul—and there were others in the trunk.

Reasonably or not, he suddenly fiercely resented every moment Leah withheld them from him.

"You waited a hellish long time to let me know of them."

"I know." He heard the hint of an apology but saw little remorse.

"Then why now?"

Leah sat on the edge of the bed, angled to face him, something she hadn't done in weeks. The derriere he'd admired earlier pressed warm and firm against his thigh. His nostrils flared from the now stronger, heavenly scents of lavender and female.

"The time seemed right."

He withheld disagreement, but not his displeasure.

As he knew she would, she went on. "You will remember that at first you were on the very edge of *death*."

"But I did not *die*."

"Praise the saints. But then you needed time to heal and gain your strength."

"And I could not have carved or read then?"

She crossed her arms. "I did not realize you were ready for more until Father gave you the stannary ledger."

"That was nigh on a fortnight ago."

"And you have been busy with that and the household ledger since, besides getting still necessary rest."

Except resting bored him to where he wanted to pull out his hair. Couldn't Leah see that?

Or perhaps she truly didn't realize he no longer needed coddling, and might not believe until after he could walk again.

"So you give these to me now to keep me busy and abed."

"Nay, I give them to you . . . because I thought . . . hoped . . . oh, dear." She looked away and took a deep breath.

Leah was anything but indecisive. He cupped her soft, smooth cheek and turned her head. Doubt and worry clouded her amber eyes, which only seemed to happen when they spoke of the past.

Sweet Jesu, was Leah finally ready to help him remember? Had she hoped he'd regain his memory when presented with the carvings and book? If so, he wanted to hear it from her lips.

"You hoped what, Leah?"

"That you would be able to enjoy your possessions without becoming overset."

Not exactly what he'd wanted to hear, but close.

"I am not overset."

She raised an incredulous eyebrow, with good reason.

"All right, I was a *bit* overset," he admitted.

"I feared you might become angered if you did not remember how to carve or read Greek."

"Is my anger fearful?"

She raised a hand to cover his, pressed her cheek more firmly into his palm. "It can be."

Leah had told him about the fight he'd been involved in aboard the ship, and had he been able to physically intimidate her brother during their argument he knew he would have.

If he hadn't been able to read the book, might he have become so angry he'd curse at Leah, or worse, for having given it to him? Had he ever been so angry with her he'd frightened her, possibly struck her? The thought appalled him. 'Struth, he couldn't imagine laying other than gentle hands on his wife.

As he did now, still cupping her cheek. She neither drew back nor stiffened nor trembled but, finally, seemed to fully accept an intimate caress.

He could evoke a tremble. With one kiss. One deep long kiss.

Leah's tongue flicked out to wet her lips, her amber eyes darkening, revealing her own struggle with sanity.

Geoffrey lost all common sense.

The slightest pressure pulled her forward. The searing touch of mouths pressed him back into the bolsters, all sensation focused on the melding of her mouth to his, the sweet taste of her that promised a delightful feast.

His heartbeat quickened at the prospect.

Never breaking the kiss, he pushed the book onto the mattress and pulled Leah up to take its place across his thighs. She squirmed against him, her softness pressing against his hard and aching sex.

He could barely breathe and didn't care. He tightened his hold both to support her and prevent any escape attempt. She not only didn't try, but gave up a soft mew of approval, melting into his embrace.

Damn his sherte and her gown. Damn splints. The wood entrapping his legs from above his knees downward had to remain in place, but the garments could be removed. He couldn't make love to her fully, without restraint. He wanted Leah beneath him, their bodies joined to the hilt. That wasn't possible for another fortnight, but he knew of other ways to satisfy needs.

Tonight he'd settle for what Leah was willing to give, and ensure she received her pleasure, too.

Geoffrey tugged the tie at the back of Leah's gown. The signal of his intent caused the tremble he'd sought to evoke, but she also stiffened slightly and broke the kiss.

"We cannot," she said on a ragged breath, leaning back enough to expose the graceful length of her throat. "Your ribs."

"Have not hurt in days."

"Your legs, then."

He ran a finger along her collarbone, noting one enticing mole on the expanse of creamy white. Nothing but an outright command from Leah to cease could have stopped him from lowering his hand to her breast. The yet covered nipple hardened instantly to a light grazing.

"I need not move my legs for what I have in mind. Have we never pleasured each other without coupling?"

Leah went very still.

If she found his suggestion repugnant, he'd not force her, though he hoped to the depth of his being she'd not refuse. "I burn. You burn. Why deny ourselves relief unnecessarily?"

Why, indeed, Leah wondered, knowing there must be good reasons why not but hard-pressed to think of them through the haze fogging her brain.

She shouldn't have sat down on the bed, shouldn't have allowed the kiss or given in to the overwhelming urge to seek succor in Geoffrey's embrace. But she had, and found it impossible to regret a moment of his enticing kisses, his possessive hold or continued stimulating touch.

When his palm again skimmed the tip of her breast, gentle yet firm and oh, so arousing, the overpowering desire for a more intimate caress overcame all caution. He wanted her. She needed him. The promise of pleasure enthralled her, and pricked her curiosity. Pleasure without coupling? How?

"What must I do?"

With a feral smile he ordered, "Remove this damn gown so I can pet you properly."

She felt the heat of his gaze the entire time she slowly peeled away her gown, all traces of hesitancy withering under his vivid appraisal and blatant approval. Emboldened, her woman's place afire, she disposed of shift and hose while he stripped off his sherte and pushed the coverlet down to the top of the splints.

Leah had bathed Geoffrey, known him well-endowed, but not guessed at the imposing length and magnificent thickness to which his male member now stretched.

Geoffrey thought he might burst under her fervent admiration alone. Then Leah softly, almost tentatively, touched him. Fingertips skimmed the tip, circled the hood, measured the shaft. His blood boiled. He almost forgot his wish to pleasure her first.

He grabbed her wrist. "Come back where you belong."

She complied, snuggled into him as she had before, but this time skin to skin. "Here?"

"Perfect."

Leah was perfection, from her golden hair to the tips of her narrow feet, just as he'd often imagined and was now blessed to behold.

He captured her mouth and petted her breasts properly, delighting in her response to both tender caresses and possessive strokes. He enjoyed every low moan, every soft hitch of her breath. Her heartbeat quickened under the heel of his hand.

She didn't lie still. While her urgent fingers raked through his hair and beard, over his chest and around his nipples, her bottom brushed against his stiff, aching penis which refused to obey orders to stand down and await its turn.

She started and gasped when he slid his hand between her legs and stroked her sweet heat. So wet. So ready. If only . . . but he yearned for a completion that wasn't possible, and 'twas far too late to turn from the course he'd set.

Leah curled inward, trapping Geoffrey's hand between her thighs, stilling his fingers. He'd promised pleasure, not this spiraling torture. Her heart pounded against her ribs; she struggled for breath. If she let him continue she'd surely die, or at least lose what little wits she had left. 'Twasn't right that the nub at the apex of her thighs served as a target for each of her tingling nerves.

"Why stop me now? You are nearly there."

She had no idea where *there* was and wasn't inclined to ask his meaning. "Cannot breathe."

He chuckled. "Then lean back."

How dare he make light of her misery? But he had the right of it, if she unfurled she'd breathe easier. Except as she moved his hand did, too, shooting her back to the top of the spiral. She squeezed her eyes shut against the intense pressure.

"Relax, Leah. Let it happen. Do not fight so hard."

He didn't know what he asked of her! She wasn't fighting anything.

She was going to explode!

Then she did. Her body convulsed, shattering into thousands of vibrantly colored pieces, scattering bits of her into the heavens, obliterating her tenuous hold on reality. She still couldn't breathe and her heart beat far too fast, and she didn't give a damn—and she understood.

Pleasure didn't adequately describe the feeling of both exquisite joy and delicious languor, a joy she'd shout out if she could find the energy. Bliss, perhaps, or ecstasy.

She wasn't a virgin, had been with a lover. Only now

she knew why a man threw back his head and groaned when he loosed his seed. The ecstasy must overcome a man, too. A mingling of pain and pleasure that she'd never known existed for a woman.

The revelation stunned her. Geoffrey had cured her ignorance in more ways than one.

"Can you breathe now?" Geoffrey teased.

Aye, she could, not enough to laugh at his jest, but more than enough to kiss him full on the mouth. She may have been ignorant, but not innocent. 'Twas his turn to suffer.

To her delight, soon Geoffrey's heart beat hard and fast under her circling palm, his breath turned ragged under an onslaught of kisses.

She touched him as he'd touched her, soft then hard, in places she wanted to touch and where she knew he wanted to be touched, stroked, petted.

"Can you breathe, Geoffrey?" she taunted.

"Have mercy, Leah," he begged.

"Do not move your legs."

He groaned.

Her hand wrapped firmly around the thick, firmly engorged shaft where she now knew every fiber of his being focused. She stroked, and within moments flung him into the mindless oblivion of bliss.

Geoffrey could take no more. He pulled Leah into his arms, held her against his chest, inordinately pleased with his wife, and with himself for taking a risk. *Mon Dieu*, if the monks were right about going blind from sex performed by the hand, he'd go to the darkness happily with the vision of Leah as she was now—contentedly pressed to his chest, her head on his shoulder, her long, unbound hair veiling them both.

Her passionate response hadn't surprised him, but the hint of innocence had taken him unaware. Obviously, if she yet retained traces of the virgin, they hadn't been married long enough to banish it completely. That pleased him, too.

Truly, he'd been blessed. He'd beaten death and would soon be whole again. His mind held knowledge if not memories, and perhaps Leah's father would let him become more involved with the stannary—an interesting proposition.

He might wish for more, but believed he could be content here at Pecham, with something to occupy his mind and hands during the day, with his lovely wife beside him in bed at night.

What more could a man ask for?

*Her love.*

Her heart pledged to him as firmly as her body.

She'd never uttered the extent of her feelings for him. Had she before and he just didn't remember? Had he ever uttered the word to Leah?

She was his wife, his mate. His possession under the law of God and man, as all wives belonged to their husbands. Love wasn't required, only consent to live together for their mutual benefit, to breed children.

He'd come to care deeply for Leah, knew she must care for him. As her love or as her mate?

As the philosophers said, great love occurred rarely. Was a great love possible for him and Leah, or did he wish for the moon?

# Chapter 10

"Where the devil is Anna?" Geoffrey grumbled from the bed. "She must be awake by now."

Leah contained her own nervous impatience by rearranging Geoffrey's carvings which graced the oak mantel. She moved the cow closer to the far edge, left the sheep and pig alone, then switched the bear and turtle. The horses, which Geoffrey intended to give her father in thanks for his hospitality, lay in the trunk.

"She is an old woman, Geoffrey. Give her time."

"I see no need for her to be here. Between us we could take the splints off."

"We could, but neither one of us has the skill to declare your bones fully mended."

"The bones are whole. Look."

He lifted his right leg several inches off the bed, heavy splints and all, in a movement too smooth for this to be the first time. Leah bit back a reprimand, refrained from asking how many times he'd previously tested his bones' strength.

"So I see. Still, we will wait for Anna. Are you sure you do not want me to ask Ned to come up first?"

"Nay." Geoffrey pointed at the door. "No more peeing in a bucket. My first walk will be to the garderobe."

She couldn't help a smile. Geoffrey had been awake for nearly an hour now, his sherte and sapphire tunic already donned. Hose and boots awaited the splints' removal. All along he'd hated the indignity of using a bucket and, apparently, had no intention of using it this morn, suffer though he might.

"I thought your first walk would be to the window, to see the ocean."

"That was before I knew 'twould take Anna an eternity to dress and climb the stairs." He smiled then. "First the garderobe, then the window, then down the stairs to break fast." He gave an exaggerated sigh. "Oh, heavenly day."

Leah agreed with the sentiment, mostly. Geoffrey looked forward to his liberation from the splints, from being carried to wherever he wanted to be. He'd spent much of the past two weeks in the hall playing chess with Ned or reading his book of Greek philosophy, or else in a chair placed outside the hall's doors to work on the carvings.

He'd completed the carvings now on the mantel, finished reading the book and begun a second—one on medicine written in Arabic. Naturally, the first thing he'd looked up was the length of time necessary for bones to heal. He hadn't been pleased when the Infidels agreed with Anna—six weeks, no less, perchance longer.

While Leah was happy for Geoffrey, his impending

freedom to wander about at will made her nervous. As long as he didn't explore the caves, she supposed all would be well. Still, she wished for her father's speedy return to deal with the possibility of Geoffrey learning more than he ought before he ought. 'Twas inevitable he'd realize what was going on. He was simply too intelligent not to figure it out when presented with a few suspicious happenings.

"Did you decide what to do about the guards?" he asked.

The abrupt change of subject brought her up short. "Not as yet."

"They should be punished, Leah, and soon. Falling asleep on duty is not tolerable."

Not tolerable at all. Leah sank down in the chair.

She'd breezed through the first fortnight of Father's absence, not so the second. Ever since Will placed his head in line with a horse's hoof—and thank the Fates suffered no enduring harm—other incidents, most of them minor, had demanded her attention.

The guards' lack of attention to duty wasn't minor. Two of them had taken naps while supposed to be patrolling the wall walk. Because Pecham was located in so remote an area, very little threatened the keep's security. However, Father demanded constant vigilance. As captain of the guard, Thuro had dutifully reported the lapse. 'Twas up to the lord—or in this case Leah in her father's absence—to punish.

"Father would assign them extra duty for a sennight, confine them to the guard tower during their free hours."

"Yet you hesitate."

Because she felt partly to blame. Discipline suffered
due to her lack of attention, which she could partly lay
at Geoffrey's feet, or rather magical hands. She'd spent
far too much time either thinking about bliss or cuddled
with Geoffrey, craving his touch, seeking succor from
her harried days.

"I am not sure any of them will take me seriously.
They have become lax in their duty. Even Thuro does
not follow me about so closely." For which she'd been
grateful and allowed without comment and shouldn't
have. "With the servants there is no problem, but the
men-at-arms are made of sterner stuff."

"You act in your father's stead. The guards know
that."

"Aye. Still . . ." She shrugged.

"Would a stern talk with Thuro beforehand help?"

"Perhaps. Father's return would be the best solution."

"True, but he is not here."

Geoffrey was. Father had told her to consult with him
about problems. She'd resisted for various reasons—
proving her worth to her father one of them. Mostly,
however, she hadn't wanted to involve Geoffrey too
deeply in the running of Pecham, not knowing how the
return of his memory would play out.

His memory, however, seemed lost forever. If the
carvings and his books hadn't jolted it loose, she
doubted anything would.

"Perhaps you should talk to Thuro and the guards."

He tried to hide what seemed triumph. Damn him,
he'd been waiting for her to ask his aid. Why hadn't he
just offered?

"If you wish it. Think you they will listen?"

Of course they would, and he knew it.

"The people like you, respect your position here. Besides, you are a man, a *big* man. If they don't listen, you have my permission to knock their heads together."

"I doubt it will come to that."

Probably not, but at least he knew he had her confidence.

Geoffrey tensed, his hands clenching. Through the open door Leah heard Anna's shuffle. Slowly she rose from the chair, not sure she was ready for this drastic change.

Anna entered the room, followed by Thomas and Ned. All three wore huge smiles.

"Good morn, milady." Anna approached the end of the bed. "What think ye, milord? Shall we have a look at those bones?"

Geoffrey's smile was tight, but a smile all the same. "I can think of no other woman I would rather have inspect my bones than you, Anna."

"Such a flatterer. Turning ye loose may not be wise."

"Only you turn my head, make my heart flutter, O beauteous one."

"Hmmm . . . well . . ." Old Anna blushed, then made her way to the side of the bed.

She untied the ropes around his right leg first, merely laying the wood down flat on the bed. Geoffrey would be horribly disappointed if Anna had to put them back on.

With gnarled hands and eyes closed, Anna kneaded the area of the break. She pushed and prodded, then asked Geoffrey, "Can ye bend yer knee?"

He obliged, raising the knee off the bed.

"Now yer ankle."

Geoffrey turned it in circles, an elated smile spreading across his face, so brilliant Leah nearly cried.

Anna nodded in approval and unwound the linen wrapped around his joints to protect them from the wood. The skin on his joints looked terrible, dried and puckered from having been under bandaging so long. Anna brushed lightly at his knee.

"Do not scratch this too much. The skin beneath will be tender. If it bothers ye unduly, I can give ye some unguent."

Then Anna circled the bed and repeated the procedure. Soon Geoffrey sat on the edge of the bed, his legs hanging free of all encumbrances.

"Anna, I shall love you forever. My thanks."

"Just ye have a care now. Them joints and muscles ain't been used in a while so will be stiff and weak for a bit. Walk slow. Up with ye, milord."

Geoffrey eased off the bed, putting weight on his limbs for the first time in six weeks. He stood there for a moment, stretched to his full, imposing height, then sat back down.

"I see what you mean," he said with a chuckle.

Anna gave him an indulgent smile. "'Twill be fine in short order."

"It had best be. I need the garderobe! My hose and boots, if you please."

Soon he was fully garbed and, at Anna's insistence, placed a hand on Ned's shoulder to walk stiff-legged out of the chamber. Thomas followed them, hauling away the splints. She heard the men's laughter, likely at some vulgar comment about bodily functions.

Leah felt like crying. Damn, she was glad for Geoffrey, so why did this deep sadness engulf her heart?

Anna gathered up the ropes and swatches of cloth. "He will be fine now, Leah. Ye watch, by nooning he should not need Ned's shoulder to keep his balance."

"So soon?"

"Tsk. I have seen many a broken and healed bone in my time, since before ye were born, in fact. Think ye I would let him out of the bed if I was not sure his legs fully healed?"

Leah held up her hands in surrender. "My apologies for doubting." She gathered her courage for the more pressing question. "What about his mind? His body healed fully, so should not his head come right again, too?"

Anna gave a sigh. "Ain't never seen the like in all my days. I thought once the lumps were gone his brain would settle back into his head proper. I suppose we should give thanks that it settled as well as it did. Most likely he will never gain back what he lost, but he seems no worse for it."

Leah had begun to suspect as much, merely wished to have her conjecture confirmed. She gave the old herbswoman a hug.

"My thanks, Anna. I do not know what I would have done without you."

"Ye would have done what ye thought right, as ye always do." She backed away. "Do not let Geoffrey come down the stairs without Ned. Now that he has his legs, he may be a hard one to hold back, even for a morn."

So Leah feared.

Anna shuffled out the door, leaving Leah alone in her

bedchamber. So empty. So quiet. Geoffrey would return anon, fill up the room again with his big body and compelling presence.

She sauntered over to the window. The ocean pounded against the cliffs, the seabirds circled. People bustled about the bailey, guards patrolled the wall walk.

Nothing had changed, and yet everything changed— all because Geoffrey could walk again. Oh, she worried about his discovering evidence of the smuggling, but more, she now lost all control over his whereabouts. Always she'd known what he was doing and exactly where to find him.

No more. He could see to his own needs now.

The physician had been wrong about Geoffrey's dying, but apparently not about the damage to his mind. 'Twas a blessing he retained the greater portion of his wits, his knowledge—even if he didn't remember how he came by it.

Leah felt more than heard him enter the chamber. She turned to see him close the door, leaving Ned out in the hall. He still smiled, no longer elated, simply pleased and at peace.

"Feeling better?"

"Infinitely."

He progressed slowly but surely to the window, placed his hands on the sill and leaned forward. To her amusement he took a sniff of salty air and a long perusal of the view.

"'Tis more rugged and beautiful than I imagined. More green, the cliffs higher, the ocean wilder."

"Perhaps everything is more beautiful to you today."

"You may be right."

He put his arm out and she slipped beneath, sliding an arm around his waist. He pulled her in snug. She felt the warmth of his breath in her hair.

"There were times I lay in that bed and thought this day would never come. I know full well my idleness and recovery were not easy on you. My thanks, Leah, for your good care."

"Pray do me the favor of not doing too much too soon. You are not fully recovered as yet."

He gave a burst of laughter. "You think not? Wait until tonight. I will show you how recovered I am."

Leah inwardly shivered with anticipation—and a moment of misgiving, though she brushed the remains of guilt aside.

She'd given him his possessions and they'd not jarred his memory. He knew of his sister but didn't remember her name, and Leah couldn't supply it. She'd told him everything she knew of him and nothing had changed.

Her sense of duty toward Geoffrey had given way to caring, then grown to love. Despite her efforts to shield her heart, for good or ill, wise or not, she'd fallen hard and forever.

Whoever he'd been before no longer existed. From a death bed had risen a man of learning, of quick temper and quicker humor. A man both gentle and strong. Passionate. Vulnerable to bouts of self-pity and yet confident of his ability to get on with his life.

A man any woman would be proud to call her husband.

She *felt* married, longed for a home of her own, babes

to cuddle—and couldn't imagine doing so with anyone but Geoffrey.

'Struth, but for mere formality of vows, and those weren't strictly required by law, she and Geoffrey were husband and wife, bound together by fate and affection. If Geoffrey didn't remember his old life, he couldn't go back to it.

Now that he'd regained his health and mobility, life held new and exciting possibilities for him, and she yearned to be a part of it.

So tonight she'd abandon the pallet on the floor for the comfort of the bed.

Make love with Geoffrey. Sleep beside him.

Pray she did the right thing for both of them.

She hugged the man she hoped to hold onto for a lifetime. "Then you need nourishment to keep up your strength. Come, let us see what Cook has concocted to celebrate this glorious morning."

Praise God, thank the saints and Fates, it felt damn, gloriously wondrous to stand on his own two feet. True, he'd been a bit wobbly down the stairs, but after a meal of spiced pottage and warm bread and coddled eggs— all washed down with an excellent wine—now, with Ned ahead of him, Geoffrey eased down yet another stairway to the keep's lower floor and the guards' quarters. Three men should be awaiting him and woe to them if they weren't.

His knees creaked less with each step, his feet becoming accustomed to his new boots. Damn fine over-the-ankle boots, the black leather soft and supple, with nary a pinch in either toe or heel.

"I suppose, milord, we shall have less time for chess."

"I fear so, Ned. 'Struth, you have become very skilled at the game."

"Aye, and now I shall lose my edge."

"Oh, we shall not give it up altogether, I warrant. 'Twill not be long before I itch for another match."

"Maybe some night after evening meal?"

"A good plan."

And it was. Ned had played as much a part in Geoffrey's recovery—particularly the messy, smelly part—as Leah and Anna. The guard's companionship had been welcome, too.

How did one make adequate payment to those people who'd saved his life and sanity? 'Twas a quandary he'd ponder later. Right now he had guards to reprimand.

He entered the guards' quarters and stepped headlong into the musky odor of male sweat and the tang of sharp steel. A sense of belonging washed over him, so strong his head spun. In his past he'd spent much time in a place such as this, he was sure.

Thick straw pallets, separated by trunks containing the men's personal belongings, lined both sides of the room's length. Maces and short swords hung on racks. Lances, point up, leaned against the wall in neat order. Long bows guarded sheaves of arrows.

He barely noticed the men gathered there as his hand reached for a sword.

The hilt warmed to his palm. He tested the balance and found it wanting. With pad of thumb to edge, he judged the weapon well sharpened.

He'd not only held but wielded a sword before, knew

a hefted lance would feel familiar, too. Had he once been the member of a guard in a lord's castle? Where? When? For whom?

No vision sprang forth, only a sense of urgency, as if there was somewhere else he should be, something important he must do.

Geoffrey didn't fight the sensation, but neither did he probe too deeply. He'd tried and failed too many times to force a memory, and battering one's head against an impenetrable wall hurt both body and heart.

"Milord?"

Ned's prod jolted him back to the task he'd agreed to perform for Leah. He placed the sword on the rack, resolved to get the job done with the least fuss.

Thuro, captain of the guard, stood beside the two men-at-arms he'd caught napping while on duty. Intolerable, and they all knew punishment inevitable. Except Thuro wasn't aware of the extent of Geoffrey's displeasure.

He addressed what he considered the worst offense first—falling asleep on duty. "I assume you both expect a penalty for your negligence the other night."

To their credit, the guards voiced no excuses, merely stood stoic in anticipation of what they knew was coming.

Geoffrey continued, "Her ladyship informs me the usual punishment is extra duty and confinement to quarters for a sennight. Is this correct, Thuro?"

"It is, milord."

"You will see the penalty enforced beginning today. Her ladyship is much distressed over this incident, and I dislike seeing my wife upset. You have until after nooning to devise a plan to ensure that such an incident does not happen again. Report to me in the hall."

The captain's eyebrows rose in surprise. His mouth opened as if to object.

Geoffrey cut him off before he could begin. "As the guards' commander in Nigel's absence, you are responsible for their behavior. If you cannot ensure the security of Pecham, then someone else must. If that someone else must be me, then so be it. Am I understood?"

Thuro's eyes narrowed, but he nodded his understanding.

Geoffrey felt a pang of remorse for further reprimanding the captain, but quickly banished it. Orders given must be obeyed—all orders.

"Her ladyship believes her father gave you a direct order to watch over her. Is this correct?"

"His lordship asked me to keep an eye out for her safety, aye."

"Then why have you ceased doing so?"

Thuro ran a hand through his hair. "Begging yer pardon, milord, but her ladyship sure don't like me following her around everywhere."

No, Leah didn't, and frankly there were times when Geoffrey didn't want Thuro hovering either. He couldn't let the captain shirk his duty, but perhaps the order could be changed and still satisfy Nigel's intent.

"What say we share the duty, then? You have charge of guarding Leah when she is not with me."

"She still ain't gonna like it much."

"Likely not, but her father's wishes prevail."

Satisfied with the outcome of the meeting, Geoffrey waved at the door leading out onto the wall walk.

"Thuro, if you would accompany me, I should like to see Pecham's defenses firsthand."

Geoffrey stepped out onto the wall walk, into the sunshine, and the wind damn near knocked him over. If not for Ned's easily grasped shoulder, he might have fallen backward.

"Perhaps we should wait until ye have full use of yer legs, milord," Thuro commented. "Not much up here to block the breeze."

*"Breeze?"*

The captain chuckled without rancor at the incredulous tone, as Geoffrey had hoped, easing the tension between them.

"When a storm blows in, ye will see what I mean."

"Then I had best enjoy the breeze while I may. Lead on."

Thuro proceeded to point out Pecham's few defenses. The keep's best defenses were its remoteness and the cliffs on the ocean side. Geoffrey hadn't before realized the keep perched on the very edge of the cliff. 'Twas a dizzying distance downward from wall walk to water. What he knew must be huge boulders jutting upward along the coast looked like mere pebbles from this height.

The captain pointed east. "The stannary lies two leagues down that road, the village beyond it. 'Tis rare we see the miners, just at feasts and the like."

Geoffrey marveled at the stark beauty of the countryside, as he had from the bedchamber window. The view out the window was spectacular, but from the wall walk one could see nigh on forever, both out and down. What must it be like to take in the view from the water's edge, to look up at such imposing heights? Could one get down to the water?

Geoffrey sought a path, and found it. "Can that path be taken all the way down to the sea?"

Thuro straightened slightly. "Aye." The man sketched a bow. "If ye expect a report by midday, I had best get at it. By yer leave, milord."

Geoffrey nodded permission, taken aback by Thuro's sudden formality and leave taking.

"You wished to see the stables, too. Shall we do so now?" Ned asked.

He took a last look at the path before following Ned, vowing to follow it at first opportunity.

Geoffrey sat in the bedchamber chair Leah normally occupied, his boots off, his legs propped on her stool, watching her flutter about lighting candles against the night. He could sit here for hours admiring the sensual grace of her movements.

"You have had a busy day," she commented, her tone conveying she thought his day too busy.

He'd never admit as much to her, but his legs told him the same. Still, he couldn't think of a minute he hadn't enjoyed after his talk with the guards, particularly relishing the visit with Thomas and young Will in the stables. After nooning Thuro had presented a new schedule for the guards of which Geoffrey approved.

Perhaps he shouldn't have insisted Leah give him a tour of Pecham, but getting to know his new home, from the kitchens and dairy to the cobbler's shop had seemed important. Or perhaps he shouldn't have gone back out on the wall walk just before evening meal, but his curiosity over the path had pulled too hard.

"Busy, but not overtaxing. Have you anything of special import to do on the morrow?"

"Nothing that does not need doing every day. Why?"

"I think it might be pleasant to go down to the ocean, view the cliffs from below."

She blew out the taper she'd used to light the candles, set it on the table. "Do you, now?"

"I saw the path from the wall walk, and Thuro said it goes down to the shore. Are there caves in the cliffs as well?"

"A few."

He'd thought so, and yearned to explore them.

"Then what say we pack a basket full of food and—"

"Hold a moment. Geoffrey, that path is very steep in places and you are not yet steady on stairs!"

"Woman, you worry overmuch."

Brow furrowed, mouth in a firm line, she crossed her arms, all set to argue. He wanted no harsh words between them, not tonight, not when he'd been anticipating soft words and loving touches.

He unfolded from the chair, placed his hands on her shoulders. "Think on it, Leah. We could take food and a blanket, find us a cozy cave, spend hours completely alone, just us and the sound of the ocean."

He meant to tempt her, maybe make her blush at the idea of making love in a cave, not elicit a wry smile.

"Us and the seabirds seeking to steal the food."

"They would not dare. I will roast any who try."

"Hah! You would be too busy capturing and roasting birds to . . . do aught else."

He cupped her cheeks, tilted her face upward, lost himself in her amber eyes.

"Then just us." He brushed a kiss across her mouth. "You, me and the ocean."

She clutched his tunic, straining upward, begging a deeper kiss. "Sounds lovely."

He gave her what she sought, a long, hard kiss, savoring the honey of her mouth, eager to please and be pleased. He untied the lacing at the back of her gown and eased it from her shoulder.

She gave a little moan, firing his blood. He bent to kiss the uncovered skin.

"But I cannot be gone from the keep so long," she said, just above a whisper. "If one little thing goes wrong, someone will come to fetch me."

He didn't want to be practical, but conceded Leah's point. Of late it seemed every time she had a moment to rest, another problem sprang up to demand her attention.

"I do not suppose you would allow me to roast an interfering servant."

Leah wrapped her arms around his neck. "That would never do. Besides, the path truly is too steep for you to try yet. Father will be home in a day or two. I will then have more time and your legs will be stronger. Can you be patient until then?"

For the cave, aye; for Leah, nay.

He removed the circlet from her veil, then the veil from her long, golden hair.

"Depends upon how well you occupy my time between now and then. I vow my patience sore tested of late."

She tugged open the ties of his tunic. "I know of a task or two you might find agreeable."

He peeled gown and chemise off her shoulders while she undid the gold-link girdle wound around her waist. "Might these tasks involve you and me and a bed?"

"Eventually." Her garments dropped to the floor, puddling at her feet. She stood before him in only short hose and garters, an erotic vision of wantonness and innocence.

Geoffrey pulled off his tunic and sherte as one, feeling the laces of his hose come undone. Warm hands slipped inside, pushing the hose down, freeing him to her touch—and she knew exactly where and how to touch to drive him wild.

They'd pleasured each other before with gentle petting and firm strokes. While he enjoyed the fondling, he was eager for more. Tonight would be different. Tonight no splints bound his legs. Tonight they could join, as man and woman, as husband and wife were meant to mate.

The pressure in his loins rose, warning Geoffrey to still Leah's busy, knowing hands or all would be over for him sooner than he intended. His body protested jerking away, yearning for more delights. With the aid of a deep breath he calmed the inner turmoil, scooped Leah into his arms, and carried her to the bed.

They landed hard, chest to breast. She swung a leg over, pressing into him, as eager as he for the coupling. Lust almost won out. From deep within he found the strength to roll Leah onto her back.

He left her there, her eyes closed and legs spread, only long enough to shuck his hose. Between heady kisses he caressed Leah's creamy skin, aroused further by the scent of lavender and female heat.

She whispered his name when he worshiped her breasts with gentle nips and soothing sucks. He cupped her moist, ready core and drew forth a long, pleading moan.

He should slow down. Take his time.

He eased away and she took advantage. Fingertips fluttered over his chest, pausing to urge his nipples to hardness before skimming down, ever so slowly downward to beneath his navel. She played there, tormenting him with anticipation, until finally grasping his shaft. Fevered need surged through him.

The night was young. Slow could wait. If he didn't take Leah now, while he maintained a semblance of control, he'd leave her wanting.

He grasped her wrist, pulled her upward to lie atop him. "Enough."

Glittering amber eyes smiled at him. "Is it?"

"Unless you want our coupling over in a trice."

"Oh, nay." She bent to nuzzle in his neck, her warm breath on his ear sending shivers down his spine.

He'd satisfy her if it killed him.

Geoffrey rolled, easing Leah beneath him. He captured her mouth, parting her lips, slipping his tongue inside to duel sweetly, erotically with hers. Her thighs clamped his hips and she arched upward, granting him welcoming access to her woman's depths.

The long-awaited entry proved glorious. Geoffrey slid inside with care but purpose, felt the power surge through him all along the journey, like a victor snatching a coveted prize. When they were joined to the hilt, she sighed her satisfaction, claimed and yet procuring exactly what she'd wanted.

He rose up, braced on his hands and gave her more. Her sheath tightened, grasping him firmly in a delightfully inescapable hold.

In rhythm old as time they rocked together, slowly at first, then quickening. Geoffrey watched Leah's eyes glaze over until she finally closed them, heard her increasingly hard puffs of breath.

He ignored the stiffness in his arms, concentrated on silencing his screaming demand for release. Just when he thought the dam about to break, Leah arched high, cried out, and melted around him. The pulse of her pleasure commanded an answer in kind, and with his own cry Geoffrey surrendered.

He eased down to his elbows, his breathing labored, sweat beaded on his upper lip, replete and elated and drained.

Leah's eyes fluttered open, her tongue flicked out to dampen kiss-reddened lips. She fair glowed, and damn if his pride didn't swell. With a soft smile she raised a hand to his cheek, stroked his beard.

"You were extraordinarily able," she purred.

"Did you doubt?"

Her smile widened. "For a moment there . . . but then you made me believe."

He thought she teased, but wasn't quite sure. Had he given her reason to doubt in the past? He had no way of knowing, and wasn't about to ask because he truly didn't want to hear he'd ever been an inconsiderate lover.

"Henceforth you must always believe."

She squirmed beneath him, stirring his loins, quickening his heartbeat.

"Always?"

"Every time," he vowed, and then slowly, patiently, long into the night, made good on the oath.

# Chapter 11

Invited to inspect the new tunnel, Leah followed the overseer and several proud miners into the hole hollowed out of the hillside.

Stout beams hewn of sturdy oak supported the entrance as well as the walls and ceiling a few yards beyond. The shallow tunnel would soon deepen, becoming narrow and slanted, when the miners began to follow the vein of ore.

'Twas dangerous work done by small, slight men who knew the pitfalls and strove to avoid them. Mishaps occurred. Luckily, no serious injuries had befallen anyone in years.

Leah picked up a chunk of ore, turned it around to judge the quality of tin, then handed it to Garth, the stannary overseer. "Father was right. 'Tis a rich vein."

Garth tossed the chunk, caught it. "Better even than we reckoned. Nigel will be pleased, and the earl."

Father would be pleased—as soon as he learned of it. He was now several days later than she'd expected. He'd promised to be home before another ship arrived, and Thuro informed her this morn that the day had come.

Sails had been spotted off the cove, the signals passed for a transfer of goods tomorrow eve if the weather cooperated.

She'd be expected at the cove as Father's agent, and could probably, if awkwardly, do whatever she must do. Except she had no idea how to explain her late evening absence to Geoffrey.

Leah glanced back at the man who'd insisted on accompanying her today. Geoffrey stood not more than two feet inside the entrance, his hand pressed against a support beam, his head ducked slightly.

He looked uncomfortable, both in body and mind. Leah had the feeling he preferred not to step any farther inside than he must, even if he fit more easily. Understandable. She knew of men who couldn't bear being inside a tunnel, who swore there was no air to breathe, that they feared the walls would cave in and they'd be trapped.

Leah shoved the unsettling thoughts aside and, knowing her duty, addressed the expectant miners.

"You have done a wonderful job, and in so short a time. I have no doubt my father will be most pleased and your efforts will be rewarded."

The miners' smiles widened.

Garth sketched a small bow. "Yer praise does our hearts good, milady." He waved at the entrance. "If ye wish, I will fetch the week's figures afore ye go."

'Twas why she'd come, as she did at the end of every week, a duty she didn't mind.

Leah smiled inwardly when seeing Geoffrey waiting

for her outside of the tunnel, probably regretting his decision to accompany her.

She didn't. Having Geoffrey at her side turned an ordinary day into an adventure, brought home the miracle of his recovery.

He fell in step beside her, matching his long stride to her shorter one, his movements smooth and balance sure.

"Interesting."

"I am glad you found it so." Leah badly wanted to ask if he'd felt unduly confined, but doubted he'd appreciate her inquiry. Likely he'd shrug off the discomfort and tell her she worried overmuch.

Garth veered off to fetch the figures; Leah headed for where they'd tied the horses.

"You promised the miners a reward. Will your father make good on it?"

Geoffrey's accusatory tone didn't sit well.

"'Twas Father's pledge I spoke of. He promised each miner two shillings reward if the tunnel was ready to be worked by month's end. They have earned their reward."

His surprise came out in a low whistle. "A lot of coin."

"Not when compared with what Father and the earl stand to profit from this vein. 'Tis ripe with tin."

He shook his head, the tips of his sable hair brushing his shoulders. "That piece of ore you examined looked like no more than a rock to me. I suppose I have much to learn about such things." He came to a halt, bringing her up short. "My apologies, Leah. I did not mean to insult you. 'Tis just . . . there are too many things I do not understand."

His healthy curiosity fascinated her. In the few days

since he'd been on his feet, she'd shown him much of Pecham and learned he tended to ask one question after another. So far answering had proved no hardship.

"Such as?"

He glanced back at the new tunnel. "How do they know where to dig? One does not just stick a shovel in a hillside and expect to find ore, I imagine."

She smiled. "You are right. 'Twould be a foolhardy way to go about it. There are signs, of course, but it takes experience to make such decisions. Father seems to have a talent for locating veins of ore, as did his father before him."

"Which makes him valuable to the earl. And Odo?"

Her brother took little interest in the stannary, preferred the excitement and higher profit of the smuggling.

"Odo tends to shun those tasks which might soil his hands, or interfere with his . . . other pursuits."

"Ahhh."

Ah, indeed. 'Struth, Leah worried over the stannary's fate when Odo inherited Pecham, as he would someday. Thank God her father was still in good health.

"If you wish to fully understand the workings of the stannary, you must ask my father. I am sure he will tell you whatever you want to know. His pride in both the men and their workings is boundless."

Leah watched him glance around the area—at the various tunnels, the dirty-faced miners in their tattered working clothes, shovels and picks strewn about, the smoke billowing from the brick smelting furnace. Did he also appreciate the skill necessary to shape the tunnel and support beams, the bravery required to do the dangerous work?

On the verge of asking, she spotted Garth coming toward them, her question lost to the business of accepting
the parchment and the uttering of farewells.

With the aid of a log she mounted her favorite mare.
Geoffrey needed no such help, swinging fluidly up into
the saddle like a man born to it.

Where had he learned to ride? Either someone had instructed him very well or he'd gained the skill with much
practice. She'd wondered the same thing about his carving.

Such questions couldn't be answered, and she found
she wanted answers. Her intimacy with Geoffrey seemed
so right. She wanted to know all there was to know about
the man she loved. Not possible unless he remembered
his past, which seemed unlikely to happen after all this
time.

The reason for this morning's outing over, Leah
sought to prolong the ride and avoid dealing with tomorrow night's problem. Besides, she wanted Geoffrey to
herself a while longer.

"Would you like to see the village?"

"Delighted."

Leah didn't remind him that he had uttered the same
sentiment when asked if he'd like to inspect the tunnel.

The village, situated in a cozy valley within sight of
the stannary, consisted of neat, wood-framed, thatched-
roofed cottages. The overseer's stone residence anchored one end while the church of St. Peter marked the
other.

As usual, some of the women gathered around the
common well to visit while the youngest children played
on the surrounding green. The older children combed the

countryside for sticks and branches, which they bundled into the faggots necessary to fuel the smelting furnace.

On the far end of the green, little Eileen stood apart, her blindness preventing her from joining the children's running game. Leah felt sorry for the girl, but nothing could be done about her lack of sight. Throughout her life there would always be games Eileen couldn't play, things she couldn't do.

As they neared the church, Geoffrey slowed to nearly a halt.

"Stained glass," he whispered, awed.

Leah glanced up at the lovely window that graced the eastern face of the church.

"Shall we stop?"

"I should like to see it up close."

She'd no more than reined in when he was off his horse and circled around to help her dismount. He stood there with his feet braced and hands raised, looking for all the world as sturdy and strong as an oak, capable of catching her with ease if she chose to fall into his arms.

A small shiver tingled along her spine as she grasped his broad shoulders. His long-fingered hands encircled her waist. She eased forward, slipped from the saddle and floated free. He set her on her feet, but not before she noticed his eyes darken, his hesitation to release her.

The air fair shimmered with sparks of awareness between them. Now was neither the time nor place to allow them to flare, but the promise of *later* urged her to rush home where she could fan the spark to full flame, divest Geoffrey of tunic and hose, press him into the mattress—

The window. He wanted to see the stained-glass window.

"Shall we go inside?" she asked, her voice rough.

"'Twould seem the sensible thing to do."

Sensible almost seemed beyond her at the moment, but she managed to climb the few steps and open the church's door. 'Twas light within, but musty from disuse. Even Geoffrey noticed, wrinkling his nose.

"The priest was granted permission to make a pilgrimage to the Holy Land." Her voice echoed in the emptiness. "He should be back by harvest."

Only a month hence. Sweet mercy, the weeks since the shipwreck had flown by and taken most of the summer with them.

He crossed the stone floor to stand beneath the towering window, staring upward at the likeness, in brilliantly colored glass, of Mother Mary and the divine babe in her arms.

"A magnificent window, is it not?"

He nodded.

She continued. "'Twas a gift to the church from the earl. I always wondered if there was a penance involved."

Geoffrey chuckled. "Perhaps. Though nobles tend to give extravagant gifts for the benefit of their souls, 'tis rare to see stained glass in so small a church." He tilted his head. "Pretty face."

Pretty and filled with joy.

Leah crossed her arms at a suddenly vivid memory of many years ago. "My mother said 'twas the delight in her babe that made Our Lady so beautiful."

Other events floated through her memory, of Masses and weddings and burials, all held at the church with

Mother Mary and babe looking on. The emptiness suddenly seemed so sad.

For a few more moments Geoffrey stared at the window, and Leah wondered at his thoughts. Was he entranced by the pretty face, or did he wonder about his own mother, or simply admire the artistry of pieces of colored glass set in lead? Finally, he strode toward her. Ready to leave the unsettling sadness behind, she went out ahead of him, and nearly tripped over Michael and little Eileen.

The miner quickly stepped back. "Beg pardon, milady!"

"No pardon necessary, Michael. I did not look where I go," she said, then bent down. "Good day, Eileen."

The girl executed a curtsey. "Good tidings, milady."

Eileen's smile could cure anyone's sadness, and Leah felt her spirits lift at this unexpected ray of sunshine.

"What do you in the village, Michael? Is it nooning already?"

"Nearly, milady. I saw ye head this way from the stannary and hoped to have a word with ye. Have ye a moment more?"

The miner's own smile headed off any foreboding of a problem. She'd had enough of them to deal with lately and wasn't looking forward to those ahead.

"Certes."

"Well, me and Eileen here, we wanted to let ye know how grateful we are to ye. Yer letting us through Pecham's gate, yer speaking to yer father on our behalf—" He shrugged a shoulder. "We owe ye more than we can ever repay, milady. Just wanted to let ye know we are in your debt."

She'd heard much the same before, from Michael's wife when she'd visited the village to see if the family settled in well. On the day her father had left.

"As I told your wife, Michael, you owe me no debt. 'Twas my father's decision to give you work, not mine."

"Aye, but if ye had not let us in the gate and put in a good word, his lordship might not have. Yer a good-hearted lady, and we thank ye for our fine home."

Leah realized arguing was fruitless.

"Then you are most welcome. Give my regards to the rest of your family."

"I surely will, milady."

They bowed their farewells and, hand in hand, headed back to their cottage for midday meal.

"Adorable little girl," Geoffrey said from behind her. "I gather she is the one Odo worried was evil."

"Aye." Leah sighed. "Unfortunately, many people believe ailments are caused by acts of the devil, blindness among them. One need only look at Eileen to see no evil lurks within her. She is such a happy child despite her infirmity."

"Mostly her parents' doing, I imagine."

Leah's stomach chose that moment to grumble. She laughed at the reminder that her own midday meal awaited.

"Come, let us hurry before my stomach protests its emptiness too loudly."

They rode side by side, allowing the horses to run at times. Eileen's sunshine warmed Leah all the way home, until Pecham came into sight.

Noticing the bustling near the gate, Leah rose up in

the saddle. A glance up at the wall walk answered her question.

Odo leaned against the stone. 'Twas truly a shame her relief and gladness at her father's return should be marred by her brother's presence.

Geoffrey saw Leah's brother turn toward the guard tower stairs and disappear, vowing that if Odo dared to utter one disrespectful word to Leah he'd break the man's neck.

"Father is home."

He heard her relief. She'd worried about her father's overlong absence. Geoffrey had wondered what estate business had taken Nigel and Odo over a month to complete, but decided it was Nigel's affair, not his.

"'Twill be nice to stand before your father and greet him properly for a change."

She smiled again. "I imagine it will."

They passed through the gate and crossed the bailey to the stable without spotting Odo. Still, Geoffrey watched all the while they gave over the horses and—his hand on the small of Leah's back—made their way to the great hall. Her brother wasn't there either, but her father was.

Leah strode toward Nigel. "About time you came back."

Nigel raised a gray, shaggy eyebrow. "Told you I would be back before I must, did I not?"

"Aye, you did, but I worried nonetheless. Have you spoken to Thuro?"

"Aye."

"Did your trip go well?"

"Aye. I even found your Mistress Thatcher and gave her your message. She sends her greetings. Now, leave off your questions while I have a look at this husband of yours."

Leah turned sideways, stepping out of Nigel's line of sight. With a full smile, she said, "I think he looks rather good now."

Nigel chuckled. "Indeed he does. Nice to see you on your feet, lad."

Geoffrey sketched a full bow. "'Tis wondrous to have full use of them again, my lord."

Nigel turned to Leah. "Is he fit enough for a walk down to the caves?"

Geoffrey had expected to take the path to the caves with Leah, blankets and a basket of food in hand, the two of them alone.

Her smile gone, Leah now stared at her father. "Is that wise?"

"I have already had this debate with Odo. Since Geoffrey is not yet ready to resume his former life, he may as well become fully involved in ours."

Geoffrey didn't know which bothered him more, being talked about as if he weren't standing there, or Leah's nervous silence, or the prickling along the back of his neck. What the devil was going on here?

Leah finally answered. "Geoffrey's legs are fully mended. Do you mind if I come with you?"

Nigel shrugged. "If you wish. Come along, Geoffrey, we have much to do before tomorrow eve."

Curiosity high, Geoffrey followed father and daughter out of the keep. Leah gave him a wan smile, as if resigned to her father's decision and apologizing for it. Confused, he matched his pace to theirs.

Leah had been right about the path. In places 'twas very steep with slippery footing, but his legs held without a twinge, allowing him to aid Leah's descent when she seemed hesitant. Nigel had no problem, as sure-footed as a goat on the slope, oftentimes getting far ahead.

When not pressed to watch his footing, Geoffrey glanced down at the foaming white waves battering the cliff. The lower they went, the louder the noise, nearly drowning out the cry of the gulls they disturbed along the way.

Around each bend and down every level lurked another breath-stealing view of the endless ocean, tugging at his concentration. Then Nigel turned to his right—and disappeared. They'd reached a cave.

Geoffrey bent over as he had at the mine tunnel and ducked inside. He blinked against the lack of light, stood his ground while his eyes slowly adjusted.

*No air.*

He dragged in a chestful of musty moistness, slowly blew it out, and tested his willpower yet again. Air filled his chest a second time. Reassuring. Somewhat.

At his side Leah stared up at him, concerned.

"Better?" she asked softly.

*She knows.*

Geoffrey fought a nearly overwhelming urge to grab her hand and get them both the hell out of there.

"I will be."

After two more steps inside he straightened upright, and that helped some, too. Only then did he realize others also occupied the cave. Nigel, of course, but also Odo and Thuro.

So this was where Odo had gone.

Odo's knowing smirk rubbed a raw spot on already tightened nerves.

Geoffrey felt Leah's hand slide into his and squeeze. He tried not to squeeze back too hard. Summoning his courage, he headed toward the men at the back of the cave.

With each step the tightness in his chest eased. He could breathe. Unlike the rough roof and walls of the tunnel, the cave was made of solid rock, high enough to accommodate his height, and showed no sign of crumbling. They were safe—for the nonce.

Odo turned back to the large wooden crate Nigel and Thuro looked down into. "All seems in order. We tested two of the torches and they lit quickly enough."

Torches? Why would one have need of torches in the cave? 'Twas dark in here, but not so dark . . . unless the caves were used after nightfall.

Again the hair on the back of his neck itched. Off to his left lay two huge coils of rope. Ladders leaned against the wall. A stack of oars rested beside a large, thick square of white canvas. A sail?

Everything he'd noticed about his father-by-marriage's finances and quality of life clicked into place, and he could have kicked himself for not realizing the obvious sooner. He was on the coast of Cornwall, for heaven's sake, where smuggling ran rampant.

Nigel hadn't purchased luxuries at a good bargain. Whatever he desired he simply had smuggled in.

Abhorrence flipped Geoffrey's stomach. He'd been sheltered by a criminal, a thief of the worst sort.

Leah knew and she hadn't said a word.

His flash of anger died quickly.

Of course she kept mum. A smuggler's success depended upon the discretion of those involved. She'd had a lifetime of practice with keeping secrets.

Had he known of the family's disreputable business before their marriage and wed Leah despite it? Had he ever cared?

"Well, lad?"

Nigel's softly uttered question turned Geoffrey's head. The man looked the same as before, still appeared the gruff but fair man he'd come to like—but found hard to respect now.

What could he say? Rail his displeasure? Hardly. Utter an approval? Nay. At the moment he wasn't in any position to do other than accept the facts as they were. That might not sit well, but for now he saw no option.

"I wondered how you could afford Persian rugs and Gascony wine."

"I keep what strikes my fancy, sell or barter the rest."

"At good profit."

"Most times. Then there are those occasions when we trade finery for favor, and that can prove valuable, too. The high nobility of England *do* like their finery. Silks. Furs. Pearls. Gems."

"All those things can be purchased from merchants."

"Not at our prices."

Nay, because an honest merchant had to pass along the cost of the various fees and tolls and duties of doing business—which Nigel didn't.

Nigel glanced down into the crate. "Test two more, Odo, then meet me below."

Still gripping Leah's hand, Geoffrey followed Nigel, grateful to be quit of the cave. As Thuro had told him a few days before, the path led all the way down to the shore—passing by two more caves—to the mouth of a horseshoe-shaped cove that couldn't be seen from Pecham's wall walk nor, Geoffrey assumed, from the top of the cliffs.

Cozy. Very private. A smuggler's delight.

"If the winds and sea permit, at high water the captain can bring his ship straight into the cove," Nigel said. "I leave the decision of when to bring the ship in to the captain. Some captains are more skilled at avoiding the rocks during rough seas than others."

Geoffrey felt Leah stiffen at the comment, but had no time to wonder at the reaction as Nigel continued.

"At this time on the morrow, we shall judge the captain's intent for making a run. Once the goods are unloaded they are hauled up to the other caves you might have noticed on the way down."

He'd noticed and been delighted to pass them by.

"You pay the captain for the goods, unload the booty, and the ship slips out of the cove and back to sea, no one of authority the wiser."

Nigel smiled at Geoffrey's summation. "Nearly right. This way."

He might have enjoyed the walk along the sand under other circumstances. Today the golden grains sucked at his boots, hindering his steps as if in warning to go no farther.

Another cave loomed ahead, this one tall and wide, a

veritable cathedral when compared to the others. No bending over was necessary, no testing of the air.

The cave contained huge tubs filled with what he now knew to be tin ore.

"Most times the captains and I make a trade, his cargo for ore," Nigel explained. "They take it to a smelter in Ireland."

Since no taxes were involved on ore, only on smelted tin stamped with the earl's seal, 'twas another source of profit.

"I gather the earl does not know of the revenue lost."

Nigel chuckled. "I would not hold sympathy for the earl, lad. As you saw in the ledger, he enjoys a hefty profit. Besides, most of what you see here comes from the miners' share."

Geoffrey didn't have to turn around to know Odo and Thuro had entered the cave. Their laughter bounced off the stone walls. 'Twas a revelation that Odo could laugh.

"Father," Leah said softly, "'tis a long, hard climb up the cliff. If you are finished, Geoffrey and I should start back up."

Nigel glanced at Geoffrey's legs. "If you think it best. We can talk later, Geoffrey. I am sure you have questions."

His legs were fine, but he took the excuse Leah provided to leave. He wanted no more revelations, no more jarring surprises.

The upward climb took more concentration and effort than the way down. Not until they'd reached the top of the cliffs did he have the calm or breath to utter a word to Leah.

"How long has your father been involved in smuggling?"

"Always," she admitted. "He surprised me, Geoffrey. I did not think he would involve you in anything but the stannary."

"I would rather he did not."

"Neither, I imagine, does Odo."

"Then why?"

"Possibly because Father did not think he could hide it from you for long." She worried her bottom lip. "More likely, he thinks of you as a second son, and deserving of his trust."

Geoffrey heard the sense of her reasoning, but wished his father-by-marriage was less trusting, his wife more honest. Leah hadn't actually lied, but she'd kept secrets.

"You disapprove," she said softly.

"Aye, I disapprove. You might have told me, prepared me."

"'Twas not my tale to tell. And did you not just imply you would rather have not known about the smuggling at all?"

She was right. He'd rather have not known, and he couldn't fault Leah for her loyalty to her father. Valid reasons for her silence. Still, he wished she'd told him.

"Geoffrey overstepped, Father." Within the cave near the cove, Odo presented his argument in as calm a manner as his rage permitted. "He had no right to discipline the guards."

"If he did so, then 'twas at Leah's request."

"Which means Leah shirked her duty. Neither had the

right to instruct Thuro to work out a new schedule for the guards."

Nigel glanced at Thuro. "Does it work to our advantage?"

"Seems to."

Nigel shrugged. "Then I shall let it stand for now."

Father's acceptance grated. Odo wanted his father to put Geoffrey in his rightful place, which was nowhere. Leah's husband took too many liberties for Odo's peace of mind.

"I still think it a mistake to have brought him down here."

"When I learned Leah had given him the household accounts, I saw little reason not to. Geoffrey would have figured it out in time."

"Another mistake of Leah's."

"She looked for ways to occupy his time, merely followed my lead in giving him sums to total. I cannot fault her for that."

Odo could and did. Father should too, except he rarely noticed Leah's faults, didn't mete out punishment for her mistakes. He'd too easily forgiven Leah for running off with Bastian. Now, it seemed, he'd not take Geoffrey to task for his errors either, and that couldn't be allowed.

"Geoffrey does not approve of our trade. You trust him to keep secret what he sees. His knowledge places us in a precarious position if he tells the right people."

"Oh, I think not." Nigel's smile was maddening. "He cares deeply for your sister, would do nothing to harm her or her family."

Odo knew Geoffrey's good will didn't extend to his

wife's brother. As of today, the man didn't look to be too pleased with his wife's father, either. Geoffrey's blatant distaste for the family's source of wealth could lead to problems. Why couldn't Father see this marriage ill-advised?

"Have you discussed her dowry with him yet, as you said you would?"

"Not as yet. Perchance this eve, over a chess board. I hear he is very good at the game."

Yet another mark against the man. The strategy of the game had always eluded Odo.

Was there no end to the insufferable man's talents?

The favor and respect Geoffrey garnered from everyone, from Father down to the serving wenches, wasn't to be borne.

n the quiet of the solar, hunched over a chess board, Geoffrey studied his options. He moved his bishop, willing to sacrifice a pawn to Nigel's knight for the prospect of a greater prize.

This game proved more challenging than those with Ned. Not only did Nigel possess a keen knowledge of the game, but Geoffrey's concentration was divided between the moves on the board and Nigel's explanation of how Pecham's finances came to be as they were.

"Miners are set apart from other workers, free men given royal privilege to search for ore wherever they choose—with the exception of churchyards and roads. Even those places they violated with their shovels." Nigel's hand hovered over the board, pondering the taking of the pawn, then withdrew. "Royal policy makes matters worse for landholders by granting miners the right to cut wood and divert streams. Many good oat and hay fields have been lost over the years. Landholders make good revenue from a stannary, but to the injury of farmers and food supplies. One cannot feed hungry people and cattle with ore."

Nigel smiled when he took the pawn; Geoffrey restudied his strategy.

Nigel continued, "During my father's time, Garth and a group of miners moved onto the land very near the present village. Bargaining with them to have a care for the land proved futile, especially since they dug on land held in fee to royalty. At present, John of Eltham, younger brother of the king, is earl of Cornwall."

Seeing no immediate threat to his strategy, Geoffrey took Nigel's castle, causing his opponent's brow to scrunch.

"By damn," Nigel muttered. "I have not played in too long. More wine is called for."

Geoffrey reached for the flagon containing what he now knew was smuggled Gascony wine and refilled both goblets. "One would think an earl might have some influence over the miners."

Nigel took a sip and leaned back in his chair. "He might if he cared to, but I know of no royal personage who puts the fate of a farmer's crop over the prospect of higher income. 'Struth, as landholders, 'twould have been in our best interest to leave the miners to do as they pleased and simply collect the taxes due on the smelted ore."

"Your father cared about the crops."

"He cared about the farmer and his family, and preserving the land in the event that the miners found little ore and moved on. So he sought a way to limit the damage." Nigel leaned forward. "He convinced the miners to cooperate by appealing to their greed. He provided them with the means to make a higher profit on their share of the ore in exchange for limiting their stannary to lands he chose. This only worked, mind you, because he also knew where to tell them to dig."

Geoffrey swirled the wine in his goblet, beginning to understand how the lords of Pecham became involved in smuggling, but not approving.

"Leah told me both you and your father had a nose for tin."

Nigel chuckled. "Not back then, but we learned quickly."

"The arrangement is an old one, then."

"A bit over a score of years. Shortly before Leah was born the first shipment of raw ore went to Ireland, serving as ballast in the bottom of an old fishing boat."

Geoffrey shook his head at Nigel's comfort over the arrangement. "How does one go about finding a trustworthy fellow to take such a risk?"

"Ah, lad, half of Cornwall is involved in smuggling and the other half benefits. 'Tis easy enough to find a captain with a boat and a sense of adventure. Smuggling is as much a part of our lives as the mining, a matter of local pride even. The Cornish have ever been an independent lot."

An illegal but tolerated trade, even accepted.

"And if you are caught?"

"There isn't a jury in all Cornwall that would convict me," Nigel declared with such confidence Geoffrey believed him.

"The earl does not suspect?"

"Humph. In all my years I have never set eyes on an earl. Twice a year we are visited by a bailiff, rarely the same man. He flips through the ledger, collects the coin due, eats a meal and is off. 'Struth, the last one was in the gate and back out within the space of a morn."

"The bailiffs do not inspect the mine?"

"On rare occasion, but they see only holes in the hill-sides and the smelting furnace. To actually learn of what they observe, they would have to know Cornish to speak with the miners, or at least have a better command of English. Most of them only know the French they see in the stannary ledger. If the earl's revenue seems within reason, the bailiffs are satisfied." Nigel put aside his wine and leaned over the board. "Now, what to do about that infernal bishop of yours."

'Twas obvious not all of the ore mined was accounted for in the stannary ledger. Not a chunk of the ore stored near the cove was recorded—unless another ledger existed. Geoffrey supposed one did exist, which revealed how much ore Nigel traded for silks, jewels, wine and the like. No bailiff had ever seen that ledger, Geoffrey was sure.

"I gather you have no trouble selling your goods."

Nigel's focus never left the board. "Nay. This last trip I traded six ells of silk and forty ermine skins to a baron for one hundred faggots to feed the smelting furnace. He gets his new robes and we need not chop down any trees. I would have had eight ells to trade, but the miner's wives wanted silk to line the hoods of their woolen cloaks. They were most disappointed that I denied them the ermine, but there are the sumptuary laws."

Incredible. One business fed the other, and where Nigel broke several laws he enforced another. Of course, llowing the miner's wives to wear ermine, reserved only for royalty, might give the whole business away.

As much as it galled him, Geoffrey had to admire the complexity of the entire scheme and Nigel's shrewdness. The miners reaped added profit and the benefit of small luxuries. Both tenant and the demesne fields assigned to Pecham remained intact, thus ensuring the food supply. Woodlands didn't fall victim to the smelting furnace, preserving soil and stream and hunting grounds.

Pecham prospered, the earl of Cornwall content.

Still, the utter disregard for the law nagged at Geoffrey's innards. Why should that be when all Nigel revealed seemed so reasonable?

Nigel looked up. "By the by, I meant to commend your handling of the guards. Thuro is a mite disgruntled, but I suspect 'tis because he did not think to change the schedule before you asked him to."

"Leah asked me to have a word with them, is all. She felt the men-at-arms would take discipline better if given by a man."

"For a woman, Leah has a good head on her shoulders—most of the time. She tends to be impulsive, but I assume you are aware of that."

Not the Leah he knew, at least not now. 'Twas the second time someone implied Leah's character to be other than what he'd witnessed for himself. Odo had used the phrase "disgraceful behavior" with regard to his sister.

Had Leah changed so much, and when?

"Leah knows her duty, and all seem fond of her, willing to do her bidding. I suspect the guards would have, too, had she felt comfortable dealing out punishment to men-at-arms."

"Which is why I felt no qualm leaving her in charge of Pecham in my absence." Nigel pushed away from the table. "Speaking of duty, shall we see if any guard sleeps?" He grabbed a candle from the ring, and smiled. "'Twill give me time to ponder your annoying bishop."

Geoffrey rose, unfolding his legs, sore not from the mended breaks but from the climb up the cliffside. The muscles needed further strengthening before he tried it again.

Instead of heading for the solar door, Nigel pushed aside a tapestry, revealing the door behind it. "Bring a candle with you. The stairway is steep and dark."

Geoffrey wasn't surprised to learn of the stairs leading from the lord's chambers down to near the postern gate. Passageways such as these ensured a lord's route of escape from the keep in times most dire.

Dark. Close. His breath hitched as it had in the tunnel and the caves. Damn, had he always had this senseless reaction to small spaces? More irritated than fearful, Geoffrey descended the stairs, one hand on the wall, the other swatting at cobwebs and nearly extinguishing his candle with his zeal, determined not to breathe more deeply than he must. At the end, sweat beaded on his brow and his heart beat so hard he wondered if Nigel could hear it thump.

Nigel opened the door and the wind rushed in, blowing out the candles and providing relief. Blessed air. Geoffrey set his candle on the floor next to Nigel's and welcomed the openness of the bailey. By the time they climbed even more stairs to reach the wall walk, he managed to regain control.

One could see forever from up here. A multitude of

stars glittered in the heavens; the white of the waves sparkled in the moon's light. Tranquillity reigned.

They walked quietly, Nigel softly hailing each guard as they approached. None slept.

Near the gate tower, Nigel halted and surveyed the land beyond. "'Tis time we spoke of Leah's dowry."

'Twas the last thing Geoffrey expected his father-by-marriage to say, and his lack of memory came back to haunt him. A bride's dowry was set before a marriage, not after, and Geoffrey hadn't given his own finances much thought, having no need of coin at Pecham. Truly, his marriage to Leah hadn't been arranged in normal manner.

"If you wish."

"She comes with moveables, naturally. Most of the furniture in her bedchamber is hers. There are chests of linens and pewter plate and pottery and oh, she can show you what she brings to set up her household." Nigel cleared his throat. "Well, perhaps some day you will find it possible to set up a household. Both of you are most welcome here at Pecham until that day arrives."

Geoffrey hoped the day arrived soon. Surely, there must be somewhere the two of them could go. Leah must know something of where they'd planned to live after they wed.

"We appreciate your hospitality."

"She owns jewelry, some nice pieces of her own and those she inherited on her mother's death." He placed a hand on Geoffrey's arm. "Should you find yourself in need of funds and think to sell the jewels, I ask you give me first opportunity to buy them back, especially her mother's brooch."

Geoffrey noted the earnestness of the plea, doubting Nigel asked because of the value of the brooch, but due to personal reasons. "Certes."

Nigel released his hold. "Leah is also entitled to two hundred pounds. All the coin and her mother's jewels are up in my solar, locked in a small chest."

The sum stunned him. "Two hundred pounds?"

"Should be enough to set the two of you up comfortably for a while, I would think."

For several years if properly managed. Combined with his own income—and he must have one if he could afford velvet tunics and leather-bound books—he and Leah were far from destitute.

"I wish I could give you an accounting of what I bring to the marriage to assure you your daughter is not wed to a beggar."

Nigel chuckled. "A beggar? I have my doubts, though I must say Leah is either most reticent on the subject, or perhaps you never told her. Some husbands prefer to keep such things secret from their wives."

Geoffrey frowned. "If I did not tell her, we may never know how to collect any income I may possess."

"Perhaps some day you will remember. Until then . . . what say we finish our game? I think I know my next move."

To Geoffrey's relief, Nigel wasn't inclined to return to his solar up the dark stairway. Instead, he continued along the wall walk, entered the keep through the guard's quarters and then up the torch-lit stairway to the great hall.

A few servants mingled by the hearth; others had already spread out their pallets and slept. Geoffrey saw neither Leah nor Odo and assumed Leah had retired to their bedchamber.

He'd rather abandon the chess game and join Leah, if only to snuggle close and hold her through the night.

'Twas rare they climbed into bed together and simply curled up to sleep. Once pressed against Leah, he couldn't keep his hands still, nor could she. Making up for lost time had proved both exhilarating and exhausting, neither of them minding the lack of sleep for having made love most of the night.

However, courtesy to her father demanded he tuck his lust for his lovely wife aside for the nonce.

Once back in the solar, Nigel took a long slug of wine and once more studied the board.

Nigel took the bait of Geoffrey's bishop. "Check."

Geoffrey momentarily thought about prolonging the game, perhaps even letting Nigel win, and found his competitive spirit too strong to temper. He slid a castle across the entire length of the board and captured Nigel's queen.

"Mate."


Leah introduced Geoffrey to the horse in which she took enormous pride. "This is Boadicea. One can still see the scar along her neck, but she is otherwise whole again, too."

Geoffrey stroked along the scar and his slight smile gave Leah heart. He'd been so quiet and withdrawn, both last night and all day today, unable to concentrate on either his book of Arabic medicine or on his carving. She'd hoped telling him about the horse, getting him out of the keep, might distract him from his disquiet over learning about the smuggling.

"Quite a bargain at six shillings," she bragged.

His smile widened. "I should say. She melded nicely into your father's stable, too, as if it were her destiny."

"I gave no thought to destiny when I bought her. All I knew is she fought so hard to survive the shipwreck, I could not allow her to become stew meat. So I handed over the shillings and hoped for the best."

"You have a soft heart, Leah."

"And an eye for good horseflesh. Father's fault, I suspect."

He gave the mare an affectionate pat, then left the stall. "Are there any coins left in my pouch?"

"Two pounds, a few shillings."

Soon there would be much more. Two hundred pounds more, which she'd learned about from Geoffrey this morn. She'd known about the moveables and jewelry meant for her dowry, but not the stunning amount of coin—and she wasn't legally entitled to any of it.

His expression pensive, he stated, "I wonder, perhaps, if we should make plans to leave Pecham."

Now she knew what he'd been brooding about all day, and Leah had to admit the same thought had crossed her mind. With two hundred pounds in hand she and Geoffrey could go anywhere, do anything they pleased. No one need ever know they hadn't exchanged vows—which no longer mattered the least to her.

Geoffrey was the husband of her heart, the man she loved. As long as they were together, they could live anywhere he wished, pursue whatever interest took his fancy.

"If you wish."

"We must have had plans . . . before."

Before the shipwreck. They'd each been on their way home to different lives.

"Nothing definite. You were to attend your sister's wedding, I to Pecham. Beyond that . . ."

"Where did we call home?"

Each question dug deeper. Too soon she'd come up empty. She knew of only one place where he'd lived, and to get there they'd have to cross the Channel again. Not a pleasant prospect, but a risk she'd take if Geoffrey wanted to go.

"You were a student in Paris. Would you like to return?"

He was quiet for a moment, then smiled wryly. "Nay, I do not believe I am ready to board a ship yet. That explains the books, though. In which line of study did I focus?"

She had no idea. "I do not think you made a final decision."

A bell rang, the call to evening meal.

Leah clasped Geoffrey's hand. "We shall give it more thought later."

Father and Odo were already seated at the dais. Leah took her place beside her father, Geoffrey next to her.

"'Twould only cost forty pounds a year," Odo was grumbling.

"A waste of forty pounds," Nigel countered. "I have no need to be called Sir Nigel."

Leah recognized an old argument and signaled the wenches to begin serving. Thus far, Father resisted taking on knighthood for himself, though his heritage and income allowed.

"Think on the honor a knighthood would bring to both you and to Pecham," Odo continued.

"I think more on the cost of the chain mail I should be forced to purchase, even more on the discomfort of wearing the infernal armor."

"'Twould not be that often, only when called to serve in the earl's forces or when at court."

"Court. Now there is a waste of a man's time." Father leaned forward, looking past Leah. "What think you, Geoffrey? Could a man embark on a more useless endeavor than to follow the king around from palace to palace?"

Geoffrey swallowed a piece of fish. "I might find it interesting, for a time."

Odo jumped on Geoffrey's answer. "Ah! You see Father. Geoffrey agrees with me."

"Nay, Odo, I do not. I said *I* might find it interesting, not your father. If you think a knighthood desirable, why not pursue the matter for yourself?"

Leah pursed her lips to withhold a gasp at Geoffrey's straight-faced, and perhaps unintended, shot to Odo's vulnerability. Until her brother inherited or married a woman of means, he had no income of his own, no coin to spend without Father's approval.

"Perhaps someday I shall," Odo said too softly for Leah's peace of mind.

The rest of the meal passed quietly. Not until they finished a sweet composed of apricots and nuts coated with honey and cinnamon did a guard, garbed in a dark brown tunic and breeches, approach the dais.

He bowed slightly to her father. "The captain makes his run, milord."

"Make ready." Father tossed down his wine before he rose, Odo with him. "Coming, Geoffrey?"

She wasn't sure Geoffrey would accept her father's invitation until she saw the challenge on Odo's face. Without a word, Geoffrey drained his goblet and rose. He made no secret of his objection to the smuggling, yet refused to appear either weak in body or unwilling to shoulder responsibility in front of Odo.

Leah resisted the urge to tell Geoffrey to have a care. He knew what he faced in the caves. Perhaps he'd find a way to avoid entering them and still salvage his pride.

She took a deep breath before leaving her chair. Such nights as these were long and quiet in the hall. The men would be gone most of the night, depending on how long the ship's captain took to anchor and how full the ship's hold.

With the servants already clearing away supper's remains, Leah headed toward Anna, sitting on a bench near the unlit hearth, a woolen blanket draped over her shoulders even on this warm evening.

"Shall I have the fire lit?"

"Nay, 'tis only mine old bones that chill, no others."

Leah eased down next to her. "'Tis your bones I care for."

Anna patted Leah's knee. "Ye have a good heart, Leah. So how goes it with ye? We have not had time to talk much."

"My fault, I fear. I did not mean to neglect you."

Anna laughed lightly. "No need to fret. I should have

been surprised if ye did not spend the time with yer husband. A strappin' big man he turned out to be, heh?"

"Aye, that he is."

"A shame about his memory, though. Does the loss yet give him grief?"

Grief? No, Geoffrey didn't grieve for his past as he had weeks ago.

"The lack of memory bothers him, but not as badly as before. I think he simply means to get on with living, make do with what he has now."

Anna gave an approving nod. "As should you."

Leah tossed a hand in the air. "And here I thought I was."

"Nay, ye merely keep yerself busy, and yer Geoffrey busy, but busy ain't the same as living."

"But . . ." The argument died a swift death. Perhaps Anna was right, especially about Geoffrey. She suspected his objection to the smuggling had led to his speculation about leaving Pecham.

He was no longer content.

"We talked a bit earlier this evening about leaving Pecham," Leah confessed.

"Did ye now? Where might ye go?"

"I suggested Paris, but that means crossing the Channel, and Geoffrey says he is not ready to board ship." Mercy, the thought of boarding a ship sent a chill up her own spine. "I cannot say I blame him after all he suffered last time."

"Geoffrey is English through and through. Is there nowhere in the kingdom ye might make home? Has he family?"

She knew only of one sister. 'Twas now a full two

months since the shipwreck and Leah doubted a soul existed in Dover who hadn't heard the legend and didn't know she'd brought Geoffrey to Pecham. Had his family made inquiry at all, someone should have arrived at Pecham's gate by now.

If Geoffrey's family didn't care enough to search for him, she refused to feel any obligation toward them.

"No family we can rely on."

Anna rearranged the blanket draping her shoulders. "Well, at least this time ye've a smart, steady man to lean on, not like that other scoundrel."

Leah hadn't given a thought to Bastian in weeks, her involvement with Geoffrey so complete she'd nearly forgotten her grave mistake.

The two men were nothing alike, neither in looks nor manner. Still, wasn't she thinking of making a similar mistake again? Leaving Pecham with a man not her husband, with no surety of a permanent future.

Only this time 'twas she who played the part of the scoundrel.

The Italian captain spoke English well enough to converse with Nigel. What Geoffrey didn't understand was how the captain and his crew of two men could navigate the waters between Spain, France, England and Ireland in what appeared to be an old fishing boat. The vessel didn't seem sturdy enough to hold the crew's weight, much less the heavy ore hauled aboard and dumped into its hold.

Geoffrey stood outside the cave that now held the night's booty and watched the boat maneuver out of the cove, grateful it was gone, more grateful he hadn't been forced to go aboard.

He felt more than heard someone come up behind him. Odo. Leah's brother made no threatening move but Geoffrey remained on his guard. He didn't like Odo, who returned the dislike.

"What keeps you out here, I wonder?" Odo asked, his mocking smile making Geoffrey bristle. "Your fear of the cave or your disapproval of the smuggling?"

A bit of both, though he'd never confess such to Odo. Besides, as confining as he found the cave, he'd been inside twice to oversee the stacking of the kegs and crates.

"I found watching the boat leave the cove fascinating. How the captain managed to avoid the rocks . . ." He shook his head, acknowledging his awe. "Are the captains all Italian?"

"Nay. We deal with five. Three English, one Italian, one French." Odo's smile vanished, replaced by a deep frown, his more usual expression. "At least we used to deal with a French captain. 'Twould be a pity to lose Bastian's good will because of Leah."

A small voice warned him not to ask because he wouldn't like the answer. Still, if Leah was involved he couldn't let the comment pass.

"What has Leah to do with this Bastian?"

"Did she not tell you?"

Not a word, at least not since he'd awakened at Pecham, his memory lost. "She might have, before the shipwreck."

Odo rubbed his chin, as if considering the wisdom of continuing, the gleam in his eyes betraying his eagerness to tell the tale. "Perhaps she did. You may even know him. Leah and Bastian were lovers. She ran away with him this past spring, and several months later came back with you in tow." Odo snickered. "I assume you either possessed more coin or better skills in bed. You will have to ask Leah why she left Bastian for you."

The sordid vision of Leah in bed with another man, writhing beneath a lover, clenched his fists.

Geoffrey battled for control over the emotional punch to his gut, hoping Odo didn't see either the anger or anguish that seared his blood. Denial screamed in his head but didn't pass his lips. He couldn't call Odo a liar if he spoke true, no matter how tempting to slam the man up against the cliff and demand he withdraw the accusation.

Odo crossed his arms. "The priests warn men to 'ware the wiles of a woman, the temptation of the flesh. One can imagine how Leah lured you into wedlock—"

Geoffrey grabbed a fistful of Odo's tunic and pinned him against the cliff wall. Fear flashed on Odo's face, his hands grasping Geoffrey's wrists and pushing to no avail. Geoffrey knew he used his greater size and strength against a smaller opponent, but the insult to Leah couldn't go unanswered.

"You will keep your vulgar speculation to yourself," he commanded. "Speak of my wife with disrespect again and you and I will cross swords, and I vow you will come out the worse for it."

Odo tried to blink away his fear. "You defend a woman who deserves no defense. My sister has the morals of a feline in heat. Did she twitch her tail under your nose, beguile you with her scent? Only a man bewitched takes the leavings of another."

The gall of the man! Surely Odo deserved a beating,

then tossing over the cliff. Geoffrey settled for giving the beast a hardy shake.

"I allow you to live only because your death might upset your father. Say one more word against Leah and I shall ignore my peaceable nature and toss you to the fish below."

Odo swallowed and glanced toward the edge of the cliff.

"You would not dare."

"Would I not? Care to test me?"

Thank God a glare couldn't kill.

"Perhaps another time." Odo released Geoffrey's wrist.

Geoffrey gave the man credit for knowing when to retreat. "Another time," he acknowledged and let go of Odo's tunic.

His brother-by-marriage shook his garment straight, then near bolted for the cave. To tell Nigel of the confrontation? No matter. He'd not back off his threat.

How much of Odo's tale was true?

By the time he returned to the keep he still hadn't decided whether or not to confront Leah.

He undressed by the light of the single candle she'd left lit for him, slid into the bed beside the woman he realized he knew too little about and yet burned for. Just as his entire past was a secret, so were portions of hers.

Leah's eyes opened, blinking away sleep. He answered the unspoken question in their depths.

"All went as planned, and I survived both the climb and the cave."

She smiled softly and snuggled into him, right where she fit best, where she belonged.

Had there been another man before him? This Bastian? Had she given her body to a lover as sweetly and thoroughly as she now submitted to him? He nuzzled in her neck, breathed in the aroma of lavender that was so much a part of her.

Perhaps Odo had the right of it. Perhaps she'd twitched her tail and beguiled him with her scent, and he'd followed and fallen as if bewitched.

Or, perhaps, he'd lured Leah away from Bastian.

She stirred against him, the hair surrounding her mons teasing his penis to arousal. Her hand slid up his chest to his shoulder, her fingertips gliding along his heating skin, leaving a tingling sensation in their wake.

So easily she seduced him. So willingly his body responded to her offering of pleasure.

In the hour before dawn, Geoffrey took full possession of the woman who gave of herself completely and with such zeal, sure only that Leah belonged to him now, that however it had come to pass he'd won the prize—not Bastian.

# Chapter 13

Geoffrey knew he should stay his course to the bedchamber, fetch the book on medicine he hadn't yet finished reading, but the angry voices coming from the solar slowed his steps. Nigel and Odo were in the midst of a disagreement, one none of Geoffrey's concern—until Odo said Leah's name as if spitting a rancid piece of meat from his mouth.

His ire again pricked by Leah's vexing brother, Geoffrey decided since neither man saw fit to fully close the door to ensure their argument private, then neither had the right to be upset if they were overheard.

"I informed Geoffrey of Leah's dowry the other eve," Nigel said, his patience clearly nearing its end. "We agreed on the terms and that is the end of it."

"Two hundred pounds is too much coin to bestow on a man we know near to nothing about. Who is to say he will not take the money and vanish?"

The insult to his honor grated, but Geoffrey held his peace.

"Hrumph. You would have me believe you worry he will abandon Leah?"

" 'Tis not unheard of for a man to receive a dowry and then abandon his wife."

"Granted, but anyone can see the two are fond of each other. If Geoffrey decides to leave Pecham, as is his right, he will take Leah with him."

Aye, he would, and the idea sounded better with each passing day—except he didn't know where to go or what to do with himself when he left.

"You place too much faith in him, Father. I thought so when you gave him control over the stannary accounts. I believe allowing him to witness the smuggling a mistake. You trust him to keep our secrets, but he has done nothing to earn your trust."

Nigel sighed. "Had I not exposed our dealings, he would have learned of them on his own. Geoffrey is Leah's husband, which makes him family. What would you have me do, Odo? Lock him away?"

Geoffrey suspected the prospect appealed to Odo.

"At least we should demand proof of their marriage before giving over Leah's dowry."

A shiver slithered up his spine.

If asked, he couldn't provide proof because he had no memory of when they'd met, why or where they'd married.

Leah knew, but likely couldn't produce proof either. Couples generally spoke vows before witnesses, but those persons resided in France, unreachable, of no immediate worth.

"You doubt your sister's word?" Nigel sounded as incredulous as Geoffrey felt.

"As should you," Odo insisted. "Leah proved her true nature when she sneaked off into the night with Bastian. She left with her lover without a word to anyone, without heed for the disgrace to herself or her family. I am given to mistrust her tale, what little she has revealed."

"Come, now. You heard their story retold all over Dover, same as I."

Odo huffed. "Tavern gossip cannot be trusted. God's wounds, the townspeople consider Geoffrey a hero of legend, and Leah an angel. Both are flesh and blood, with faults aplenty, Leah in particular. To hand over her dowry before knowing more, without some proof of her story, to my mind lacks sense."

The silence nettled. Did Nigel give his son's vehemence credence?

Having heard enough—too much—Geoffrey quietly backed up toward the stairway, unwilling to pass the doorway and reveal his presence.

Geoffrey had never doubted he and Leah were husband and wife, not from the very moment of his awakening. Her actions since supported his belief. 'Twas simply unbelievable a woman would do all those things for a man not her husband.

Possible, he supposed, but not probable.

Brother and sister were continually at odds. Questioning the validity of the marriage was just one more way Odo sought to upset Leah.

Or to upset Geoffrey. Perhaps this was how Odo intended to repay him for their quarrel on the cliff. Perhaps Odo's doubts were hatched of spite, hoping to drive a wedge between Geoffrey and Nigel.

Still, some of what Odo said made sense.

'Twas true Geoffrey had done nothing to earn Nigel's trust, except with regard to the stannary accounts, which Geoffrey knew to be correct because he checked every entry and sum. Why then was Nigel willing to trust a man with no past with both his daughter and her dowry?

Nigel put great faith in the notion that a member of the family deserved trust. Still, with no proof a marriage had taken place, perhaps Nigel should use more caution, as Odo advised. Two hundred pounds was, indeed, a large sum of money to give to a man they knew nothing about.

Certes, put in Odo's place, wouldn't he have advised his own father to ensure his sister's husband a trustworthy man before bestowing the dowry?

Geoffrey ran a hand through his hair. Somewhere in the kingdom lived a sister whose face he didn't remember, whose name he couldn't recall. A sister whose impending marriage had been the reason for him leaving France.

Had she made inquiry over his whereabouts when he didn't arrive for the ceremony? What of his parents— alive or dead, caring or not?

Leather hinges creaked. Snapped from his musings, Geoffrey found the presence of mind to walk forward, as if he'd just come up the stairway. Odo strode out of the solar, looking much too pleased, and nearly bumped into him. Geoffrey felt the heat of a sudden glare, but within Odo's glare flashed a hint of fear. A good sign. Fear made men cautious, and fear of a husband's retaliation might make Odo wary of speaking harshly to Leah.

Odo said nothing, continued on his way down the stairs as if Geoffrey hadn't been there. The slight was irksome, but of no import. Only Leah's opinion of him, and her father's, mattered.

Geoffrey paused by the solar door. Nigel stood near the window, looking out at the ocean as Leah had done so often when watching over Geoffrey. Briefly he wondered if 'twould be best to leave matters be, but then stepped into the solar.

"Nigel. A word?"

His father-by-marriage turned, a haggard weariness marring his features. "Geoffrey."

"Not only have I never doubted my marriage to your daughter, I also give you my oath that I will never abandon Leah."

Nigel's eyes narrowed. "You overheard?"

"The door is open. Anyone passing by might overhear."

Nigel glanced at the still-open door, which Geoffrey left open a-purpose, not caring if anyone overheard. 'Struth, if Nigel insisted he shout both his faith in Leah and his oath of constancy from the guard tower he'd comply.

A soft smile eased Nigel's weariness. He waved a hand at the table on which sat a small chest. "In the chest are the jewels and the coins that make up Leah's dowry. You may take them now if you wish."

Geoffrey crossed his arms. "Perhaps you should wait to give over until your mind is at ease over Odo's objections."

"My mind is at ease, though I thank you for your oath. Odo may harbor doubts and suspicions, but not I."

"As Odo said, you know nothing of me. Hell, I do not even know myself."

"Your loss of memory yet troubles you."

"I try not to allow it, but at times it haunts me," Geoffrey admitted. "If I could give you proof of the marriage, I would."

Nigel ambled over to the table and lifted the chest's lid. He withdrew a gold brooch studded with sparkling gems; clear diamonds, blood red rubies.

"I believe I once told you, Leah tends to have a good head on her shoulders." He flipped the brooch in his fingers. "She was all of twelve summers when her mother died. Leah never asked for her mother's keys, and I never gave them to her, she simply took them. 'Twas nigh on a fortnight later I realized what she'd done, that she strove to ease my burden by taking over her mother's tasks. The girl never did learn to weave well, but she ensured my stew spiced just as I liked it. She stood toe-to-toe, hands on hips, with any servant who dared move too slow for her liking."

In the ensuing silence, Geoffrey tried to picture Leah as a mere child, striving to fill a void she likely wasn't prepared to fill.

Nigel's thumb caressed the center diamond. "I allowed her to struggle through it all. I did not shield her from Odo's growing discontent. I should have arranged a betrothal when she came of age. In much I failed her."

He reverently put the brooch back in the chest. "I may not have heard you exchange vows, but I witness your devotion to each other every day. Leah may have given in to a whim when she ran off with Bastian, but she had the good sense to come home with you, even if you were half dead."

Geoffrey suppressed a shiver, not wanting to think of

what might have happened to him if Leah hadn't searched for him and pulled him off that plank, given him a chance to live.

"I owe Leah my life. I owe her a great debt for that alone, one I cannot repay."

"Ah, but you will lad. Have you not just given me your oath that you will never abandon her? Being a good husband to her will satisfy your debt, and perhaps atone for some of my neglect." Nigel closed the chest. "Take the dowry, hold to your oath and all will be well."

Geoffrey took a long breath and picked up the chest, not lifting the latch to further inspect the contents. If Nigel trusted him to keep his oath, then he'd trust Nigel to give over the entire dowry.

"Geoffrey, if you would, I have another task for you."

He noted the subtle shift in Nigel's mood, the stern set of his jaw. "What might that be?"

"Since you already know the contents of both the household and stannary accounts, I ask you to verify the accuracy of all of Pecham's accounts."

Damnation. The only other account was of the smuggling, the part of living at Pecham he found most disturbing. He sought a way to refuse.

"Odo will not approve."

"I prefer Odo did not know."

Ye gods. Nigel would make this request only if he suspected something amiss.

"You suspect . . . errors?"

"That is what I wish you to tell me. I am aware you do not approve of what we do, but I would like to make use of your talent with numbers all the same."

Nay, he didn't approve, preferred not to become any

more involved with the smuggling than he already was. 'Struth, he'd feared being asked to accompany Odo to sell the recently obtained goods, which consisted mostly of wine destined for inns and churches within Cornwall. Odo would be gone two, maybe three days at most.

Geoffrey couldn't think of another good reason to refuse, so with the dowry chest and the smuggling ledger in hand, made his way to the bedchamber, praying Odo had made no errors—either careless or a-purpose.

Leah leaned against the wall walk, knowing she had chores to attend, but couldn't command herself to budge.

Below, outside of the curtain wall on a grassy field, the men-at-arms held weapons practice—Geoffrey among them. Sweet Jesu, the man looked like and handled weapons as well as a warrior out of the troubadour's tales.

Where the guards wore short brown tunics over their breeches, Geoffrey had shucked his long tunic and sherte, leaving him bare-chested; black breeches hugged his trim hips and muscled thighs.

He towered over most of the men-at-arms, evidence of a heritage different from the men of Cornwall. Yet the guards accepted the man with the sable hair and beard who wielded a sword with controlled flair.

Leah no longer doubted the strength of Geoffrey's legs. He moved with a natural grace and speed when warranted, as now in his current match with Thuro. Steel clashed against steel, the two men grinning like fools while they tested each other's skill.

She'd watched weapons practice many times, but had never before worried so hard over where a sharp blade might take a bite, draw blood. Her stomach flipped even though she knew her fears groundless. Thuro wouldn't purposely harm Geoffrey, and Geoffrey obviously knew what he was about, enough to protect himself from a well-aimed slice.

On board the ship, Geoffrey had mentioned his studies in Paris. Where had he honed his skill with a sword?

Leah brushed the troublesome question aside, much preferring to concentrate on the play of Geoffrey's muscles within his sweat-sheened chest and arms.

Glorious. Magnificent. Dangerous, both to her heart and to his opponent on the field. His foolish smile had gone feral, no longer testing Thuro's skills but challenging.

She sensed company on the wall walk. Father. He came up beside her and leaned over the wall to observe.

"Poor Thuro," he commented. "He did not know what he faced when he taunted Geoffrey into crossing swords."

Geoffrey pressed Thuro hard, too hard for Leah's liking. Then Geoffrey stepped back. With a fist on one hip, his sword flailing under Thuro's nose, he spat out a string of names so vile they made her blush.

Father chuckled. "That should get Thuro's attention."

As well as the attention of most of the guards, who halted their practice to crowd around Geoffrey and Thuro. Neither man seemed to notice, too intent on each other.

Geoffrey continued. "Get your elbow up, for Christ's sake, or my sword will slice off a piece of you I doubt the wenches wish you to lose! Now let us try again slowly, and see if you are able to protect your manhood."

Thuro looked about to tell Geoffrey to go to the devil, but when faced with the swing of a sharp blade, angled his sword to deflect the blow, his elbow high in the air.

"Better," her father murmured.

"A lame attempt, Thuro! Again," Geoffrey ordered.

Leah winced, but watched the lesson, for lesson it was. Not until the fifth try did Thuro get his elbow in a position that pleased Geoffrey.

She nearly joined in the crowd's cheer at Geoffrey's verbal approval and jovial slap on Thuro's back.

Pensive, Father asked, "Has Geoffrey earned his spurs?"

Geoffrey a knight? She'd never given the possibility a thought, found nothing in his trunk to indicate a knightly rank. Still, given his prowess with a sword . . . 'twould explain much if he'd received a knight's training.

Certes, a wife should know of a husband's knighthood.

"If he did, he never said so."

Father eased back from the wall, then glanced over his shoulder down into the bailey. "We may soon have our answer."

Stable lads led four horses toward the gate. Behind them a mule pulled a wagon loaded with blunted lances and a quintain—the devices necessary for tilting.

Knowing how her father's mind worked, Leah couldn't help voice her growing suspicion.

"You test Geoffrey, as you did with the ledgers. Did you order Thuro to taunt him onto the field?"

"Aye."

No hint of apology tainted the admission, as if he had

every right to do as he pleased to whomever he pleased—which Leah grudgingly admitted he did. As lord of Pecham, Father's word was law and when his mind was set, he'd not be moved from his resolve or purpose.

Geoffrey shared that trait, an irritating quality, yet likely inherent to every man in a position of authority. His handling of Thuro suggested he'd previously given lessons in swordplay, perhaps commanded men, and Father sensed the abilities and sought proof.

"To what end?"

"Your brother seems bent on obtaining his knighthood. He'd do well to seek Geoffrey's aid."

"You consider having Odo knighted?"

"I would if I thought him prepared. He may do well dancing attendance at court, but soon or late he would be expected to enter a tournament or prove his worth on a battlefield. In that he would fail, and suffer the derision of those men he holds in high esteem. 'Twould break him."

Unfortunately, Odo did not take correction well. Thuro had stood his ground when Geoffrey raised his voice. Odo might have tossed his sword on the ground and walked away in a fit of pique.

"Odo will not listen to Geoffrey."

"He might, if the prize is great enough. Look, Geoffrey cannot resist."

The quintain—the target for the lance—now stood at the far end of the field, its thick wooden crossarm in position to knock man from horse if not hit with a faultless strike.

His arms crossed over his chest, Geoffrey watched the

more daring of the men-at-arms charge the quintain, cheering those who succeeded, laughing at those who landed in the dirt.

She'd begun to wonder if he truly intended to participate when he hefted one of the lances, set it aside, then proceeded to test several others until he settled on one. He strode directly to the largest stallion and swung up into the saddle.

To Leah's amazement, he didn't charge the quintain, but spun the horse around to gallop across the field and over the drawbridge. He reined to a halt in the bailey, below the wall walk where Leah stood.

Her nether regions warmed to the sight of him, a feast for the female eye, a half-naked delight. All male animal, sleek and powerful, temptation on horseback.

To make matters worse, he grinned up at her, mischief lurking in his sapphire eyes.

"I beseech thee, milady! A length of ribbon, a scrap of lace—any token of favor you might bestow upon your humble, unworthy champion."

Flattered and flustered, Leah inwardly scoffed at Geoffrey's claim of humility, wondered for how long he'd known she watched him. 'Twas unreasonable for her pulse to race at his playfulness. Champion, indeed.

She untied the amber ribbon from the end of her braid and released it to float down to his outstretched hand. "Have a care for your ribs."

He tied the ribbon securely to the lance, then tilted it toward her in salute. "Your faith in my prowess gladdens my heart."

"'Ware the crossbar, O mighty champion."

"As my lady commands." Bowing low over the saddle, with the merest nudge of his knees he backed the horse, then wheeled and sped back to the field.

Father chuckled. "Tournament manners, nicely performed."

"Which only means he apes them."

"Think you?"

She'd benefited from Geoffrey's chivalrous bent and bravery on the day they'd met aboard an ill-fated ship; he'd risked his life to save hers. He wore his pride and honor like an ermine-trimmed cloak, for all to see and heed. Knightly attributes all.

"A man need not be a knight to possess chivalrous qualities."

Father gave a disbelieving huff and turned his attention to the field where Geoffrey took position to challenge the quintain.

The stallion pranced, eager for the run. Leah gripped the stone wall and tried not to worry.

Powerful thighs gripped the steed, commanding it to stillness. The lance lowered. Geoffrey leaned forward—and charged. Leah covered her face, her heart beating in rhythm with pounding hooves—except she couldn't help but peek through her fingers.

The lance splintered under the force of the blow, jarring rider and horse too much to avoid the sweep of the crossbar. Both went down in a swirl of dust and flailing limbs, the horse regaining his feet almost immediately. Not so Geoffrey.

Leah held her breath until Geoffrey finally rose and reached for the broken lance. He untied the ribbon, flung the remains of the weapon aside and mounted the horse. As he called for the quintain to be reset, then for Thuro to hand up a lance, he wrapped her ribbon around his wrist.

"Daft man," she muttered, the determination of his set jaw leaving no doubt he'd try again, as many times as he must until he succeeded.

There wasn't a damn thing she could do but watch.

To her great relief, she was forced to watch only once more. The lance hit the target squarely with a solid thud. Horse and rider escaped in perfectly timed form.

Pleased with himself, he sought her approval with an upraised, ribbon-wrapped wrist and bewitching smile. Unable to do aught else, she waved, eliciting a cheer from his appreciative admirers.

Father straightened. Leah prepared for his gloat. Instead, he placed a hand on her shoulder and squeezed. "He is a good man, Leah. You did well, perhaps better than I might have done for you. Perhaps leaving you to choose your own path was not a mistake on my part after all."

He walked away before she could swallow the lump that formed in her throat.

Almost more stunning than the small show of affection was the approval of her judgment—high praise she didn't deserve.


Geoffrey dipped cupped hands into the water basin in the guard's quarters and washed the sweat from his face.

He hurt all over, and damn if it didn't feel good.

He'd given good account of himself except for that first pass at the quintain and that was Leah's fault. He reached for a towel and paused, forced to admit the miss 'twasn't Leah's fault at all but that of his own distraction.

True, he wanted to succeed to impress Leah, but he'd also been visited by an awareness impossible to ignore. The cheer of the crowd. The gaiety of color on fluttering banners and nobles' garments. The mingling odors of metal, horse and meat pies. For mere moments he'd wandered into the midst of a tournament, enough moments to ruin his concentration.

As if he knew the feeling of participating in a tournament.

As if he'd done so often, but oddly enough, found no joy or satisfaction in the competition.

He'd given in to Thuro's goading to find out how well he could use a sword. Sweet Jesu, somehow the practice turned into a lesson he didn't know why he felt compelled to give. The urge to correct Thuro's fighting form had sprung forth and he acted on the impulse. Nigel had every right to berate him for taking the liberty.

These odd feelings and sudden impulses took him unaware, reminding him of a life before Pecham but not revealing details. Damn but he wished his head would settle, wished either his memory returned fully or ceased taunting him with vague images.

Geoffrey drew on his sherte and overtunic, then picked up the amber ribbon he'd set aside before washing.

The ribbon's hue nearly matched Leah's eyes.

'Twas unwearable now, stained with both dirt and the sweat from his wrist. She'd been pleased by his request for the favor, even as she cautioned him to 'ware the crossbar.

*O mighty champion.*

A true champion better protected his lady's token of favor. Next time he would.

He took the stairway up to the great hall, quiet now between meals. Neither Leah nor her father were to be found, both still outside somewhere. He resisted the urge to find either, knowing he'd put off a disagreeable task long enough. The smuggling ledger awaited his perusal.

Forcing himself up yet another stairway, Geoffrey noticed the twitch in his side. A nasty bruise bloomed where the crossbar hit, a bruise he'd not allow Leah to see if he could help it. She'd want to poke at it, put on a poultice—remind him he'd not heeded her cautions.

The smuggling ledger lay on the bedchamber table, beneath the chest containing Leah's dowry, both right where he left them this morn, next to the book on medicine. He opened the book, preferring to read more on a fascinating study of leprosy. But study must wait.

The ribbon dangled from his fingers. What to do with Leah's unwearable ribbon? Ruined yet precious.

'Twas senseless to keep it, but he couldn't discard it—this length of silky ribbon the color of Leah's eyes, so charmingly bestowed at his request. After realizing she watched from the wall walk, moments after ripping into Thuro, he'd sought to favorably impress her. She'd warned him to have a care for his ribs—Leah still worried overmuch—but the delight in her eyes warmed him clear through.

Geoffrey brought the ribbon to his nose. His ripe sweat almost overwhelmed Leah's mellow lavender, but still the scents mingled, much as they melded when coupling.

He was fortunate to have a wife who suited him so

well, both in bed and out. Beautiful. Caring. Passionate. Sensible, yet able to play.

He draped the ribbon over the chair to dry, would decide what to do with it later.

Leah might suit him well, but another member of her family did not. After setting the dowry chest set aside, he settled into the chair and opened the smuggling ledger.

"All right, Odo, let us see what you have been up to."

# Chapter 14

"Milady, do you know of his lordship's whereabouts? I hoped for a chess game."

Ned's request for a bit of Geoffrey's time and attention rankled Leah. After participating in the weapons practice the other day, Geoffrey seemed intent on hiding in the bedchamber, reading—or so he said. Yet the book of medicine rested in the same place on top of his trunk as it had three days ago. The only sign he touched it was her hair ribbon marking a page.

He'd brushed off most of the dirt, then placed the ribbon in his book as a reminder of her. A bit of romantic fancy wrapped in shades of chivalry. His refusal to discard the ribbon touched her deeply.

"He is up the stairs."

Ned tilted his head. "Is he ill?"

"Nay, merely busy." But busy with what? "I will tell him you seek a game. Perchance after evening meal?"

"Whenever he might have time. I do not wish to intrude."

Ned bowed and took his leave, and Leah considered intruding. 'Twasn't like Geoffrey to spend so much time alone. He liked the company of others, delighted in riding over the countryside on a swift horse, had enjoyed the weapons practice. 'Struth, she was surprised he hadn't gone to the stannary with her father.

Leah glanced about the hall. Satisfied all was nearly ready for nooning, she took to the stairs. If naught else, she'd make Geoffrey aware of the impending meal.

She chided herself for considering to announce her entry to her own bedchamber. Forswearing a knock she opened the door.

Rolls of parchment and thick ledgers littered the room—on the table, the bed, even the floor. Geoffrey sat cross-legged on the rug, a large, bound book she didn't recognize balanced on his knees.

He looked up, startled. He said nothing, merely stared at her with those blue eyes that changed color with his mood. She saw his surprise, but also another emotion she couldn't quite identify. She closed the door, knowing something was wrong but not sure what, then spread her hands to indicate the mess.

"What is all this?"

He closed the ledger on his lap, glanced around at the strewn parchments and books. "The entirety of Pecham's accounts for the past five years."

The *entirety*? Dear Lord. The book he held must be a smuggling ledger.

Only one person could have given it to Geoffrey, and Leah wasn't sure she wanted to know why her father saw fit to have Geoffrey look at the ledger.

Odo would toss a fit if he knew. Those were his accounts to keep current.

Leah pushed several parchment rolls toward the middle of the bed, and eased onto the mattress so not to disturb Geoffrey's arrangement of scrolls.

"I gather Father asked you to have a look."

"Aye." With a frown, Geoffrey rose to his feet, leaving the ledger on the floor. "Your brother is not an honest man."

The statement wasn't a revelation.

"Neither is Father. Both engage in illegal trade."

"Your brother is the worst of the two. He—"

Geoffrey pursed his lips. Leah waited for him to continue. He didn't, and his reluctance prodded forth a feeling of dread.

"Geoffrey?"

He shook his head. "I should speak to your father first."

She should let the matter be. The accounts other than those of the household were none of her affair.

"You found something in the smuggling account not to your liking, and it troubles you."

He took a deep breath, crossed his arms. "You must promise to say naught to Odo."

"I know how to keep a confidence."

Geoffrey had no idea of the truth of that statement. The secret she kept from Geoffrey was likely far worse than the one he asked her to withhold from Odo.

He nodded. "Odo robs your father and the miners of their proper share of the smuggling profit."

Her gasp brought her up off the bed. "Are you sure?"

"'Tis my great misfortune to be absolutely sure." He

waved a hand about the room. "Given what I have learned of Pecham's affairs, and what I see recorded— and what is not recorded—I know Odo takes for himself a portion of funds each time he makes a selling trip. Not much, just a little, but enough to add up to a hefty sum over the years."

He nudged the smuggling ledger with the toe of his boot. "I am also sure your father suspects Odo's theft, merely wants me to confirm his suspicion. What vexes me is your brother's advising Nigel not to trust *me* when all along *he* is the one unworthy of trust."

Leah didn't know what to say. She couldn't defend Odo, but couldn't condemn him either. Poor Father. Neither of his offspring had proved worthy of the trust he placed in them, and 'twas hard to say which child offered up the worst of sins.

"Will your father return from the stannary today?"

"Likely, but one can never be sure."

"Let us hope he does. I would like to talk to him this eve, give him time to decide what course to take before Odo returns on the morrow." He stretched his arms up and back, working the muscles in his shoulders. "I suppose I should also put this mess in order."

He talked of scrolls and ledgers, not the mess of their lives. What would Father do upon learning of Odo's theft, and what would Odo do when accused? Whatever happened, Pecham's peace was about to be disrupted. Not a pleasant prospect.

"The mess will keep. Come eat first."

Geoffrey smiled. "Is that what you came up to tell me, to come down for nooning? I will not perish from missing a meal, my dear."

"Perhaps not, but I have grown accustomed to ensuring you eat and sleep properly. Besides, I have missed your company these past days. So has Ned. He requests a chess game."

He took the few steps that separated them, ran a finger over her chin. "Feeling neglected?"

She thrilled to his touch, as always.

"I care not what you do with your days as long as your nights are mine."

He cupped her cheek, bent forward. His warm breath teased her lips, making them tingle before he kissed her gently, a mere brush of mouths.

"We could bolt the door, turn day into night," he said, his voice low and seductive.

Her nether regions heated. Desire swirled, deep and tempting. The man had no shame when it came to coupling. No matter the time or place, he was ready to oblige. And able. Oh, so able.

"Nooning—"

"Can wait. I would rather feast on you."

Leah snuggled against him. His arms wrapped around her in an encompassing embrace.

Making love might provide relief from his thoughts, but better they should escape the chamber, give them both distance from the problem for a time.

Not that she wanted to put out the ignited fire, merely let it smolder. She'd learned the value of anticipation. Her body would now hum pleasantly for hours, and when they did finally come together, she would match him in vigor.

Besides, if she didn't go down for nooning, someone would soon be looking for her.

"I am expected in the hall. After we eat we can come up and clear the bed."

"The meal had best be worth the wait."

Leah eased out of his arms and clasped his hand. "Cook roasts you two doves."

"Dove, hmmm?"

She tugged, he followed, closing the chamber door behind them. The meal passed in pleasant fashion until near the end.

The hall's door burst open. Odo strode in, his garments soiled as if he'd been rolling in dust. He approached the dais, his gaze locked with hers. Leah steeled her resolve to withstand whatever comment he might make, reminding herself not to call him a thief.

Nothing could have prepared her for his news and order.

"Father is dead. Ready the hall for the vigil."

Denial screamed in her head, threatened to overwhelm her. She heard her eating knife clatter to the floor. Geoffrey swore.

*Father cannot be dead. He is at the stannary!*

Odo turned and began to walk away. Her anger flared hot and bright. She shot out of the chair and caught up with him near the stairs, grabbing hold of his sleeve to halt him.

Leah found enough voice to ask, "How?"

Her brother's face twisted with the agony she felt. "The new tunnel caved in. I escaped. Father . . . did not. We had to dig him out."

Her heart ripped open, the pain intense, tears unstoppable. All she could do was stare in disbelief at her brother, willing him to take back the words. Odo remained silent, offering neither denial nor comfort.

"Where is he?"

"Cart. Outside." He stared down at his trembling hands. "I need to wash. I need—"

Odo jerked away and bolted up the stairs.

Geoffrey's hands landed gently on her shoulders. She nearly collapsed under their weight, wanting to turn around and be held, weep against his chest. But not yet. She swiped at her tears, commanded her knees to hold.

"Do you want me to see to him?" Geoffrey asked softly.

*My father. My duty.*

"Come with me?"

"Whatever you wish."

She wished her father would walk through the door, tell her Odo lied.

Her hand secure in Geoffrey's Leah went outside. A cart waited at the bottom of the long stairway. She was aware of people milling about the cart, but saw only her father—white with dust, eyes closed, motionless.

Only hours ago he'd broken his fast then ridden out of Pecham on Boadicea into an unusually bright morn.

Her breath caught. Geoffrey's hold on her hand tightened. She descended the stairs slowly, reaching deep within for strength, drawing on Geoffrey's.

Anna stood at the foot of the cart, her hands covering her face. Leah touched the old woman's shoulder, all the comfort she could give for now, too racked by her own grief.

Father wore no shoes. Where were his shoes?

Geoffrey asked Garth what had happened.

Garth twisted his cap in his hands. "We were washing the mornin's diggings when Odo rode in. When he complained there was hardly enough to wash, Nigel took him to the tunnel to show him why we dug slow. Next thing we knew dust was a-pouring out the mouth. I thought sure the both of 'em were under the rubble. Got down on my knees and praised God, I did, when Odo walked out, coughin' up dust but alive."

How unfortunate that her brother—Leah banished the selfish wish before it fully formed. 'Twas unconscionable, sinful, to wish for one death over another.

Garth's disbelief and anger poured forth. "I do not understand why the beam split! 'Twas sturdy, I swear." He raked a hand through his hair. "I swear! His lordship woulda said the same."

Geoffrey asked, "You are sure the beam broke?"

Garth took a long breath. "Odo said he saw it give way and then the ceiling came crashin' down. Damn near buried them both."

Leah shook with horror of what her father must have suffered, wanted to hear no more for now. "Was anyone else hurt?"

Garth shook his head. "Nay, milady. Only yer father and brother were in the tunnel."

One death to deal with, then. There could easily have been more. A dangerous way to earn one's coin, mining. Father had loved it so.

*My father, my duty.*

Leah snatched at the refuge of duty, the sense of purpose when all seemed senseless. She'd done the same at her mother's death and found a bit of peace.

Prepare the body. Hold the vigil. Were there enough

candles about to light up the hall through the night? Order the cook to prepare a feast for after the burial. So much to do in so little time.

She glanced around at the men-at-arms, chose one. "Ned, we shall need a priest come morn. Hie you to the abbey and beseech the abbot's good will."

With the aid of prayers, to the dread of living, on the morrow they'd lay her father next to his wife for all eternity —their son now lord of Pecham.

Ye gods, what a terrible thought.

As Nigel's heir, Odo became lord of Pecham. As Leah's brother, he now possessed legal power over her fate.

Leah glanced up at the man whose presence as her husband protected her from Odo's whims.

"Bring my father inside, Geoffrey."

He kissed her knuckles before he let go, his concern for her clear in his eyes.

Leah climbed the stairs, her duty clear, blanking her mind to all else but bidding fare-thee-well to Nigel of Pecham.

Geoffrey followed Garth out of the lord's bedchamber and adjoining solar, leaving Leah, Anna and two servant girls to prepare Nigel's body for the vigil and burial—a wretched task normally performed by the women of the keep.

Garth halted in the passageway, his shoulders slumped. "I will go back to the village, set the miners to digging his lordship's grave."

The despondent overseer sought a way to work

through his grief, and his perceived responsibility in Nigel's death.

"I swear, Garth, I saw no flaw in the beams the one time I was in the tunnel."

He'd studied them, thoroughly, before he'd stepped inside, and judged them solid enough to hold the walls and roof in place.

"Yet there musta been a flaw or his lordship would still be alive." Garth's shoulders rose a bit. "I will be back later to keep vigil. Beggin' yer leave, milord."

Geoffrey nodded, releasing Garth to his tasks and grief.

Once alone in the hallway, Geoffrey wondered what to do with himself. He'd prefer to go back to Leah, but he'd likely just be in the way.

Where was Odo? His bedchamber? Likely, and best he stay there a while. Damn the man. He'd told Leah of Nigel's death in the harshest, bluntest possible way, with no regard for her feelings whatever. Then run off, leaving Leah to deal with all as best she could. The ruddy coward.

Geoffrey wondered what task he could perform to ease Leah's burden, and came up with nothing except dealing with the mess he'd made of their bedchamber. He stepped into the chamber, the parchment scrolls and ledgers still scattered everywhere, right where he'd left them.

A waste of two days. The study and figuring for naught.

Nothing he'd learned truly mattered now. Upon Nigel's death Odo became lord of Pecham—everything that didn't belong to the earl of Cornwall belonged to

Odo. True, he'd cheated the miners as well as his father, but as his father's heir and now solely responsible for the smuggling, Odo could do as he wished with no one to gainsay him.

Geoffrey was spared the ordeal of confirming Nigel's suspicions, and Nigel spared the *knowing* of his son's thefts, but damn, 'twas a hell of a way to go about it.

He'd miss Nigel. Their chess games. Their talks. For all Geoffrey disapproved of the smuggling, he'd liked the smuggler, admired the man's earthy wisdom and humor. He felt his heart twist, and knew Leah's suffering surpassed his own sorrow by leagues.

Had Nigel suffered? He hoped not, but could well imagine the terror of being unable to breathe, to know death imminent from lack of air. Geoffrey knew the feeling, having tasted it when he'd entered the tunnel and caves.

Geoffrey cleared away the lump in his throat, shook off the dread, and gathered up the scrolls and ledgers holding household accounts. These he'd place in the solar where they belonged along with the stannary accounts.

He stacked the stannary ledgers, wondering why Odo had been out at the mine. Had Odo finished his selling trip, coming home early—or cut the trip short a-purpose?

Only Nigel and Odo had been in the tunnel at the time of the collapse. The two had argued about Leah's dowry before Odo left Pecham. Had the argument continued, perhaps touching on Nigel's suspicions of Odo's thievery? And had Odo taken the opportunity to end it permanently?

The possibility chilled Geoffrey. Odo might be a thief, but a murderer? His own father?

Sons had done away with fathers or brothers for inheritance rights before. Had Odo done away with Nigel to save himself shame and punishment?

Or was his own sorrow seeking to place blame where none existed. Perhaps the beam was flawed and no one had seen it.

Perhaps another talk with Garth and an inspection of the beam was in order.

Geoffrey picked up the smuggling ledger from the rug. So much money involved. So much proof of illegal trade. Until he satisfied his suspicion over Odo's involvement in Nigel's death, he'd keep the smuggling ledger and to hell with Odo's feelings on the matter.

Geoffrey opened his trunk and laid the ledger atop the book of law he hadn't yet had the chance to peruse. Under his garments he placed the dowry chest, glad Nigel had seen fit to give it to him. Given Odo's animosity, Geoffrey knew that if the chest wasn't already in his position, he'd have to wage a battle for it, either legal or physical.

*Take the dowry, hold to your oath and all will be well.*

Nigel's words still echoing in his head, Geoffrey closed the trunk and snapped shut the lock, knowing he'd hold to his oath for no other reason than he loved his wife.

Geoffrey wasn't surprised at the depth of his emotions. From the first he'd admired her beauty and sought succor in her compassion. Now he couldn't imagine what his life might be like without Leah by his side.

At times he'd felt like half a man without his memory. Without Leah he'd be nothing at all.

The woman who claimed his heart entered the chamber quietly, seeming composed. She removed her veil and circlet, tossed them on the bed and smoothed back her hair.

"How do you?"

"Anna arranges a trestle table as a bier, then we will have Father . . . carried down to the hall." She bit her bottom lip, blinked back tears. "I could see . . . on his head where . . . the beam struck. I do not think he suffered."

The tears fell and Geoffrey could stand no more. He pulled Leah into his arms and held her tight while she sobbed her grief.

The lord's bedchamber smelled of death even though his father's body had been removed. A thorough airing was called for before he ordered his belongings moved in.

From his father's trunk, Odo pulled out a thick chain and hung it around his neck, the gold medallion landing at mid-chest where it belonged and shone nicely against his black tunic.

Lord of Pecham—the title fit, too.

True, the earl must confirm the inheritance, but Odo saw no obstacle in gaining approval. Both he and Father had been careful to ensure the earl had no reason for complaint of Pecham's revenue, the only thing the earl cared about. The only thing a clear-thinking man *should* care about.

As for the wealth and title he inherited, both were important to the future he desired and deserved. Now he could take on his knighthood, attend the king at court, and marry far higher than he'd been able to reach before.

He had no choice now but to marry quickly, provide Pecham with the next heir.

Odo dug deeper in the trunk, and the longer he searched the more his ire rose. The chest wasn't here. The brooch was gone.

Damn, damn, damn Father!

He slammed shut the trunk lid.

He was sure he'd convinced his father to withhold the dowry until after obtaining proof of Leah's marriage. But then, Father had always favored Leah, given his daughter everything she wanted while he forced his son to work hard to earn a pittance.

Or was Father to blame? Leah had been in this room for some time, preparing the body for the vigil. She'd likely rummaged about in this very trunk to fetch clean garments in which to garb their father.

She could well have come across the chest and taken it.

Either way, the little whore couldn't keep it! Especially their mother's brooch. 'Twas worth a fortune, and necessary to his plan to obtain a suitable wife, especially now that he could aim higher. He well knew how very susceptible high-born ladies were to pretty jewels. He'd sold them enough over the years.

Leah had done nothing to deserve the brooch except to be born. As firstborn, as the male heir of Pecham, *he* was entitled to the brooch, not his sister.

'Twouldn't be easy to reclaim the dowry, not with Geoffrey hanging about. After all he'd tried to discredit

Geoffrey, a man he disliked and mistrusted, and the lout now possessed the brooch.

What rotten luck! If only he'd come into the chamber ahead of Leah and gotten hold of the chest before her— but he'd thought he had time to change garments and wash away the dust and ore. He hadn't been thinking clearly, not after his near escape.

Too close he'd come to resting on a bier with his father.

Too many times since hearing the beam crack and watching the tunnel fall into itself he'd revisited the horror of tumbling wood and blinding dust, felt his bowels churn and panic rise. Only by swift reaction and a few feet did he escape his father's fate—death—which he couldn't have prevented had he tried. Everything happened too fast, in the space of a few heartbeats.

He hadn't wanted to go into the tunnel to begin with, but Father had insisted. Who the devil cared *how* the ore was dug out of the tunnel so long as the miners dug out enough to satisfy the needs of the smuggling captains?

No one could blame him for saving himself, not under those circumstances. Better one of them lived. Better the younger than the older. Fathers died and sons inherited. 'Twas the way of things.

Odo drew a long breath, calmer now. As lord of Pecham he must withstand the vigil and burial with solemn dignity, and he'd best get down the stairs and see to his duty. The problem of retrieving the brooch would have to wait for the nonce. There had to be a way to get it back.

He left the chamber, confident he'd soon discover the best way to go about the task.

\*     \*     \*

Geoffrey stood near the great hall's main doors while Odo and Leah said their private farewells to their father. Across the hall, Thuro took a position next to the doorway to the guard's quarters. Once Leah and Odo finished, the servants, men-at-arms, miners and farm folk would be allowed into the hall to mourn and keep vigil if they chose.

Nigel lay on a black-velvet draped bier set up at the foot of the dais, surrounded by thick flickering candles. He looked at peace, and Geoffrey hoped that was so.

Leah knelt in prayer, her head bowed. She'd cried so hard and long in the bedchamber Geoffrey didn't think she had any tears left to shed. She'd tucked a small piece of linen up her sleeve, but hadn't yet pulled it out.

Odo stood in somber silence at the head of the bier. Already he assumed the position of lord of Pecham, flaunting a huge golden medallion . . . nay, not flaunting. Pecham's people needed some sign that their lives would go on as always despite Nigel's death. Such visible assurances as a medallion calmed fears.

Still, Geoffrey didn't think Odo deserved either the lordship or the power that went with it, inheritance rights or no.

Leah rose and spoke quietly to her brother. "I will allow the others in now if you are ready."

Odo never looked at her, merely nodded.

She glanced about the room—likely ensuring all in readiness—then came toward Geoffrey. Her eyes were red but dry, her face composed but pale. Her small, sad smile made his heart ache.

"'Twill be a long night," she said.

Not as long as she thought. Geoffrey intended to force Leah to rest, if only for an hour or two. He'd not have her collapse because she'd overtaxed her strength in the name of duty.

He waved a hand at the hall's doorway. "Shall I let the others in now?"

"In a moment."

Her gaze locked with his, as if looking for something within the depths of his eyes.

'Twas disconcerting how easily she perceived his moods, knew his needs and guessed at his wishes before he could voice them. Were those talents all wives shared, or did Leah just know him so well?

What did she look for now? He wished he knew.

She took the scrap of linen from her sleeve, wound it around her fingers. "While I prayed, I realized I never told my father how much I . . . cared for him, respected him. I shall always regret never saying the words."

"I am sure he knew."

"I hope so." Her amber eyes went soft, and within their depths he caught his own reflection, and nearly melted under the rightness of the image. "I do not want to chance regrets with you, Geoffrey. No matter what path or twists our lives may take, I want you to know that . . . I love you."

Nothing she might have said could stun him more. Her declaration reverberated through him. Joy swelled his heart to near bursting. Speechless, he held out his hand.

She backed up a step with a shake of her head.

"Nay, if I touch you I will start crying again and I would rather not. This may not have been the best time or place to tell you, but I wanted you to know." She waved at the door. "You may open the door now."

After a nod to Thuro, she turned and walked toward the kitchen, where the servants awaited permission to enter the hall.

*Leah loves me!*

He nearly ran after her, anxious to tell her that he loved her, too, had known for some time now. Her beauty, her spirit, her gaiety and even her tears—he treasured them all. He loved so many things about Leah he'd never be able to list them all. Damnit, he adored the woman, and just possibly that's why he'd married her.

He'd have been an utter fool not to.

But he stopped himself from rushing forward, preferring to choose a time when he could wrap her in his arms, hold her close, and be sure whatever tears she shed were of joy and not of grief. She'd blurted out her feelings in an effort to stave off regret. The next time it happened there'd be none of that, only two people declaring their love for love's sake alone.

The servants entered the hall through the kitchen doorway, most pausing to say a few words to Leah. The men-at-arms more formally filed across the room toward Odo, gave respectful bows to their new lord.

Reminded of his duty, Geoffrey opened the hall's huge oak doors. Without stood a large crowd of miners and farmers, their families with them. Some faces he recognized, others not. They filed past him, most with a simple greeting, acknowledging his status as Leah's husband.

Garth entered, still distraught. Later, after most of the people took their leave, Geoffrey intended to ask the overseer about the tunnel's support beams. After further thought on the matter, Geoffrey doubted Odo possessed either the strength to budge a beam from its supporting position, or the courage to risk his own neck, but he had to be sure.

And once he was sure, he would again talk to Leah about leaving Pecham.

She might be willing, even anxious to leave, but not until after every ritual was performed, her father buried, the will read and executed to her satisfaction. Only then would she consider her duty to her father and to Pecham done.

In the meantime, he'd keep Leah close, watch Odo, and ensure the dowry chest and smuggling ledger stayed locked in his trunk.

# Chapter 15

Those affected by Nigel of Pecham's will gathered in the solar, somber and silent while the priest broke the red wax seal on the rolled parchment Odo gave him.

Leah's head ached, a dull throb at her temples. If Geoffrey hadn't insisted in the wee hours of morn that she close her eyes for a few minutes, she might not now be sitting upright.

She'd thought sleep impossible, but she'd drifted off for a few hours, awaking only when Geoffrey gently roused her in time to prepare for the burial.

Father Ambrose, sent over by the abbot, had kept the service at graveside short but respectful. Leah found it comforting to think her father and mother were now rejoined.

Geoffrey stood nearby, hovering as he had for most of last night, like a dark guardian angel. She felt protected, but yet a bit uneasy over his attention.

Mercy, she'd blurted out her deepest emotions in a

most irregular manner at a poor time. The man must think her so addled he felt compelled to guard her against further stupidity.

Not that she was sorry he now knew of her love, even if it stunned him to speechlessness. She did love Geoffrey, more than was good for her, she supposed. He cared about her, had shown her so many times in various ways, but she shouldn't have hoped to hear the words back no matter how much she craved them.

Odo cleared his throat, loud in the silent chamber.

The priest looked up from the documents, glanced over the people gathered. "Before I begin, does anyone here doubt the state of Nigel of Pecham's mind when he made his will?"

Anna, Garth and Thuro all shook their heads.

Odo waved a dismissing hand. "My father's mind was sound. I only have you read the will before us all so no misunderstandings occur."

Leah understood the necessity. Contention over wills had caused deep rifts in families, the cost of contention in the courts depleting coffers until there wasn't a shilling left to fight over.

The priest began reading her father's last wishes.

As was common, Nigel of Pecham rewarded those people in positions of responsibility who'd served him long and well. He made generous awards to the herbswoman, the stannary overseer and the captain of the guard—fitting tributes, Leah thought.

Not so Odo, whose eyes narrowed and frown deepened with each bequest, as if confused by them. Why so? Surely he'd expected the awards.

"To Geoffrey, whom I acknowledge and accept as my daughter's husband—"

"Hold!" Scowling fiercely, Odo snatched the will from the priest's hand.

Startled, Father Ambrose asked, "Is aught amiss?"

Leah clutched her hands in her lap, realizing her father must have changed his will very recently to include Geoffrey—and hadn't informed Odo. Had her father also changed the bequests awarded to his favored retainers? 'Twould explain why her brother had seemed puzzled.

"Do you challenge the validity of the will?" the priest asked. "Is this not his lordship's style of handwriting?"

She held her breath, felt Geoffrey's hand tighten on her shoulder.

Odo flung the parchment back at the priest. "'Tis written in my father's hand."

"You will honor the terms?"

"'Twould seem I have no choice!"

Leah thought Odo might leave the room in a fit of temper, but he merely turned his back on everyone in the room and began to pace, hands behind his back, eyes downcast.

No matter his agreement, she feared he already schemed against honoring the bequests. Still, Odo had declared the document valid before several witnesses, had stated their father of sound mind. Both would work against him should he decide to contest the will.

The priest continued. "To Geoffrey, whom I acknowledge and accept as my daughter's husband, into whose care I have entrusted her welfare and her dowry, I give thee another treasure to hold safe, that of the mare Boadicea."

Leah's throat tightened. She felt like crying again, and couldn't help but smile up at Geoffrey, noting his own pleased smile.

"To Leah, my beloved daughter, I grant the sum of one hundred marks to aid the setting up of her own household. May God grant you and your husband many years of joy."

*Beloved daughter.*

She blinked back tears. She'd treasure the words more than the coin.

"To Odo, son of my loins and heart, I grant thee . . ."

Leah half listened to the listing of property—rugs and furniture, personal items and a wealth of coin and pewter plate. Then the discharge of duties as lord of Pecham, the responsibilities for the keep, the farms, the stannary, the village and its people.

What wasn't stated in the will frightened her most.

With father gone, Odo legally became her guardian, possessed the power to decide her future. Only Odo's belief in her marriage protected her—along with one small phrase in the will.

By handing her into Geoffrey's care and giving over the dowry, father had as good as betrothed them. All the marriage lacked was a pledge between she and Geoffrey to live as husband and wife, whether before witnesses or not.

For herself, she cared not if she lived in sin, but others would condemn her for fornicating with a man not her husband.

As she had so often, she again considered telling Geoffrey of her deception. Her dishonesty gnawed at her innards. She could hardly condemn Odo for his greed, his selfishness and dishonestly when she was guilty of much the same.

Geoffrey squeezed her shoulder, a gentle prod out of her thoughts. He bent low and whispered, "Come, food awaits."

The priest had finished, was rolling up the parchment.

One more duty to perform—the feast held to honor her father's memory. She rose from the chair, determined to see it through. Geoffrey took her hand and tugged her toward the door. Leah held fast, eyes on her brother, without whose presence the feast couldn't begin.

He now stood near the window. Unmoving. What was he thinking, staring out at the ocean? Did he, too, miss their father? Perhaps, but more likely he grieved over Father's generosity.

"Odo, 'tis time to go below."

Leah shivered as he strode past her, his cold expression more fearsome than his anger.

That night, while Leah readied for bed, Geoffrey opened his trunk to put his book of medicine inside. With the smuggling ledger and dowry chest atop his own belongings, the book didn't fit well enough to allow closing the lid. He rearranged, exchanged the bigger book for the smaller law book. Better, but now what to do with the law book?

He put it on the table. There should be room to pack it with Leah's belongings. Or perhaps they'd leave all but the most important things behind, just get out of Pecham and worry about the rest after they settled someplace.

On the morn he'd tell Leah of his decision to leave

Pecham, after they'd both rested, when grief wasn't so fresh and painful.

The past two days had been long and wrenching. Leah looked ready to keel over. Nigel's death had rocked him, too. Normal reactions to a death, he supposed. The sorrow was palpable, most especially in the keep, everyone affected in differing ways. Some wept, some turned inward, all mourned.

Garth could hardly raise his chin from his chest, blaming himself for Nigel's death. The miners had studied the broken beam and discovered a fault within the wood that caused it to break, ending Geoffrey's musings over Odo's direct involvement in Nigel's death.

Odo might not have murdered his father, but the man's demeanor was still insufferable. Leah's brother treated all and sundry with an arrogance and disdain that boded ill, especially for anyone who dared cross him. No longer checked by Nigel's level-headed influence, Odo would prove unendurable.

Leah came toward him, a weary wraith in white linen. Her fingertips glided over the gold lettering on the book's spine.

"This is written in French, is it not?"

The question puzzled him. She should know the book written in French. "Aye. Did you read it?"

"Dear me, nay. I am not well educated in the language."

"But you use French in the household accounts."

"A few words only." She smiled wryly. "I doubt any book of yours contains the words for eggs or cloth or oats."

His confusion melted away. She'd been taught those words she needed to know to fulfill her duties, no more.

"Not this book."

"What is it about?"

"The workings of the law."

Her mouth tightened. "A timely subject. You may wish to see if the book contains advice on wills. I fear Odo very displeased with my father's."

So he'd noticed, and would deal with Odo if he tried to withhold anyone's rightful bequest. Another problem to ponder over and discuss with Leah. But not tonight.

He slid his arm around Leah's shoulders and steered her toward the bed. For now she needed sleep.

"Coming to bed?" she asked, sliding beneath the coverlet, her eyes already drifting shut.

"Aye." He'd be willing to wager she'd be asleep by the time he removed his boots. He brushed aside her silky blond hair, kissed her forehead. Her sigh made him smile. "Sleep well."

She didn't answer, and he hadn't even begun to undress.

Knowing he wouldn't fall into slumber as quickly as Leah, his thoughts once more homed on their future.

Where to go? Given the money in the dowry chest and Nigel's added bequest, they could go anywhere, perhaps visit a few towns, look them over, examine the possibilities. They could go back to Paris, as Leah had suggested, but the mere thought of stepping aboard a ship turned his stomach.

He'd obviously studied philosophy, medicine and law. Of them all, law seemed to him the most interesting profession to take up to support them.

Geoffrey lowered into the chair, pulled the law book in front of him. Surely he could make a decent living by writing wills, drawing up deeds, representing lords in land disputes.

He flipped through pages, skimming along words, wondering if perhaps he had, after all, once before decided to make law his profession.

His eyes burned—awake too long to try to read by dim candle glow. He shut the book, pushed it aside, then noticed the corner of a piece of parchment jutting out of the bottom.

Curious, he pulled it out.

His pulse quickened as he read the message—a request to attend the wedding celebration for his sister. Eloise.

Geoffrey pressed his palms to the table, a useless effort to remain calm as a little girl's face took form—a pert nose, large blue eyes, dark hair to match his own.

*Eloise. My sister.*

Her face matured, transformed into one of exquisite beauty, a touch of the girl remaining—her sweet innocence tinged by a hint of mischief.

Geoffrey closed his eyes to hold onto the single image, but lost it under the deluge of other people and places as memories of his family flooded back.

His mother, long dead; his father, alive. His siblings. A keep in Warwickshire.

Geoffrey crossed his arms on the table and put his head down, breathing deep, palms sweaty, head light. Where before he'd experienced vague awareness of his past, here was reality, solid memory.

He'd both craved and dreaded this moment of revelation, torn between wanting desperately to know who he was and where he came from, fearing he wouldn't like what he learned. Unable to slow the flood, he allowed the wave to wash over him, knowing he'd emerge alive and intact—but changed.

Success and failure. Joy and sorrow. Triumph and defeat.

The emotions tore him asunder as events in his life took form, faded, and another grabbed his attention. Two and twenty years worth of life opened up, whipped around him, and then settled—the storm was over within heartbeats that seemed an eternity.

Gently, he probed at his identity.

Sir Geoffrey Hamelin, son of John and Elizabeth, born at Lelleford, his father's holding in Warwickshire.

He could see the stone keep, larger than Pecham, surrounded by two curtain walls, more heavily guarded. The bailey teeming with people. The tiltyard where he'd learned the use of sword and lance, training for his own knighthood. A nursery chamber, where he'd caught the love of learning.

His breath hitched on a child's image of his mother, blurred by the distance of years. Soft, fragile, she'd died of childbed fever after giving birth to a stillborn son.

His father burst into view, demanding his son's attention in the same overbearing manner he did in real life. Sir John Hamelin, the bane of Geoffrey's existence, the man he'd never been able to please. Their heated arguments had led to a final separation, one of Geoffrey's making.

He shoved his father aside, those memories too

painful to deal with all at once. As he had often in the past when troubled, he sought out his siblings.

Julius, the eldest child and heir, strode through Geoffrey's memory with graceful but purposeful steps. A proud bearing, a warrior's body, a face women swooned over. He took his oath of chivalry seriously, an admirable quality that caused their father despair.

Jeanne's visage was hazy. At their father's command, she'd been wed at a tender age to a man Geoffrey remembered as having white hair even then, nigh on eight years ago. He'd seen very little of her after she'd gone off to live with her husband.

Eloise wouldn't meekly submit to an unsuitable marriage, even if the fight cost her dearly. The youngest, still vulnerable to their father's whims—

Geoffrey raised up and reread her message. He'd missed the wedding. She'd been married nearly a month already!

Damn! Had Eloise freely consented to the marriage or been forced to accept a husband their father chose?

He'd intended to confront their father over Eloise's marriage if he must, knowing Julius better suited to the task but too far away to reach home on time.

Julius' visage sharpened, and Geoffrey again saw his brother as he appeared at their last meeting, several months ago now. He'd stopped in Paris on his way to Italy, not to order or cajole his wayward brother into returning to Lelleford, just to see how Geoffrey fared—or so Julius said.

They'd spent two days seeing the sights in Paris, and two nights enjoying the lively, bawdy entertainments the city offered. Then Julius took his leave, resuming his pilgrimage.

Julius had never said why he felt compelled to make a pilgrimage. Had it been his brother's idea or their father's?

'Twould be like their father to send Julius out of the country if he believed his eldest son might object to some wild, loathsome scheme of his—like selling Eloise to gain a stronger foothold at court, or get his hands on a piece of land he coveted. Father wouldn't have dreamed his younger son might return home to interfere.

Not Geoffrey, who'd escaped to Paris and to the university when his father demanded he enter holy orders, his only contact with home through the rare letter from Eloise.

Again he read her message, heard the faint yet detectable plea for his presence at her wedding. His gut twisted.

John Hamelin's mocking voice rang in his son's head. *Certes, you failed her. I expected no less from you.*

Geoffrey's hands clenched into fists. *I would have been there had I not broken my legs and lost my memory!*

*A poor excuse. What might you have done if you arrived? Eloise is my daughter, to do with as I see fit. No law in that damn book of yours could have stopped me.*

Geoffrey tried to banish both voice and visage, but John Hamelin stood his ground despite his son's efforts.

*I would have tried.*

*Without success. You never did fight hard enough to win.*

*Not so. I escaped your plans for me, did I not?*

*Only for a time.*

'Twas his greatest fear about returning home—that he wouldn't be able to leave, that somehow his father would bend or break his will. Geoffrey ran a hand through his thick hair, the prospect of a tonsure still disagreeable.

*I am free of you, Father.*

*Only because I did not come after you. Think you I did not know where to find you? Eloise never could keep a secret.*

*Why did you not come fetch me back then?*

The voice went silent, mocking him yet again by not answering the question Geoffrey had wondered over. He'd spent nearly all of his first year in Paris glancing furtively over his shoulder, fearing his father's wrath.

After arriving in Paris, he'd written Eloise, knowing his younger sister would be most upset over his disappearance. Nay, Eloise couldn't keep a secret and, frankly, a knight's little daughter didn't receive a missive without half the keep knowing of a messenger's arrival—without his father being aware, and likely reading the message before giving it to Eloise.

*Do you know I robbed your coffer for the coin to pay my passage to Paris?*

Again silence.

His father's image faded, so Geoffrey moved on—to Paris.

The glorious university. His shabby room above a tavern. The struggle for funds to pay for books and lectures and food. His ability to carve had saved him, most unexpectedly.

Geoffrey got up, took the bear down from the mantel. Burly and finely detailed, it looked much like the first one he'd made just to keep his hands busy—and then, much to his surprise, sold for several florins—to a drunken count, who'd taken the bear home to his wife as a gift to appease her anger at his wastrel ways.

The countess not only forgave her husband but came looking for Geoffrey, seeing more in the statue than the rude image of a bear. She'd wanted more, paid more. Soon her peers wanted the little carvings, too, and paid dearly.

He returned the bear to the mantel, among the rest of the animals he'd carved for Leah, for his own pleasure.

Geoffrey tried to move on, but some wall blocked his path.

He couldn't bring up a memory of Leah, or of the shipwreck that nearly claimed their lives. 'Struth, while he knew every word of Eloise's message, he didn't know how or when he'd received it.

Most of his memory had returned, but not all. A portion remained hidden behind that damn thick wall.

Frustrated, he reasoned that if Eloise's message prodded forth so much of his memory, then something else in the trunk might unlock the rest. The most important.

He opened the trunk, set the dowry chest and books aside, knowing they wouldn't be of help. He pulled out garments, all of which he'd worn and meant little. His coin pouch—nothing in it except the coins Leah had told him it contained. Knives and whetstone. A pouch containing two bars of lavender-scented, French-milled soap. Leah's soap?

The horses. They were among his finest work, would fetch a pretty price among Paris' nobles, but his purpose in carving them eluded him.

Nothing in the trunk helped budge the annoying wall.

Leaving the trunk's contents scattered on the floor, he went back to the law book and fanned the pages. No more notes stuck between the pages.

Damn.

So what was the last thing he remembered clearly? At what event or season did his memory stop?

Carving. He'd carved a statue of a cupid for the countess as a gift to her husband. Spring. Early spring. No memory of Leah, then, so they must have met later.

He tucked Eloise's message back in between pages of the law book, considered waking Leah to tell her the good news—but then he'd have to tell her the bad, that he still didn't remember her. More than anything he wanted to remember the day the two of them had exchanged vows, the day beautiful, loving Leah had become his wife.

The gap in his memory between early spring and midsummer rankled hard.

The room was suddenly too small to hold both his elation and ire. Quietly, so not to disturb Leah, he left the bedchamber and made his way out to the wall walk.

The misty air chilled him; the wind cleared his head.

After carving the cupid for the countess, what then?

He'd attended a lecture, could envision the crowded lecture hall and the man who spoke, but couldn't name the topic.

Geoffrey shook his head. 'Twould be a very long night if he must try to force memories day by day. Surely there must be a better—

*Scarlet silk.*

His stomach churned.

Leah clung to him, frightened yet brave.

*Get off the ship. Get Leah off the ship!*

Smoke. Fire. The thunder of breaking wood.

Leah screaming his name, over and over, the sound ripping at him because he couldn't get to her.

*Sliding across the deck. Down. Down.*

*Horrible pain. Drowning!*

Geoffrey swayed against the wall and held his breath, able to do naught but hang on through the onslaught. Again he stood on the ship's deck, clinging to the rail, his stomach roiling. A woman in a scarlet silk gown took pity on him, talking to him to distract him from his illness.

He'd met Leah on the ship.

*Not my wife.*

His emotions warred with what he now knew to be true.

*Not my wife.*

He'd been deceived by the woman he'd felt compelled to see safely into one of the boats. A stranger.

She'd *lied*. To him. To her father. Everyone had believed her tale except Odo. Gads, her brother had been right after all to demand proof of the marriage—a marriage that had never happened.

Leah's deception cut a deep, bloody swath through his heart. He'd saved her life and she repaid him with lies. No wonder she hadn't been eager for his memory to return—'twould expose her ruse, reveal her deceit.

Damn her lovely hide to hell.

Geoffrey shoved against the wall, the temptation to rush back to the bedchamber and shake Leah awake and demand an explanation so strong he nearly gave in. He'd never hit a woman, believing them the weaker sex and worthy of a man's protection—a consideration Leah no longer deserved.

He couldn't return to the bedchamber and face Leah with his temper this high. Though he might want Leah to suffer as badly as he, he'd not do her murder.

He hurt. Dear God, he hurt. No one, not even his father who could wound him with a word, had ever injured him this deeply.

Geoffrey turned his face to the wind and cold mist, willed his ire to ease.

*Sweet Jesu, Leah, why?*

Only yesterday she'd said she loved him and he'd believed her. Even now he wanted to believe the woman who'd saved his life, nursed him tenderly, stolen his heart, loved him. She'd slept with him, made love with him, done everything a loving wife ought—except all along she played him for a fool, betrayed him.

Aboard ship, even before their first meeting he'd noticed her sadness, which turned out to be sorrow over a man, one who she claimed to love and hadn't loved her in return. Now he knew who that other man was, her lover, a smuggling captain named Bastian.

Damn her lying tongue, her fickle heart.

What a dolt he'd been to believe Leah different from her father and brother, an honest member of a family of thieves.

She'd duped him thoroughly and deserved punishment for her deception. Geoffrey knew he didn't have the right to determine what that punishment might be. As Leah's closest male relative, Odo possessed that right.

A chilling, sobering reality.

No wonder she'd chosen an odd time to declare her

love, right after she'd realized that without Geoffrey standing as her husband, she'd be at the mercy of her brother's whims. Odo was now her legal guardian, could do with her as he wished. Marry her off to whomever he pleased. Send her off to a convent. Ravage her dowry.

Geoffrey doubted she loved him so much as she needed him—a large, solid buffer between her and an uncertain future.

He rubbed his hands over his bearded face, the facial hair he'd let grow because Leah expressed a preference for it. He'd done so much to try to please the woman who'd saved his life, cared for him so tenderly. All Leah's concern, their intimacy—no woman could fake all that, could she? He remembered the night he'd dared suggest she should have left him out in the Channel, her horror and tears, and how good it had felt to finally hold her against him.

That night he'd yearned for a great love, and now . . . now that his memory returned some demon inside him wanted his true life to fade back into the darkness, yearned to again believe the love he'd thought they shared remained pure, untainted.

But nothing could ever wipe away the tarnish. How could he ever again trust her? Without trust, how could love flourish?

Truly, he should leave at first light, stuff everything in his trunk into a big sack, tie it to Boadicea—the mare willed to him quite legally—and make for home. Abandon Leah to whatever fate Odo decreed.

But as much as he despised her lies, could he leave Leah to suffer her brother's whims?

And he'd given Nigel an oath not to abandon Leah.

He'd given Nigel the oath when believing Leah his wife. Now that he knew the truth, was he honor bound to keep the oath?

Perhaps not, but if he broke his own word, discarded his honor, he'd be no better man than Odo.

The ring of boots on stone alerted him to an approaching guard. Thuro, making his inspection round.

"A miserable night, milord, for standing at the wall."

Geoffrey kept his answer short, willing Thuro to keep walking. "Aye."

Thuro came to a halt. "Her ladyship asleep? Hard day."

The man had no idea how hard, and Geoffrey wasn't about to tell him. "Tomorrow will be less trying."

Thuro frowned. "Nigel's passing will not soon be forgotten."

"'Twill be hard to become accustomed to his absence."

Those at Pecham had no choice in the matter, but Geoffrey did, and the sooner he could leave Pecham behind the better.

Except he'd given that damn oath to Nigel.

The captain glanced out into the night, in the direction of the noisy ocean. "I would not stay out here too long without a cloak, milord. Chill goes right through a man after a while. I bid thee a good night."

An inane conversation, saying nothing, yet calming in a way Geoffrey couldn't fathom.

He would *not* regret getting his memory back and getting on with the rest of his life.

A life without Leah.

He'd mulled over plans for the future, all considering

Leah in the mix as his wife and helpmate. But he'd fallen in love with a woman who certainly didn't deserve his love, not even his forgiveness. And now?

*Go home.* Why bother? With Eloise already married he couldn't do a thing to help her.

With the sharp clarity of his life spread out before him, he realized he'd used the excuse of Eloise's situation to do what he should have done years ago. Go home. Repay the coin he'd once stolen to make his escape.

Attempt to mend the severed relationship with his family.

That could only be accomplished if John Hamelin now accepted that his younger son had grown into his manhood and wouldn't be forced to accept a father's dictates.

He would go home and confront his father, soon. First he'd keep his oath to another father, Nigel. He couldn't abandon Leah to suffer harshly at the hands of her brother.

Perhaps, if Fate leaned his way, he'd have both his emotions and plan of action well in hand before dawn.

# Chapter 16

Confused by the mess, Leah packed Geoffrey's trunk. 'Twasn't like him to leave his belongings lying about.

What had compelled him to rummage through his trunk in the middle of the night? Books, clothing, dowry chest, smuggling ledger—nothing seemed to be missing.

She left the law book on the table because she guessed he'd want it later.

Her concern and puzzlement grew when she didn't find Geoffrey in the great hall breaking his fast. She swallowed the lump that formed in her throat and put a hand over her aching heart upon seeing her father's empty chair. 'Twould take time, likely months, to become accustomed to his absence, just as after her mother died.

She turned away from the sadness and went out to the stable. Boadicea stood in her stall, and the stable lads reported not seeing Geoffrey this morn.

He had to be somewhere in the keep, and with each

passing moment she became more determined to find him. Something was amiss. She could feel it in her bones.

Leah left the stable and glanced around the bailey, then up along the wall walk. Geoffrey stood near the center of the east wall, gazing out over the ocean.

Perhaps nothing was amiss after all. Perhaps he'd only needed quiet moments with his own thoughts, his own grief. He'd been fond of her father despite his disapproval over the smuggling. And Leah understood the desire to seek solitude when battling mind demons. She did it often, and she, too, found the rhythm of the ocean comforting.

Leah briefly considered leaving him alone. Except she suspected he'd been out here for more than moments and his emptied trunk preyed on her mind. Too, grief was an emotion they could share, help each other muddle through. In the minutes it took to climb the steps for her to reach him, he neither moved nor glanced her way as she approached.

"Good morn." The greeting didn't come out cheerfully, but then her grief was too fresh for cheer.

Still he didn't turn to her. "Sleep well?"

Anger, barely controlled, simmered in the question.

Foreboding nearly sent her racing for a safe haven. Except, of late, her safe haven existed within Geoffrey's embrace.

"Aye. And you?"

"Too much on my mind to sleep." He shoved away from the wall, yet stared off in the distance. "I began reading the book of law and, to my surprise, found stuck

ithin the pages a message from my sister. Her name is
oise."

The cause of his anger. Now that Geoffrey knew his
ster's name, he wanted to know more about her. How
ustrating for him to know so much and yet so little.

She'd forgotten about the scrap of parchment she tried
read while kneeling beside Geoffrey in the warehouse,
inking it notations he'd made during a lecture.

What could she say to comfort him? No words
emed right. Learning his sister's name brought back
I the pain he'd tried so hard to put behind him.

"A lovely name, Eloise."

"A lovely young woman, too, last I saw her." He fi-
lly glanced her way, and Leah winced under his fury.
he married damn near a month ago, about the time my
lints came off. 'Tis now far too late for me to save her,
fe."

Geoffrey's harshness splintered her already broken
art into sharp shards.

*He knows I deceived him.*

The earth tilted beneath her feet, threatening her bal-
ice, much the same as had happened aboard the ship,
ssing them both into a situation neither had planned on
cared for.

Tears welled in her eyes. She'd been foolish to be-
ve this day of accounting wouldn't come, to hope her
wouldn't have consequences.

He waved a cutting hand in the air. "Have you noth-
g to say? No excuse, no explanation?"

She'd never figured out how to defend the indefensi-
e.

"I did what I thought best."

Incredulous, he asked, "Dear God, Leah, best fo
whom? I trusted you! From the moment I awoke,
trusted you with my very life. And now . . . now afte
months of believing . . . ah, hellfire. I thought you dif
ferent from the others, but you are no better than Odo o
Nigel, without honor or conscience. Why, by all that i
holy, did you see fit to drag me into your miserable life?'

The insult to her father's memory stung. Reminded o
those agonizing days after the shipwreck when forced t
make quick choices, Leah felt her ire rise. He had no no
tion of how often and hard she'd battled with her con
science.

"I had no choice but to remove you from the ware
house. I knew not who you were or how to send word t
your family. Where should I have taken you but hom
with me?"

"Anywhere!"

An answer bred of anger and resentment. She'd ha
nowhere else to go but home.

As he'd been on his way home.

In that instant she became aware that she again face
a stranger, not ill of body this time but sick of heart. H
looked like her beloved Geoffrey, tall and broad an
handsome and, except for the beard, much as he'
looked on the day they'd met. Except there was a har
cast to his expression she'd never seen before, an edge a
sharp as a sword to his deep, rumbling voice she'd neve
heard.

Geoffrey, but changed. Complete. Whole. A man wit
family and a purpose in life that hadn't included her unt
that horrifying shipwreck, his life-threatening wounds.

"You would have died without proper care. You saved my life and I could not abandon you."

"Ah, an act of mercy was it? Haul the half-dead man home and tell your family he is your husband. A bald lie. What if I had not lost my memory, caught you at your lie in the beginning? Did you think I would not dispute your claim?"

His loss of memory had only prolonged the deception. At the time she didn't think he'd live to even know what she'd done.

"I believed you would die! For nearly a sennight I believed the physician's declaration that you could not possibly overcome all of your injuries. Mercy, you were so ill and battered I feared I might have to bury you along the road."

"My apologies for disappointing you."

His sarcasm bit deep.

Nay, this wasn't the same man who often cajoled her into a smile, who made apologies if his words turned harsh. There would be no softening this time, no regret for raising his voice or hurting her feelings. She ached for the Geoffrey who'd shown her how to truly love, who'd so gently coaxed her into bed last eve.

"You never disappointed. I admired your tenacity, the way you ignored your pain and dealt with the loss of your memory, your absolute surety of overcoming any hindrance."

"You so admired me that you deceived me in vile manner. Why, Leah? What did you hope to gain?"

If Geoffrey demanded an explanation, then she'd give him one—the truth. 'Twas clear he now hated her. What matter if he despised her thoroughly?

"To save face. By claiming you as my husband I hoped to salvage some measure of my reputation." Only partly true. She lied for Geoffrey's sake, too. "And to ensure Odo would not convince my father that you deserved no better than a stall in the stable in which to take your last breath."

"Your father did not lack compassion."

"So it turned out, but on the day I returned home I was not sure Father would even allow me back in the keep. I had hurt him, embarrassed him by leaving Pecham with . . . Bastian."

With a sneer he turned away, again contemplated the ocean. "The man you told me about aboard ship. Odo saw fit to relate that sordid tale the other evening. So now I know the identity of the man you said you loved but didn't love you in return, whom you'd left before latching on to me."

He hadn't told her he knew about Bastian, and Leah could imagine how Odo must have told the tale—without a qualm over how it might sting. Sordid to be sure. Still, she hadn't *latched* on to Geoffrey the way he thought, far from it.

"The townspeople in Dover, even the physicians, assumed you and I were wed. Had there been anyone, friend or family, into whose care I could have delivered you, I would have—gladly. Bringing you home with me made an already difficult situation nigh impossible."

"So by claiming the false marriage you hoped to ease your way into your father's good graces without paying a penalty. What of after, Leah, when you knew I would survive? You went to great lengths to perpetuate your deception, even fornicating with me."

Leah almost slapped him for his crudity. "Perhaps I *should* have left you on that damn plank."

The words out, she couldn't take them back, and trying to explain only gave him further excuse to lash out. He'd judged and condemned her, nothing she might say would change his mind.

She gathered up the shreds of her dignity. "I assume you wish to leave forthwith. I will arrange a carter to haul your trunk."

"Not as yet. I swore your father an oath that I would not abandon you and I will keep my word."

When had he made such an oath, and why? No matter. He'd given the oath thinking the two of them bound in wedlock, and she'd not hold him to an oath he loathed to keep.

"Since you are not my husband, any oath to my father does not bind you."

"Perhaps not, but I intend to keep it all the same. Tell me. How did you intend to explain my leaving to Odo?"

Ye gods. Odo. Fear mingled with her heartache and threatened her composure.

"I will tell him the truth."

"That ought to please him."

"Likely. 'Twill give him an excuse to . . ."

She couldn't voice her concern over her brother's possible reactions.

"Beat you? Show you the gate? What will he do, Leah?"

If Odo had been lord of Pecham when she'd brought Geoffrey home, he'd not have been as forgiving as her father, would likely have turned her away. And now?

There were too many possibilities to sort through, from locking her away, to banishment to a convent.

One thing was for certain. Given her tarnished reputation, he'd not be able to marry her off easily. Not a comfort.

"I know not."

"Which is why I stay until after you confess to Odo. You deserve a punishment, but not an overly harsh one. I will not leave until all is over."

He'd decided to stay because of an oath sworn to her father, not out of concern or affection for her. Act as her protector as he'd once been, her rescuer. Out of duty or sense of chivalry.

Only look at what had happened after the last time he'd done so. And whatever made Geoffrey believe he could stay Odo's wrath to begin with, much less after he left?

Geoffrey held no authority at Pecham, no means to sway Odo from whatever course he chose. Still, if Geoffrey was determined to stay, she'd be a fool to not accept whatever protection his presence afforded.

"Then let us be done so you need not suffer this miserable place and my displeasing face longer than necessary."

Geoffrey gave an aggrieved sigh. "Would that we could. Odo rode out early this morn to visit the stannary. I assume he inspects the beam that killed your father."

A reprieve. One she could do without. "This eve then."

"So be it."

His anger had faded, though his disgust with her remained. He'd never forgive her, and that might be the worst punishment of all.

She owed him her life, should thank him for the joy of his company these past months. She'd learned much about honorable men, and now knew the difference between infatuation and love. He wouldn't believe any expression of love, but he might accept an apology—which she owed him.

"Do you remember on the ship, you told me that one must do what one must to keep body and mind in balanced humor, despite the opinion of others? I went about it badly, but that is what I tried to do, for both of us. I never set out to hurt or deceive you, and I am sorry for . . . well, I am sorry."

Clinging to what little pride she had left, she turned to leave the wall walk.

"Perhaps not this eve," he said. "I see sails near the cove."

Lovely. Just what she needed. More time to contemplate Odo's punishment and regret her mistakes. More time to look at Geoffrey's handsome face, memorize every angle and plane to hold in her memory when he was gone. More time to keep from throwing herself on his mercy, beg his understanding and forgiveness.

The last an utterly foolish notion. In his present mood he'd either laugh in her face or simply turn his back— neither of which she could bear.

"Then we will not need to wait until this eve. If a ship is due in, Odo will ensure he returns on time to meet it."

"I would swear your father expected no more ships until spring."

She squinted against the sparkling light of sun on water, but the ship was too far out to see clearly.

"Not all ships passing close to the cove belong to smugglers. Perhaps you see a fishing boat."

"Perhaps," he echoed the word, his doubt clear.

Not even in this small thing was he willing to take her at her word, and his complete distrust stung.

From the cove's shore Odo waved a greeting to the smuggling captain he hadn't expected to see for several months, if ever again. While displeased with Bastian for not keeping their agreement about Leah, he valued the captain's trade enough to feign a measure of courtesy.

In an outlandish display of prowess, the lean, black-haired Frenchman skittered down the rope ladder to the small boat, as graceful and surefooted as a spider on its web. He stood in the boat's bow, smiling hugely, while one of his crew rowed him to shore.

"Hail, *mon ami!* 'Tis delighted I am to see you again."

Odo knew better. If Bastian made this second trip of the year to England, in the chill of autumn, it wasn't to visit a *friend*. He wanted something.

Bastian leapt from boat to sand. Odo held up a hand to stave off the man's widely spread arms. Father might have tolerated the captain's greeting embrace, but Odo wanted nothing to do with the disconcerting intimacy.

"We had an agreement, Bastian. What happened?"

The man gave a huge sigh. "Leah made her way back to Nigel, then, as I assumed. Is your father very upset with me?"

Naturally, Bastian's first concern was for the state of

his money pouch, for any hindrance to their trade. Odo liked the way the man thought.

"Father died. We buried him yesterday morn. 'Tis *my* wrath you must face."

Bastian put a dramatic hand over his chest, and Odo almost believed the look of sorrow. "*Non!* This cannot be so! Nigel no longer among the living? Ah, Odo, how sad. How unfortunate. I shall miss him deeply. Do you inherit all?"

Odo crossed his arms. "Most all. There would have been more to inherit had you kept our bargain, which I paid you good coin for, and which you now owe me."

Bastian's smile returned. He waved a dismissive hand. "We had a most unfortunate misunderstanding. Women. How beautiful they are, and how quick to temper. I shall simply lure Leah back onto my boat and all will be well."

"A nice plan, Bastian," Odo scoffed. "What the devil do you intend to do about her husband?"

His eyes went wide. "Leah has married another? *Mon Dieu!* My heart breaks in two."

Odo's patience thinned at Bastian's pretense. His already bad mood darkened.

His wretched day started with an inspection of the beam that nearly killed him along with his father—all because Geoffrey asked Garth too many pointed questions at the wake, causing the overseer to request Odo to inspect the beam.

Going back into the tunnel, reliving those terrifying moments of its collapse, proved an unpleasant reminder that he hadn't been buried under the rubble due to a twist of fate and quick thinking. He'd escaped death within a gnat's breath.

No matter how many times he told himself he'd done right by saving himself, he yet saw the plea on his father's face for aid.

The vision would fade with time. Soon he'd not recall the moment his father realized death imminent, that the son allowed fate to choose without hindrance.

Then Bastian had the gall to sail into the cove during full daylight. Added to his lack of discretion, Bastian showed no regret for allowing Leah to escape him. 'Twas enough to goad any man to anger.

"I should break your fool neck for your carelessness."

"Ah, but then I could no longer bring you silk and pearls. Is our trade not worth more than your desire for a pithy dowry?"

Bastian didn't know the worth of the dowry, especially the brooch, which Odo hadn't yet given up on reclaiming.

"So why are you here, Bastian?"

"I bring you silks and pearls so exquisite you will not be able to contain your joy. And . . . there is a little matter I must settle with Leah. But come, let us make a bargain first."

Odo took the tempting bait of greater profit for the year, but didn't bite too hard. "Let us see what you value so highly. If I deem your goods worth buying, we will unload after night falls."

The ells of silk in the ship's hold were well worth buying, as were other items the captain offered. Bastian, for all his bravado, knew his trade.

Their bargain sealed—one that made up for Odo's

loss on their failed agreement—he climbed out of the hold.

"Be ready at the usual time."

"As you say, *mon ami*. Now . . . a small matter. Since a husband may not appreciate the presence of a wife's previous lover, might I impose on you to make a request of Leah?"

Odo couldn't hold back a jibe. "Lost your daring, Bastian?"

"I merely appreciate the delicacy of the situation."

He scoffed. Bastian didn't want his nose bent or jaw bruised. Either would mar the man's too-handsome face.

"What request?"

"I should like my money pouch returned. Perhaps the man your father married Leah off to will make good on the coin she stole."

"Father had nothing to do with her marriage. Leah found her own husband, in France, after she left you."

Bastian's brow scrunched. "After she left me? *Mon Dieu,* the lady wasted no time. A hasty courtship. Barely days!"

Days? His suspicions over Leah's marriage reared up. "Explain."

The captain told of how Leah caught him in bed with a whore—the unfortunate misunderstanding. She'd stolen his money purse and stamped off.

Bastian shrugged a shoulder. "I thought she would return, but the lady's ire burned too hot. Naturally, I wished the coin back—so when she did not return by dark, I inquired of her whereabouts. She had left Rouen with a peddler headed for Calais. When I reached Calais, I learned she spent my money for passage to England."

"How long after leaving you did she board ship?"

"Three days."

Either Leah met and married Geoffrey very quickly indeed, or Bastian was mistaken.

"You are sure 'twas Leah who bought passage?"

Bastian took offense. "A lovely golden-haired woman gowned in scarlet silk is noticed on the docks. I have no doubts."

What man in his right mind—not that Geoffrey possessed a working mind—married a woman he'd known for mere days, perhaps hours if they'd met in Calais?

*Had Leah lied?* Certes, he'd encouraged his father to demand proof of the marriage, hoping to put off the granting of the dowry until he could find a way to get the brooch for himself. He'd never seriously doubted Leah's claim—until now.

'Twas possible Leah concocted the tale, foisting a dying man on the family as her husband in order to collect the dowry. Had Geoffrey actually been dying, or were his injuries as severe as Leah claimed? Had Geoffrey truly lost his memory, or was the ruse part of their planned deception?

Odo didn't particularly care. Leah's entire dowry was again within his grasp if the two weren't wed. He could almost feel the brooch warming his hand, see the admiration glowing in his future wife's eyes.

"Bastian, pray do me the favor of coming up to the keep. You can make your own claim to Leah."

"Ah . . . her husband?"

Might not be her husband, and thus of no consequence.

\*     \*     \*

Their argument on the wall walk hadn't gone unnoticed or unheard. The tale spread with the swiftness of a Cornwall wind. Leah endured the looks of either shocked horror or humiliating pity with bile in her throat and her chin raised.

Only to Anna did she haltingly, quietly relate her fears over her brother's reaction. While stirring some vile-smelling concoction in a kettle bubbling at the hearth, the old woman had listened with quiet acceptance, without commenting on Leah's stupidity.

"So what are ye going to do, dearie?"

Leah relieved Anna of the ladle, dipped it into the kettle and gave a stir. "Put my head on a block and wait for the axe."

"That be too clean for Odo. The man prefers to see a body suffer."

"Then I will just hand him a whipping cane."

"Let yer chin droop and he will beat ye with it sure." Anna's eyes narrowed. "Ain't like ye to let yer chin droop."

Leah agreed, but damn, she was too tired and numb to spar with her brother. The hollow where her heart had been threatened to engulf her. Talking to Anna brought a measure of peace; the confession to Odo would be a battle.

"His authority over my fate is absolute, Anna. Whether my chin droops or no, he may do as he pleases."

Including beating, or locking her away, or banishment, or any number of degrading punishments meted out at his whim.

"Too bad ye cannot talk Geoffrey into marriage. 'Twould save a wealth of trouble."

Absurd. He'd never agree—a good thing. She'd be hard-pressed to endure his rejection in the days he stayed. To do so for a lifetime? Unbearable.

"He can barely deign to look at me much less consider marriage. He despises me, as I knew he would."

"Still, he slept with he. His honor—"

Suddenly realizing the bend of Anna's thoughts, Leah interrupted. "You are not to approach Geoffrey with a suggestion of marriage. I forbid it, Anna. No meddling."

The old woman sighed. "As ye wish. Truth to tell, I will miss the lad. Good looks and a fine mind. Ain't seen the like in an age."

Leah dared a glance across the hall. Geoffrey stood near the stairway leading down to the guards' quarters, speaking with Ned and Thuro.

He stood within the same room and already she missed him.

Not only wouldn't Geoffrey look at her, but he hadn't even spoken to her. She'd learned of his full identity from remarks made by the servants to whom he did speak.

Sir Geoffrey Hamelin. A knight. A scholar studying in Paris, his main interest in law.

No wonder he'd been so bothered by the smuggling, the illegal trade rubbing harshly against his natural inclination toward legality.

He'd reclaimed his identity in appearance, too, by scraping off his beard. Nothing else could have proclaimed his severance from her as forcefully as ridding himself of the facial hair he'd allowed to remain merely because she liked it.

While all seemed so hopeless, Leah snatched a moment of satisfaction from the rubble. Sir Geoffrey Hamelin had come through the ordeal hale and hearty. Only a small scar on his forehead remained as a reminder of his severe injuries. Tall, strong and vigorous, he appeared very much the man she'd met aboard an ill-fated ship.

"I shall miss him, too." She swallowed the renewed threat of tears, handed the ladle to Anna. "What do you brew, Anna? The stench burns my eyes."

"Yer Geoffrey, he told me of an unguent for burns mentioned in his medicine book. I don't hold with heathen ways, but I cannot see the harm in giving the unguent a try."

Not only she but the people of Pecham had to stop thinking of Leah and Geoffrey as belonging to each other. Had she gone about the business differently . . . well, no sense mourning now over what might have been.

"He is not my Geoffrey."

"Hard not to think of him any other way."

The hall door opened, saving her further comment. Odo strode in, and behind him, Bastian.

Leah's stomach flipped. For a moment she forgot to breathe.

"Holy Mother of God," Anna said softly. "What brings *that* scoundrel to Pecham?"

Money. The only reasonable explanation—whether Bastian wanted back the coin she'd stolen from him or whether he had goods to sell to Odo. She'd truly thought to never set eyes on the whoreson again, that the possibility didn't even exist until spring. Yet here he stood, as darkly handsome and cocksure of himself as ever—traits she'd once found appealing.

"'Ware yer chin, girl."

The warning jerked Leah's attention back to her brother, who stared at her with a frightening degree of glee. Which could only mean that after talking to Bastian he suspected her deception.

Odo then glanced around the hall, spotted Geoffrey, and hurried toward him. Bastian shrugged his shoulders, raised his hands, palms up with an apologetic smile— then followed Odo.

Her first impulse was to rush up the stairs to her bedchamber and hide, but Leah forced her feet to hustle in the other direction. Whatever was said she needed to hear, if only to prepare her own defense.

Odo stopped within an arm's length of Geoffrey. "This is Bastian, Leah's lover, the smuggling captain with whom she fled to France. From the tale he tells me, 'tis nigh impossible for you and Leah to be married. My father chose not to demand proof of your marriage, but I fear I must insist."

Geoffrey glanced at Bastian. His expression darkened, but so briefly she wondered if she'd imagined it. She came to a halt several feet from the men, close enough to hear them but out of striking distance.

"I am aware that Leah and I are not wed."

The blunt, flatly delivered admission only momentarily stalled Odo's bluster. "How could you be aware if you have no memory, or is that a lie, too? I begin to won-

r if the two of you purposely devised a scheme to dupe
⌐ father."

"I regained my memory last eve. Had you not gone
t to the stannary I would have informed you this
orn."

"Last eve, hmmm? I find the timely recovery of your
emory rather convenient. One might say unbeliev-
le."

"I give you my word of honor, as a knight." At Odo's
arply arched eyebrow, he added, "Sir Geoffrey
amelin, son of Sir John Hamelin of Lelleford, in serv-
e to King Edward."

Leah bit her bottom lip, hoping Odo possessed
ough sense to respect the rank, if not the man. She
n't like the gleam that suddenly lit his eyes.

"Then as a man of honor, you should marry the
oman with whom you have fornicated for these past
eks."

How like Odo to have quickly calculated the possibil-
⌐ that Geoffrey's rank, and possible wealth and con-
ctions could prove useful to him. She opened her
outh to voice her objection; Geoffrey spoke first.

"In light of Leah's deception, I feel no debt of honor
marry her. However, an oath I swore to your father
nds me to ensure her well-being. Have a care when you
cide Leah's fate. I will not allow anything over harsh."

That damn oath. Though she'd heard about it earlier,
didn't hurt any less to know why he acted as a buffer
tween her and her brother.

Odo visibly puffed with indignation. "'Tis within my
ght as her guardian to do whatever I deem proper. You
ve no right to interfere."

"Nigel gave me the right when he begged me keep m
oath. A knight honors a pledge given. You would do we
to remember the tenents of chivalry if ever you apply t
the king for your own knighthood."

Odo blanched at the subtly delivered threat.

Leah now knew how Geoffrey planned to contr
Odo's actions. As a knight in service to the king, Geof
frey could interfere with, possibly block, her brother'
aspiration to knighthood.

Did Odo crave the rank enough to bend to Geoffrey'
will?

"You will allow I am within my rights to demand th
return of Leah's dowry."

Geoffrey nodded. "You may have it when I am as
sured Leah will come to no harm."

Geoffrey's audacity to withhold the dowry burs
Odo's pretense of civility. Fury bloomed on his face, th
veins in his neck drawn taut. The struggle for contr
took long moments.

"Come, Bastian, we have goods to unload," he said
the words deceivingly calm.

Bastian frowned. "'Tis yet daylight."

Odo hissed, "I know the time of day, you fool."

With violent strides Odo left the hall, Bastian in hi
wake.

Leah knew she'd never see a pound of the dowry onc
Odo possessed it. He'd beggar it, which probably didn'
matter anyway. With two black stains on her reputatio
and a pittance of a dowry, no right-minded man woul
offer for her, which suited her fine. 'Twould be impossi
ble for her to be a proper wife to one man while anothe

held her heart, though he didn't want it anymore, perhaps never had.

And for the nonce he held her dowry. He also possessed another thing that rightly belonged to Odo—the smuggling ledger, which Leah thought the stronger weapon to use to stay Odo's hand.

Geoffrey stared at the hall's door. What she wouldn't give to have him look at her just once more without disdain. To have him put his arm around her and tell her all would be well. A hopeless fantasy.

"Will you give Odo the ledger when you give him the dowry chest?"

"I doubt he knows I have the ledger. 'Twould be best you do not tell him." Geoffrey stirred then, a shift of weight, an ease of muscle. "I have much to do while Odo is occupied. Stay out of his way until after I return."

With the command issued, Geoffrey headed down the stairway to the guards' quarters.

The order rankled, but also contained good advice.

The easiest way to stay out of Odo's way was to hide in her bedchamber, the door bolted. Tempting, but cowardly.

'Struth, if she'd learned naught else from this mess 'twas to deal with a problem head on instead of evading it. Better to see trouble coming than be caught unaware.

# Chapter 17

Geoffrey reined in Boadicea near a copse of trees to give the mare a rest. After dismounting, he looked around to get his bearings. Insides churning, he'd headed out of Pecham without a clear destination in mind.

His stomach had settled, his anger subsided. Mostly.

Now, if he could manage to evict the vision of Leah making love to Bastian, he might be able to think straight again. 'Twas one thing to know she'd given herself to a lover, quite another to come face to jowl with the smuggling captain she'd admitted to loving.

'Twasn't his concern any more who Leah loved, or whom she made love to. Only his oath to Nigel bound him to protect her as best he could from her brother's uncertain temperament.

He should despise Leah. He couldn't look upon her without his anger igniting, yet he was still powerfully drawn to the conniving woman. Infuriating to be so torn between wanting to strangle her and hold her tenderly.

To scream his disappointment until she cowered and cried, then soothe away her fears and tears with whispered endearments.

His feelings didn't make sense, but then he'd never dealt with the demon jealousy before, a devil of an emotion he loathed to admit held him with sharp claws. He might no longer want Leah for himself, but he didn't want Bastian to have her either.

So what did he want—besides to run Bastian through?

Keep the oath given to Nigel, then go home. There might be nothing he could do for Eloise now, but he still had to face his father. Depending on John Hamelin's disposition, he'd either stay or go back to Paris. No matter which, he'd try to forget this misadventure in Cornwall.

A damn hard thing to do, because he'd leave a part of himself here at Pecham, with Leah.

Given time and distance he'd no longer remember Leah's face clearly, nor crave the heat of her body under his. He'd no longer hear the sound of her laughter, nor become instantly aroused at the scent of lavender.

He might even forgive himself for being blind to her faults, for becoming so besotted he saw only the good in her and not the bad. 'Twas still difficult to believe a woman who took such a keen interest in everyone at Pecham could prove so selfish and dishonest.

Aye, time would cure his longing for the woman who'd stolen his heart and then trampled it under underfoot.

Boadicea nudged his shoulder, ready to be off again. The horse loved a wind-chasing gallop, so he'd allowed Boadicea her head. She'd carried him to this spot not far from the miners' village—a longer distance than he'd intended to ride.

He should return to Pecham to deal with Odo.

Leah's brother might be harder to control than he'd first thought. Geoffrey believed his presence at Pecham and the withholding of the dowry kept Leah safe, for now. But what of after he left? Odo hadn't strongly reacted to the possibility of not being able to obtain a knighthood. Perhaps he didn't want the knighthood badly enough to keep him from harshly punishing his sister.

Stronger measures might be necessary.

Geoffrey knew he could ruin Odo by sending the smuggling ledger to the earl of Cornwall. Except by ruining Odo he might also harm the rest of Pecham's people—not fair.

Hard to tell what the earl might consider just punishment. The earl would be within his rights to toss Leah out of Pecham with her brother, or he might have pity and claim her wardship—giving the earl the right to marry her off as he saw fit, perhaps to the new lord of Pecham.

There had to be a better solution where Geoffrey could maintain more control over Leah's fate.

He'd thought of one way—withhold both the dowry and ledger to ensure Odo's continued cooperation, but the plan presented problems. He would need help from one of Pecham's people, from someone more loyal to Leah than to Odo. And he'd be putting that person in harm's way.

Anna would do, except the herbswoman was both too

old and too easily suspected—and directly under Odo's nose.

Geoffrey dismissed the men-at-arms and servants, though a couple might be willing. Ned, perhaps. Or Mona. But again, to hide the chest and ledger within Pecham and swear either guard or serving wench to secrecy, put them in too much danger from an irritable lord upon whom they depended for their daily bread.

Best to hide the booty outside of Pecham's gate where someone couldn't either accidentally or a-purpose stumble upon it—especially Odo, who'd likely tear the keep apart searching.

Too bad the priest from the village church hadn't yet returned from his pilgrimage. But then, not every member of the clergy could be trusted, and Geoffrey loathed leaving the task of guarding the chest and ledger to someone he'd never met.

Which left the farmers and miners. He'd seen many of the tenant farmers, but didn't know them. Of the miners he knew Garth best, but the man had been loyal to Nigel, would likely be loyal to Odo as long as the profits flowed.

Profits flowed even as Geoffrey mused over the dilemma. Odo and Bastian would be done unloading the ship soon, with Odo returning to the keep. Pecham was too confined a place for Leah to avoid her brother for long.

He'd best get back, mind his duty.

He mounted and nudged the mare forward, noting the position of the sun, confident he'd make Pecham well before midday meal.

No longer would he sit at the dais next to Leah as he

had since healing enough to take meals in the hall. Tonight he'd not sleep in the bed they'd shared. 'Twould be agony enough to sleep in her bedchamber on a pallet, a sword at his side in case Odo decided to try something foolish.

If only Leah hadn't lied. If only his memory had returned before Nigel's death he'd not be bound to her, her well-being none of his concern.

Out of the corner of his eye he caught a glimpse of St. Peter's bell tower. He'd been in the church twice. The first time with Leah, to admire the beautiful stained-glass window. Then again on the day of Nigel's burial.

Gads, was it only yesterday morn when he'd stood within the shadow of the Virgin and Babe, his arm around Leah's shoulders, listening to prayers for swift passage of Nigel's soul to his Maker's side? So many people crowded into the church, shoulder to shoulder— men and women, old and young—standing together to mourn under the color-dappled light of the stained-glass window.

Geoffrey took a deep breath, suddenly realizing the perfect place to hide the chest and ledger, and the one person he knew he could trust with the secret.

Leah slowly descended the cliff path, clutching her skirts with fingers hampered by rope-wrapped wrists, her mouth doomed to silence by a swath of binding linen.

If she could get her hands free, she'd knock sense into Odo's head. If she could speak, she'd curse him to everlasting hellfire. The most she'd managed was a kick to his shins, and for that she suffered a stinging cheek—but damn, she'd do it again if Odo got close enough.

As for Bastian, she'd kill him just as soon as the chance arose.

She'd been a fool to agree to Odo's plea for a private word in the solar. He'd duped her with a soft voice, false sincerity for treating her harshly over the years, and feigned desire to set things aright.

He'd sighed, aggrieved. "You and I are all the family we have left. Father would have wished us to make amends."

She'd taken his bait and swallowed it whole, hoping they could regain a measure of the fondness they'd shared as children.

Instead, Odo had overpowered her, hustled her down the stairway from the solar to the postern gate where they met Bastian—by design. Now she trekked down the path to the cove—Bastian ahead of her, Odo behind—struggling to keep her balance.

If she tried to escape now, she feared Odo would push her over the cliff and be done with her. Well, perhaps that wouldn't be so bad if she could manage to take her ruddy brother with her.

Leah twisted the rope around her now raw wrists. The knot *had* to come loose so she could free her hands. She had to escape when they reached the cove's shore, give Geoffrey more time to rescue her.

Where the hell was he, anyway? She didn't doubt he'd come after her once he knew her gone. He'd keep his oath to her father. Except as far as she knew he was still outside of the keep, enjoying a ride on Boadicea while she tried to avoid being dragged onto Bastian's boat.

To think she'd boarded that same boat willingly not several months ago—which she would *not* have done if she'd known Odo paid Bastian to woo her, entreat her to run away with him.

Fool. Simpleton. How had she not seen through Bastian's charm to his traitorous heart? How had she not realized her brother cared so little for her that he'd resort to kidnapping to be rid of her?

She skidded on a loose stone, her boot sliding toward the edge of the cliff. Sweat of fear mingled with that of exertion. She barely righted her balance.

Bastian heard and stopped. To catch her? Certes, he would catch her. If she fell over the cliff he couldn't collect payment for taking her back to France.

Satisfied his villainous fee wasn't in immediate danger, he started down again, this time kicking the occasional stone from the path.

The farther down, the closer the cove, the more ominous the boat. Possible paths of escape narrowed down to none. High cliffs lined the horseshoe-shaped cove, the only path up them the one she trod. With Odo blocking the path, she'd not get around him.

All she could do was run along the shore until one of the men caught her, fight to gain time.

To what end? If Geoffrey didn't come . . . Leah fought the threatening despair. The sharpness of her bravado dulled as her anger waned. What if Geoffrey decided she was too much trouble to rescue, that he'd done what he could to protect her and would do no more?

Then she'd have to get out of this mess on her own.

Allowing Odo a victory simply wasn't to be borne, not when the cost to her was so high. She didn't know what Bastian planned to do with her once they reached France, assuming he didn't toss her into the Channel along the way.

Fighting panic, she wondered if she could talk Bastian into releasing her. Perhaps, if she offered him more money than Odo gave him. The contents of her dowry chest should be more than sufficient enticement. But then, if he wished to continue to trade with Odo, a lucrative arrangement for them both, he'd not be swayed.

The moment her boots touched sand, she hiked her skirt up as high as she could manage and ran past Bastian.

Odo swore, called her a fool. Perhaps he had the right of it, but she wasn't stepping foot on Bastian's boat without a fight.

The soft sand slowed her progress. Already her rag-stuffed mouth was dry, her throat sore. She heard her heartbeat, and the men giving chase.

Odo shouted, "Be sensible, Leah. You have nowhere to run!"

Right again. As soon as she got to the end of the strip of sand that lined the cove she'd have to stop, nowhere to go but up. Climb the cliff? Impossible.

Nearing the huge cave used to store ore, she ran faster. Perhaps she could hide behind something stored there or squeeze into a crevice, prolong the chase until either Geoffrey found her or she eased the damn rope from her wrists.

*Geoffrey! Hurry!*

As if he could hear. And if he could, would he heed her plea? Aye, if only to keep his oath.

Leah sped into the cave, breathing labored, frantically searched for a place to hide.

Not a barrel or crate or even tub of ore offered succor. With winter coming on and no ships expected, the cave stood empty. A crevice, then. Any small concealing crack in the rock walls would do. Nothing. Not a fissure.

Trapped. Damn.

Odo laughed, his degrading pleasure at her failure echoing through the cave. She spun around to glare at her tormentors. Backing up, she let go her skirts and reached for the strip of linen binding her mouth. Thankful he'd not thought her worth the waste of finer cloth, she tugged at the loose weave until a small rip heralded her success.

"Have something to say to me, Leah?" Odo taunted. "A protest, perhaps? 'Twill do you no good."

She tore away the linen, spat out the rag. "Beast."

He shook his head, coming at her, his hands clenching. "'Tis with sorrow I bid thee a final farewell. The contents of your dowry chest, however, will ease my pain over your parting."

Her back hit the cave wall. "How touching, coming from a man who cares for naught but himself."

Odo kept coming. Leah turned her head and braced for a strike, wishing she could melt into the rock. He grabbed her chin, forced her to look at him.

"Not true, but of no import." He seized her bound wrists and flung her away from the wall.

She stumbled, caught a toe in her skirts. Pain shot

through her knee and elbow as she landed hard, the rope cutting deeper into her wrists.

Bastian bent over to grasp her upper arms to help her stand. "Ah, little dove, you give your brother no choice but to deliver you into my care."

His care she could do without. Bastian's touch repelled her, but right now she had no choice but lean into him until her knee took her weight. 'Twasn't broken, but pained.

"We waste time," Odo complained. "If I ever again see her face, Bastian, you had best avoid England's shore."

A sweeping threat Odo couldn't make good on. His authority didn't extend beyond this small cove on Cornwall's coast, no matter how much he wished it otherwise.

"You suffer delusions, Odo. You *will* see me again."

With a foreboding sneer he said harshly, "Not if Bastian keeps his bargain this time."

Leah forgot about her pain, her anger. All dissolved with the confirmation of her worst fear.

"You hate me so much you wish me dead?"

"Your very existence keeps me from having all I deserve. Why should I not want you dead?"

"But I have nothing—" Except her dowry. Was that why he'd turned so grim and unpleasant over the years? All because of greed, for a few coins and jewels?

"You begrudge me my dowry?"

He glanced up, a plea heavenward for patience. "The brooch, Leah. I will have the brooch."

She knew the piece of jewelry he coveted, their mother's diamond and ruby brooch, worth a fortune and which Odo had always admired greatly. "Why did you not ask Father for it?"

"I did. He refused to give over. 'Twas always you he favored, would not see I needed the brooch more than you." He huffed. "No more will women turn me aside, not when gifted with such a fine token of my wish to marry."

Leah opened her mouth to tell him no piece of jewelry could compensate for years of marriage to a loathsome man, but Bastian jerked her arm and pushed her toward the mouth of the cave.

"Hush, now. 'Twill be quick and painless, *cherie,* I promise you. Can you walk?"

Bastian uttered endearments while he spoke of death.

She limped along the sand, searching the cliffs. No sign of Geoffrey, no hope of rescue. Bastian helped her into the bow of the small boat and took up the oars.

"Until spring, *mon ami!*"

Odo pushed the boat off the sand, sending it into the cove.

Leah raised her chin, stared at her brother. "A coward pays another to do that which he has not the courage to do himself." Did she imagine his wince? "Hear me, coward, you *will* see me again, if only as a shade come to haunt you!"

He didn't retort, merely turned his back and started up the path, no doubt to enjoy his evening repast.

Bastian chuckled.

Leah leaned forward. "You find this amusing?"

"You always did have spirit, Leah. 'Twas why I let you live the first time."

Her spirit, or because she'd let him take his pleasure

any time he wanted? Leah decided now wasn't the time to tell Bastian he wasn't as good a lover as Geoffrey. She glanced at the boat now a few feet away. Time ran short.

If she had the least idea of how to swim she'd leap over the side, delay again. But she didn't, and her wrists were bound. She'd surely drown.

"I can give you a fortune if you take me back to shore. Two hundred pounds. Jewels of good quality, probably some you sold to my father."

Interest flashed, then vanished. "*Non.* My apologies, *cherie,* but if I do not keep my bargain with Odo this time, my reputation suffers. You understand, *oui?*"

Boat bumped up against boat. Bastian called up to his crew to lower hauling ropes. Desperate, Leah again searched the shore. No Geoffrey.

"Come, Leah. Up."

The idiot wished her to climb up the rope ladder draped over the side of the smuggling boat. She raised her bound hands, arched an eyebrow.

Bastian drew a wickedly long, pearl-handled dagger from his boot and sliced through the rope binding her wrists. Her hands tingled with sharp pinpricks that defied easing.

Hand over hand she climbed, contemplating the dagger he'd surely slid back into his boot. The right boot, on the outside. She paid heed to how she swung her legs over the railing. Right foot first, outside up.

Her feet on the deck, she took her best guess at where Bastian's boot would clear the rail, where she must stand to have a chance to grab at the dagger. Dare she try to give Geoffrey more time to rescue her?

Dare she not?

Leah braced her feet, ignoring the crew member not a few feet off, ready to haul in the small boat.

Bastian climbed the rope. If her plan worked, she'd soon have him at *her* mercy, and if not she wasn't any worse off than she was now.

'Twas as if the very walls of the keep mourned.

Geoffrey felt the heavy sorrow as soon as he walked into the hall. The few servants about prepared the tables for evening meal with slow steps and without the usual chatter.

Leah wasn't in the hall. Unusual for this time of day.

From upstairs he heard cursing, the voice Odo's. Concern for Leah's whereabouts rising, he took to the stairs. The sound of something heavy hitting the plank floor of the solar quickened his pace.

Odo stood near the oak table. Geoffrey recognized the ledgers scattered about, noted the emptied chest where Nigel had stored the estate's important documents. He knew what Odo searched for and didn't find—the smuggling ledger. Geoffrey crossed his arms and leaned against the door frame, enjoying the man's upset.

"Something amiss, Odo?"

Startled, Odo looked up. "Naught that concerns you." He tossed a parchment roll onto the table. "Truth to tell, you will be delighted to hear that your duty here is done. Since Leah has again fled to France with Bastian, you may now give me the dowry chest and be on your way."

The vision of Leah with Bastian returned full-blown and clawed at his innards. The lying, scheming bitch had . . . Geoffrey tamped the vision and accusation down hard. He'd never fully trusted Odo, shouldn't now.

Somehow he managed a false calm. "I find it hard to believe she returned to a man from whom she fled."

Odo tossed a hand in the air. "I tell you Leah left with her lover. If you disbelieve me, go look for her, and after you do not find her, I expect the return of the chest."

Geoffrey backed out of the room, unsure of his next move, unwilling to allow Odo to see his turmoil.

Leah had run off with Bastian once before, and Geoffrey couldn't help wonder if after his bad-tempered treatment of her these past two days, she might well have decided to do so again.

Anna stood outside Leah's bedchamber, a tear sliding down her cheek. Now he understood why the grief he'd sensed in the hall seemed so deep and fresh. The people mourned not only for Nigel but for the loss of Leah, too.

The old woman motioned him forward. He obeyed, his emotions bouncing between hurt that Leah could so easily take up with her former lover and anger that she'd left him without a word of farewell. Unreasonable emotions, both.

Anna stepped inside the bedchamber, Geoffrey followed.

She wiped away the tear. "Yer lordship, if Leah truly left with that scoundrel, 'tis my belief she did not go willingly."

Sweet Jesu. Of course. What a dolt he was for not considering the possibility sooner.

"How long has she been gone?"

Anna raised a helpless hand. "The boat may yet be in the cove. If ye hurry . . ."

He grabbed her shoulders, kissed her forehead, plans already forming. Possibly he placed Anna in danger from Odo, but saw no choice for the nonce. Someone had to guard the dowry and ledger, and there wasn't time to enlist anyone else.

"Stay here. Bolt the door. Let no one in but me."

Geoffrey ignored the temptation to confront Odo. If the boat wasn't in the harbor, if he couldn't get to Leah—he pushed the thought aside. With long strides, not bothering to hide his intent, he made his way down to the guards' quarters, strapped on a sword, and ran toward the postern gate.

He flung open the gate and sped to the path, his pulse pounding. His boot skidded on a stone, forcing him to concentrate on his footing down the steep path, not looking up again until he neared the cave used to store smuggled goods, where he could get a clear view of the cove.

A boat bobbed on gentle waves, no sails raised. Until those sails fluttered to catch the breeze, he had time to reach Leah. He didn't question his good fortune, just watched for raising sails. Near the end of the path, he slowed, noting the lack of activity aboard ship.

He didn't see Leah, or Bastian, or any crew. 'Twas as if the ship was deserted—unlikely. The small boat used to come ashore floated in the water, ropes attached to bow and stern, ready for hauling up.

The lack of activity worried him, but 'twas to his advantage if no one peered over the side to spot him in the water.

He kicked off his boots while unbuckling the sword belt, his hands unsteady. The last time he'd been under water . . . the Channel, no use of his legs, salt stinging his burned arms.

He tugged off his tunic.

Again he tasted blood in his mouth, heard screams of men dying. Fire and smoke. No air. He couldn't breathe.

*Drowning.*

Geoffrey took in a deep breath and gathered all of his will to focus on what he must do.

This wasn't a storm-chopped channel, just a calm cove. He wasn't injured, had use of his legs, knew how to swim.

Leah was on that boat, and only he could rescue her.

Geoffrey strapped on the sword belt at the top of his breeches and eased into the water.

Cold. Salty. Blood raced through his veins, pounding in his ears. Panic seized him. He glanced at the boat, suddenly so far away. No one stood on watch. No one would see if he turned around and . . . Leah, he had to get to Leah.

What if Odo told the truth, that Leah made the decision to return to France with Bastian? What if she truly wanted to be with her lover?

He had to find out, if naught else to inform Anna, to keep faith with his oath to her father.

To see Leah one more time before they parted ways.

A fortifying deep breath. A long glide down into the depths of the cove. The water surrounded him, threatened to drag him under so far he'd never surface. His arms and legs remembered how to stroke and kick while memories flashed by in horrifying clarity.

His body cried out for air. He denied the plea, knowing it best he stay under as long as he could hold out, the whole distance to the boat if possible.

He kicked harder, pulled with greater force, until

through squinting eyes he spotted wood. Not until touching the boat did he surface, careful to make no noise that might alert those on board.

Geoffrey eased up the rope ladder, wary of the eerie silence. He peeked over the side into the boat, and nearly burst out laughing in both amazement and relief.

Across the deck, Leah sat on a barrel, Bastian on his knees in front of her, both facing him. She held the smuggling captain captive, holding a long dagger to his throat. Two crewmen sat cross-legged at mid-deck, their hands in their laps.

Leah's smile washed over him. "You come at a good time. My arms tire."

In a tone filled with relief, Bastian said, "Please, Sir Geoffrey, do come aboard."

He swung over the side, a host of questions begging answers. The moment his feet hit the deck his stomach grumbled a protest. Damn, but he hated boats.

Sword drawn, he crossed the deck, giving the unmoving, quiet crew members a wide berth.

Leah looked disheveled, but unharmed. Bastian appeared the worst off, his face pale as cream, a narrow stream of dried blood marring his throat where Leah must have nicked him.

Geoffrey angled the tip of the sword toward Bastian. "You do not intend to move, do you?"

"*Non.* The she-beast may truly slit my throat."

"Your crew?"

"Will stay where they are, as I ordered. No one will hinder you, I swear."

Leah huffed, eased the knife away. "She-beast, indeed. You deserve to have your throat slit."

With a heavy sigh, Bastian folded forward, palms to the deck. Leah rose from the barrel and slipped the dagger up her sleeve—exposing a raw red wrist. Tempted to chop off the head of the man at his feet, Geoffrey grabbed Leah's hand and inspected the damage. Leah tugged, and he let go, fearing he'd hurt her further if he hung on.

"They look worse than they feel," she said softly.

He didn't believe her, knew the man responsible for the rope burns wasn't Bastian, who'd risen up to sit back on his heels.

Leah shot a hand toward Bastian. "The coin purse. You did not earn your fee."

"I propose a trade. My dagger for the purse."

Geoffrey waved the sword. "She deserves to keep the dagger, nor are you in a position to bargain. Give over, Bastian."

Uncomplimentary French phrases accompanied the transfer of funds. Leah withdrew a few coins and tossed them on the deck, her seeming calm beginning to crack.

"This should cover what I owe you, *oui*?"

Bastian glanced at the tip of the sword. "As you say."

Geoffrey didn't understand why Leah gave Bastian the coins—one of many questions that could wait until they were ashore. He put a hand on Leah's shoulder, she backed up to match his steps toward the ladder. Neither Bastian nor his crew made any attempt to stop them.

She was more hurt than she'd let on. She limped.

"Your leg hurts. Can you make it down the rope to the boat?"

"I have done this before, remember?"

Aye, he did. Another ship, another boat, another body of water to cross to safety.

She swung her leg over, caught the ladder with the toe of her boots, then paused to tell Bastian, "You may not need to avoid England altogether, but you may wish to shun Cornwall."

Bastian actually chuckled. "Such are the fortunes of the trade, *cherie*. My regrets to your brother."

Down in the small boat, Geoffrey untied the ropes and manned the oars. From above came shouted orders to raise sail and haul up the anchor. By the time he reached shore, the bile in Geoffrey's stomach began to churn.

"Are you all right?" Leah asked, her head tilted, trying very hard not to smile.

He managed a grunt, then leapt over the side to drag the boat onto the sand. With his hands at Leah's waist, he lifted her out, put her down—and couldn't let go.

Leah's bottom lip trembled. Her hands snaked from his shoulders to around his neck, holding him captive. Senses reeling, he surrendered.

The kiss began hard and turned near violent. Leah clung to his wet body that even though exposed to the ocean breeze hadn't a prayer of cooling. Not with Leah safely in his arms, not with her mouth greedily answering his.

No other woman had ever responded to him as Leah did, with abandon. No other woman fired his blood, muddled his mind, caused him so much suffering, both painful and sweet. Even as his body strained toward the sweetness, his heart whispered of her betrayal.

He couldn't let her enchant him again.

Geoffrey reluctantly broke the kiss. Leah yet clung to him, her cheek against his bare shoulder, the aroma of lavender filling his senses.

"I knew you would come if I gave you enough time."

Guilt raised its ugly head. "I should not have left you alone with Odo."

"Not your fault. Mine." She backed away. "'Twill not happen again."

"He paid Bastian to take you back to France."

She turned to watch the smuggling boat clear the mouth of the cove, break free into the ocean. "Aye, as he did the last time, too. I feel such a fool."

Geoffrey tossed on his tunic, slid into his boots, knowing well what it felt like to play the fool.

He allowed her to limp up the path until he could no longer stand to watch, then picked her up. She raised a questioning eyebrow, but didn't protest. With Leah cradled in his arms, he trudged upward, his legs feeling the strain—no less than he deserved for allowing her abduction.

She laid her head on his shoulder, the scent of lavender strong, her warmth seeping through his garments. "What now?"

"I will take you up to the bedchamber where Anna can tend your wrists and legs."

"And after?"

He knew how to end the situation in final, indisputable fashion. It hadn't appealed, so he'd dismissed it out of hand, concocted other means to check Odo.

Which nearly cost Leah her life. Did she suspect, as he did, that she might never have made it to France? His gut twisted so hard he nearly dropped Leah.

To truly keep his oath he'd have to gird his loins and accept his fate, which was what Nigel intended for his daughter all along.

Could he ever forget the agony caused by her deceit? Could he ever fully trust her again? With his life, with his heart? Perhaps, given time . . .

"We marry."

# Chapter 18

T would be easy to tighten her arms, bury her face in Geoffrey's neck and agree. Here within her grasp was a dream come true—marriage to the man she loved, who she could joyfully keep a home for, bear his children.

Her body still hummed from his rough kiss, uncontrolled and possessive, like a champion claiming a prize for his victory.

She'd not mind being fully claimed if she thought any affection could again bloom between them. Just as affection hadn't prompted his kiss, no heartfelt emotion prompted his decision to marry her.

Duty and honor demanded he keep his oath to her father, the same oath she'd counted on to bring Geoffrey to the cove to fetch her off the boat.

She didn't want a forced marriage; wouldn't force a marriage on Geoffrey.

"Pray put me down."

"Your leg is injured."

They were still on the path but close to the top of the cliff. "My knee no longer hurts so much. I can walk."

Geoffrey put her down.

She eased away from those strong arms she'd never feel around her again. "We cannot marry."

"'Tis the only sure way to protect you from Odo. We take vows, you come to Lelleford with me, we leave Odo to his fate."

She heard both ire and resignation, but no affection—and she accepted the blame.

"Go home, Geoffrey. Your duty here is done. Your oath is satisfied."

He crossed his arms, arched an eyebrow. "Leah, Odo paid Bastian to remove you from Pecham, permanently. Do you truly believe he meant to take you to France?"

"I feared the worst, at first, but while Odo may have paid Bastian to do away with me, I doubt he would have done so."

He flung a hand toward the cove. "The man is a criminal, a smuggling captain, a scoundrel whose greed likely matches Odo's! What in the name of all the saints makes you believe he would not sacrifice you to the altar of his profit?"

A slow realization of Bastian's true intentions had stunned her. How to explain?

"Bastian did not take the dagger away from me when he could have, several times over. When I told him I intended to wait for you to come for me, he made it easy to hold him captive."

"That does not make sense."

"Oddly enough it does, knowing Bastian." She searched for the sense she'd made of his actions. "Bas-

tian is driven by profit, and part of the reason for his un-
seasonable visit was to repair any damage done to his
trade with Pecham. I also think some small part of him
wanted to know if I managed to get home."

Geoffrey scoffed. "That supposes the man has any
sense of honor, to feel guilt over taking you from home
the first time."

And he'd taken her to France instead of committing
murder.

"Odo made the same bargain with Bastian then as
now, and Bastian did not keep his part of the bargain. I
truly believe if I had not snatched Bastian's dagger he
would have taken me to France and, well, I am not sure
what, but I would have lived."

Geoffrey's skepticism didn't fade. She went on.

"Bastian did not want responsibility for my fate any
more than you do. By allowing the rescue he ensured my
safety by handing the task of guarding me back to you."

He quietly contemplated, then asked, "Why let you
hold a dagger to his throat?"

An easy one to answer. "His reputation would suffer
greatly if his crew thought their captain possessed a soft
heart—not a good thing to have bandied about on the
docks among fellow traders. Bad enough he needs to
deal with the tale of a woman getting the better of him,
but a blade pressed to his throat makes the tale more ac-
ceptable."

"A blade you nicked him with."

"I did not intend to, but I was . . . awkward." She
smiled, remembering poor Bastian's reaction. "He
yelped, cursed at me, then decided a small cut to display
not such a bad thing. 'Twas part of why I repaid the coin

I stole from him in Rouen, an apology of sorts for his injury."

"The pittance you gave him will not make up for his loss of the contents of the money purse, or of his trade with Pecham."

"I should not worry overmuch about Bastian's loss. He will find another man along Cornwall's coast to bargain with. As he said, 'tis the fortunes of the trade."

Geoffrey ran a hand through his drying hair. "I suppose what is done is done, though I fail to understand why you thought you owed him any consideration at all."

A small debt repaid, not worth arguing with Geoffrey over. Her debt to Geoffrey was much higher and she prayed he'd now accept payment.

"I owe you a debt, too, for my rescue. Release from your oath should satisfy it."

He began walking, she followed, her knee better though sore.

"I swore the oath to your father. 'Tis not satisfied until I deem it satisfied."

Even if he must marry her. Whenever Geoffrey deigned to look at her she saw disdain and disappointment. Her distaste for the prospect of a forced, loveless union rose.

"I refuse your offer of marriage."

He didn't speak again until they reached the top of the cliff, the keep a short walk away on level ground.

"Odo tried to have you murdered and may do so again. With me you would be safe."

"And we would both be miserable. Nay, Geoffrey. No marriage." Perhaps if she denied him often enough, 'twould hurt less. "Go home to your family. See your sister. She must be horribly worried over your whereabouts."

"My sister did not know I decided to attend her wedding. My family believes me still in Paris."

Which explained why no family member awaited his arrival in Dover, why no one had come to Pecham looking for him. They didn't know about the injuries he'd suffered for her sake.

"You should still go home."

"Not yet. If you will not agree to marriage, then I will carry on as I intended before. I am not leaving until I am sure Odo will not attempt to harm you again."

"How?"

"Best you know none of the particulars so Odo cannot force answers from you."

Stubborn, infuriating man—who led her toward the postern gate. Damned if she'd sneak into the keep.

"Do as you like, but I intend to go through the main gate. I want Odo to know I am coming and fret over my promise to cut out his black heart."

The corner of his mouth twitched. "As you say." He angled his steps toward the main gate. "Intend to use your newly acquired dagger?"

Leah nearly blushed remembering her awkwardness, her shaking hands. "'Twas a miracle I did not cut myself from stem to stern when I took the blade from Bastian. Best I leave the wielding of sharp weapons to others."

"Wise decision." He slowed to a halt, cast her a reflective glance. "If you wish to make a grand entry, then we should do so to full effect. Tuck the dagger into your girdle."

She carefully slid the dagger from her sleeve and eased the blade beneath the gold links encircling her waist, next to her father's money pouch. "Like so?"

"Now push up your sleeves."

'Twould expose her raw wrists for all to see, exactly what Geoffrey had in mind, and she approved his reasoning. A blatant appeal for sympathy wasn't uncalled for. The image she presented to Pecham's people would be remarked upon and remembered.

Her wounds in full view, she lengthened her spine, lifted her chin. "Shall I limp, too?"

"Only as is natural." He stepped back, looked her over. "A shame your gown is not torn, but 'tis soiled, which will do."

She smiled. "The daughter of Nigel returns a bit battered but not broken. 'Twill be . . . interesting to see how Odo reacts."

"Have a care when you accuse him of—"

"He would only call me a liar, and some will believe him. I have a different strategy in mind." She looked Geoffrey over. "'Tis a shame your breeches are nearly dry. Is the sword and scabbard still wet?"

He reached up under his tunic, unbuckled the scabbard, then wrapped it over his tunic so the wet leather showed. "'Tis water-marked enough so any of the men-at-arms will notice. What do you intend to do?"

Bring Odo to a reckoning for his sins against her, very publicly, using both Bastian's fee and the people of Pecham against him. 'Twas a risk, but she knew if she didn't strike back swift and hard, he'd consider her weak and ripe for another blow. His next blow might truly prove fatal. She'd *not* give him the opportunity.

Nor did she intend for him to get his hands on their mother's brooch. The wretch! Imagine believing that one piece of jewelry, though magnificent and costly, would win him a wife.

"I intend to have a fine time spending Bastian's fee. Ready?"

"Nearly. Are you aware Odo explained your absence by telling everyone you decided to go back to France with Bastian?"

So she'd assumed. "My thanks for not believing him."

His mouth thinned. "I confess to doubt, then Anna expressed her belief you would not go willingly. 'Twas then I realized Odo's scheme."

His doubt proved his lack of faith in her judgment, and that hurt more than Odo's treachery.

"I owe Anna a debt then, for sending you down to the cove."

"As do I. I told her to remain locked in your bedchamber until I returned. Best we go set her free."

Geoffrey waved a hand at the gate. Resolved, Leah led the way, her head high. As she hoped, the guards at the top of the gate tower saw her coming, their eyes narrowing at her dishevelment. Those people within the bailey, who got a closer look, pointed at her wrists and whispered their shock among them.

A glance upward revealed her brother in the solar window, looking down into the bailey. He ducked back as soon as their gazes met. Ruddy coward.

By the time she reached the keep's steps, a crowd followed her and Geoffrey. She put a foot on the first stair, then changed her mind and direction—to under the solar window.

"Odo! I return as I said I would. Come down to the hall, brother dear. I bear gifts."

Climbing the steps hurt her knee, but the promise of sweet revenge pulled her upward. The household servants turned to gape at the mass of people entering the hall.

Odo wasn't in the hall, hadn't accepted her challenge.

Geoffrey leaned close to her ear. "Shall I bring him down?"

"Free Anna first or she will fret until she sees me safe."

She motioned forward the nearest serving wench. "Find Thuro. Tell him his attendance is required."

The girl bobbed a curtsey. "'Tis good to see you, milady. We . . . worried."

Good to know. After the girl scurried off, Leah crossed the hall, drew the dagger and money pouch from her girdle and placed them on the front edge of the table up on the dais. A commotion near the stairs drew her attention. Anna came to her, tears in her eyes, arms open. Leah gratefully accepted the old woman's embrace.

"Oh, Leah. Praise God and all the saints. I *knew* ye'd not take up with that scoundrel again."

"Your belief in me saved my life, Anna. My thanks for sending Geoffrey to my rescue."

"Knew he would get you back, I did. Good man."

With a final squeeze, Leah backed out of the embrace. Anna's eyes narrowed on raw wrists.

"Yer injured. Damn bastards. I will get my salves."

"Not yet, Anna. Stay a moment."

Thuro entered the hall, pushed his way through the crowd, as puzzled and curious as everyone else. "You sent for me, milady?"

"I have something for you. We wait only on Odo."

His gaze landed on the table's edge. "Bastian's dagger," he said before reaching up to reverently touch the money pouch. "Nigel's."

"No long Bastian's dagger but mine. You recognize it?"

"Seen it many a time. He always let the pearl hilt stick up over his boot, handy like. What do you with Nigel's purse?"

"I took it from Bastian. Thuro, did Odo and Bastian trade goods for ore this morn?"

Thuro nodded, a frown forming. "A good deal of ore, all that remained in the cave. To my mind, Bastian got the best of the bargain."

"Ah. Well, perhaps Odo knows how the pouch came to be in Bastian's hands."

Thuro's expression told her he'd thought of a reason.

Leah glanced around, both amazed and amused at their reactions to her.

As had happened in Dover, people observed, listened and speculated. With very few pieces of information they made assumptions about what transpired.

She'd allowed everyone in Dover to believe as they wished—and they'd created a legend. Geoffrey was bound to come out the hero of this tale, too. 'Twas her brother's involvement in the tale she needed to ensure they got right.

Odo stormed down the stairway into the hall, Geoffrey at his heels, sword drawn. Apparently Odo required persuasion to quit the solar, face his sister.

Her brother strode toward her, reviving her fears in the cave of being struck. Except this time her hands weren't bound; this time she didn't face him alone.

Geoffrey stood guard, indeed, keeping Odo from getting closer than several feet away. How Odo felt about having a sword drawn against him in his own hall he didn't reveal, his focus too intent on her.

"So, once more the whore returns," he spat out. "Tire of Bastian again already?"

The taunt pricked her ire; she batted it down. Without retort she stepped up onto the dais and circled the table, then eased into the lord's chair and picked up her father's money pouch, suddenly angry that Odo had used something of her father's in his unholy plot.

Odo appealed to the crowd. "Not only a whore but a thief! See you how she flaunts her wickedness? Certes, she stole my father's pouch to take with her to France. By robbing me she robs us all."

To the questioning murmurs, with more calm than she felt, she asked, "Have you been careless with the key to Pecham's coffers, Odo? Father used to keep the key on a chain around his neck so no one but he could open the chest."

Her brother's hand eased toward his chest, his face burned red. Not only a coward but a fool to make such an accusation.

Leah opened the pouch and spilled the contents onto the table. Pounds, shillings, marks—Bastian had commanded a generous sum to do away with her. 'Twas both insulting and flattering.

She picked up a silver mark. "Lovely, is it not? Part of this hoard is mine, of course—"

"Nay. What belonged to Father now belongs to me."

Greedy bastard.

Leah began making three stacks of coins.

"Not quite everything, Odo. Others are entitled to a share of our father's wealth. He made several bequests in his will. Thuro, Anna, have you received those grants yet?"

They shook their heads.

"Nor have I, and I would wager Garth has not seen a shilling of his bequest either. I propose we correct my brother's oversight now." She focused on Odo, who'd gone pale. "Unless, of course, Odo objects to your receiving your due."

"They are . . . entitled."

"They most certainly are. Thuro, Anna, accept these bequests given by my father for your good service, lo these many years. Might I beg a favor of you, Geoffrey, to ensure Garth's share delivered to him as soon as you are able?"

He grinned. "As milady wishes."

With a sweep of her arms, Leah gathered in the remaining scattered coins. "This is my share."

Odo finally broke his silence. "You are only entitled to one hundred marks."

And now she had him. Sweet revenge.

So why did it hurt to see her brother brought low?

Mercy, he'd tried to have her murdered. She had to expose his nefarious plan or risk another attempt on her life. Only if the people of Pecham knew the extent of her danger from her brother would they solidly rally around her, protect her.

One shouldn't need protection from another who shared one's heritage and blood.

"Aye, I am due one hundred marks by the terms of our father's will. How do you know, Odo, how much I now claim for myself unless you knew how much money the pouch contained to begin with?"

She wanted to say more, accuse him of filling the pouch and handing it to Bastian. 'Twas damn near more than she could bear to keep silent, allow the whispers to turn to murmurs, the surprise shift to disgust.

Odo heard it, too. She'd never seen him so dazed, so confused. Finally, his pride could no longer stand the heavy weight of their loathing. He turned heel and strode toward the hall's door, people scooting to the side to get out of his way.

Thuro shouted orders to clear the hall. Geoffrey sheathed the sword into the water-stained scabbard. Anna fussed about an unguent for the rope burns.

Suddenly so tired she could barely sit up, Leah rose from her father's chair, her chin up, her knees trembling. The room spun, the light dimmed.

She heard Geoffrey shout her name just before all went black.

Geoffrey knew the difference between winning a battle and winning a war. To Leah went the day, in rather stunning fashion, but men like Odo always managed to regain an advantage and strike again.

'Twas still up to him to provide for Leah's continued safety. Assured that Leah's fainting resulted only from exhaustion and she was now well-tended and under tight guard, Geoffrey used the excuse of delivering Garth's bequest to ride into the village. On the way out he steered Boadicea into the churchyard.

The village's streets were near deserted, the miners and their families tucking into evening meals. To do what he must, he need disturb only one miner, and that on the sly.

He wrapped Boadicea's reins around a Celtic cross in the shadows of the graveyard, then made his way to a cottage not far up the road. Moments later he returned with both the miner—who'd agreed to become guardian of the chest and ledger—and the tools needed to complete his task, no one else the wiser.

"A fine steed she be," Michael said of Boadicea. "His lordship did love that horse."

Geoffrey took down the bundle strapped to the horse's rump. "That he did. Did you know Leah bought her for Nigel?"

"Aye. Tales of such nature are retold over and again, even down here in the mines. I hear the mare is yours now."

Reminded of how quickly news spread, of his need for haste, Geoffrey shifted the bundle. "I ask much of you, Michael. If you cannot bear the burden, say so now."

Michael's admiration and loyalty rang in his voice. "For her ladyship I would take on any burden. Let us be done before we are seen."

By the dim light sifting through the stained-glass window, Geoffrey and Michael pried up a large, flat-topped stone out of the church's floor with a miner's pick. All

the while Geoffrey related the tale of the day's events—
the same tale now being bandied about at the keep—and
impressed upon Michael the danger Leah might be in if
her brother ever got hold of either of the items they
buried.

Michael forced the shovel into the dirt. "A nasty man,
Odo."

"A dangerous man, too. You must take great care to
never let him know where the chest and ledger are hidden, for your own sake as well as Leah's."

"I will take care. I have a family to think of."

A wife, two little girls—one of them blind. Aye,
Michael had better reason than some to keep his silence.

Michael carefully removed only as much dirt as necessary. Geoffrey eased the oiled cloth-wrapped bundle
into the hole, packed dirt around and over it until sure
the stone would fit as evenly as before.

By the time they refitted the stone and scooped up the
unused dirt into Michael's ore-washing pan, 'twas nearing dusk.

Michael gave the stone a final stamp. "Come morn, I
will make sure the stone looks and sets right, get up any
stray dirt. No one should be able to see what we have
done."

Geoffrey hoped not. "Now, how do we mark the
stone? They all look so much alike."

"I were thinkin' on the problem. If we chip or otherwise mar it, sure as day follows day someone will notice."

"Think you can remember which it is?"

"Beggin' pardon, milord, but as ye say, tellin' one
from the other after a space of time might be a bugger.

Now, all these stones, they might look much alike, but I would wager a bucket of ore that they do not *feel* the same, and I know just the one who could pick it out if'n I ask her to."

"Eileen."

Michael nodded.

A cold chill washed over Geoffrey at the thought of putting so much trust in a child. Over what Odo might do to a little girl if . . . nay, had to be another way.

"I know what yer thinkin', milord. I mulled on it too, her being involved. Still seems the most sure way to me, and Eileen, well, 'twould be no more to her than a game."

"A hell of a game." Geoffrey wished he'd planned a step further. To involve the child didn't sit well at all. "Perhaps . . ." But there was no perhaps, no other way to mark the stone.

"You are sure, Michael? This is your daughter we speak of."

"Ye put a foot on that stone and I will be back anon."

Geoffrey placed his right foot on the stone. Michael picked up the washing pan and shovel and took them with him.

Alone in the silent church, Geoffrey looked up at the Virgin and Babe. He'd purposely selected this area of the church to bury the chest and ledger. Somehow, having the Mother Mary looming over the treasures, watching over them, seemed fitting.

Geoffrey knew he was doing the right thing. For himself, for Leah. Even for Michael, who felt honored to be of special service to Leah.

A good plan, in a good man's hands, and soon in a little girl's.

None of it would be necessary if Leah had agreed to marriage. Geoffrey had yet to decide if he was more relieved or angry or hurt—aye, hurt damnit—at her refusal.

Common sense should have led her to accept. Marriages for convenience, for money, for power happened all the time. A marriage to keep her safe from her brother's authority seemed the best way to fulfill his oath. But then, her reasons were sound even though based on emotion.

He couldn't force her to accept him.

Now, if Leah were with child—but she wasn't. She'd had her flux only a sennight ago and they'd not made love since. A good thing. Nothing held him at Pecham but his oath.

He heard father and daughter on the steps of the church before they entered.

"Here we be, milord." Michael closed the door behind them, and hand in hand, they crossed the floor. "You remember Sir Geoffrey, Eileen?"

The pixie with the coal black hair and staring gray eyes dipped into a curtsey. "Milord."

Without moving his right foot, Geoffrey scrunched down. "Good tidings, Eileen. 'Tis fine to see you again."

"Father says ye wish to know how *I* see with my hands."

"A very special talent. Will you show me?"

"What do ye wish me to see?"

Michael saved him from answering. "Here, Eileen, the stones on the floor. Can ye tell one from the other?"

"Tsk. O'course I can."

"A test then," Michael went on, motioning Geoffrey back. "Start with this one where Sir Geoffrey stood."

On hands and knees Eileen *saw* the stone, her nimble fingers running over bumps and ridges, seeking the edges. When done, Michael guided her to the surrounding stones, and as Geoffrey watched he began to believe the girl would only think she played a game to prove her ability to two disbelievers.

Michael turned the girl around a few times, bringing forth giggles, then asked her to find the original stone. She did, her success beaming in the shadow of the window.

"This one, Papa. Sir Geoffrey stood on this one."

"Well done, girl."

Geoffrey agreed. "My thanks, Eileen. I stand enlightened."

"Ye are most welcome, Sir Geoffrey." The girl turned to her father. "Papa, would you lift me up so I can touch the lady's foot again?"

Michael chuckled as he did her bidding. "She likes the feel of the glass."

Guided by her father, Eileen found the piece of glass where the Virgin's foot rested on a scarlet pillow. "Someday, when I be bigger, I want to touch the baby's foot."

"'Tis not to be, little one. By the time yer arms are long enough yer ole Papa will not be able to lift ye."

"Oh."

Geoffrey judged the distance needed as only a few inches. "Michael, perhaps I can be of assistance."

"'Twould be kind of ye, milord."

He hadn't held a child in many a year, not since long before leaving Lelleford for Paris—one of his sister Jeanne's babes, and he remembered being so scared he'd drop the baby or squeeze it too tightly.

Michael handed over his daughter, her body small but not so breakable. Warm and innocent, with a healthy heft and gray eyes that could not see.

"Oh, I am high up! Ye must be very tall, milord."

"So I am told." Geoffrey stepped up to the window, adjusted his hold to lift the child higher. "Reach now. Stretch. There, the babe's foot."

She giggled her delight. "I did it, Papa! I did it!"

Geoffrey hadn't prayed in years, not for himself or for another. He did now, not for a miracle to restore Eileen's sight, but a special blessing to keep her safe from dangers her lack of sight presented.

"Aye, that ye did. Come, Eileen, 'tis time Sir Geoffrey returned to the keep. Night comin' on."

Already he'd lingered overlong.

With a shyness she'd not displayed before, Eileen asked, "Might I see ye first, milord?"

At that moment he'd not have denied the girl anything. Gads, some father he'd be, so susceptible to a child's whims.

"You may."

Small hands, tender fingers, fluttered over his forehead.

"Ye have a scar here, like his lordship. Does yers hurt?"

"Nay, no longer."

She saw his eyes, his nose, his cheeks. Her brow creased.

"Maybe Mama does not see ye aright. She said ye had a beard, all full and bushy like."

"Your mother sees fine. I only recently scraped off the whiskers."

In a fit of pique because Leah had convinced him to grow it out, because she'd liked it.

Her hands stilled. "My thanks, milord. I would know ye again."

He couldn't help it. Geoffrey hugged Eileen before he gave her back to her father.

"Take care, Michael."

"And ye, milord. Fret not. All will be well here."

Convinced the chest and ledger under good guardianship, Geoffrey left the church. Once mounted, thinking of all he had yet to do at the keep, he paused to peer at the freshest grave in the churchyard.

"I did all I could, Nigel," he whispered. "What happens now depends on Odo."

# *Chapter* 19

S he'd insisted on being present when Geoffrey confronted Odo, so now Leah sat in the same chair she'd occupied during the reading of her father's will, trying not to fidget.

Odo slumped in a chair behind the desk she would always consider her father's, manipulating a silver mark between his fingers, his scowl deep.

Geoffrey stood behind her, his hands resting on the back of her chair, his warning to Odo already delivered.

If anything untoward happened to her, the hidden smuggling ledger would be sent to the earl of Cornwall.

In a low, steady voice, Geoffrey stated, "The guards have shifted their duties to ensure someone watches over Leah at all times—"

Odo's head snapped up. "You have no right to order my guards about!"

"I gave no order. They took the duty upon themselves. As for the dowry, when Leah has need of it, she will have it. Put it out of your mind, Odo, for you will never see it again."

"You have no right—"

"As you had no right to try to have Leah murdered."

Defiant to the end, Odo huffed. "I did not. I paid Bastian to take her to France and ensure she stayed there. If he told you aught else, he lied."

Leah couldn't believe what she heard. "You told me yourself, in the cave. How dare you—"

"Then you heard wrongly."

Geoffrey put a staying, steadying hand on her shoulder, the message clear, so she refrained from further argument. Already her brother twisted the tale to fit his delusions. Soon the marks on her wrists would heal, the people of Pecham would lose the sharpness of their current anger. Even the guards would eventually see no reason for steady vigilance.

Eventually, Odo might even be able to coax some of them into believing his version of the tale.

'Twas galling, but possible.

"No matter," Geoffrey said. "The chest and ledger are well hidden, under excellent guardianship. Mind your actions, Odo, or risk exposure of your trade."

"You tricked one of our good people into treason. I shall strive to be merciful when I find the hiding place and discover who."

Geoffrey chuckled. "Have at it, Odo. All that rummaging about should keep you well occupied for several years."

"You went out to the village to see Garth earlier. You hid them somewhere near the mine."

"Could be. Or perhaps I stuffed them into a hollow

tree trunk along the way, or buried them under a farmer's turnips. Or maybe they are under a stack of hay in the stable."

"Then they are in none of those places."

"But you will never know for sure unless you look."

Odo's scowl deepened.

Believing Geoffrey finished, Leah rose, unwilling to stay longer in Odo's presence. Besides, Geoffrey wished to leave on the morn and there were preparations to make, and she was determined to help him without becoming emotional.

She would *not* weep. They'd pack his belongings, say farewells, make a swift, clean break of each other and be done. No sense wallowing in melancholy, wishing for the impossible.

Out in the hall, a man-at-arms stood near her bedchamber door. 'Twas disconcerting, but she allowed for the need.

Geoffrey followed her into the chamber, closed and bolted the door. "That went well."

Leah noted his lack of anger or bitterness. He was no longer the confused but accepting gallant who'd struggled with his loss of memory, nor the distraught and furious man who'd berated her on the wall walk. He seemed to have come to some accord with himself.

Perhaps, now that he'd fulfilled his oath, he found his peace. Nice that one of them had done so.

"I will not ask you of the hiding place or who agreed to act as guardian. You are right, 'tis best I do not know. Not that I am not curious, but I shall trust you chose well."

He smiled softly at that. "I believe I did. As I told

Odo, should you have need of your dowry, it will be delivered to your hands, not his. You may need to be careful about guarding it until giving it over to your ... husband."

She noted the hesitation. He'd offered marriage, she'd refused, and had no intention of changing her mind. After he left on the morn, went back to his family and life, she'd never see him again, and that was for the best. 'Twas painful enough to know what she passed up by setting him free.

She needed something to do before she started weeping.

"Shall I arrange for a cart for your trunk?"

"Nay, too cumbersome." His smile mixed with worry. "Wait until Odo realizes I take Boadicea. I warrant he will rage, accuse me of thievery."

Damn, she'd miss the horse, too.

"Let Odo rage. All know Father gave her to you in his will. You are entitled."

"When your father bestowed the gift, he thought us wed."

"No matter. A gift is a gift. Or consider her payment for rescuing me a second time. Which reminds me." Leah crossed the room to her clothing chest, withdrew her father's money pouch, shook out a palm full of coins. "You are also entitled to the funds I spent in Dover."

"I have no need of your money."

"Perhaps not, but now all of my debts are paid. Pray take it, if only to allow me to fulfill a penance I know the priest will impose for my sins."

He hesitated a moment more, then held out his hand. She was careful not to touch him during the transfer.

"The priest will be back from his pilgrimage soon, will he not?"

"He planned to return before harvest, if all went well. The farmers will begin within a fortnight."

And the days would get colder, and the nights colder yet.

Leah put the money pouch away, heard the jangle of coins emptying into Geoffrey's. When she turned from her chest, he knelt before his trunk, opening it.

If he planned to go on horseback, he couldn't take the trunk. She peered over his shoulder at the items inside.

"You will need a large sack."

"A grain sack should do."

He lifted out his treasured books. She remembered unwrapping them, wiping them off after their dunking in the Channel. He'd since spent many pleasurable hours lost within their pages.

"I do not see your oiled cloth."

"I found another use for it."

She opened her mouth to ask what, but then knew. He'd wrapped the dowry chest and smuggling ledger before hiding them, protecting new treasures.

The room shrank, the walls closing in fast. If she didn't get out she'd come undone.

"I will find you a grain sack."

She had the door unbolted before he said, "Have a care."

The guard would follow her. Geoffrey knew that, so she saw no reason to answer and risk his knowing how close she came to tears.

On her way to the kitchen she fought to regain composure, enough to locate a sack and tell the cook to prepare a packet of food to send along with Geoffrey. As an afterthought, she set a scullery maid to filling him a wine skin.

His books needed to be wrapped. She could think of no better purpose for an ell of indigo silk.

With silk and sack in hand, she entered the bedchamber, determined to get through the rest of his packing and departure without making a fool of herself.

The trunk was emptied, that which he intended to take with him stacked on the floor. Geoffrey stood near the mantel, in his hand the bear he'd carved.

"If you do not object, I should like to give this to Anna. I always meant to carve her something special, but . . ."

He hadn't found the time, and now he was leaving.

"I am sure she will be pleased with the gift. Here, I brought wrapping for your books."

He put the bear on the edge of the mantel and took the silk. "Rather fine wrapping."

" 'Twill serve the purpose. You might give it to Eloise, with my best wishes for a happy marriage."

Geoffrey nodded, then bent to his task. Knowing she'd just be in his way if she tried to help, she lowered into her chair. The silence grew oppressive, gave her too much privacy in which to mourn her impending loss.

"I always wondered about your family, your sister in particular."

He took a long breath, then gave out a small laugh. "Eloise is the youngest of us, with eyes and hair to match mine. I always think of her as a nymph, slight and fragile, which seems to have no bearing on her temper." He shrugged a shoulder. "I have two older siblings, Julius and Jeanne—and my father, of course. As happened to you, my mother died when I was a child."

Admitting a bit of envy, she commented, "You are fond of them all."

He stuffed the wrapped books in the sack, then the horses. "Of my siblings, aye. My father and I have our differences. Here." He gave her the lavender-scented soap. "I intended to give this to Eloise as a wedding gift, but with the silk . . ."

She set the cakes on the table, knowing she'd think of him every time she used them, not that he'd fade from her thoughts anytime soon. Into the sack he shoved his spare garments and the pouch containing his carving tools. Almost done.

Leah rose, her hand trembling as she reached for the small statues—the adorable little sheep, the humorous turtle . . .

"Nay," he said. "Keep them, or give them away as gifts."

She pursed her lips, lowered her hand.

He stood up, gave the bag a shake, then wound the twine that had once bound his books around the top of the sack. Would that she could crawl in there, too, count herself among his belongings. She could, with just a word, accept his proposal.

He let go of the sack. "If things here get too bad, send word to Lelleford. Even if I am not there, Eloise will know how to reach me."

The oath again. Always the damned oath.

"You have done all you could."

With a sigh, he said, "Most all. As your guardian, Odo has rights I could do naught about."

To marry her off, send her to a convent.

"But he will not harm me, nor get away with locking me in the north tower. For that I thank you."

He hefted the sack over his shoulder. Tonight he'd sleep on a pallet in the hall or down in the guard's quarters, no longer her lover or protector. She supposed he'd spend some time with Anna and Ned tonight, say farewells to whomever he might feel obligated to take leave of.

By the time she rose on the morn he'd be gone, on his way home.

With unsteady hands, she handed him the bear. "Go home, Geoffrey. Be happy."

His hand on the latch, he paused to look back, his eyes brilliant sapphire, his mouth soft and sad. He stared at her for a moment before he shook his head slightly and issued his last order. "Bolt the door."

Then he was gone.

Through unstoppable tears she slid the bolt into place, crawled into her lonely bed and pulled the covers over her head.

On the morrow she'd be brave, deal with Odo, carry on with her duties about the keep, do whatever must be done.

But not tonight. Sweet mercy, not tonight.

Leaving Pecham hadn't been as easy as it should have been.

Even now, three days later, with the awkwardness of this morning's return to Lelleford behind him, Geoffrey stood on the battlements and missed the roar of the ocean and Cornwall's almost constant wind. More, he couldn't help wonder about and miss the people he'd left behind.

Taking leave of Leah—best not to think about how much he'd longed, at the end, to take her in his arms and ask her to reconsider the marriage. He might have if he wasn't sure Leah would refuse again.

All along he'd planned to break ties cleanly, then some demon forced him to offer to return to Pecham if she needed him. Dry-eyed and stoic she'd told him to go home, be happy.

He'd come home. But happy? Not for a long while yet.

He should put the misadventure in Cornwall out of his mind, concentrate once more on convincing his father that he wasn't about to enter into the Church. The thought of a tonsure still made him cringe.

At least Father had been pleased with the horses, though Geoffrey didn't admit carving them, telling John Hamelin they were carved by a sculptor currently enjoying popularity among French nobility.

As for Eloise—Geoffrey wished he'd been here for the ill-fated wedding ceremony. He could only imagine her horror when her groom dropped dead at her feet on the church steps.

"There you are." As if his thoughts conjured her, Eloise floated toward him, a vision of grace and elegance rivaling that of a French countess. "I searched all over for you. One would think you could be considerate and make yourself more readily available to your neglected sister."

Her wide smile and teasing blue eyes belied her petulance. He lifted one arm and she glided into his side for a brief but hard hug. Garbed in saffron, his vibrant sister smelled of a sharp spice, an invigorating tang to the senses. The lavender soap he'd purchased would have been all wrong for Eloise.

"I beg pardon, but 'struth, no one could neglect you for long."

She laughed lightly. "I choose to accept that as a compliment no matter how you meant it. And now I must beg your pardon. Father sent me to find you and drag you into the solar."

Geoffrey nodded, acknowledging her reluctance to issue the expected summons.

"Then let us walk slowly so you can tell me about the wedding. I heard only tidbits of what happened."

She tucked her hand through his crooked elbow and sighed heavily.

"'Twas the strangest thing. One moment Hugh was alive, then the next dead. His eyes rolled back and over he went." Geoffrey felt her small shiver. "Hugh wasn't old, the same age as Julius. He possessed a mild manner, seemed healthy enough. Yet the physicians say his heart just stopped."

Their brother Julius was twenty and six, hardly old. "You were content to marry Hugh?"

"Oh, aye! I had no objection to him at all. Courtly manners, a knight's rank, heir to his father's vast estates—which our father thought his most attractive trait. He truly was easy to talk to, a pleasant man all around." Her expression went dark. "Unlike that bothersome half-brother of his. Now, if Father had betrothed me to Roland, I might have strenuously objected."

Eloise let go his arm to hike up her skirts. All the way

down the stairs Geoffrey considered her opinion of
Hugh, who in his view sounded . . . dull.

"If Father covets an alliance to the St. Martens, might
he consider betrothing you to Roland?"

"Heaven be praised, nay! Roland is too far down on
the list of heirs for consideration. May all of his other
brothers lead long lives!"

They entered the passageway to the solar, the gloom
relieved only by Eloise's presence.

"Enough of me," she ordered. "What of you? Such an
ordeal you have been through. I gather you fully recovered from all of your injuries."

Only his heart still ached.

"Aye. The people of Pecham took good care of me.
My body healed well before my mind did."

"How awful to lose your memory. How horrifying to
not remember who you were, where you belonged.
Thank God you finally regained your senses and came
home to us."

He'd told his father and sister the barest details of the
shipwreck, his injuries and memory loss, said little of the
woman who'd tended him. Beyond her name and her
role in his recovery they didn't need to know more about
the woman he'd fallen in love with, who'd betrayed his
trust. The woman he'd have married if she'd but said the
word.

She'd shot an arrow into his heart every time she'd refused him. He should be glad, relieved. He wasn't. Every
time he thought of her he missed her more, and he'd
thought of her too often.

Geoffrey applied his will to a change of subject.

"'Tis your fault my memory returned."

"Mine?"

"Your message about your wedding was tucked into my law book. The moment I saw it, everything came back."

And his whole world had fallen apart.

Enough. No more. What was done was done.

"I am glad I played some small part in your recovery, though it pains me that my message also placed you on that ill-fated ship. 'Twas harrowing for Leah, too, I imagine. 'Tis fortunate for you she was sensible, cared for you after. You saved her life, then she saved yours. How very romantic."

"Romantic? You make much more of it than there is. Leah and I did not suit, just like you and Roland."

She stopped, halting his steps. Those clear blue eyes looked up at him, studying, judging.

"Roland is a disagreeable toad. Leah sounds like a nice woman—must be to have endured your foul disposition while you were ill. Did the two of you not get along?"

"My disposition was not foul, I will have you know, and Leah and I got along well enough."

"Is she ugly as a boar?"

"Nay."

"Is she married?"

"Nay! Eloise, have done. We simply did not suit."

She crossed her arms. "What did you do to offend her?"

"Me? Offend *her*?"

"I know you, Geoffrey. You can be the most single-minded, stubborn man on God's earth. You must have done something to put her off." Her expression softening, she put her hand on his arm. "You care for Leah,

Geoffrey. I can hear it when you say her name. What happened?"

Too much . . . and not enough.

"I asked Leah to marry me and she refused. End of tale."

Geoffrey entered the solar, seeking the solace of an outright battle with his father, except his father wasn't there. Damn if Eloise didn't follow him into the chamber. And she thought *him* single-minded.

Her soft voice heralded her approach. "'Twould be the end of the tale if you did not hurt so badly. You are also one of the most loyal and loving of men on God's earth. If Leah refused you, then she must not have loved you as she ought, and for that she is a fool and you are best off without her."

He was half a man without her, his body in one place and his heart in another.

"Leah is no fool. She . . . she once told me she loved me, and at the time I believed her."

"And you love her."

"With my whole heart."

Having said it aloud, his aching heart bled.

Eloise settled into a chair, gave him that expectant look he might try to resist but would fail. So he told Eloise almost everything from the time he awoke in the solar—leaving out the details of intimacy—up to the rescue from Bastian's boat and Leah's victorious skirmish with Odo in the great hall after.

Eloise held up a hand to halt the story. "So you proposed marriage between the cove and hall, as a way to protect Leah from her brother."

"Leah refused, and tried to release me from the oath to her father, which I refused to do."

"Naturally." She rose, ambled toward him. "I know there is more to this tale, but as I see it, your Leah was most practical. I do not excuse her for her lies, but I understand her reasoning. We women *do* find ways to cope with ill-tempered men. Geoffrey, if you can forgive Leah, then you might wish to go back and restate your proposal. Only this time, do so with love in your heart and voice."

"She knows I care for her."

"Does she? Or does she merely know you were prepared to do your duty and keep your oath? Not once in your proposal did you happen to mention that she meant more to you than duty, did you?"

He took a long breath, his pulse beginning to pound. "Nay, I did not. I was—"

"Witless. Gallant, but witless." She tossed her hands in the air. "Admit it, you botched the proposal. Had you told Leah you wanted to marry her because you love her, not by some misguided sense of duty, you would not be standing in father's solar about to argue your unsuitability for a position in the Church."

The irritating nymph had a point.

"If I were married, I could not take clerical vows."

"Convenient, is it not?" She flounced across the room. "I shall see what keeps Father." She stopped at the door. "By the by, in payment for my silence I expect an invitation to the wedding and the honor of being godmother to your firstborn."

"There is no sense in asking her. She would only refuse me again."

"I pray she does not, for your sake as well as mine. I truly would not mind having a sister-by-marriage who sends me gifts of such exquisite silk."

Such as Eloise, unafraid to speak her mind even when it got her into trouble. But then, as the youngest, she'd always been allowed more freedom than he or their older siblings. She hadn't had to worry whether or not her brothers would berate her, or worse. Neither he nor Julius had wished either of their sisters harm, certainly hadn't tried to have them murdered.

They'd all had to cope with their unruly father.

Forgive Leah? Aye, perhaps he could. He could understand her doing what she must to protect herself. The weapon of her lie had wounded him, which she hadn't intended. She'd striven to keep body and mind intact in the best way she knew how.

Truly, hadn't he done the very same when deciding to escape his father's domination by running away to Paris? He'd sneaked into this very solar, stolen enough coin for passage and board and food for a few months.

Even on returning home he'd evaded opening himself to further ridicule.

On his father's large, dark oak desk sat the horses, his peace offering. He'd turned coward when not admitting them his work, crediting some unknown sculptor, afraid his father wouldn't like or appreciate them if their true maker was known.

Too, he'd berated Leah for doing, as she'd said, the best she could in a difficult situation. She'd apologized, tried to make amends . . . which he'd shunned.

Nay, no saint, he.

Would Leah accept him if he told her he loved her, or use

Bastian's dagger to cut out his heart and stamp on it? Could she forgive him for being quick to judge and condemn?

Only one way to find out. Return to Pecham. Tell Leah he loved her and ask, maybe beg her to reconsider.

Sir John Hamelin, knight of the realm, adviser to the king, the father he'd feared most of his life, entered the solar with all the regal bearing of his nobility.

How odd that his father reminded him of Nigel— barrel chest, graying hair. Gruff. Purposeful. Willing to use whatever means, even illegal, to obtain his ends. Except Nigel's concern had been for Pecham's people, where John Hamelin schemed to further himself. Like Odo.

The comparison bothered him immensely.

"About time you came home. Sit, lad. I have a proposition for you."

"If the proposition requires me to take a position in the Church, I must decline."

Father lowered into the chair behind his desk. "Touchy as always. Hear me out first." He waved at the horses. "Nicely done, by the way. How odd you should have such a talent. You never showed such leanings as a boy."

'Twas Geoffrey's turn to sit. "You know them my work?"

Father folded his arms, leaned forward. "Certes I know. Do you think I do not know where you lived, what you studied, who your companions were these past years?"

Not all of that information could have come from his letters home to Eloise.

"You had me watched."

"The occasional observation, to ensure you neither starved nor did yourself irreparable harm. To your credit, you did better for yourself than I thought you would, and your study of law is particularly impressive."

Geoffrey remained silent, both stunned and resentful. On the one hand he'd proved himself to his father, on the other John Hamelin had provided a net into which his son could fall. 'Twould indicate he cared about his son, but Geoffrey knew 'twas to ensure the son didn't overly embarrass the father.

"I warrant you also paid my knight's fee all this time."

"Certes. I saw no sense in allowing your rank to lapse when you might someday have need of it."

More like his father would have need of it. Done and done.

"Your proposition?"

"Adviser of law on the personal staff of the Archbishop of Canterbury."

John Hamelin reached high indeed. Having a son at the right hand of one of the most powerful archbishops in the kingdom would be quite an achievement, raise his level of influence among his peers, with the king. No matter what it cost the son.

"The position would require I become a priest, and I cannot do that if I am married."

"You are not married."

"I intend to be if she will have me."

His father took a deep breath. "Son, if there is a woman you desire you can have both. Few churchmen are without their housekeepers and mistresses, several have sired children and acknowledge them."

A common occurrence, indeed, but not for Geoffrey—who could well imagine Leah's reaction to *that* proposal, and the imagining made him smile.

"Nay, Father, I fear the lady would be offended."

"Who?"

"Leah of Pecham."

"The young woman who nursed your injuries? I gather her attentions proved . . . amiable. If she has already shared your bed without benefit of marriage, why would she not do so again?"

He should take umbrage on Leah's behalf, instead his smile widened. "Because I was witless. Begging your pardon, Father, but the only position I aspire to now is that of Leah's husband."

Father tossed a hand in the air. "What harm would it to do ask her? Perhaps she will see the advantages of the wealth and power to be obtained."

Leah might well see fit to toss him off a cliff.

"I assure you she will not agree."

Father leaned back in his chair. "Has she connections? A dowry of any size?"

Geoffrey knew where this line of questioning led, to from whom Leah's family held their land right down to a count of the sheep on the farms. If his father truly wanted to know, he could find out. Right now Geoffrey had no patience for it.

"Not enough to suit you, but enough for me." He rose from the chair. "Besides, 'tis of no import if she refuses me."

"Then would you consider the position with the Archbishop?"

If Leah refused him, then he might as well become a

priest, take vows of celibacy, because he'd never love another woman as deeply as Leah.

"I will consider it."

Eloise entered his bedchamber, waved a hand at the items on the bed waiting to be stuffed into a sack.

"In need of help?"

Geoffrey tossed a second pair of wool breeches on the bed. "Nay, nearly done."

"I wish you could stay longer, though I approve of your haste."

"Three days of Father's harping are nearly all I can stand." He'd have left two days ago if not for the torrential rains that turned roads to rivers, making travel dangerous for both horse and man. "One would think it necessary to life itself to establish a connection to the Archbishop of Canterbury."

"You know Father. Always willing to take advantage of an opportunity." Uninvited, Eloise sat down on the bed. "You will remember what I said about the wedding."

Geoffrey wished he were half as confident as Eloise of Leah's accepting his proposal.

"I will remember to send an invitation. If not, Leah will remind me. She is as curious of you as you of her. I fear the two of you will get along well."

"She is very nice, then."

*He'd known it all along, but had refused to admit it for several days.* "Very."

She nodded, satisfied. "Are you taking your books?"

Geoffrey glanced at the shelf he'd put them on. "Nay, I shall leave them here." No sense taking all of his belongings only to have Leah point him to the road, tell him to go home. "If I need them I will send for them."

"Might I see the message I sent you? 'Twas in your law book, I believe you said."

"Certes. Any particular reason?"

"Only to see what prompted you to remember us. I forget what I wrote."

He took down the books, put them on the table. As he opened the law book and drew out the message, Eloise came to stand beside him.

"Beautifully written. I am sorry I was not here."

Eloise bit her bottom lip. Her eyes glistened. "I, too. But it is past." She reined in her emotions, ran a finger over the leather biding. "This is law. What are the others?"

"Arabic medicine," he said, placing the book in front of her. "The other is Greek philosophy."

"You learned both languages in Paris? How wonderful! I always thought I might like to . . . ah, what is this?"

Eloise opened the book to reveal an amber ribbon, a bit soiled, but precious all the same. He'd forgotten putting it in the book.

"Leah's hair ribbon." He picked it up, ran it through his fingers, caught the scent of lavender. "Her token for my lance."

"You never cared much for tournaments, though you acquitted yourself well."

"Not a tournament, just practice in the tiltyard. 'Twas a silly thing to do, I suppose, but I asked Leah for a token and then promptly made a fool of myself."

Her eyebrow arched. "You missed at the quintain?"

"Landed flat on my arse."

"Oh, Geoffrey, how romantic! I ask you, how could a woman possibly turn aside her champion?"

How possibly? Too easily. She already had.

Geoffrey wrapped the ribbon around his wrist, knowing that if he didn't win Leah over at his first pass, he'd likely not have another chance.

# *Chapter 20*

O do wrapped the thick rope around a stout tree, and with frenzied fingers secured it with a knot he'd learned in his youth from a man of the sea. He gave a mighty tug to ensure the knot tight, the rope would hold his weight.

"Odo, this is madness," Leah stated, her exasperated tone making him all the more certain of his conjecture. "Do you truly believe Geoffrey hid the ledger and chest on the side of the cliff?"

For the past sennight he'd searched every other possible hiding place, from fresh diggings at the mine to hollow tree trunks to—he was chagrined to admit—under piles of hay in the stable. Now he stood at the edge of the cliff on the verge of victory.

Once more he glanced down, squinting against both sun and wind, and caught the flash of metal, which had to be the chest's latch. Leah could feign concern for his safety all she wished. He knew better. She must know the chest and ledger were down there and tried to talk him into not going after it. He'd not be fooled.

"I do." With all his strength he heaved the coiled rope over the cliff, gratified to see the end dangle within mere inches of his destination. "And once I have the prize in my possession, I will have the coin to purchase my knighthood and send you off to a convent."

Her eyes darkened. "And the brooch with which to woo a wife. Have you ever thought, Odo, that perhaps if you were less disagreeable you might not need to bribe a woman into marriage?"

He'd slap her for such insolence if not for Thuro and Ned, her two self-appointed guards. Once Leah was gone, he'd deal with those two harshly.

Once more he tugged at the thick rope. Secure. After one more glance down, he began his descent.

True, he'd accidentally caught the flash of light off the dowry chest's metal clasp, but as soon as he saw it he'd known what he found and laughed at Geoffrey's stupidity for not burying the items deeper. The harsh winds that whipped Cornwall's coast must have blown away the fresh dirt to expose the latch.

Feet braced against the side of the cliff, Odo eased downward, hand over hand, one step at a time. In a few more feet he'd reach the small ledge where Geoffrey must have stood to dig the too-shallow hole.

His arms strained. Muscles burned. Sweat beaded on his brow and palms. He didn't worry. If Geoffrey could climb down and back up this cliff, so could he.

His foot touched the narrow ledge. With both boots on solid rock, he found a handhold and let go of the rope.

To his left rested his prize, his victory.

He bent down and brushed away dirt to uncover the chunk of metal.

Not the clasp of a dowry chest.

Sonofabitch.

Leah would surely gloat, this time, at his failure.

Anguish rose in his throat, begged for release, but damned if he'd give her the satisfaction of hearing his torment.

After several deep breaths, resigned to more searching, more digging, he reached to his right for the rope the wind had played with and now dangled beyond his fingertips.

He shifted his weight, leaned right, stretched out.

The rock beneath his foot crumbled.

Few attended the burial. Fewer mourned.

Leah stood by the grave, her eyes now dry, while the miners shoveled dirt over the shrouded body of her brother.

At least death had come instantly and likely painless. He'd snapped both spine and neck.

Thuro had been reluctant to order any of his men-at-arms to risk their own necks to retrieve the body. Those who'd stepped forward to offer, Ned the first of them, had done so out of sympathy for her, because their lady couldn't bear to leave Odo's body to rot and feed the seabirds.

Most everyone who'd attended the burial had already returned to their everyday activities. She'd not ordered a feast served tonight in Odo's honor, fearing too many might use it as an excuse to celebrate.

To the continued scrape of shovels in earth, Father

Donald approached her. The poor priest had returned last eve from his pilgrimage, just in time to attend to Odo's burial this morn. He didn't yet know everything that had happened during the past months, but would likely hear all before the day was over.

He took her hand. "My condolences, my lady, on the loss of both your father and brother so quickly together. Your pain must be nigh unbearable."

Aye, she mourned the loss of her father. Visions of Odo tumbling down the cliff gave her night terrors. She'd rather not speak of either.

"'Tis good to have you back, Father," she said. "Pray, come up to the keep, sup with us. I should like to hear of your pilgrimage to the Holy Land."

"Ah, my lady, the sights I have seen! A place so hot 'twould seem the devil's own hell. A wondrous, horrid place, the desert. Blessed, I was, to walk where our Lord lived."

Leah nearly cringed at the newly acquired fervor in his eyes. Her penance might be harsh indeed. 'Twas a shame he'd not accept her suffering of this past week as atonement for her sins.

Geoffrey's departure had left a hole in her soul and an emptiness in her heart. Every time she looked at his statues on the mantel she cried, yet couldn't remove them from where he'd left them.

She glanced at where the miners were now nearly finished. "We should also discuss grave markers for both my father and brother."

"Certes, my lady, whenever you wish. Have you informed the earl of Cornwall?"

Yet another duty to perform, one she hesitated to do immediately.

"Not as yet."

"Best sooner done than later. 'Tis not good for a holding to be without a lord."

On Odo's death, she inherited Pecham, became somewhat of an heiress. 'Twas rare a woman was allowed to rule a holding of any size or wealth in her own right, and she didn't doubt the earl would press her to take a husband, perhaps choose one for her. An unappealing prospect.

Thuro and Anna waited for her in front of the church, standing by the cart used to haul Odo to his final resting place. Hoping her brother had at last found peace, Leah turned to leave.

"Milady? A word?"

She glanced back at Michael, leaning on his shovel.

"Of course. What is it, Michael?"

The miner stared at the priest. "A *private* word."

Her curiosity pricked by Michael's audacity, she waved toward the cart. "If you would wait by the cart, Father Donald, I shall not be long."

The priest huffed. "New man, is he not?"

"New, but highly skilled with a grand family. Do not judge him harshly."

Giving way to her show of favor to the discourteous miner, the priest reined in his pique at being dismissed. With a nod, he headed toward the cart.

She tilted her head at Michael. "Not a good idea to offend Father Donald. What made you do so?"

Michael smiled. "What I have to say is for yer ears alone, milady. Would you join me in the church?"

Unable to resist the mystery, Leah followed him into the empty church, to under the stained-glass window.

In a conspiratorial whisper, he told her, "They are here, milady. Beneath yer feet. Think ye can keep the priest busy long enough for me to dig 'em up?"

Dig what up?

Sweet Jesu! What other than the chest and ledger?

Leah glanced down, incredulous. "Here? Under this stone?"

"Or the one next to it." He winked. "Worry not, milady. I know how to figure it out."

Leah fought to banish the inappropriate, likely sinful vision of Odo rolling over in his grave. She couldn't help but grin at Michael.

"'Twas you Geoffrey trusted as guardian."

With pride, he said, "Aye. Sir Geoffrey did not say what to do with 'em if Odo passed on, but since the danger is now past, I see no reason not to give 'em back to ye." Then Michael's feet shuffled. "Beggin' yer pardon for bein' forward, milady, but ye should let him know what happened."

Perhaps she should, but 'twould require further thought. Geoffrey might be pleased to know all turned out well, for the most part, or displeased she intruded on his life again.

"I will consider it, Michael. My thanks. And I shall invite Father Donald to partake of some fine Gascony wine while he tells us of his pilgrimage, which will likely last far into the night, which means he will not return until morn. Enough time for you?"

"More than enough. I will wait until all have departed before I begin. Expect me at the keep on the morrow."

He leaned his shovel against the wall and left the church with a lilt in his step.

Still amazed, Leah looked down at the stone.

By law, miners were not allowed to stick a shovel in roads or churchyards. Certes, by digging Odo's grave they skirted on the illegal. To dig in the church itself, with the Holy Mother and Christ child looking on? Audacious. Yet Geoffrey and Michael had done just that, and Leah couldn't tell which stone had been disturbed. 'Twas so well done no one would ever have suspected, not even the priest, who awaited her outside.

Resigned to a long evening of entertaining Father Donald, Leah left the church—to find Geoffrey standing in the road where she'd expected to see a cart and other people.

Geoffrey.

His sapphire eyes held her captive, heart pounding and knees ready to melt. She'd missed him desperately, had seen him so many times this past sennight—in her dreams. Now he stood before her as braw as ever, and she feared to move or speak on the chance he might vanish, prove a mere apparition.

"I sent the others to the keep." He glanced at the new grave. "When I rode up I feared . . . that was you."

The hitch in his rumbling voice revealed his upset, thinking Odo might have harmed her despite his efforts to protect her.

She chanced her voice. "Odo."

"So Anna told me, and how he died. She said you tried to stop him, witnessed his fall. I am sorry for that, but cannot mourn his passing." He tilted his head, studying her. "Yet you shed tears for him. Why?"

Her dazed state clearing, she wondered why Geoffrey came back. To see how she fared, obviously. Because of his oath or because he truly cared? There had been so many angry, hurtful words between them, but there had been laughter and loving, too.

Which did he remember most? They stood but a few steps apart. Was the crevice too wide to cross?

"Odo was not always malicious. I remember a time, when we were children, when he actually smiled at me on occasion. That was the brother I mourn."

Geoffrey withheld comment, but he seemed to understand when so many others didn't, and she loved him all the more for it.

He nodded toward the church door. "Michael showed you the stone?"

"He saw no reason to keep the secret any longer. Michael plans to dig them up tonight and bring them to the keep on the morrow."

"Good man."

"He is. I was right to trust you."

Geoffrey shook his head, his mouth tight. "Nay, I made a serious error in judgment. I forgot . . . I neglected to . . . ah, hellfire."

He tossed down the horse's reins and stepped over the crevice as if it never existed. His large, warm hands cupped her face, his expression now so tender she forgot to breathe.

"I must beg pardon for being such a hard-headed, obstinate fool, for all the loathsome things I said in anger. I love you, Leah. If you can find it in your heart to forgive—"

She grabbed hold of his tunic, pulled him down and

kissed him hard and full, passionately, until sure Geoffrey couldn't possibly doubt that he was her world, her joy. She knew her tactic worked when his arms came around her, pulling her in so tightly not even Cornwall's wind could find a crack to whistle through.

'Twould be lovely to stand here the rest of the day in this sweet haze, wrapped in his embrace, his mouth on hers. But kisses had a natural life of their own, and she had yet to remind Geoffrey she loved him.

After releasing his mouth but not his tunic, she was gratified he seemed muddled in the head, too. "I love you, Geoffrey."

"Can you still, after all those harsh words?"

Her forehead fell to his chest, the ugly words they'd flung at each other ringing in her ears. "I must beg your pardon, too, for what I did, the things I said. I hurt, and wanted you to hurt as much as I."

"The wounds went deep because we cared so much. 'Tis good, in a way, to know."

"So we do not rip each other apart anymore."

"That, too, but knowing love is shared binds us, and means you have no choice but to marry me."

With her forehead on his chest, she could feel him hold his breath, and he couldn't see her smile. She'd denied his offer so many times, damning his oath, which had no bearing anymore. Geoffrey was free of all obligation and still he'd come back—and he loved her. 'Twas all she'd been waiting to hear.

"This time I think you mean it, so I suppose I must."

With a huge sigh of relief, he declared, "Praise the saints. You have no idea how frightened I was you would tell me to go home again."

She slid her arms around his neck, smiled up at him. "My champion knows no fear . . . except, perhaps, of closed-in places."

"When you are with me even the closed-in places are bearable."

"You once suggested a basket of food, a blanket and a cave."

He smiled then, kissed her again, gently this time but no less stirring than the last. "What say we begin with a larger space, like your bedchamber?"

Fine with her, except . . . "I fear I invited Father Donald to sup with us and promised Michael to keep the priest occupied well into the night. 'Struth, he may even now be learning that we lived together as husband and wife for several weeks. He may even be waiting for us at the drawbridge to serve up a lecture and insist we take vows immediately."

"I gather no roasting of an interfering priest is allowed either."

"Uhm . . . nay."

Geoffrey hugged her tightly before grabbing her hand and pulling her toward Boadicea. Leah gave the mare a loving pat before taking Geoffrey's outstretched hand. From beneath his tunic's sleeve she caught a flash of amber silk wrapped around his wrist.

She glanced up. "My hair ribbon."

"Your token brought me good fortune once. I saw no harm in testing its power again. A knight seeks every advantage when vying for his lady's favor."

Amused, but very pleased, she allowed her knight to pull her up onto his lap. Cradled across his thighs and against his chest, she snuggled in for the ride home.

He nudged the horse forward. "We shall have to put the priest off for a bit, not that I am not anxious to make you mine, but I did promise my sister an invitation to the wedding." He chuckled. "Do not be surprised if she shows up in a gown of indigo silk."

"She liked the cloth?"

"Termed it exquisite, I believe."

"Good." Leah's thoughts raced ahead to what else must be done. "We must also notify the earl. Because I inherit Pecham, I believe I must ask his permission."

Geoffrey reined the horse to a halt, frowning. "Any reason to believe he will not grant it?"

"I see no reason why not. You are of knightly class, and my father as good as betrothed us in his will. The earl might consider it a boon you have already earned the respect and loyalty of everyone in the holding. More importantly, how do you feel about becoming lord of Pecham?"

After silent contemplation, he said, "How much of that loyalty will remain if I ended the smuggling?"

He had a point. So much of Pecham's financial good health depended on the smuggling profit.

"Perhaps you could wean them off, say a ship per season."

"A possibility. 'Twould not hurt so much, and my sister is truly fond of the silk."

"No need to decide immediately. And truly, if you wish to name a castellan here, go somewhere else, take another position, I do not mind."

He threw back his head and laughed. "Oh, my father has suggested one, but I will not tell you about it until after we are wed. I should hate to anger you so soon after we have just found accord."

His kiss was long and deep, and Leah thrilled to the strength of their accord.

"I love you, Leah. Always will. On my oath."

Another oath that he intended to keep, and Leah vowed to do right by Geoffrey, too. No more lies, no more secrets.

"And I you, with all my heart."

He nudged the horse into motion again. "So, how soon can we wed?"

Leah knew which part of "wed" he most looked forward to, the wedding night, as did she.

"I should think a fortnight sufficient."

Geoffrey's groan reflected her own feelings. "If I must keep myself away from your bedchamber for a full fortnight, I may go mad."

So might she. Just the thought of having Geoffrey back in her bed heated her woman's places. "Perhaps we can find a way to smuggle you in there a time or two before the ceremony."

The gleam in Geoffrey's eyes promised he'd find a way.

Content, Leah glanced toward where the keep now came into sight. So much had happened since she'd returned from France—some bad, some good. Pain and sorrow aplenty, but joy and happiness, too.

So many changes, yet some things remained the same. The gulls cried among the cliffs; the wind tugged at her cloak. Yet no matter the changes to come, now she would face them with Geoffrey, her knight, her love. Two bodies and minds in harmony.

Approaching the gate, Leah felt a sense of rightness, that she and Geoffrey could truly make a good life together, whether here at Pecham or anywhere else he pleased.

"The first time we three passed through this gate, we were all a sorry sight. You lay on a blanket in the cart, broken and barely breathing. Boadicea truly looked like stew meat on the hoof. I was disheveled and so frightened for all of us."

"Frightened now?"

Leah snuggled against Geoffrey with a sigh. "Nay, never again. Not if we are together."

With a victory cry he nudged the horse, and together they galloped over the drawbridge.

# About the Author

SHARI ANTON'S secretarial career ended when she took a creative writing class and found she possessed some talent for writing fiction. The author of several highly acclaimed historical novels, she now works in her home office where she can take unlimited coffee breaks. Shari and her husband live in southeastern Wisconsin, where they have two grown children and do their best to spoil their two adorable little grandsons. You can write to her at P.O. Box 510611, New Berlin, WI, 53151-0611, or visit her web site at www.sharianton.com

More
Shari Anton!

❧

Please turn this page
for a preview of
*ONCE A BRIDE*
available wherever
books are sold.

# Chapter I

The summons was delivered in Sir John Hamelin's pointed manner by a nervous squire. Father wished to see her in his counting room. Now.

Confident she could defend each of yesterday's purchases at the village fair, Eloise Hamelin's boot heels clicked briskly over the passageway's plank floor.

Maintaining a castle as huge and well-manned as Lelleford required certain purchases. Sir John Hamelin earned coin in abundance and his youngest daughter enjoyed spending it. The arrangement worked well for them both. She spared him the task of making mundane purchases, like spices and kegs of ale, sacks of various grains, barrels of salted fish—staples of the winter food supply—and other necessities. For her trouble he didn't begrudge her the occasional trinket.

Yesterday's trinket consisted of several lengths of utterly lovely, finely woven wool, a purchase which she deemed vital, and likely the reason for this morning's summons.

Merchants from all over England attended the fair and made their goods readily available for her inspection only once a year. She'd taken full advantage. Most of the wool would be sewn into winter tunics for her father. Even under ordinary circumstances she'd be remiss to send the lord of Lelleford back to the king's court—to enjoy the grand festivities of Christmas—garbed in less than elegant fashion.

The remaining wool was for her own gowns, suitably styled and elegantly trimmed. She hadn't yet told her father of her desire to accompany him to court, waiting for the right moment to make her request without risking outright denial.

Perhaps the time was now. She would judge his mood, then decide how to state the reasons why he simply *must* take her along.

Eloise didn't doubt Sir John Hamelin intended to contract a betrothal for her while at court. What better time to negotiate a marriage than while mingling among the high-born men of the kingdom? 'Twas her destiny to marry well, and she accepted the duty of a knight's daughter to her family.

Except *this* time she wanted a look at her intended husband beforehand, to ensure him healthy and strong—unlike Hugh St. Marten, a wealthy but weak-hearted heir to a baronage, who'd fallen over dead at her feet on the church steps before uttering his marriage vows.

Even now, two months later, the sorrow over Hugh's death lingered, and the humiliation still stung. She'd do whatever she could to avoid seeing pity in people's eyes, hearing them mutter "poor Lady Eloise" when they thought she didn't hear. Once had been more than enough.

She paused outside the accounting room's door. With a flight of hands over her emerald velvet gown and a quick tuck of a rebellious strand of long, sable hair back into her braid, she ensured her appearance without fault.

Spine straight, chin set, she rapped on the heavy oak door.

"Eloise?"

Even muffled her father's voice held a sharp edge. Perhaps this wasn't the right time to make her request.

"Aye, Father."

She heard the bolt slide. The door flew open into a small chamber that always smelled of crisp parchment, pungent ink and beeswax candles.

Eloise noted her father's bright fury mere moments before he grabbed her arm and pulled her into the carnage.

She gasped, unable to comprehend why parchment scrolls littered the dark oak desk and spilled onto the floor. Why an overturned bottle dripped indigo ink onto the brown robes of unconscious Br. Walter, who was sprawled face down beside the desk.

Ye gods! Was he dead? Nay. The young cleric breathed, though shallowly. Her hand trembled as she bent toward the bloody gash at the monk's temple.

The door slammed, causing her to flinch.

"Leave him be!"

Too confused to do aught else, Eloise withdrew at her father's sharp command. Fury darkened his dove gray eyes to pewter, a near match to his thinning hair. Never before had she seen his barrel chest heave so rapidly, nor had she felt so fragile in his imposing shadow.

Desperate to make sense of the senseless, she ventured to ask, "What happened?"

He waved a meaty hand at the monk recently retained as his clerk. "Yon dolt proved unworthy of my trust. You can do what you will with him after I am gone."

"Gone where? Why?"

He strode toward the desk and began to shove parchment scrolls into a black leather pouch.

"Best you do not know of my whereabouts. As for why?" He glared at Br. Walter. "I have been declared a rebel. Even now the earl of Kenworth comes to make the arrest."

A rebel? Unbelievable. Impossible!

Stunned, she could only stare at her father. Surely, there must be some mistake, but for the life of her she knew not where to place the blame.

He closed the flap on the leather pouch. "Show Kenworth no resistance. Allow him through the gate. Give him free roam of the castle. Feed him. Serve him our finest wine. By all the saints, bed him if you must, but give him no reason to seize Lelleford by force!"

Eloise snapped out of her stupor.

"Dear God, Father, what have you been accused of?"

"Treason."

Her stomach roiled, her knees nearly buckled. A conviction on such a high crime demanded gruesome punishment. Hanged, drawn and quartered.

From a trunk in the corner he lifted out a gold chest encrusted with rubies and set it on the desk. Eloise knew well what the coffin contained. Coins. Pounds and marks. Into his money purse he scooped two handfuls, then pulled the string taut and tied the pouch to his belt.

Father was truly running away, leaving her to deal with both a wounded monk and a hostile earl.

He closed the chest. "Sew some coins into the hems of your gowns and cloaks in the unlikely event you are forced to abandon Lelleford. By the grace of God, perhaps Julius is on his way home and can take charge on his return."

Julius. Her eldest brother. Off in Italy on pilgrimage. It was useless to wish he'd walk through the door *now*.

"Father, there must be some way to resolve—"

"There is, but not with the earl of Kenworth. He and I have been at odds for too long. Do not send to Jeanne or Geoffrey for aid. There is naught either can do to assist me and the fewer of my children involved the better." He snapped up the leather pouch bulging with scrolls. "I'll take Edgar with me. He should be readying horses."

Eloise now understood the squire's nervousness when he delivered her father's summons. Edgar must have witnessed heated words between John Hamelin and Br. Walter, possibly knew how the monk had been injured.

"What of Brother Walter?"

"The wretch will live. Do nothing to restrain him. All you need do is feign ignorance of my affairs and all should be well."

She'd never felt more ignorant or frightened. This couldn't be happening, but her father moved toward the door to make his escape. Near panic battled with anger over his abandoning her to this perilous predicament.

But if he didn't go, he could very well be hanged in his own bailey with his own rope.

A lump formed in her throat, tears welled in her eyes. Damn. Now was no time for sentiment. Sir John Hamelin, a knight of the realm, a heretofore trusted adviser to the king, would find a way to dispute the charge and avoid hanging.

She must concentrate on her part in this calamity, fulfill her duty.

"Do you know when the earl will arrive?"

"Likely before evening meal."

Only a few hours away. Not enough time to prepare, but all the time given her.

"You had best hurry, then."

Father flicked open the latch. "I shall send word when I deem it safe. Do as I have told you and all will be well. I place great trust in you, Eloise. Do not fail me."

Failure was unthinkable, not in this instance or any other. "Have I ever?"

He tilted his head; his expression softened. "Nay. Of all my children only you have shown unfailing loyalty. Have a care, daughter."

"Godspeed, Father."

He opened the door slowly and peered both up and down the passageway before he strode out.

Eloise leaned against the desk and took several deep breaths to settle both mind and body. She lacked time for either outrage or self-pity. What to do first?

Br. Walter sprawled on the floor, still unconscious, the blood on his temple drying dark and garish against his pale skin. An untrustworthy man according to her father.

He deserved whatever misfortune befell him for whatever part he'd played in her father's downfall.

Nay, not downfall. Merely an adversity her father must set right. Surely he had allies who would aid his defense.

Treason? Unthinkable! Too often Father praised young King Edward's policies, and been effusive over Edward's military prowess after England's victory over Scotland at Halidon Hill. 'Twas against all sense for her father to betray the sovereign he admired.

*Do nothing. Feign ignorance.*

Gads, did Father know what he asked?

Likely, because he'd seen fit to issue pointed instructions for her behavior. As for not sending to Jeanne, well, he was right about her sister's inability to help. Many years ago Jeanne's husband had forbidden her to contact her father and wouldn't lift a finger to aid him now.

But why not Geoffrey? Her brother and father didn't get along well, but tolerated each other. And Geoffrey had studied law. Perhaps, if events turned too sour—

The monk stirred, moaning.

The churl didn't deserve any show of concern, but show it she must if he were to believe she'd simply come upon him, found him wounded—didn't know he'd somehow betrayed her father.

She knelt and put a hand to his shoulder. "Brother Walter, can you hear me? Can you awaken?"

He opened his eyes, dazed. "L-lady . . . Eloise, I—"

"Do not try to speak yet. You must have tripped on your robes and hit your head on the desk. Can you sit up?"

He braced on an arm and rose slowly, shaking his

head as if settling his brain into its rightful place in his skull.

Once he seemed balanced, Eloise moved away from the monk she'd dearly love to toss in the dungeon, but was under orders not to restrain.

Br. Walter glanced around the room. Looking for Father?

She righted the ink bottle. "Tsk. Such a mess you made. I dare say Father will not be pleased if he sees his possessions in such disarray. But come, I will take you down to the hall, fetch a cold rag and posset for your head before we attempt to tidy the room."

"Where is . . . Sir John?"

"I know not." Was her father in the stable? Had he yet passed beyond the gate? She swallowed the lump threatening to choke off her air. "Are you able to walk?"

The monk sighed. "I believe so."

Eloise watched him struggle to his feet, unable to muster any compassion. She'd ease his aches, then wheedle information out of him. Truly, she didn't want to face the earl of Kenworth without some notion of how to deal with him.

*Do nothing.*

'Twas the hardest command to obey. Truly, of all that had transpired, she didn't understand why her father deemed it best to run from a confrontation with the earl. Why not secure the castle, place added guards on the crenellated battlements, deny the earl entry?

From the time of the Conquest, Lelleford had withstood both outright attack and long sieges. With winter coming on, the earl couldn't keep his force in the field long without suffering many hardships. Lelleford's storage rooms bulged from the recently completed harvest; both wells were deep and flowing. 'Twould be the perfect time to take a defensive stance.

Even with the threat of hanging, running away seemed cowardly, and she'd never known her father not to stand his ground.

Eloise eased toward the door, giving the monk time to find his legs, deciding her father must be taking the right course of action. She had to trust he knew the best way to deal not only with the earl but with the charges against him.

So she'd feed the invaders, serve them wine—but not bed the earl. Surely Father hadn't been serious. He couldn't have meant for her to sacrifice her virginity to the enemy simply to keep the earl entertained. The unappealing prospect that her father had meant every word he said churned her stomach again. If the earl wanted "entertainment" to forestall actions against Lelleford or its people, could she meekly submit?

The question chewed on her nerves all the way down to the great hall, where she decided that, for now, she would tend the monk and obey her father's other orders, and pray she'd give the earl of Kenworth no reason to take Lelleford, or her, by force.

Traveling with the earl of Kenworth compared favorably to traveling with the king—both liked their comforts and provided commendably for those in their retinue.

Sir Roland St. Marten ate his midday repast in the earl of Kenworth's large tent in the company of William and his knights. Without, the squires and men-at-arms dined on hearty if less sumptuous fare.

One would think the company traveled for pleasure, not on serious business. William, earl of Kenworth, seemed in no hurry to reach Lelleford, take Sir John Hamelin into custody and haul the traitor off to Westminster for judgment.

Roland thought Kenworth misguided in his belief that, with surprise in his favor and John's ignorance of the charges against him, the knight would allow the earl to enter the stronghold and then give over peaceably to the inevitable arrest.

John Hamelin wasn't the type of man to roll over and whimper like a beaten dog. More likely the earl's force was in for a lengthy siege. Having spent several days at Lelleford, Roland knew the fortress strong and well-manned. Hamelin could avoid seizure for months if he chose.

But that was the earl's problem. The aging but still imposing magnate had the duty of capturing the traitor. Roland's duty was to take charge of Lelleford in the king's name and ensure the holding suffered no setback while its lord stood trial. Easy enough to do, providing him with a fortuitous opportunity to advance his standing in King Edward's eyes while earning a reward for good service. The king, Roland knew well, could be very generous to those men who did his bidding with satisfactory results.

The earl popped the last bit of lamprey into his mouth and washed it down with a healthy swallow of wine. The ensuing belch complimented the cook and signaled the end of the meal.

Kenworth set his goblet on the table and grinned at the group attending him. "Let us hope Lelleford's cook is as skilled as mine own. I should hate to come so far only to be forced to endure thinned stew and meek wine for my supper. Tell me, St. Marten, do the cooks at Lelleford make good use of spices?"

Since he was the only one of the company who'd been inside the keep, such inane questions were usually directed Roland's way. Would that the earl were more concerned with the keep's defenses, the size of the storage rooms, the number of men Sir John could send onto the field.

Roland had learned immediately upon joining the retinue that Kenworth harbored no concerns over possible obstacles, and so far he'd managed to refrain from voicing a dissenting opinion.

Roland's first lessons upon entering the king's service had been to keep his own counsel when among the magnates. The dukes and earls of the kingdom took council from only their trusted advisers and each other—and then did what they pleased anyway.

It pleased the earl to dismiss John Hamelin, an old adversary, as no more than a thorn in his paw, easily plucked out and tossed aside. Given the many times the two had tangled in parliament, Roland could only wonder at the earl's arrogant and likely incorrect reasoning.

"I found no lack in Lelleford's hospitality, either in the comfort of the beds or quality of the victuals served." At the hint of the earl's displeasure, he quickly amended. "You must remember I was at Lelleford when the Hamelins wished to make a grand impression on my family. No doubt the meals and company are not always so excellent and gracious as are your lordship's."

"I should say not." Kenworth leaned back in his armed chair. "A near miss, that. If Hugh—rest his soul—had lived, you would now be related to the traitor."

The shiver of revulsion Roland allowed to show was genuine. "I praise God for his intervention, though I wish He had done so in a less dramatic fashion."

To this day he could envision his half-brother's death, see Hugh's enchantment with his bride dim to pain, his eyes roll back in his head just before he collapsed. Hugh St. Marten had died in ignoble fashion, sprawled face down on the church steps at his bride's feet.

Eloise Hamelin hadn't shed a tear over the man who worshiped her beauty and would hear no argument against her once he'd set eyes on her vibrant charms. Roland had tried to warn Hugh, and failed, to his everlasting grief.

The earl's fingers drummed the chair's arm. "One might wonder if not God, but a mortal being of unsavory character and low morals, intervened."

Given the suddenness and timing of Hugh's death, Roland had suspected treachery, too, but been disproved to his satisfaction. "My father's physicians assured us 'twas Hugh's heart at fault, not villainy of any kind."

"A shame, that. Had villainy occurred, you would now be in a position to avenge Hugh's death. Such an opportunity does not come often."

Wary of the earl's tone, Roland sought to make his position clear. "I have no personal quarrel with Sir John other than his treachery toward our beloved sovereign."

"Ah, but personal quarrels are the most satisfying to

settle." William abruptly rose. "If we are to sample Lelleford's hospitality this eve, we must be off. Ready the men."

Roland followed the other knights out of the tent, their exit a signal to all to break camp. He headed for the horses—his particular assignment on this journey—to ensure them properly cared for. Not a hard job due to the efficiency of squires who knew their masters' horses were highly prized possessions. Even now the squires and grooms scrambled for saddles, including Timothy, Roland's own squire.

Odd to have a young man at his beck and call, doing those tasks Roland had always done for himself until recently.

With little to do but observe, Roland mused over the earl's relish for settling personal scores, fearing the earl was up to no good. No matter what quarrel William, earl of Kenworth, planned to settle with Sir John Hamelin, Roland couldn't allow the earl to do Lelleford or its people any harm. The king had been most specific in his instructions.

However, magnates possessed a tendency to act in their own interests if they thought they could get away with taking justice into their own hands.

If the earl decided to hang John outright, there wasn't much Roland could do to stop him. For that matter, though he'd been given charge of Lelleford by the king himself, if the earl chose to loot and pillage, what could one man do?

How very odd if he found himself commanding Lelleford's men-at-arms and archers against an earl!

'Struth, odder events had happened this past year, like

his knighting after the battle of Halidon Hill, where he'd been in the wrong place at the right time, guarding a king's back.

A year older than the two and twenty king of England, and a bit taller and broader in the shoulder than the imposing sovereign, Roland had found himself swiftly thrust into events of historic proportion. Such rare opportunities for the third son of a knight's second wife didn't present themselves often or in such magnificent form.

He'd acquitted himself well on the battlefield, earned the king's admiration, friendship and rewards. He now owned several horses and all the necessary weapons and armor needed by a knight. All he required was an income rich enough to keep them.

Which was why, Roland was sure, Edward set him to this task. A man could earn great rewards in royal service if he served the king well.

Roland planned to begin his upward rise by faithfully completing his given task, if the damn earl of Kenworth didn't take it into his head to cause mischief—or worse.

The earl's tent tumbled to the ground. Soon tent, poles, furniture and foodstuffs were being loaded into the baggage carts, and men prepared to take their places in line. Roland made his inspection of bridles, bits and straps. Sure neither the knights nor the earl would lose his seat from a squire's carelessness, he approached his own horse and squire.

"All is ready, Timothy?"

With a toothy grin, the tow-headed lad of ten and six bowed at the waist. "Aye, Sir Roland. You can tug all you wish and not find a loose or misfit piece anywhere.

'Twould not do for the knight in charge of the horses to fall off his own, now, would it?"

Roland couldn't withhold a smile. "Impudent imp. What news?"

Timothy furtively peered around Roland's huge black stallion to locate the earl's squire.

"There is something afoot," the lad said just above a whisper. "Gregory knows, but he is not saying, just smiling like he hoards a secret. Could be the rest of us are wrong, and I dislike speaking ill of my fellow squire, but . . ."

"Then speak no more. Speculation does us no good."

"My apology, milord, for falling short of my task."

Roland grasped the squire's spindly shoulder, still amazed a lad so slight, though tall for his age, could heft a saddle to such a great height as a stallion's back.

"You did not fall short, Timothy. You cannot inform me of those things you do not know. Keep a sharp eye and ear. 'Tis all I ask."

With his chin set in determination, the squire nodded, then bowed off to see to his own mount.

Roland swung up into the saddle and nudged the stallion forward. Near where the line began to form, the earl spoke earnestly to the two men assigned to ride ahead and beg a night's hospitality at Lelleford for the earl and his retinue.

Would John Hamelin open the gate, or tell Kenworth to go to the devil? Given an open gate, would the earl arrest Sir John with the dignity due his stature, or do mischief?

Roland wished he knew, but he'd learned no more

over a meal with the knights and earl than Timothy had from the squires and grooms.

Perhaps there was nothing to learn. Perhaps he feared treachery when none was forthcoming.

Perhaps cows gave wine and sheep gave linen.

His instincts hadn't failed him yet. The prickling on the back of his neck yet nagged. He was rarely wrong about people, been proved right time after time.

The earl of Kenworth intended to torment Sir John Hamelin just as surely as that man's daughter had intended to rule Hugh.

Truly, 'twas a mercy Hugh had escaped that particular noose, wrapped in silk and gently tightened, but a stout rope all the same. Her sunny smile disguised a heart of ice; her courtly manner concealed a will of steel. Behind her beautiful face lurked a shrewd, cunning mind.

Roland smiled, looking forward to the moment when Lady Eloise Hamelin learned that Hugh St. Marten's "disgusting toad of a brother" had been given royal authority over her home.

'Twould be an interesting test of wills to see who prevailed over the weeks ahead, a contest he had no intention of losing.

# THE EDITOR'S DIARY

*Dear Reader,*

Trick or treat? For both Angelina Mercer and Leah of Pecham, the two go hand in hand as deception leads them both to a love more electrifying than they could ever have imagined in our two Warner Forever titles this October.

*Romantic Times* raves **Annie Solomon**'s work is "dark, riveting, and emotionally dense . . . one powerful read" so get ready because her newest Warner Forever title, **DEAD RINGER**, will knock your socks off. Angelina Mercer is Federal Agent Finn Carter's last hope. His hunt for a dangerous weapon has led him to her door with a proposition that could be her salvation or destruction. But it is surely her only chance to learn the truth about the birth mother she's been searching for her entire life. In return, she must infiltrate the inner sanctum of a tycoon's Montana ranch, walking the dangerous line between deception and discovery. With only each other to trust, Angelina and Finn must watch their every step because one false move could mean the end of their growing love . . . and certain death.

Leaving the thrilling world of espionage for medieval England, we find **Shari Anton**'s Warner Forever debut **THE IDEAL HUSBAND**. *Rendezvous* says "she creates a spell that keeps her readers captured" and you'll be under her spell soon too. After all, what could be more romantic than a heroic husband risking his life to save his beloved from a shipwreck? But the gravely injured man Leah of Pecham tenderly cradles is not her husband but a gallant stranger who fearlessly came to her rescue. Honor-bound to care for Geoffrey's health yet certain he cannot survive, Leah decides to take him home to Pecham. There she will make everyone believe he is her lawfully wedded husband, washing away her dishonor and averting her father's wrath. And Leah will discover just how delicious—and how dangerous—a lie can be for Geoffrey grows stronger and more seductive each day . . .

To find out more about Warner Forever, these October titles, and the authors, visit us at www.warnerforever.com.

With warmest wishes,

*Karen Kosztolnyik*

Karen Kosztolnyik, Senior Editor

P.S. Next month, Warner Forever offers you two titles that will make you think twice about being nice: Leanne Banks presents a hilarious romance about a bad girl whose life is turned upside down by a sexy neighbor and a special bundle that appears on her doorstep in WHEN SHE'S BAD; and Melanie Craft makes her writing debut with TRUST ME, an endearing story of a veterinarian who's a soft touch...until a client's brooding and gorgeous grandson accuses her of being a gold digger.